I RETURN

Doris Leslie

SAPERE
BOOKS

I RETURN

Published by Sapere Books.

24 Trafalgar Road, Ilkley, LS29 8HH

saperebooks.com

ISBN: 978-0-85495-541-1

BOOK ONE: THE HOUSE OF THE RED DOOR

Prince of sweet songs made out of tears and fire,
A harlot was thy nurse, a god thy sire;
Shame soiled thy song, and song assoiled thy shame,
But from thy feet now death has washed the mire,
Love reads out first at head of all our quire,
Villon, our sad bad glad mad brother's name.
Swinburne

ONE

There are those who have already told my tale, not as I tell it now to you, but from my Testaments both great and small, my ballades, rondels, scraps of verse, my jargon; for to some I live as poet and to others poetaster who say I gabble like a goose among the swans. And there are some who wash me white and raise me high and name me an immortal son of France, to split my sides! I, who since my zenith waxed and waned and sank to darkness, lay forgotten until they dug me up out of the dust. Pity that a man must die to live, but better I should rot in God's good earth even though my grave be God-forsaken, than I should creak and dangle on a rope at Montfaucon with crows pecking at my stinking rags of flesh and staring eyeballs, a fate as well deserved by me as by many of my fellows not so lucky to escape it.

Yes, I've thieved and starved and whored and loved along with rogues and vagabonds, and killed a man — in self-defence, or he'd have had my guts.

So take warning you who read what I've to say, and in your mother tongue, not mine, that I am not for the squeamish nor for puny prigs nor smirking snarling critics, no, nor bawling Toms; and should I slip a word that falls amiss to startle you I will oblige your prudery, if any such exists, hypocritically, today, which it didn't in my time.

You may have heard how Rabelais created in my image one Panurge, and how that I in my old age (who never lived to an old age) did retire to St Maxient under a good honest abbot of Poitou. As Rabelais draws me, I, or Panurge, was *dry as a red-*

herring, lean as a rake, and like a poor lank slender cat walking gingerly as if he trod on eggs. And he says of me, or of Panurge, that he was *of middle stature, not too high and not too low with somewhat of an aquiline nose made like the handle of a razor. And withal he was a very gallant proper man of his person only that he was a little lecherous and naturally subject to a kind of Disease which at that time they called Lack of Money, and this notwithstanding he had three score and three tricks to come by it, of which the most honourable was in a manner of Thieving, secret Purloining and Pilching, for he was a wicked lewd Rogue, a Cozener, Drinker, Royster, Rover and a very dissolute and debauched Fellow if there were any in Paris; otherwise in all matters else the best and most virtuous Man in the World...* And that's how Rabelais, who lived long after my time, did hand me down for all posterity as Panurge, my living spit. You can read it for yourself in *Pantagruel*, Book Two.

But to that learned medico whose huge laugh rings through the ages I was a shade, a myth, a legend; yet although I am a shade I am neither myth nor legend, for what I give to you is truth or as near as I can come to truth, which I never was particular to tell... And now I know all I still know not myself.

You remember my Ballade?

I know flies in milk
I know pelf from silk
I know cloud from the sun
And good wine from the tun
I know fruit from the tree
I know Love's heresy
I know Death and Life are the same,
Je congnois tout fors que moymême.

I was born under Saturn in the year that your English goddams, or *godons* as we called them, roasted alive our Jehanne de Lorraine for a witch. So like us to stand for five centuries humming and hah-ing before we decided to saint her.

I never knew my father then, but I do know him now for a lackey in the Château de Montcorbier. My mother, too, served the Montcorbiers for whom we are named, for it was the custom for serfs and dependants to call themselves after their *seigneurs*.

It has been said I was a bastard; that I can disprove. My father married her in time, and just in time, that I be born in wedlock. And so I see them, young and bravely deep in love, set out to seek their fortunes, poor innocents, in Paris. I see her, little angel that she was and is, in heaven, though I gave her hell on earth, trudging along those rough-hewn roads of our barren lovely land laid waste by a hundred years of war. Yes, I see those two in the eternal now, he supporting her small body, big with me kicking at her womb impatient to be out, and she so staunchly footing it in shoes worn down to shreds leaving a track of blood from her sore broken feet as she went, halting at the wayside to rest and feed herself and me with roots torn from the ground, or turnip tops thieved by my father from the ragged fields. And to this day when all of my beginnings, before I drew my first breath, is remembered, I have the taste of those same turnip tops gobbled by my mother, and the dry crusts of bread offered at a cottage door by peasant women no less starved than she, but pitiful of her condition… So to the gates of Paris.

How did they live in blackest poverty, the pair of them, in that squalid cellar of a dark and narrow house in a dark and narrow street long swept away on Time's relentless tide?

Within those bare four rat-infested walls, where she writhed in her travail on a pallet of straw, I burst from her a week too soon, yelling my protest at this cold, unkindly world so cruel in contrast to the warm familiar cavern that for nine months had been my home.

My father, in a rare fuss, I'll be bound, delivered her, washed me in the hot bath-water bought from a seller of such with the *sol* flung at him by a goddam for holding his horse. The first sound I heard was the cry of the *estuveur* down in the gutter below:

'Seignor, qu'or vous alez baingnier
Et estuver sans delaier;
Li bain sont chaut: c'est sans mentir.'

There must have been some delay, or *delaier*, in the bathing of me by my father unaided, for all that my mother endeavoured to guide him while I screamed myself puce and might well have passed out or passed over, but that my father, having severed my cord, seized and swung me round and round, mid-air, before I choked. Then, once put to my mother, I took comfort and suck, subsided and gurgled and slept.

Paris! Whose war-distorted beauty shines through the haze of distance like a jewel set in a frame of tarnished silver: a little captive city mastered by the English, the hub and storm-centre of France. But enemies more bitter than your goddams were the plague and starvation that followed the wars. Trees died, birds died, and little children died crying, *'Doux Jesu, je meurs de faim et de froit.'* And wolves, driven hunger-mad in that coldest of all winters, came out of the woods across the frozen Seine to fight with and devour the scavenger dogs in the streets, and carry off dying babes snatched from their dead mothers. Yet neither death nor disease nor disaster could stifle the quenchless soul of Paris; nor of my little mother when the plague felled my father and left her to fend for me alone.

Upheld by her simple faith in God and our Blessed Lady, she battled on, undaunted, in a town bled dry as a squeezed orange by the ravages of war. The miserable pittance she earned by sewing cere-cloths for the dead, or cleaning the houses of citizens left wifeless by the plague, scarce sufficed to fill my empty belly nor to feed herself. She starved that I be fed. And for our warmth and comfort in those frost-bound winter months we had our Church of the Celestines. There, before the altar of the Holy Virgin, she would kneel with me beside her. The frescoed walls depicted, on the one side, the promised glories of heaven, on the other the torments of hell. At these, in terror-stricken fascination, I would gaze, dazzled by the candlelight and glow of colour from stained glass that seemed to bring the naked damned to awful life, sizzling and gyrating in the torture of the flames, served by little gloating devils. The golden haloed angels and rosy cherubim entwined among the luscious trees of paradise were, to me, despite their loveliness, a trifle tame beside infernal demons whom one could seize by their tails and fling in the fires to grill them in their turn and grapple with and overcome himself, Sathanas… One dared not give voice to such a thought, dared not recognise its ugly head raised like the serpent to tempt you with its wickedness, but there it was and there was I, shamefaced, bowed and praying to St François, my good patron saint, to intercede for my forgiveness. And I would snuggle close to my mother for protection and cross myself to ward off Satan's minions.

I can see her now, my little mother, her thin mouse-hands uplifted. I hear her whispered prayers, and you can hear them too in the ballade that I wrote for her to our Blessed Lady: *Dame de ciel, regente terrienne, recevez moy, vostre humble Chrestienne…* You know how it goes. They are for ever quoting it in old French and new French and, execrably, in English. 'I am a poor old woman…' (She wasn't all that old.) 'I have no learning. I cannot read, but in your Cloister I can look upon a painted Paradise where angels sing with harps and lutes, and I see hell where the damned burn in everlasting… Between fear of the one and joy of the other I turn to thee, great Goddess, to save me, a worthless sinner, and in You, sweet Princess Virgin, I live and I will die.'

I can't give it to you in your barbarous tongue as I gave it in mine to my mother, but she cherished it and if it brought her some solace for all the sorrow I brought her, so let it serve.

I was still a child of the gutter when the English left Paris for ever. While nominally our masters, your troops, underpaid, demoralised and as sick of us as we were of them, deserted their regiments, causing disintegration, chaos, and revolt to force Willoughby, your Commander-in-Chief, to withdraw his garrison of some fifteen hundred men-at-arms. What use to keep them kicking their heels in the Bastille when they were not looting or raping or rounding up loiterers after the curfew? And besides which, the Burgundians and Armagnacs who, since Agincourt, had been fighting like mad dogs among themselves in Normandy and round about the very walls of Paris, a worse fear and menace even than the wolves, had licked their wounds and patched, in part, their quarrels. The Duke of Burgundy and Charles VII, our Jehanne's Dauphin, fell on each other's neck at Arques to join forces for one last whack at the goddams. You didn't stay to meet them. Willoughby was wise enough to get out quick before we brought our reinforcements up from Rouen. Pursued by a howling populace, you marched out of our gates, the King's men at your heels, and Paris belonged to France again.

But Charles didn't stay long with us. One look at our devastation, one whiff of the stench from our unburied dead, and the filth of the streets and the rot of it all were too much for his stomach. He retched up his heart and was off, and left our city starving still and battered, but not broken. Never that!

Lord, how we rejoiced with dancing and singing and burning of your effigies on bonfires, hanging them on wick-lamps above doorways that you couldn't get in or get out for the ragged scarecrow with a soldier's helmet on its head, and me and my fellow *gosses* digging at it with sticks and a pike-staff you had left behind. At every street corner a galaxy of candles blossomed on the shrine of Our Lady to turn night into golden day. How we hooted and yelled as we followed the goddam's retreat, shouting, 'There they go, the sons of a sow, with their tails tucked into their trunks!' For we had it firmly they were forked of tail, cloven-footed as the devil's spawn.

So we were quit of you, and a thanksgiving followed with a solemn procession through the town headed by the princes and prelates of the church and the university, with all of us out in our best rags to watch, subdued of our joy and our cheers, since this was a holy occasion. I was there with my mother, pushed and jostled by the crowd and saw nothing but men's legs and women's skirts, I being so little. And how they stank, those fishwives from the Petit-Pont, when we found ourselves jammed in among them who had come to give God-blessings with all others for this miracle. And miracle it was on that blustering rainy day as I can swear to, having seen with my own eyes, that not one of the candles held on high by the priests above the heads of the people were blown out despite the downpour of rain and the wind. I was whimpering and whining because I couldn't see more than the lighted candles, could only hear the chanting and the tramp of feet, until a bearded fellow in a rain-soaked leather jerkin turned to take and hoist me on his shoulder.

'Up you come,' he bawled at me. 'Sit here and look and thank Almighty God, His Son, and Mother for this most blessed day!'

I knew him for the locksmith, des Cayeux, father of Colin, one of my playmates. You'll hear more of him later.

From my perch on his father's shoulder I saw that long procession pass in all its gilded splendour of cope and vestment, scarlet banners, boys in white, pink-faced and swinging censers to lend an aromatic sweetness to the tainted air, and a silvery sun glinting through the rain clouds.

Women fell on their knees; men wept, and the locksmith blew his nose between his fingers. I tugged at his hair and shouted above the chanting, right into his ear that was dirty enough to grow mustard and cress in it. 'Where's Colin?'

'Colin,' I was told, and heard him gulp as if he swallowed a rock in his throat, 'is somewheres hereabout.'

I saw him then, crouched between the legs of a juggler in tattered parti-coloured hosen with patches of flesh showing through the holes. I called to him, 'Colin, hey! Colin!' But he couldn't or he wouldn't hear, stuck there on his knees and picking his nose to pass the time, for he couldn't have seen a thing more than petticoats and calves.

A carrot-headed, sallow, freckled boy was he, with little shifty eyes set close together and a nose like a small shallot onion. But he was strong and sturdy and well nourished, his father being in a good way of business.

Through the town and into the gracious arms of Notre Dame, with that sun-gleam like a glory on her grey twin towers, the procession passed. My mother, tears pouring down her face, grabbed me when the locksmith put me down.

'Come, hold my hand. Stay fast by me or I'll be losing you here in the crowd.'

It took us a full hour to get home in that multiple mob under those tall gabled houses leaning over in streets so narrow that from an upper window you could shake hands with your neighbour across the way. And a noise and clatter and hullaballoo to deafen you, with mountebanks and mumpers come out to join in the jollification, and peddlers palming off their tawdry stuff on stout burgomasters' wives in their square-bodiced gowns and heart-shaped headgear. All the blades of the town were out in full fig, and full drink. They weren't hard up, neither, more than the English had drawn off them with loaded dice. Swaggering along, rubbing shoulders with the rabble and for once unheedful of us and our dirt, they went, nor, as was their habit, if we brushed against them, did they kick us disgustfully aside. One of them, reeling drunk, chucked me a sol before he turned about to spew his wine in the gutter. I was down on hands and knees to catch the coin where it rolled, while my mother stammered out her thanks, 'God bless you, *Seigneur*,' between his bouts of heaving. Very fine they were too, these gentlemen of Paris in their boots of soft Spanish leather drawn over their bright coloured hose, their hair falling in love-locks on their shoulders, perfumed with musk and amber, their eyes slantwise for the doxies of the town who came at them with whispers. And here too, was that old hag known to us all as La Belle Heaulmière, shuffling along, grubbing in the muck for rotting cabbage leaves or fish-heads, pursued by the jeers and howls of urchins, myself not the least of them, who, having wriggled free of my mother, scooped up a fistful of dog's turd to sling at La Belle amid squawks from my fellows and Colin too — he had come after us — yelling filthy jibes at her; and then my mother darting up to take me by the arm and clout me one over the ear, rounding on Colin and the others in a blaze. 'Leave her be, poor soul! She done you no harm, let be, I say!' And laid about her to the nearest, and again to me with the flat of her hand and the threat, too often threatened that I knew it for what it was worth, 'I'll give you over to the *godons*,' for some of them had stayed behind for a final clearing-up and clearing-out.

And as tribute to that pox-ridden old drab who, when the century was young had queened it over all other famous courtesans as the mistress of Nicolas d'Orgement, Maître de la Chambre des Comptes, I wrote for her my lament to beauty lost, forgotten, '*Les regrets de la Belle Heaulmière.*'

It was she who first taught me my letters. None knows of this till now, but I ask you, why should that verminous old trull have stuck in my memory to make of her a poem that those who write of me declare to be one of my finest? That's as maybe. Yet I wrote it from my heart in gratitude to her and in pity's token of her kind.

How well I remember one day in the spring of the year 1438. The snows had melted and winter's clutch had loosed its hold on Paris, leaving the wreckage of its passing in famine, brigands, those devil's hordes that prowled the city's walls to break through and kill a *sergent à verge*, what you would call a policeman, and in broad daylight, too. Then they seized all they could lay hands on and got off with their loot. It made no odds to us who always starved, but the tradespeople and burgesses who had never suffered much of want, went short of viands, bread and wine, while we ate cabbage-stumps and turnip-tops and the less noxious weeds that sprouted on the dung-heaps.

My mother brewed nettles to make bouillon for me, and with any luck I grubbed for and was thrown a mess of pigs' swill; but the wolves, as ever, were our greatest fear in those long frozen winters. There was one, we named him 'Sansqueue' because he had no tail. A man-eater he was, though he found women, as do others of his sex, more tasty. He devoured fourteen juicy morsels — and God knows they hadn't much of flesh on them — between Montmartre and la Porte St Antoine; and golloped a baby torn from its mother's arms, while she, poor wretch, stood screaming in her anguish to bring the *sergents* and neighbours there with clubs to batter him to death. And for our rejoicing he was paraded through the streets on a barrow. I and some of my fellows threw stones at him yelling, 'Sansqueue, king of the *godons*, be damned to you in hell!'

But when spring danced again with a savour of sweetness from the woods, where primroses peered out to greet the sun, then we, whose only playground was the gutter, went joyously unfearful of dead Sansqueue and his howling brothers in the woods.

Yet I was more often alone than with my playmates, preferring my own company to theirs when I walked the crowded streets. My favourite haunt was the Petit-Pont. I would climb on to the parapet and watch the swirling river down below, racing on and ever onwards to the sea. And there was more to watch than that. My eyes and ears were busy to catch the sight and sound of those that thronged the bridge; a never-ending file of red-gowned burgesses and learned Sorbonnical doctors; whining beggars exposing their sores; a leper with his clackdish — one shrank away from him! — a brown-frocked friar, fingering his beads, a string of rowdy students from the university, chasing a pair of painted mopsies, beautiful to me as the knight's dame carried in her litter by four lackeys and attended by an enviable page in scarlet livery, well-fed and rosy-cheeked. I cocked a snook at him and got a mouthful of spit in return from behind his lady's back.

But despite the great empty hole in my belly, I could feast upon the grim and graceful loveliness of Paris: grim and weighted with the burden of her sorrows, stricken with a leprosy of evil, where men were broken on the wheel and thieves and felons boiled alive in the swine-market; yet lovely withal as a queen, clothed in her five hundred silvery spires and towers piercing the sky; her palaces with gardens stretching green aprons to the Seine. For, in spite of her suffering and squalor, there were palaces and pleasure grounds and tennis-courts of nobles hard by the palace of the King, although he cared less for Paris and his people than if he were King of the Turks...

Then, while I sat precariously balanced astride the fretted stonework, I heard a voice beside me croak a warning above the noise and clatter of the bridge.

'Take care, my little one, you don't fall in.'

I turned and saw La Belle Heaulmière toothlessly grinning, her hair in wispy elf-locks, her mouth awry, but her eyes — I had never seen her yet at such close quarters — held a light as though a candle had been lit behind a curtain.

I gaped at her and crossed myself, for talk gave it La Belle was a witch; and indeed there was witchery in those young-old eyes of hers that still held a mist of blue like bluest water under rain. And staring at her, scared of her, I leaned backwards and would have lost my balance from the grip of my knees on the parapet that I bestrode as on a horse, had she not laid her hand on my arm to steady me and pull me off my perch.

'How now,' she squawked, 'come down, I say, come down!' with that in her voice for all its rasping wheeze that had, surprisingly, the timbre of *grande dame*.

So there we were, I fronting her, bare-footed on the cobbles, she, leaning on her stick for she went lame; I so little, she so tall above me. Her face was lined and furrowed as a medlar, and the stench of her! But the stink of bodies, quick and dead, was no new stink to me.

'What do you look for,' she asked, 'in those deep waters?'

And I, digging my toes in the dirt and shifting my eyes from hers and that light in them, mumbled, 'Just ... looking.'

'To find perhaps a golden fish — or, better still, a fairy? Or maybe you search for him who comes to all of us in time.'

'Who,' I faltered, glancing all ways at once, 'might he be?'

'He is the twin brother of Life,' she said, and grinned aside to nod as if she shared a secret with someone standing by. 'And his name it is called Death. But,' she added quickly — she may have seen me quake — 'we need not fear him. He is loving-kind to those who wait to welcome him.' And she wagged her crazed old head that I thought to see it tumble off and roll there at my feet.

I was in a taking, I can tell you, and shook so that my teeth began to chat. At which she reached her hand, on which the veins stood out like blackened cords, to take my paw and chafe it, comforting, and told me, 'Haro! What fools we are to fear him, hey, my little? As for you, good Brother Death won't call you yet. Life, his twin, is more to be dreaded than he, being full of false promises to trip you up and let you down and gnaw your vitals, as wolfish as old Sansqueue. But he who looks to make profit from those he favours, holds much in store for you.' She touched my forehead. 'Here. A fine rich hoard, I'm thinking.'

And willy-nilly, with another bolt-eyed look around my shoulder lest I see Colin or the others come to shame me, I found my hand gripped in her claw and myself walked off beside her. Down the thirteen slime-greened steps to the river she led me, I dumb as a boot. The tide and the sun were low for the afternoon was waning, and a rainbow iridescence shone in the ribs of the mud. I sat crouched beneath the arches of the bridge. La Belle, whose teeth had fallen out and whose mouth had fallen in that it was for ever on the move as though her tongue searched her shrunken gums for their lost fangs, lowered herself on a snag of rotten wood.

Around, behind, before us the city's hum was as a hive of bees, Titanic, with a carillon of church bells rising sweetly above the raucous cries of street vendors, the chattering of fish-fags, the song of the washerwomen beating their linen in the waters of the Seine… Roofs and roofs; a myriad of gabled roofs clustered like starlings under the sky, their lower stories scrolled in carven fantasies of satyrs, fauns, and nymphs garlanded with flowers; for the master builders of my medieval France joyed to decorate their work with cunning craftsmanship. And everywhere the gaily painted signs swung creaking in the breeze, to add their patterned colour to that perpetual mosaic.

Recent rain had left a shine on weathercocks, spires and towers; and to the southward of our Gracious Lady, Notre Dame, the tower of the Bishop glimmered in the brassy light, receiving the last of the sun.

Shadows lengthened; that of La Belle presented to my frightened fancy the proportions of an ogress, swollen out of all her skinny shape as she were fattened — on what? The flesh of children, and soon, perhaps, on mine? *Not much to pick from my bones in any case,* thought I.

And as if she took that thought from me to fling it at the mewing gulls circling to swoop upon the river's refuse: 'Why,' she asked with her nod and grin aside, 'do you shudder from La Belle who once so well deserved her name? Not always was I as you see me now. Figure to yourself my hair of gold, my skin as tender white as swansdown, my breasts pink-tipped as hawthorn buds. Oho!' she laughed awfully, with one yellow fang caught on her lower lip (and *that* can't bite, I soothed myself). 'How comely was I then. Where — where is that lost beauty which made fools of all men, savage with desire of me and of my body. See it now!'

She rent her rags to show her withered breasts, scabbed with disease and dirt. 'See these shrivelled teats and these —' hideously, she cackled lifting her tattered skirt to show her bony thighs — 'see these flanks o' mine, specked and spotted like two rank flyblown sausages. But look and see again.'

I looked and saw again, in her bleared old eyes, the ghost of loveliness, so that in manhood's years I wrote of her: *Qu'est devenu ce front poly … ces cheveulx blond, ce beau nez droit…* You'll find it all in my Great Testament:

…Ces gentes epaules menues
Ces bras longs et ces mains traictisses
Petiz tetins, hanches charnues
Eslevées, propres, faictisses
A tenir amoureuses lisses

Where are those slender shoulders, those long arms, those subtle hands, those tender breasts, those smooth firm hips that lift enticingly to Love's approach and hold him close to rest appeased in my fair pleasaunce…?

Strange — but *is* it strange, in view of my environment, that I, poor starveling, should be offered my first crumbs of knowledge from the mud of the Seine, taught me by a prostitute? No, no, I wrong her. She was of the *hetaerae*, beloved of the Greeks; and she, once queen of courtesans, died a palsied hag to be buried in a pauper's grave. She, who told me, speaking not to the gnomish child there beside her, but to my other self, my alter ego:

'The homage of great nobles have I refused. For why? Because I loved a pimp, a blackguard thief to whom I gave my all and in return got naught but kicks, blue-black on my white flesh, so much desired and so dearly bought that he might squander what it earned. What did I have from him, dead these thirty years, more than love's harsh bitterness, while I live on, warped, sour, dried as an old smoked herring? What did I gain from loving, heart and soul, if that dark thing that lurks in me *is* soul?… I'll tell you, *gosse*, I had a son, a boy who lived to be your age, and then I lost him of the plague. You have a look of him and of the father who begot him from the dregs of my heartbreak…'

Something of this did my other half record on an unerased palimpsest while still I cast about me fearing to see Colin, for the April sun was slow in setting and the light clear to find us there.

Presently her droning ceased. She took her stick and drew, in the wet mud, signs mystic to my unschooled eyes as those our Lord drew in the sand for his disciples: $A\ B\ \Gamma\ \Delta$ and which in very fact were Greek to me.

So that's how it began; and for the next few weeks, whenever the tide was low, so would I and La Belle seek and meet each other, she to draw letters in the mud and I to gobble them like some wide-mawed fledgling swallows the worms its mother offers. But this did not last long. I knew that soon or late I would be shadowed by my fellows.

And I was.

They came whooping down the steps where I sat at the feet of La Belle Heaulmière, reciting, as she bid me, Alpha, Beta, Gamma, Delta, and the Latin-French equivalent in ABC, which now I had by heart, when suddenly a stone whizzed past her head. She ducked. I started up and saw the gang, with Colin leading them to dance around us screeching like the damned, fisting up handfuls of mud to throw at the pair of us, jeering, 'See the old trollop at her tricks, playing her tune on his codpiece!' followed by a volley of pebbles and a jagged piece of wood stuck with rusty nails, this time to strike and topple her sideways and over, with blood in a red stream from her temple.

I saw red then, myself — and was up and at them hurling all my puny weight at Colin, so much heavier and stronger than I, but I got him down, mad as I was with rage, to pummel him, until he, too, was bloody and crying 'Pax! A mercy!' while the others turned tail with half-hearted boos, and chary of me who must have looked like one possessed, spluttering curses and mud from my mouth and black in the face with the filth they'd flung. I had Colin by the throat and was yelling at him.

'You louse-begotten son of a whore, cry mercy well you may!' But seeing his eyes bulge and him gasping to choke himself, I loosed my hold and dragged him up to shoot a full right-hander at his jaw and lose him a tooth, though most of them, like mine, were in their milk stage, wobbling to fall out easy and make him blubber he'd go tell the *sergents* and his father.

'Go tell them, and the devil too — to burn you! And if you come at this old crazy bag again I'll see you stewed in boiling oil in the swine-market where you belong!'

And with a parting kick from me, off he went with a hand behind him for protection, and full of cries and screeching like a virgin who'd been raped.

When I was certain quit of them I knelt beside La Belle, to lift her sunken head. Her lids were shut, her face a queer dark grey, and she breathed like she was snoring.

I got up and dashed to the river's brink, tore off my shirt which was patched and darned that it came away in strips, and these I wetted in the water and ran back to splash the drops on her face. I saw her toothless grin and heard her voice, weakly: 'Did I sleep and dream of other days? *Mais, où sont les neiges d'antan?* ... Yes, that stuck in my mind to remember.

Her hand went fumbling to the cut on her forehead. She drew her fingers from it, scarlet-stained. 'Haro! What's this? And what's to do?'

With unease I said, 'Yes, you slept ... and fell, madame.' For instinctively I always called her that. And I trickled more water on her poor bleeding face and brushed away the wisps of hair, and found her eyes on me unblinking, while her head still tried to nod, her mouth to grin, and she to say,

'Brave *gosse*. There, that's enough. St François holds you in his heart and so do I. Now help me up.'

I helped her up and told her, 'Lean on me, madame.'

'Sure I will,' she said. 'François. You might be my François ... Did I tell you I had a boy like you, named for that same blessed saint who loved all things that fly or crawl, and turned away from worms lest he should tread on them? Not the least of God's creatures, nor even me, so worn and weary...'

I let her ramble on in her breathless croaking voice, not hearing half she said, but this I did hear and have not forgotten:

'To us, who limp along the downward years there is no life but memory, while we squat at our hearthsides watching the dying embers of our wintered youth leap up in one last eager clutch before they sink to ashes, dust to dust ... I'll leave you here.'

I had got her, step by step, on to the bridge and across it, unnoticed in the hurry of the twilight; for men and women, boys and girls were out to snatch what they could take of each other in dim corners, down dark alleyways or in the crowded taverns where harlots vied for custom with the lure of drink and dicing; or to the Cemetery of Innocents, euphemistically named, where the city's lights-o'-love held their trade's monopoly among the dead.

And as always when we came to the Rue de la Juiverie where stood the Pomme de Pin, that most ill-famed of all the taverns in the town, she left me. She would never let me take her to her den, some rat-ridden cellar or ditch that was her home.

Thereafter, though I sought her whenever Seine tide was low, I sought in vain. She came no more... No more save in my thought of her as I gave it to you and your world.

TWO

One evening some weeks later, when my mother returned from her work, she found me with a piece of charcoal that I'd pointed with a flint, busily engaged in 'dirtying my walls,' she complained, 'fresh washed this morning, too!' with the river water she carried in a pail from the Seine. 'I can't leave you alone five minutes but you don't get into mischief either here or in the streets.'

'It's not mischief, it's the ABC,' I said; for since I had no Belle to teach me I needs must teach myself. 'Don't rub it off.' But she did, with a rag dipped in the pail — there was not much water left — to make a worse mess of the wall than before. Whereupon she rounded with a clout on my ear to turn it red, and flopped on a stool with her apron to her eyes.

'Dear Jesu! Is there no end to my misery? The boy has learning in his heart and none to teach him. Blessed Virgin, of your Grace, give him guidance.'

I put my arms about her and my cheek to her cheek. It was wet.

'Why do you cry, *ma mère*? Don't cry. I have learning in my head, not in my heart. Words come to me in rhymes, and letters too. They dance about in colours. A is white and B is pink — *couleur de rose* — and C is grey like clouds, and D is yellow, and my name, François, is green and —'

'There, there!' She hugged me close; then put me from her, gazing fearfully into my face. 'God send he's not sickening,' she whispered. 'What letters and what rhymes come to you? Tell.'

I couldn't tell. 'I only know that,' I pointed to a bottle filled with goat's milk given her by a neighbour, 'last time we had milk you left a cupful out for me and I saw a drowned fly in it and made a rhyme and tried to write it in the letters I had learned. But I couldn't write it. I could only hear the words singing a song in my head.'

'Who,' my pale mother asked, 'learned you your letters?'

I told her who.

'Dieu, Dieu,' she whispered, 'is this to be believed? He's sure bewitched. The poor soul's dead. How could she have —'

'Dead?' I squealed. 'So that's why I've not seen her since those beasts of hell set on her down by the river.'

My mother, helplessly staring, laid a hand on my forehead. 'You're hot. Show me your tongue.'

I showed her my tongue.

'Nothing wrong with that,' she muttered, and opened my shirt, baring my chest to see if I carried a rash. Finding none, ''Tis a sickness of the mind,' she resignedly declared. 'God's will be done.'

'I'm not sick,' said I, impatient of this fuss, 'but why can't you understand? I *must* know my letters and so learn to know myself. Sometimes I feel outside myself as if there was another François standing over me. I'm frightened when I feel that other one … outside, and I have to run away from him and shout to drive him off.'

'The saints preserve us!' gasped my mother.

I went on, 'So when I saw the fly drowned in the milk something came to me — like this.'

And while my mother crossed herself murmuring, '*Sancta Maria,*' I lisped to her my jingle:

Je congnois bien mouches en laict
Je congnois le beau temps du laid
Je congnois pourpoint au collet
Je congnois quand tout est de mesme
Je congnois tout fors que moymême.

'But I can't *write* it,' I grizzled. 'I only know my letters what I learned from La Belle Heaulmière. Alpha, Beta, Gamma —'

'The child's raving!' cried my mother, 'what, oh, what to do with him?'

'Can't I go to school? Let me,' I pleaded, 'go to school. Why can't you send me to school?'

'School! And I earning scarce enough to feed let alone clothe you fit for school. Blessed Mother, have pity on this innocent!'

She rose from the stool, our only seat more than the straw pallet where we slept, she as often on the bare boards as on the bed, for I kicked in my sleep, she said, to waken her, and growing boys must have room to stretch.

'What's to eat?' I asked; always a burning question this.

'Ah, now, I've a surprise for you,' she said with false cheer. 'I've been given half an onion and a fine large crust.' She displayed her spoils to my avid eyes. 'I'll make a soup of nettles.'

'I'm sick,' said I, 'of nettle soup.'

'Flavoured with onion,' she wheedled, 'it'll be good and tasty. Wait and see.'

I waited and saw, when she'd boiled the water and the onion and the grey mouldy crust to dip in it, that tasty and good enough it was for me.

'I'm thinking,' said my mother when we'd finished, or rather when I'd finished, for I guzzled the soup and she, God bless her, ate but one quarter of the crust, 'that I'll find out

27

tomorrow when I go to market —' though what she thought to buy there with no money, heaven knows, unless to cadge a fish-head off one of the *harengères* — 'if there's a parish school that'll take and learn you.

I tipped the wooden bowl upside down to lick the last drops from my palm, saying, 'Colin goes to school.'

'Colin's father can afford to pay for his son's schooling. Those that pay can have.' She stroked my hair from my forehead. 'I'll put the curry comb through this tonight, and do you go dirtying my walls again with the hoof-marks of the devil I'll skin the hide off your back, I promise you.'

Then she washed and combed me, searching carefully for nits, and put me to bed ... I see her now by the light of a tallow wick, hemming a shroud, her thin shoulders bent, but not with age; starvation likely. I see her waxing the coarse thread on a reel that she kept in a leaden box along with her bodkins and needles and what-not. I see her now with the glory of her love for me about her.

Next evening, while I waited for my supper, nothing like so good a meal as the night before, since she'd only got a cabbage stump and herring-head to give me, my mother, watching while I ate, burst out with: 'A miracle has happened — is happening! Our Blessed Lady has answered my prayers.'

She launched forth in a tale of how, 'while I stood waiting my turn at the fish-stall of Mère what's-her-name, the one with the wart on her nose —'

'— with four bristly hairs growing out of it?'

'Tush, child! I didn't go looking for hairs. And presently I found myself jostled from my place by — who d'you think?'

I *couldn't* think, beyond that the cabbage stump and herring-head had given me the hiccups.

'None other,' patting my back and bidding me 'roll up your eyes and hold your breath. You shouldn't eat so fast — none other,' my mother said, 'than Mademoiselle de Bruyères!'

'Her what — hic — has that great big stone outside her house?'

'*Le Pet-au-Diable,*' prompted my mother. 'But why she keeps and treasures it as holy, and with such a name too — and what it was came over me but seeing her buy a whole codfish enough to feed you for a month with a loaf in her basket and onions and a bunch of herbs to stuff it with and so —'

My mother, bless her life, and all her life was nothing if not voluble. Once start her off and you'd have to chase along with her, your ears alert for any stray word dropped. 'And so,' she said, 'stop hiccupping. Hold your breath, I tell you.'

I held my breath and let off a belch to lose what little I had gathered from her talk beyond the tag of it.

'And,' triumphantly, 'if that is not a miracle, what is? Just fancy Mademoiselle de Bruyères knowing him! One has heard of him, naturally, yet would never dare approach him, though she can, having sat at his table and broken bread with —'

'At whose table — hic?'

'Why, at Father Villon's table, boy. I knew this, mind, but amn't one to go on hands and knees claiming even so distant a kinship as might be on my mother's side and on your father's too, God rest his soul, he and I being first cousins once removed, though they do say it gives you idiot children.' On which immense admission she closed her lips.

I opened mine. 'Who is Father Villon?'

'I'm telling you, aren't I? Mademoiselle de Bruyères heard me say to the fishwife — Don't do that! Dirty!' she leaned across to slap me who was picking out what I could find between my naked toes to suck the taste, salt and sour, from my fingers,

'Ugh, you *dirty* —! A whelp has better manners. I can't be forever washing you. Now what was I saying when you put me out? Ah, yes. I was saying I did envy her — may I be forgiven — that fine fish with money enough to buy up the whole market she being worth, as talk gives it, at the least five hundred *écus* which she keeps in a casket buried in the ground under her precious Pet-au-Diable. I wonder she's not robbed or murdered and I plucked up my courage for love makes a mother bold to say, "Of your goodness, mademoiselle, I have a boy — a clever boy with a wish for learning and only seven years and if so be it you can of your obligement, mademoiselle, being so high above a humble person as to tell me of some charitable institution —" she given to good works to save young girls who are fallen in bad ways and —'

'What bad ways?' again I interrupted.

My mother pinkened. 'No bad ways for you to know — "Not that I wouldn't gladly pay for his schooling, in work," I told her, "or maybe a scholar from the university to teach the boy to read and write in return for cleaning his room and mending his hose," but mademoiselle was haggling with the fishwife over the price of the cod and I thought she hadn't heard me in all the bawling of the market, but she did and turned sharp as knives to say, "Father Villon takes in boys to teach, though I doubt me he'll take yours," as if I were too lowly for his interest, which indeed I am, though you, my heart, are not.'

My mother's eyes caressed me with that in them of the adoration of the Magi. 'And then I asked her where this Father Villon may be found. "*À la Porte Rouge* by St Benoît-le-Bientourné," she yapped in a voice like the ravens of Montfaucon, but she can't help her voice at her age, poor soul, being past her prime and bearded — now she *does* grow hairs on her face if you like. "Thank you, mademoiselle, God bless you, madame," I said. '*À la Porte Rouge,* St Benoît-le-Bientourné.' I repeated it all the way home. And do you call that a miracle,' my mother concluded, 'or don't you?'

Miracle or not, it was to prove the turning point in my young life.

That same afternoon, having been scrubbed all over till my body was a-tingle, and clothed in my one decent shirt and a worn old leather jerkin, gifts in lieu of payment for the sewing of a cere-cloth from a widowed baker whose shop my mother cleaned, we presented ourselves at the House of the Red Door.

It was opened to my mother's timid knock by a formidable person in a starched white coif who told us curtly, 'You've come out of hours. The Father sees no beggars after midday.'

My mother, undaunted, stood her ground. 'We are no beggars, madame. If the Father is at home will you please to tell him that I, of his kin, am come on a most urgent matter.'

'A likely tale!' The door was all but slammed on us, but my mother could fight for her own.

'A tale,' she said, 'that he'll hear when I tell it.'

'You'll not tell it today. If you care to call tomorrow before noon —'

I was dodging, tiptoe, to see, beyond the wardress of La Porte Rouge, a lean, black-frocked figure emerge from the shadows of the stone-walled entrance.

'What is it?' he enquired, peering from behind his spectacles, first at my mother in a trembling curtsy, and then at me with my thumb in my mouth. A tall imposing figure of a man was he, his face bearing the delicate markings of age, his shoulders a scholastic stoop.

'What is it?' he testily repeated. 'Who is this woman?'

'One who asks to speak with you, Father, and spin a pack o' lies.'

Once more, the door was all but shut on us. Father Villon, advancing, intervened.

'Let us prove these lies. Come in, my daughter, and say what you would have me hear. This way.'

White Coif, quivering with internal indignation, drew aside to let us pass. My mother, tightening her hold on my hand, followed the priest where he led us to a room lit by two long windows of richly coloured glass through which the sun's rays stained the book-lined walls interspersed with tapestries depicting the nativity and crucifixion of Our Lord. There were stools grouped around the carven chimney-piece and a great oak chair like a throne. I had never seen such grandeur, although, in fact, the house of Father Villon in the cloisters of St Benoît was no better than any modest dwelling of a Canon of the Church.

'Be seated, my daughter,' he said to her; and beckoning to me, standing first on one foot then on another, over-awed, 'Come here, my little one.' He seated himself. 'Is this your son, madame?'

My mother wet her lips. 'My only son, Your Reverence. He is all I have. I am a widow woman, Father, of the Montcorbiers. My husband too was a Montcorbier and on his mother's side of the des Loges.'

The priest nodded; his eyes, under shelving brows, rested on my little mother clasping and unclasping her thin, work-worn mouse hands. Placing the fingertips of his together he appeared to ruminate.

'The Montcorbiers — um — yes, I too am of that kin. So it would seem,' the grave lips offered her a smile, 'that we are distantly related.'

'Yes, Father, which is why,' my mother quavered, 'I have dared to ask of — to ask advice of Your Reverence. I have no means nor ways to teach him, and being as he —' taking courage from that smile, my mother went careering on — 'as he is apt to learn and knows his letters and can count up to a hundred having taught himself and I hoped if you could place him in some school, pray, Father, if you could of your great kindness I would repay you in —'

He held up his hand. 'Not so fast, good woman. Let me take the trend of this. You say the boy is apt to learn but as yet he has no learning. You have lived in Paris how long?'

'We — my husband, God rest him, who died of the plague — came here during the English occupation. My boy was born in Paris. I was near my time then and he left orphaned in his first twelve months and little to keep us going in those hard days before the English went, and ever since though Our Lady knows I've worked for him but cannot earn enough to pay his schooling yet I promise that I'll pay in —'

Again the flow was interrupted quietly. 'Why did you not come to me before?' And although he spoke to her he turned the spectacles on me.

'I did not know,' my mother faltered, 'where you lived until I was told today in the fish-market by Mademoiselle de Bruyères that you of your charity might perhaps...' her voice dwindled... 'so I came.'

'To seek and to find.' His smile broadened as he drew me to him, placing me before him at arm's length. 'You wish to be a scholar, François, do you?'

'Yes, Father, if you please.'

We must have presented a curious contrast: the kindly priest, his greying tonsured hair swept back from a high-domed forehead, the mouth austere but tender as a woman's; and the starveling waif, its eyes unchildishly furtive, too big for its pinched face, yet between the two a bond, recognised by the one and still to be discovered by the other; the sympathetic union of minds, perceptive and receptive, of Mentor and Telemachus… Father Guillaume of revered memory, how much of me, so undeserving, do I owe to you and your forbearance!

So there we were, met face to face for the first time, while he gently led me through my inquisition. I gave him all I'd garnered from La Belle Heaulmière, the ABC in Latin-French and the *Pater, Ave, Credo* learned at my mother's knee. But when she bade me, 'Tell the Father of the rhymes in your head,' I could not. My mind was empty. Yet it seemed he'd raked enough of virgin soil to find it good for planting and to pronounce his verdict.

'The boy is intelligent beyond his years. I am prepared to tutor him.' I heard my mother draw a sobbing breath, and stole a glance at her where she sat, leaning forward, her mouth a little open, her jaw a little dropped. 'On one condition,' he amended, to sink me, 'that he lives here with me in my house.'

That was the gist of it, much of which I could not follow. I only knew that the Father decreed I must leave my mother and live with him away from her, a prospect that did not overjoy me.

I ran to her. 'No, *no!* I'll not leave you. I won't. I'll not stay here without you.'

'Darling heart — if for your good and as the Father says —'

'I don't care! I won't — I won't!'

Her arms held me; her tears fell to mingle with mine. 'It is your own wish, dear one, that you be taught. Father Villon has offered to teach you — Father!' She looked over my head at him; her prematurely wrinkled face, so pinched and small, was like a pitiful monkey's. '*Mon Père*, of your grace —'

The priest was standing over me to take me from her arms. 'It is God's will that you should come to me, my son. I will care for and cherish you, and your mother too, who is my kinswoman. You will not be parted. You shall see her every day.'

My mother was on her knees to him. 'God bless you, *Mon Père* — bless you! I'll live to see him yet a Clerk in Holy Orders —' she caught at my hand, blindly fumbling for hers through the torrent of my tears. 'Who knows where the good Father's teaching may not lead you?'

Her love-besotted eyes envisioned my future, glorified beyond her dreams... Franciscus, Prince among Princes of the Church, clothed in gold, purple or scarlet, leading a procession of priests to the altar of Notre Dame. A bishop, a cardinal! Boys of lowly birth, born to poverty, had risen to such heights, so why not he, her son, whom the Father had taken to himself to guide and foster? What honour. What triumph! And what rich reward for her years of sacrifice and toil...

The dream was shattered by a howl from me. 'I won't — I won't stay here! I want to be with you!'

'So you shall, François.' The quiet words rang through my ears like a knell. 'You will share your life with your mother and myself.'

Some sign must have passed between them as she tottered to her feet while still I howled, 'I won't — I won't!'

An authoritative hand was laid on my shoulder. 'François, my son — for you will be my son, and I your father, not only in God, but in name. François Villon.' And to my mother, 'Go, my daughter, leave us now.'

'Yes, Father. Dear Jesus give me strength to bear it.'

A last embrace, a fevered clinging kiss, and she was gone.

THREE

White Coif, none too graciously obeying orders, was my nurse. Talk of my mother's scrubbings — ouch! I came to hate the sight of the wooden tub brought to my bedside — yes, I slept in a real bed in a closet adjoining that of Father Guillaume. I had a tunic of fine cloth for high days and holy days, a cap with a falcon's feather, and a new leather jerkin with a woven belt of red and green to wear on other days. I had three meals a day — I, who had been lucky to get three meals a week! Black bread, roast pig, roast duck, fresh milk, frumenty and rice. I stuffed myself at table under the watchful eye of Dom Guillaume who bade me not to tear at my food with my fingers like a wolf-cub, and was emboldened to remind him that a wolf-cub had no fingers. For which impertinence I received a cuff, was sent to my room with a book of the Seven Penitential Psalms, and told to master and repeat the first three to him next morning.

That I couldn't read a word of them must have escaped the good priest's notice. I came to know him absent-minded, which in later years was found to be not to my disadvantage.

White Coif — her baptismal name was Blanche, though I never called her anything but *Madame* to her face and *La Vache* ('the cow'), inexcusably, behind it — would take me every day to spend an hour with my mother. There she would leave us together, her nose turned up and her lips pulled down at poverty personified.

How eagerly my mother questioned me; how she gloated on my finery, rejoiced to see me 'swelled,' she said, 'like an overfed puppy and growing at least an inch a week.' Doubtless some exaggeration, but no doubt that if small for my age and thin as a lath, I was not now the weaselly rat of a child who some months before had been adopted by good Father Villon.

I soon became accustomed to my new life in the House of the Red Door. It was not unusual for the Canons of the Church to take young boys and school them for the university. If the child were orphaned he would more often than not be placed in one of the free primary schools of Notre Dame. Dom Guillaume, however, having appointed himself my father, tutor and spiritual guide, deemed me worthy of a better education than that afforded by the parish school.

I was his sole pupil; he took no more boys once I was installed in the care of the good priest. You will often hear of him from me as 'good', for if ever I knew a living saint he was one. Why, then, in that sanctuary where no evil thought or evil deed could penetrate, did I, so responsively protean, not assimilate at least a moiety of that deific example? Why? Not only because I chafed against the fetters which bound me to a cloistered life. Even at that early age I was inherently explorative, ever seeking to appease an insatiable curiosity concerning myself and the world beyond those walls wherein I stayed so comfortably imprisoned. Yet I was facile enough to earn the Father's approval, who, however, did not scruple to whip me should I come to him with lessons unprepared, trusting to luck and my retentive memory to satisfy my tutor. I could scan a page of Latin and construe it with the greatest ease, and if I faltered I invented, to earn me a sore bottom for a week.

Dom Guillaume, though the kindest of men, was the sternest of taskmasters. Having gauged my capabilities he led me through a severe curriculum that, besides strict religious instruction, included the Donatus — the standard Latin grammar of my day — the *Doctrinal,* the Latin grammar which Rabelais noted as one of the school books of Gargantua; and the *Ars Memorativa,* that I bequeath in my Little Testament to fools and their follies. Finally, with my interpretation of the Mass and its ceremonies and all such preliminary grounding for the future of a priest, my mother's dream was about to be fulfilled and I destined for a Clerk in Holy Orders.

With that end in view Father Villon entered my name as a scholar of the Faculty of Arts.

To the very young Time crawls along the uphill path of adolescence; a month, a year, five years drag on, halting step by step, and then — each step forgotten. Only to the very old does Time pursue its course with such merciless velocity that all count of Time's passing is lost at the crossroads of life's journey, where the present joins the past with no milestone to point into the future.

So with me these borderline years, between the child and the youth in care of Father Villon, went at snail's pace. I had no young companions. I was forbidden to walk the streets alone, and if I did sneak out Nemesis followed on my heels. Well do I remember one particular occasion when I managed to escape the vigilance of the Father who had been summoned to a deathbed while Madame La Vache, no less vigilant than he, was busy in the kitchen having left me, as she thought, deep in my books in Father Villon's study.

Suddenly, seized with a nostalgic longing for the gutter, I pushed aside the heavy volumes and was up and through the window in a trice. No great effort for a youngster — who had been used to shin up eight-foot walls to rob an orchard — for me to clamber down, hand over hand, using as a ladder the thick branches of a vine that helpfully festooned the sill.

I landed on all fours in a bed of herbs — the friars were famous for distillery. You drink the liqueurs of the Benedictines to this day, yet nothing so good as that brewed by the brothers of St Benoît-le-Bientourné.

Brushing mould from the knees of my fine red hose, I was up and off like a cat into that maelstrom of narrow crowded streets, and so by a short cut, remembered, I came to my old haunt, the Petit-Pont.

There, slouching arm-in-arm with some other young toughs, I ran straight into Colin. He hadn't changed more than in height and breadth; he was snub-nosed, carrot-headed, freckle-faced as ever. He didn't know me but I knew him, who with a kick at my shins flung at me, the equivalent of, 'You *******
bastard, who do you think you are? The Dauphin himself? Barging into me, blast you!'

His *confrères* guffawed. I was surrounded by gibbering faces. One dragged off my cap and stuck it on his head; another got me by the arm to twist my wrist so painfully as to bring water — not tears — to my eyes. I stifled the yelp that sprang to my lips to give him back as good as I was given, in a trick learned from Colin in the past, by ducking low to drive my head into his tenderest parts, and that hurt him good and proper! He yelled and let go, and Colin, coming close, seeing me without my cap and, despite the fringe of hair cut square on my forehead by La Vache and clubbed under to fall sleek and clean and shining black either side my face, cried, 'God's truth! If it's not that rat Montcorbier, turned gentleman — a jay prigged out as peacock. Have at him, fellows, go on!'

A scrimmage followed there on the bridge with me in the midst of them, buffeted, jostled, pummelled and pulled till I thought my arms would be wrenched from their sockets, and all of us causing a shindy to bring the *sergents* on us with their batons and — worse than any policeman — Dom Guillaume.

His visit to the dying had brought him across the bridge and, his work done, he leisurely pursued his homeward way. It would be my accursed luck that the only time, worth speaking of, in which I'd dared play truant, he should come upon me there, and with that lot.

My nose was bloody and spreading half across my face, my tunic torn, one eye bunged up, my hose pulled down, while all unaware of the holy man's presence, invective, long dormant, poured from me at my assailants in shrill urchin treble, to fall on the shocked priest's ears.

'François!'

That voice, that tall, black-frocked figure with a face of stone! A hand was clamped on my shoulder, the hand of God, condemning.

Colin and the others fell back, swiftly to disintegrate; and I, battered, bruised, disgraced, was marched away.

I will not harry you with details of my punishment, well meted, and as well deserved; of my solitary confinement standing, for I couldn't sit, locked in my little room with the Seven Penitential Psalms, a cup of water and a crust of bread to bring me, the sinner, to awareness of my sin; of my tearful rage and vows of vengeance against those hell-hounds who had beaten me one against five in the first round, although, I told myself, I could have laid each of them flat, given time. Good living had tightened my muscles. If I could only have another go I'd knock the stuffing out of them, the swine! May they fry in everlasting, damn their souls... And while I, nursing my sores and bruises, frenziedly communed within myself, I heard the measured step of Dom Guillaume approaching, and was at

41

once on my knees dismally to recite at *haut voix* the *Miserere*.

The key turned in the lock.

The Father, grave and quiet, stood in the doorway. His spectacles were pushed up to his forehead, sure sign of inward agitation. His pale, pink-rimmed eyes blinked in sorrowful reproach. His voice, sepulchrally solemn, intoned: 'Are you aware of your wickedness? Do you realise the pain and grief your shocking conduct has caused me, your benefactor?'

'Yes, Father. *Miserere, O, miserere,*' I gabbled, feigning sobs, head bowed.

'That,' said he, 'is all very well, but what are words? Is your heart repentant?'

'Yes, Father. The devil tempted me. I told him *Retro me Sathanas,* but he wouldn't listen. He sent his imps to waylay me.'

'François, I perceive here somewhat too vivid an imagination. It is no great crime for youth to seek its natural outlet in high spirits. Even I at your age — hem! — and all boys throughout all time, turn rebellious, on occasion, to defy authority, but —'

He drew a deep long sigh and felt for his spectacles, a wandering hand at his nose, to find them gone; and while he searched around, 'They're on your forehead, Father,' I advised him.

'Ah, yes.' He took them off, wiped and adjusted them, peering. 'It was the unclean words you uttered, François, that wounded me so cruelly. Words from a foul mouth and, God forfend, from a foul heart.'

'My heart isn't foul, Sir. It isn't. I didn't speak those words, the devil spoke them for me.'

The devil was always my scapegoat and whipping boy. And now I blubbed in earnest, fearing another whigging; and a nice mess I must have looked with blood trickling from my nose to be sucked down in gulps with my tears.

The Father neared me, saying anxiously, 'You're hurt.'

'Only in spirit, Father. What if my nose is broken —' I saw him start — 'if only my spirit stays staunch? But it doesn't. It is shattered, it is torn. I'd suffer more than a broken nose if you will forgive me. I'd be boiled alive and roasted at the stake or eaten by wolves sooner, Reverend Sir, than offend, disgust and wound you. I have sinned exceedingly. *O, miserere, miserere, mea culpa, mea maxima culpa.*'

Warily I watched the effect on him of this. Yes, I was glib enough, even though not yet in my twelfth year. My tears had ceased but I could draw upon a ready fount to melt a flint, and Father Guillaume, bless him, was about as flinty as a slab of butter. I wept. I grovelled at his feet. '*Retro me Sathanas.* Yes, yes, I am unclean, foul mouthed. Dear Lord Jesus, take these ugly words from me and never let me spew them forth again. I confess all. O my good Father, absolve me, scourge me, beat me —'

At this he made a forward movement. His hand felt for the switch he had brought with him, stuck in his girdle. I quailed, doubtful if my backside, which already carried weals like ropes, could stand up to any more. I had learned from past experience that a switch could vex me worse than any birch.

'Bend over,' came the curt demand.

I let him have his way… Twenty-four god-blighted strokes in all. I counted them between set teeth. Mind you, in anticipation of further chastisement, I'd stuffed my trunks with shavings before he locked me up; small enough protection in all conscience. *And that's quite enough from you, you old so-and-so,* I said. But this I did not say aloud. What I did say when he'd finished and I, still snivelling, faced him, was: 'God bless you,

Father, for your indulgence. I deserved forty-eight o' them, not twenty-four.' *Which,* I told him silently, *is the only kick you schoolmasters can get out of teaching a pack o' whelps like us.*

He was speaking. 'If you can repeat the Seven Penitential Psalms to me tomorrow morning without fault, I will absolve you. In the meantime I will send Blanche to you with bouillon and a plaster for your nose.' Concernedly he felt it. 'I think it is not broken, unless it be the smallest fracture, which at your age will soon mend. I am immeasurably grieved by your deplorable behaviour,' he added, hiding the switch in the sleeve of his gown, 'but you must ask Our Blessed Lady to intercede with one higher than I to forgive and absolve you, even as I, His humble servant, do, and will, when you confess and I am assured of your repentance.'

So much for that; yet the incident had an immediate effect upon my future.

My name, as I told you, had been entered for the Faculty of Arts. The canonical influence of Dom Guillaume, however, gained me the advantage of hastening my entry a few months earlier than the regulation age of twelve; and I have no doubt he relinquished his sole charge of me with the least regret.

Since I had no legal right to my adoptive father's name I appear in the Register of the Faculty of Arts under my patronym, Franciscus de Montcorbier. The Faculty demanded a fee of two sols Parisis per week, willingly paid by Dom Guillaume in preparation for my ultimate entry to the university.

My early training as a Faculty scholar differed not one whit from countless others of my age. We were treated alike, flogged alike, grounded alike in the school curriculum, dressed alike in long gowns to our ankles, hoods well over our eyes, and thumbs in belts; and all of us went tonsured.

O, the pride of my mother when she saw me for the first time gowned and hooded with that little bald patch on my head. I still visited her daily out of school hours at the house hard by Notre Dame where, thanks to Dom Guillaume, she was lodged. He had some private means and owned certain house property which he leased to yearly tenants, but I know for a fact that one of them owed him at least eight years' rent which he never attempted to claim. Instead he made it a stipulation that my mother should occupy two of the rooms rent free, inclusive of her board and keep; an arrangement readily agreed by his tenant, who considerably gained by the transaction.

And now my mother need never want for food again, for you may be sure the Father subsidised her board by a weekly hamper; nor need she work her poor little fingers raw at her sewing. But she could not sit, she said, with hands folded in her lap and nothing to do; so we find her nursing the sick, bringing bouillon and bread to the hungry, caring for those who had nothing when she had been given so much... 'So much,' she would say, the ready tears springing, 'so much more than I ever asked for or hoped. Only to see you a scholar was all I prayed of Our Lady, and look what great bounty She has bestowed upon me, Her humble Christian ... You must write a prayer for me to Her, François. You will?'

'Yes, Mother, I will, one of these days.'

And one of those days, years after, I did write her a prayer: the prayer that gives her to you on her knees for all eternity.

FOUR

We were spartan, we boys of the Faculty. Inured, as we were, to frost-bound winters, we suffered a freezing hell in those stone-walled schoolrooms with nothing but scattered straw to protect our numbed feet from icy pavings. No charcoal brazier to warm us. Lord, no, we mustn't be coddled.

I had my special cronies, notably Colin des Cayeux who, from his primary school, had been entered for the Faculty in the same year as myself. Another, one Regnier — or, as known to us, René — de Montigny. A hardened young dare-devil was he, utterly unscrupulous, possessed of a charm to melt stones and incite me, a susceptible youngster, to follow blindly where he led. These two and I formed a triad defiant of discipline to harry our masters, in particular those of less sterner stuff than Maistre Jehan de Conflans, our Procurateur or, as you would call him, 'Headmaster'.

No great harm, you would say, in ragging our teachers as boys through time immemorial have done; and if I had stopped at that... Yet maybe if I had turned from sinner to saint you would not have had that other self of me to give you life in the raw as I lived it and wrote it out of the depths of my bitter experience, culled from my reckless adventures. No, I wouldn't have missed one vagabond moment of all that I grabbed with both hands to fill me and drain me and fill me again, even when sunk to the depths with Death at the door of my dungeon, to have the laugh of him where he stood in wait for me beside the gallows' rope.

A choice selection were those friends of my boyhood. Colin, as you know, was the son of a locksmith and from his earliest days had evinced an inordinate interest in the intricacies of locks and keys. From watching his father at work his supple fingers had acquired much technical skill, later to be turned to useful purpose.

I had two other intimates, worthless enough though worth mentioning: Jehan, nick-named le Loup, and Casin Cholet. Jehan's father was a bargee, Cholet a wine cooper's son; and both, for all their felonious careers as jailbirds and night-hawks, ended not on the rope nor in the boiling pot, but as Sergents of the Châtelet, officers of law. Cholet, however, got what he deserved when he was flung into prison, deprived of his office, and publicly whipped at the crossroads of Paris. But I, on my travels, missed that.

A mixed bag were these four to whom I gravitated, by magnetic force of contrast to that guarded life of mine in the saintly aura of St Benoît. From René de Montigny, three years older than I, the only one of us born an aristocrat, I learned too much and too early the enticements of the alcove where René was received with open arms, having money to spend pilfered from his father's purse.

I, an onlooker, and even before my childish treble had deepened to a harsh distressing croak, marvelled at his wit, his repartee and his audacity, could envy his handsome looks that won favours from girls of the town. Too young to know them for what they were I was ravished by their beauty, in particular one, Ysabeau: arrow-slender, sloe-eyed, with hair like black satin and little provocative breasts moulded firm as green apples to her skin-tight flame-coloured corsage... Her face floats before me and is gone, to return again long after.

With René I visited the Pomme de Pin, the most popular ordinary in Paris. Not often was I honoured with an invitation to sneak out to this haunt when I should have been in bed, and, as my good father believed, fast asleep, to be treated by René to wine and a woman.

My first initiation at a certain house, of which you are going to know more, was a miserable failure. With inward trepidation and outward bravado I, primed by René, made my fumbling approach to find, despite all her tricks and beguilements, that I was shamingly unreciprocal. Judging me more than my years with my pointed precocious gift of the gab, for I could reel off a verse, impromptu, at any moment's notice, she took offence most violent when I shied from amoral invitation to conceal what she would have.

Dragging me from her couch she displayed me to the company saying — no, I can't repeat it, but sufficient to convey that I might, when developed, satisfy a tapeworm. Then she rolled me over, stripped me of my trunks and spanked my backside good and hard… René laughed the loudest.

Thereafter I feared and loathed the ladies, choosing instead to follow Cholet and Jehan, the Wolf, on their nocturnal sorties to the moats around the city walls. The vine that crept along my window was always there at hand to let me down and help me up. Sometimes Colin would come with us, never René, who preferred more adult exploits at the Pomme de Pin or that whore-market, the Cemetery of Innocents. Once well away from the sleeping cloisters of St Benoît and Father Guillaume's snores, I would join the other two, or three, at the strip of weed-grown water where Jehan's father moored his barges. Then we would loosen from its chains a dredging boat and go paddling round about to snatch at a stray duck or goose, for the farmers owned the best part of that narrow circular canal. Not for the comfort of my belly, never now hungered, did I enjoy to steal, but for the fun of poaching. Le Loup, Cholet, and Colin would take their spoils home to be roasted and fed them by their mothers, but I dared retain no booty, for how account to La Vache for a dead duck or goose? You may believe I was bone idle both in class and out of it. Learning came too easily with me who, never at a loss for a ready answer in lessons unprepared, could turn to some advantage my facility. In exchange for a sol I would write René's essays, hand a crib to Colin to keep up his sleeve when he sat for his exams, and managed to scrape through my own with flying colours until I neared the time to take my Baccalauréate.

I see myself as then I was: lean, raw-boned, narrow-chested, with eyes deep in, a mocking satirical mouth and a one-sided smile showing teeth white as peeled almonds in a sharp-featured face tanned by all weathers.

Father Guillaume, revered in high society, visited the best houses in Paris, to which I, as his adopted son, would also, on occasion, be invited. Then, ears alert for chance words spoken and held for future reference, I would sit below the salt aping the manners and affected Parisian French of the noblesse. Tonsured and gowned I'd stay mum and polite, never speaking until spoken to, when I would bring out a phrase, twisting their words to my own with a rapier cut to discomfit Dom Guillaume, baffle the men, and win me a look from the women, appraising, to be boldly as appraisingly returned.

I no longer feared the ladies. Stolen ducks and geese were but poor substitutes for more appetising highly seasoned game. While, at home of an evening *à la Porte Rouge*, Father Villon droned and burbled with his brethren over their cups of mulled wine, I, at my books, could see between the beautifully illuminated text the more beautifully illuminated face of Ysabeau, of Jehanne, Marion l'Ydolle… and one other. A sip, a taste of each had taught me something, if not all, of passion's witchery and nothing yet of passion's emptiness. How I ached to appease the fever in my blood in the arms of … her name is forgotten, but not the warmth of her kisses, the scent of her hair, the ecstatic prolongation of desire to culminate in consummation's frenzy with its gentle aftermath of convalescence. Hell's torment! When would those dried-up old pedants be gone, taking with them their rusty dogmatical creeds as sole bed-mates, while I fused and flamed, re-living those hours from darkness till dawn with… what in the devil was her name?

Presumably sunk in my studies, mouthing the glorious Latin, far less lovely to me than the gamine chaff of Ysabeau, Jehanne, Marion and that other, I would wait, counting the leaden minutes till those wine-bibbing priests would be gone. Father Guillaume, still passing the flagon, re-filling, head-wagging, discussing canonical theories, kept them hard at it, when, a trifle top-heavy and more than ever talkative, they would talk themselves into their cloisters.

Then the good Father, rosy with Beaune, yawning and pointing me to the door with a 'Not in bed yet, boy? Don't study too hard. Sleep is the breath of life — uh-uh-a-a-ah —' and taking his candle he would light me and himself up the stairs to bless and to give me goodnight at the door of my closet.

There would follow for his hearing, through the wall, a murmur of my prayers, a telling of my beads, a creaking of my bed as I laid myself on it fully dressed, while I listened for a similar performance from the Father's room. So soon as his deep breathing turned to snores I was up and through the window, climbing down the grapevine, and away. No more than a matter of minutes was it to slip across the road to join René, Colin, Cholet and the Wolf, at the Mule, another of our favoured rendezvous where a girl could be bought for a throw of the dice … Ah! I have the name of that one now: Guillaumette, a red-headed, hot little piece with a mouth like a flower, a laugh like a song, and a mole … yes, I remember that mole, teasingly placed on her *mons veneris*.

Small wonder that despite my quick assimilation I all but failed my Baccalauréate. The usual age to take the Bachelor of Arts degree was anything from fourteen to sixteen. I was near upon eighteen when I stood before the black-gowned examiner answering questions on the Organon of Aristotle, *Les Topiques Boèce, le Doctrinal, le Grécisme*, skimmed through and memorised at the last minute.

If my foster father were grieved that I passed without honours he showed no sign of it beyond a sigh, a shoulder pat, a kindly, 'Eh well, my son, you have passed the first step on the rung of the ladder to your doctorate, God willing.'

If God were willing, I was not. The taverns had for me far more attraction than Aristotle's metaphysics or Platonic dialectics. The university, a city in itself, was less a seat of learning than a prison house to us, the hare-brained, who preferred the warmer welcome of the taverns to the dry as dust logic of the schools.

The Pomme de Pin, the Spinning Sow, the Nun-Shoeing-the-Goose, the Mule, the Popinjay, the Trois Chandeliers, were but a few of the signs that called us in to drink, to gamble, and to play at love through those dizzy joyous nights that can only come to youth bursting its bonds on life's threshold.

There were other amusements than these: the Feast of the Fools, when the whole city ran riot and sober Provosts and Churchmen, themselves turned foolish to strut and giggle in procession crowned with roses; the Gingerbread Fair and the Fair of St Germain, the Fair of St Laurent that went on for a week to end with a grand finale in the Cemetery of Innocents, where boys and the girls of the town tumbled each other on the graves of the dead, and where that great charnel house of skulls grinned down at us from the heaps of whitened bones, disinterred and hoisted on the roofs of the cloisters to make room for more recent burials.

Around the whole length of the cemetery wall was frescoed a memento of that awful plague which swept through France and Paris, within living memory of some. It was in 1426, a few years before my birth, that the grisly mural of La Danse Macabre was first conceived. All Paris came to watch the artists climbing ladders, splashing colours from their palettes to recapture that massed epilepsy of a frenzied people, maddened with fever, rotting with disease, to dance their dance of death.

Old men, lipping their tankards, still talked of it as told them by their fathers, how one, roused from his stupor, would utter a wailing clarion cry to start that hideous revel when, linking hands to form a human chain, others would join in solemnly at first, then, gaining impetus as madness seized them, they would dance through the streets and out through the gates of the city. Convulsed with demoniac laughter, their bodies heaving and twisting in grotesque contortions, on and on they danced a serpentine demented saturnalia, far into the quiet open country, dancing till they dropped and lay jerking, gasping out their dying breath until another chain would come, with shrieking glee, to trample them.

The madness passed, but its tradition lingered, enshrined on the cemetery wall, a peep-show for gaping farm yokels to wonder at on feast days, or a promenade for fashion, watched by those piled grinning death's heads; or a fairground for mumpers; a troubadour twanging his lute, a fool in his motley, and jugglers and dwarfs, jostling the stall-holders shouting their wares, offering sweetmeats and all sorts of gimcracks; pet monkeys, caged songbirds, and tinsels and laces and spices, pomanders and pies.

Light-hearted, light-fingered were we, the raffish young bloods of Sorbonne, as swift to rifle the purse of a drunk as to rifle the skirts of a girl.

So we come to a day at the end of the year 1451. I was due, in the following spring, to sit for my Licentiate, but having frittered time away I was no nearer passing it than I had been before. We — that's to say René, Colin, and a fellow they brought with them, Guy Tabarie — were making a night of it there at the Mule.

A snoutish, stocky, goggle-eyed fellow was Tabarie, and garrulous — Lord, how he talked! He had money to spend, but we won't ask how he came by it, standing drinks all round and full of a jaunt he had devised to do with a great stone, le Pet-au-Diable, that stood outside the house of Mademoiselle de Bruyères.

'For I tell you in confidence,' he bawled, that all heads turned to listen, 'she keeps a crock of gold under that stone.'

I pricked up my ears, having heard the same from my mother long ago. I jogged his elbow. 'Not so loud.'

And René, glowering, told him, 'Shut your trap. If there's gold about I'll be the first to find it, and if you're lying, I'll ram your teeth down your ******* throat, you sot.'

Tabarie, belching, made shift to say, 'It's no lie, it's — umph
— fact. She buried five hundred *écus* in the earth under that —
yip!' He belched again, excessively.

'Hold it, hold it,' growled René. He cast a glance around the
company who, raking in their winnings from the dice to go
lurching up the stairs with a girl, paid no heed now to us. 'So
what's to do,' he downed a flagon from its spout, 'and who's to
do it?'

'Not I.' Getting myself off the stool I drained my cup. I was
full as a goat, but I had sense enough to tell them, 'The old girl
sets store by her precious Pet-au-Diable, and as for burying
gold underneath it — how d'you think she'd dig it in there
without rooting up the stone? It weighs heavy as'n el — an
el'phant. Her money's safe in her coffers or under her mattress,
and no man's like to rape her for it in her bed, unless it be
Tabarie who'll — who —' I managed to achieve — 'is just
about as able as a jellyfish.'

And Colin guffawing, said, 'That reminds me of the tale of
the nun and the friar.' Which he proceeded bawdily to tell,
while I, refilling my cup from a flagon fresh ordered by
Tabarie, poured wine down my throat and left them to it.

Dawn was breaking, curfew ended, when I let myself in at
the Red Door, to be met by Father Guillaume in his shift. He
held aloft a lighted taper. His bare skinny legs were like those
of a stork, and he peered at me myopically with his
unspectacled eyes.

I was none too steady on my feet and must have stank pretty
high, for I saw him draw back with a look of disgust.

'So this,' he said, low-voiced, 'is how you pass your nights,
glued, as you say, to your books. Where have you been?'

'I was working, Father, until an hour since,' I answered
carefully, lest my words should slide, 'and then, as I'd had

neither bite nor sup all day, so deep was I in my st-studies and not wishing to dish — to disturb la Va — Madame Blanche, I went over to the Mule to eat.'

'And drink.' He uttered a deep groaning sigh. 'How do you expect to pass your finals while you resort to taverns and low company, staying out all night?'

'But, Father —'

'No.' He raised a hand. 'I'll not hear your false excuses. I know what I know and am wounded to the core. Look,' he pointed to the window, greying in the morning light, 'another day, and, as all your days in this past year, it will be wasted.'

'But, Sir —' I tried again, 'I sh — I shwear I've been at — work —'

'At devil's work, who finds much work for idlers.'

Another deeper sigh that seemed to rise up from his bowels, turned to water doubtless from accumulative shock; for this was not the first time he had waylaid me in the dawn, poor harassed, gentle gentleman. What untiring patience and saintly forgiveness were his. He had long ceased to thrash me now that I bordered on manhood; and did I in my heart despise his indulgence? Maybe. Had he shown a sterner front, which was not in his nature to show, having that in him of goodness which, when carried to excess, is akin to weakness, I might have chosen a better, cleaner way of life... But why speculate? We are as we are, and I am that I am, still seeking to find and know myself.

With a tug at my heart I watched that tall stooping figure grope its way up the stairs. I heard him close the door of his room, and feeling dizzy with a heaving of my stomach, I went out into the garden, a square grass plot in front of the house. The night dew lay like gauze on the green and the faint cheep of waking birds heralded the morning.

I stood breathing in the fresh frosty air to revive me, and heard, above the chime of bells from churches near and distant, the first stirring of sleep from the city: the raucous cry of street hawkers; the ring of hoofs on cobbles as the laden pack-mules clattered in from farms beyond the walls; and from our four thousand taverns disgorging the night's revellers, a boozy concerted cacophony of song, of drunken brawls, and women's laughter... Paris, my Paris! In all her moods, for all her dirt, her mud, her squalor and her smell — *Dieu*, how she smelt! — despite Authority's attempt to quell her stench and cleanse her gutters, I loved her, yes, I loved her for her beastliness, her bawdiness, her loveliness, the Gothic majesty and beauty of her churches, the all-embracing grandeur of Notre Dame, and for our great old university that nurtured me.

'François.' Father Guillaume was alongside, habited for early Mass. 'Do you not wish to rest and feed yourself after your —' he paused to add with gentle irony — 'your night's hard work?'

'Sir, no, I thank you. I am due to attend my lecture.' And how I got through the day, writing and answering questions on the Bucolics and Averroes' Commentaries with a mouth like a lime kiln and a head as if a dozen imps were beating at my temples with vicious little hammer-strokes, I do not know.

But when the class closed I was out again to make another night of it and this time to some purpose, if purpose you'd call it to go howling through the streets, tearing down house and tavern signs, to mate the Spinning Sow with the Nun-Shoeing-the-Goose. Harmless enough fun, you'd say, but the *sergents* didn't think so. Led by their chief constable, that pompous ass Henri le Fèvre, they descended on us in a body. We hadn't a chance, being unarmed. His stalwarts fell to with their batons to bludgeon us and scatter us in all directions, who had nothing to give in return but our fists. There was not much to choose between the beaters and the beat. The officers of law seemed completely to have lost their heads for, despite that we, the students, went tonsured and therefore were supposed to be protected from attack, they struck us down, regardless. One of us got a fractured skull, and a dozen more were bleeding from dagger thrusts and blows. A fine to-do! I was lucky to get away with nothing worse than a black eye.

Leaving Colin, de Montigny, and others of Sorbonne's desperadoes still hard at it battering the *sergents* who, at le Fèvre's orders, had placed barricades of chains across the streets to catch escapists, I slipped down a side alley to a house I knew, or rather that de Montigny knew, and where in my calf days I had been once, but not twice, entertained.

You remember I told you of my lamentable first initiation? The house was still there, marked by a red light over the door.

The house of *La Grosse Margot*.

And was she fat! Overpoweringly fat, with laughter sparkling out of her like wine; handsome too, after her fashion, dark eyed, black-haired, full bosomed, with the skin of a sun-warmed peach; and when not in her cups to let fly her tongue, a good-natured hearty soul; not old, not very young. Such was she as I later came to know and give her to you in the Ballade of her name.

The door was shut but the red light in the lantern above it showed the house still open to chance custom. I knocked and was admitted by a sprig of a girl whom I saw to be, dismayingly, a child. I asked if madame were receiving visitors. She nodded her head, sucking in her underlip, staring up at me with narrowed eyes under brows darker than the primrose-coloured hair that framed her pale, rather dirty little face.

'Rose! Marthe Rose! Who then — who is it?'

The fruity voice of Margot shrilled from an inner room, followed by the lady herself, waddling, arms wide, her teeth exposed in a smile of professional welcome.

'You are late, messire, but never too late for me.' And eyeing me over, one hand on her hip — or that part of her anatomy where her hip should have been were it not encased in rolls of flesh beneath the scarlet, too-tight-fitting gown — 'You have been here before, my dear, yes? I never forget the faithful.' She gave me a leer and a wink; then, before I could answer, she turned to the girl. 'Shut the door, Marthe Rose. And you, sir, come in. I have not much to offer you at this hour, for all my girls are already engaged, unless it be Big Joan of Britanny, one of my choicest, greatly in demand. You know her — or know of her?'

'But certainly, madame, I know La Grande Jehanne,' I replied with more assurance than veracity.

The hood of my gown, torn in the mêlée, had fallen back to reveal my tonsured head. Margot showed more teeth. 'So la! An *escholier* out on the spree. I heard the noise of it. *Sacré diable*, what a row! And so you are come to finish your fun, and where better than here with Fat Margot? Is that it?'

It was not it at all, nor had I so much as a sol to pay for my 'fun' had I wished to, since my pouch had been snatched in the riot, as I found when I felt where it should have been clasped to my belt. It was gone, and my week's dole from Father Guillaume of three whites gone, too.

'Rose! Bring wine for the gentleman. This way, messire — what is the name?'

'Des Loges,' I told her promptly.

'But of course! You are a regular habitué.'

I didn't contradict her. I was dog-tired and the blow on my eye was hurting like hell. She soon spotted it.

'You've been busy, I see. We'll put that right at once. Marthe Rose, fetch a slice of raw meat from the buttery.' The child pattered off. 'Come then, come, *chéri*.'

The greedy hands of Margot urged me to her chamber, an untidy room and none too clean. A tumbled bed, giving evidence of recent use, stood in one corner. A table containing four empty flagons, two wine cups, and dishes strewn with gnawed chicken bones betokened remains of a meal. I, too, could have done with a meal, having gone short of my supper, but was offered none.

Margot pulled forward a joint-stool, bade me be seated and seated herself on the bed. The child returned with two flagons of Beaune. I watched her clear the dishes, her face a blur in the flickering flame of wan rushlights. Such a young wisp of a thing, like a white moth in the clutch of a clumsy stag beetle — the thought came to me with swift revulsion as I glanced from her to La Grosse Margot. What, I wondered, was she doing here? A servant girl, or novice in madame's academy learning her trade?

Unfastening the front of her gown, Margot sighed contentment. 'That's better. I was laced too close.' She produced the unlovely sight of two enormous globes with nipples suggestively tinted. 'You like me — yes?' A ghastly leer, 'or would you prefer to see Big Joan — tall as a tower and a trifle skinny, yet most efficient? She's gone to bed, but I can call her if you wish.'

'No,' I said in haste, 'don't disturb the Big One. I am — um — charmed, madame,' I ineffectually declared, 'with — you.'

'Which,' her smile slipped, 'is evident.' And to Marthe Rose, now returned with a lump of raw mutton, 'Give me that,' she snapped, and slung it at my head. 'Here's a plaster for your eye.'

I caught it deftly, wincing at the touch of the 'plaster' on bruised flesh.

The child slid me a sidelong glance from eyes green as a cat's. Her nose had an impudent upward twist, her mouth was up-tilted too, blunt-cornered, inviting — did she know how inviting? — with the dawn of an impish grin as she watched me tenderly nursing that lump of raw meat on my eye.

'Goodnight, madame … messire.' She bobbed to us both.

'Don't forget,' Margot bade her, 'to put out the cat. It messed in the kitchen last night.'

'Which I had to clear up, *merci*.' And with a sniff of that comical nose off she went.

'Little slut,' remarked Margot dispassionately.

'But,' said I, 'she'd be a beauty were she washed.'

'And sly as they make 'em, believe me. Looks mild as milk, and isn't. Far from it. Wait till I get her going. They'll be lining up for her — hey, what's this?'

I had removed the meat from my eye to make better use of it, bolted in two bites, raw though it was.

'So hungry are you, *chéri*?' Margot juicily chuckled. 'Why didn't you tell me?' And, exploiting herself in a posture unmistakable, 'if you're still unsatisfied —' another of those leers — 'I can feed you something tastier.'

Repressing a shudder I refilled my cup and asked, 'Where did you find her?'

'Find — oh, that! You'll have to wait for her if she's what you're after. She's not going cheap. Her mother was one of my girls, very good at her job, but she needs must fall in love, silly bitch, with some young dandiprat, and went to live with him. And when he left her she ate rat poison. She'd placed the child with a farmer out yonder,' nodding vaguely northward, 'who put her to keep his geese, but after he took him a wife he threw the child out. One of the girls — Big Joan it was — found her wandering barefoot on the Petit-Pont and brought her here. Joan told me she was Hélène's child. She'd recognised her, having seen her with Hélène at the farm. I've only had her a few weeks. She'll be worth a fortune when she's ripe. She's still a virgin — not yet fourteen and young for her age, so I haven't the heart to hand her over until she is *au fait* — you understand. Some more wine?'

I said, 'Margot, sweet, deliciously fat Margot, I've been robbed of my purse and haven't a sol to pay for my wine — or my pleasure.'

'Pah! The wine — you know how you can pay me for that.' She stretched herself, licking her loosened lips, rolling her eyes and murmuring thickly: 'Of all men I love a student. So young, so virile. Des Loges — is that your name?'

'One of them.' I stood up, having had enough of this, and her. 'Margot, lovely, irresistible and tempting though you are, I am under a vow to refrain from temptation as penance.'

'For what?'

'For so many sins I can't count 'em.'

'Well, if there's nothing doing —' accepting lack of business in good part, she returned her proffered wares to their cache — 'or,' I was reminded before she re-fastened her gown, 'if you're out of funds you can have credit.'

I shook my head. 'You credit me with more than my worth, as unworthy of your — ah — manifold attractions.'

She flashed me a smile through a yawn. 'Tell you the truth I'm shagged out myself. Such a run on the house as we've had this week, and ever since the brat came here. Those sods! I can't keep her back much longer and that's a fact. It's the old ones who want her, and they have the money.'

'Put the bottle down to my account,' I told her grandly. 'I'll be in again, for to tell *you* the truth I only came here to dodge the police. There's merry hell going on in the Place de Grève.'

'I believe you. I heard it. It's giving over now. What the devil are they up to, then, chasing round the town like scalded cats? One of my young gentlemen came along here earlier tonight with a bloody nose, a gashed cheek and like yourself, lost of his purse, so he said. Caught up in it, he was, a precious Jemmy-Jessamy, stinking of scent. What's his name now? You must know him. They call him the Bastard. He's always popping in and out of here but no use with the girls though he tries his best, poor ******. "Ooh, Margot," he says, "Ooh, what a *dreadful* business — my clothes all spoilt — such a *rowdy* lot of students, smashing everything they see. I'm all in *rags*. I beg — I *beg* your comfort."' She took off his mincing tones to the life. We laughed together and split a second bottle on the strength of it.

'Come again soon,' Margot said, 'and maybe I'll have something to offer worth your while, or my — wiles.' She yawned again, to show the arched cavern of her mouth down to her uvula. 'You look as if you need some sleep, and so do I. We can't burn the candle both ends, and your candle seems to be —' again that raucous laugh — 'burnt out.'

'But there's plenty of wick for re-lighting.' And I kissed her full on her moist red lips, disengaged firmly, and left her.

Under the porch at the door I stood awhile listening. The air was still, shadows blacker than the night. All sounds of recent turbulence had died as if smothered by the mist rising corpse-cold from the river. Only the distant hum of taverns stirred the silence in that darkened hour before dawn.

I shivered, hugging myself in my cloak, waiting, ears at the ready for the Watch, when behind me I heard a breathless whisper.

'Sir … if you please…'

I turned to see the girl Marthe Rose, with nothing on her but the scantiest of shifts, eyes wide in the shadows, her hushed voice pleading, 'Take me with you … I can't … I can't stay here. I'm frightened … those dirty old men…'

I stepped forward to glance up at the black windows. No light from them nor in the window of Margot's room on the ground floor. Again that whisper, urgent now. 'Messire, I'll die if I stay here.'

You will, a thousand deaths, thought I between a second and a second. 'Come, then.' I caught her up in my arms and made off with her wrapped in my cloak. So light, so thin and bodiless was she, I might have been carrying a ghost, but I could feel the beat of her heart against mine like that of a captured bird.

Her hand came out to clutch at my shoulder. 'You are taking me — where?'

'Out of the frying pan, maybe,' I said, 'and into the fire. We'll see.'

The House of Mademoiselle de Bruyères, by the Church of St Jean-en-Grève, was all in darkness when, by devious ways to avoid prowling *sergents*, we arrived. She, lying placid in my arms, seemed to have fallen asleep.

That great stone, le Pet-au-Diable, the pride of la de Bruyères, had not, in the first riots, claimed the students' attention. That was yet to come.

I had brought Marthe Rose to the only haven I could think of other than the house of Father Guillaume, where it would never do to take her, for how explain her away to Madame Blanche? No, better far she be placed with this rich widow whose singular hobby it was to save *filles de joie* — or at least those who were willing to be saved, of which the majority were not. But now that we were here my heart misgave me. Like all other houses in that highly respectable neighbourhood, that of Mademoiselle de Bruyères was shuttered, closed, and somnolent. The November sky showed not a star, no moon, and but for the fitful gleam of candles on the shrine of Our Lady outside the Church there was no light, scarce enough for me to see the door barred with iron, nor the bell for which I groped but could not find.

I set the child down and knocked my fist against the oak with no result. I groped again, found the bell and pulled it, heard a distant clangour, heard no more.

The night was lifting. Soon it would be dawn, and I with a half-naked girl, my tonsured head proclaiming me a student, to be discovered by the Watch and brought before the Provost.

'Here goes, then,' I muttered, and raised a shout of: 'Madame! My lady! For the love of God, your pity.' And again I pulled the bell, hanging on to it with all my might. Marthe Rose was in the giggles.

At last I heard a faltering step and a mumbling voice: 'What's to do?'

'There's all to do,' I called. 'I must speak with madame. Open me the door.'

There was a creaking and scraping of bolts, more mumbles, and then a face, old, skew-eyed, bald-headed, appeared in the aperture followed by a bent and scraggy shape. He held a hand-lamp, and by its light surveyed us with every expression save that of alarm obliterated from his countenance.

'Who are you,' he quavered, 'that comes so boisterous to rouse honest folk from their rest? Lord, Lord! You be one of them from Sorbonne who since curfew have brought hell about our ears.'

'Not I — not on your life. I was not among the rioters,' I denied loudly. 'I insist that I see Mademoiselle de Bruyères. This poor child whom I found strayed, lost, starving on the Petit-Pont —' I shot a look at her to bid her hold her tongue; no need to have warned her. She played up to me at once, with sobs.

'Yes, sir, 'tis true. This good gentleman — he found me — oh, oh, oh —' Heart-rendingly she wept.

'Mademoiselle de Bruyères would never,' I said, 'turn away this little lost one. Go tell madame that François Villon is here. She knows me.'

Yes, she knew me, but she knew him whose name I bore much better, a name that opened every door, and this door was no exception.

We passed in. The old serving-man motioned us to a stone bench in the vaulted hall, lit candles in bronze sconces and went off muttering, 'I'll tell madame, but she'll not thank me for waking her at this hour.'

She certainly did not. From above I could hear an altercation.

'Why did you not bid him take the girl away and come back tomorrow at a reasonable time?'

Mumble, mumble.

'Dolt-head! You know perfectly well I see no one until after noon. What? A child? ... Eh, well, if it is a child ... and a student, you say? Speak up. Who? ... Ah, Villon! Sent to me from the good Father, doubtless. Why didn't you say so then? Marie, Marie! Fetch me a wrap... Drat the girl! Marie!'

While this was going on, Marthe Rose, all eyes and ears for it and still wearing my cloak, sat with her little bare toes curling up from the cold stones. Her hand came out confidingly to mine; a whisper drifted: 'Villon — is that your name? You said it was Des Loges.'

'Ask no questions and you'll hear no lies.'

Again that impish smile. 'I've heard lies enough already. *You* didn't find me on the Petit-Pont. Big Joan it was who found me.'

'You forget. It was I. You swooned, were all but dead of hunger and I brought you here this very night. You understand? Starving you were.'

'Starving I was when Big Joan found me almost three months ago. Who's telling lies now?'

'That's quite enough from you!' I hissed. 'You asked me to take you away from Fat Margot and I've done it, but back you go to her if you so much as raise a squeak to put me out. Now then, would you rather stay here or go back?'

'No!' She shivered. 'Not there. I'll never go back there. Those horrible old men pawing me and slobbering —' She glanced up and around, awed by the evidence of sombre wealth; the wide stone stairs, the suits of armour, the high windows of painted glass, the heraldic coat-of-arms above the chimney-piece. The husband of Mademoiselle de Bruyères had been notary to Charles VI.

'This,' she said, 'isn't a house, it's a palace.'

'Which being so, behave yourself as one befitting a palace, and not as a goose-girl brought up in a sty.'

'I wasn't brought up in a sty, but I have been a goose-girl. How did you know?'

'That's telling.'

'*She* told you.'

'She didn't. I have the second sight.'

'Are you a wizard?'

'As much a wizard as you're a witch.'

'I'm not a witch.'

'You are.'

'I'm not!'

'You are… My damoyselle of the twisted nose.' I tweaked it.

She wriggled. 'My nose isn't twisted.'

'It is, like the tail of a sow.'

'Well! I'm…'

'Shut up!'

I who had retained her hand, soft and boneless in mine, released it and was busy with my rosary, eyes prayerfully lowered, as Mademoiselle de Bruyères, in a wondrous purple wrapper, swept down the staircase followed by her maid and preceded by the serving-man lighting her way.

Stout, buxom, elderly, moustached was Mademoiselle de Bruyères, with a face like a pie in which were stuck two large blackcurrants for eyes. Those eyes, quick and brighter than her years would have warranted, were fixed, first on me still busy with my beads, and then on Marthe Rose who, at my sotto voce injunction, 'Curtsy to the lady,' stood, and demurely bobbed.

'Madame.' I started up, bowed low, and launched into my tale of this forlorn waif, born and bred on a farm, thrown out by a cruel parent to fend for herself and found by me and saved, in her innocence, from worse than death. 'The victim, madame, in her frailty and purity, of evil men and women always eager to seize upon such unsullied ones as this.'

'Poor child, poor little unfortunate.' So moving was the story I had spun that Mademoiselle de Bruyères was in tears. 'I will take and teach her and find her a post with good people. Reared on a farm, you say?'

'Yes, madame. Her father, a widower, married again and the stepmother ill-treated and starved her, and made her mind the geese. Is that not so, Marthe Rose?'

'Yes, messire. And mind the pigs, too, and curl the sows' tails and —'

'So you realise, madame,' I went on in a hurry, for I did not like at all that grin of hers, whose lips were shaping to improve upon my recitative with one better of her own — 'you will readily appreciate, madame, that I could not allow this innocent to stray any farther afield, and knowing of your charitable works and your great heart, I took upon myself to bring her here and give her to your mercy.'

'An act worthy of your priestly Father's guidance, Messire Villon. Come, child.' She beckoned her; and Marthe Rose, letting fall my cloak, stood there with her shift dropped from her shoulders.

'Tush, tush! Dear, dear!' Madame was in a fluster. 'The child has scarce a stitch on her. Marie!'

The maid hurried forward to cover the half-nakedness of Marthe Rose while I stood unseeing, eyes down, a hand at my beads, to murmur, 'Madame, God will bless you, nor will you regret this day's work, for day it is.' I pointed to the window where the first streak of morning drew a rosy haze across the dimly glowing colours. 'And I must to Mass, and then to my studies. *Adieu, madame.* Marthe Rose,' I sternly bade her, still standing downcast, the picture of modest simplicity, 'you should be grateful all the days of your life for this good lady's grace.'

Bowing to madame I backed; but as I turned to the door where the old serving-man stood to usher me out, I saw, from the corner of my eye, Marthe Rose slip behind the lady to touch her impudent up-tilted nose with her thumb and waggle a finger at me.

FIVE

Those riots, or 'rags', as your undergraduates call them, did not end on that night in November. Worse was to follow, instigated by de Montigny, and in this I swear I had no part. I don't ask you to believe me in view of what came after, for, despite my name as poet has redeemed my name as man, mud sticks.

I was, however, at the Pomme de Pin with René, Tabarie, and the rest, when they conceived their latest plot in defiance of Authority.

Ripe for vengeance on the police who had so severely punished them in their most recent skirmish, the students of Sorbonne decided to give La Ville something 'more meaty' thus René, 'to dig their fangs into', than the theft of a few tavern signs, all of which, by the way, were restored to their owners intact.

I had brought my tablets to the Pomme and was jotting down notes gleaned from my lecture that morning, since, with my finals drawing near, it behoved me to apply myself in some sort to my studies successively for the Licentiate and Master of Arts degrees. I had loafed and frittered and fooled away years that should have been put to the storing of knowledge, but the only knowledge I had garnered hitherto was neither theological, classical, medicinal, nor remotely in the region of the law.

Not interested was I in the babble of Tabarie who still harped on his theme that gold for the digging could be found under the Pet-au-Diable; nor did I pay much heed to René's brag, for he was ever forward in the tussle between gown and town — 'if La Ville asks for trouble then, by God she'll get it —' until, 'This shall be our plan of action to set the *sergents* on another tack. I'll detail half a dozen to go for the taverns again, making just enough row to draw off the police. Then while they're rounding up that lot, we'll make for the Pet-au-Diable. The old bag will be in bed by the time we get there, and apart from her doddering man-servant, deaf as a post, she has only women in the house. So, fellows, who's with me?'

A chorus of 'I! I! I!'

'And you, François?' René leaned across the table. 'Are you with us? There's work afoot of more profit to you than all of your piddling verse.'

For, having done with the logic of pedagogues, at least for one evening, I chased an elusive motif for a ballade to do with the women of Paris. Chin in my hands, I was stuck for a rhyme to *ny'y savant guères*, and not very happy with 'haranguères', but it had to stay, wanting a better, as you'll find in my Great Testament.

'Go on, shove it up your arse.' René made a grab at what I'd written, but I, too quick for him, was on my feet to stuff the tablets into my pouch with the rejoinder, 'What profit to me from your follies, you fool, more than the hangman's noose?'

'Right.' René too was on his feet, one hand at the hilt of his dagger, thieved from a *sergent* in last week's brawl and carried, against university rules, hid on his person during the day to be flaunted in taverns at night. 'So now,' his teeth were bared in a snarl, 'we know you for what you are.'

Smiling I lifted my goblet. 'What am I?'

He spat me as smiling an answer: 'Blackleg.'

'Then take this,' said I, 'from Blackleg to White Liver who'll pillage and rob an old woman undefended.' And into his face I flung the contents of my cup. At which he came at me, dagger drawn, overturning joint-stools and the table with a crash of drinking vessels, and a squeal from Tabarie.

'Have a care, de Montigny! He'll peach on us, the scug.'

At once the room was in an uproar. Diverted from their play with women and dice, men closed round us in a circle. I seized a stool and held it as a shield, for I went daggerless and René knew it. So did I, when he flung himself upon me to prick my arm with his blade between the stool's legs.

The landlord, de Turgis, grey-haired, and grey about the gills where he should have been red, came hurrying to part us. 'Young gentlemen, pray! I cannot allow — the Watch will be after you — giving my house a bad —'

His words, falling from him in terror-stricken jerks, were lost in the shouts of the company, hot for a fight, taking sides with and bets on the winner.

I looked to come off the worst of the two and would have stood no chance had I not seized the opportunity to thrust my knee in René's crutch, and, while he doubled with a howl, I wrenched his dagger from him, stuck it in my belt, and before he could recover breath I was through the ring of yelling spectators. They tried to hold me but I hit out right and left and got away with little more than a cut or two and a trickle of blood down my arm. No time to staunch it, for René's backers, done out of the odds in his favour, would be after me to finish the fight of which I'd had enough.

The streets had thinned to the warning of the curfew from Notre Dame. Soon Sorbonne's curfew would reverberate its answer. The *sergents* were emerging from the Châtelet, armed with staves and lanthorns, on the watch for thieves, loiterers, tricksters and beggars, those of the homeless, poor devils, who slunk to hide themselves under the butchers' stalls in the meat market, hopeful of a bone, a chunk of offal, or a lick of the blood drying on the cobbles from the carcass of a slaughtered sheep. Not a light shone along the lampless ways, and in very few of the houses.

Keeping a look out for the Watch, I footed it warily, making for La Place de Grève.

The old serving-man answered my knock. Yes, madame was within. And to his trembling question I said, 'Tell madame that Villon, François Villon, would speak with her. Look sharp.'

Looking as sharp as his hobbling gait and his years would allow, he went to deliver my message. I sat on the stone bench in the dimly lighted hall and heard from close behind the arras, a girl's young voice, tunefully clear as that of a thrush, singing, *'Ma doulce amour'*.

I waited; and presently the arras stirred to reveal a door, half-opened. There she was in a garment of some sort of cream woollen stuff, her hair in a coif, her mouth in a widening welcome.

'You … messire! I prayed Our Lady you would come, but never hoped you'd come so soon to see me.'

Her eyes, lit by the candles' gleam, danced to her words, while I, for once, was lost of them with a sudden strange up-bounding of my heart. For a moment only, while I collected myself to say, 'It is not you I come to see, but now that I'm here let me look at you.'

She tripped across the flagstones and stood before me; those eyes — were they green or grey or yellow? — changing colour in the flicker of the light, and stilled now of their dance. Her hands were devotionally crossed on her little breasts, but I saw her tongue slide in her cheek to the drooping of her lashes.

'Well,' I said, 'madame has done wonders in a week. Are you happy here?'

'Happy? What's happy? I've plenty to eat and plenty to do, waiting at table and learning my manners and shrived by the priest and mustn't say this and mustn't do that, and sent to bed early and up with the sun. She's at me from morning till night. Is that happy? I'd liefer mind geese.'

'You should be in bed now,' I said sternly.

'So was I in bed till I heard you come in.'

'How?'

'My room is over the porch and when you came to the door I knew your voice — I'd know it in a million — and I dressed myself quick and here I am. Did you hear me singing? If *she* heard me singing that song I'd be whipped. The girls used to sing it at Fat Margot's. One of those dirty old men gave me a white when I sang it to him with the words Margot taught me.'

She wrinkled her nose, drawing back her upper lip like a puppy dog about to bite in fun. Then hearing a heavy step on the stair and the words, 'Who?... Messire *who*? Speak up, man!' in the deep rasping voice of madame, she clapped a hand to her mouth and darted away, turning as she slid behind the arras to whisper, 'Don't tell on me, will you?' And was gone.

'Ah, Messire Villon! What a pleasure. I was about to send a message to your good father asking him to sup with me this week any night at his convenience. And you, too, sir.'

I bowed profoundly. 'Enchanted, madame.'

'Come into the warm. It is cold out here.'

I followed her to a large apartment opening from the vaulted entrance hall. The walls of polished stone were partially curtained in finest tapestry. Fresh-strewn rushes covered the floor, giving out an aromatic scent. A pan of charcoal on the hearth offered a comforting heat. A long oaken table, set with a flagon of wine, silver goblets and a dish of fruit, stood in the centre of the room. Between the high windows, a dresser displayed various vessels of gold. So, thought I, Tabarie had reason to presume that gold for the digging might be found beneath the old girl's Pet.

'Be seated, messire.' A plump white hand, embedded with rings to the knuckles, waved me to a settle beside the chimneypiece. The lady sat facing me in a high-backed chair.

'I am sure,' said she, 'you will be glad to hear that the girl you brought to me is shaping well. She is docile, willing to learn, and although woefully ignorant — she can neither read nor write — she has a keen moral sense,' I cocked an eyebrow, 'which most of the lost ones I seek to save from perdition, have not. However, this child, thanks to you who succoured her before she was led astray, has retained her — ahem! —' the lady coyly coughed — 'her maidenhood. Sir, oblige me by taking a stoup of wine.'

With no reluctance I obliged her. 'By Our Lady's Grace, Mademoiselle de Bruyères, you have an excellent good vintage.'

'You are very welcome, sir.' Plucking at the hairs on the first of her two chins, she absently acknowledged my appreciation. 'I wonder now if you or Dom Guillaume are acquainted with a Madame de Vaucelles.'

The name struck a note of reminder. Toying with my empty cup I answered, 'I have heard my father speak of Dom Pierre de Vaucelles of St Benoît who is also Master of the College of Navarre.'

'Yes, I know of him, and she to whom I allude is, I believe, a relative of Father de Vaucelles. This lady has offered to take Marthe Rose into her service — not just yet, of course, for she is gauche, untrained, but when she is more *au fait* — you understand?'

'Perfectly, madame.' And I was uncomfortably aware of an echo from Fat Margot's self-same words, but with, one hoped, a less equivocal interpretation.

'Pray, sir,' abandoning her chin, Mademoiselle de Bruyères offered me the dish of fruit, 'I can recommend these grapes from my vine.'

I refrained from expressing my preference for the grape distilled, and accepted, with homage, the poorer substitute.

'The girl will be well cared for by Madame de Vaucelles,' I was assured. 'You will appreciate, messire, that while I have in my house at present no *protégée* but Marthe Rose, there will be others whom I rescue from iniquity. Not often do they come to me untainted as is this child. I feel it were neither right nor proper that she be brought into close contact with these fallen ones. Do you not agree?'

'Madame,' I rose from my seat to make her a devout obeisance, 'I am in complete accord with and greatly touched by your most charitable magnanimity.' I lifted my empty goblet. 'Allow me to help myself to wine that I may drink to your health and your good works, madame.'

'But certainly, messire.' The lady filled her cup to return my toast. 'I hope you will persuade Father Villon to give me the favour of his company.'

'With all my heart I thank you in the Father's name. But I have this to say, dear lady.' And, my tongue loosened by madame's fine Barsac that mixed not well with the inferior stuff sold by de Turgis at the Mule, I said it. 'While you, of your bounty, save the Mary Magdalenes of this sinful city, you have not thought to save yourself.'

'Sir!' Wrathful resentment blazed from those blackcurrant eyes. 'Do you dare insinuate that I —' A mottled flush suffused her pastry-coloured face, so very like a pie.

'No, no, my lady, no!' I hastily assured her. 'You misunderstand me. I am come to apprise you of danger. You are known to all Paris for your charitable works and, if I may suggest, for your considerable wealth. If you will take what I advise in your own interest, madame, you would do well to have about your house some more able-bodied younger man than your aged servant, endowed as you are with ineffable charm and unique attractions.' Again, exaggeratedly, I bowed, watching the effect of this on the receding red of indignation replaced by a simper too painfully girlish. 'One who would deem himself honoured,' I rashly pursued, 'were he permitted the right to protect you from importunate admirers and unwelcome interference — one who would guard, shield, and fight for you, if need be, with his life.'

I think by this time I was rather drunk; and as always when wine worked in me, after the first maudlin stages of slurred speech, I became loquacious and repetitive. On I rushed. 'One, who given the right — I say the right, madame, to stay beside you —' *and keep an eye on Marthe Rose*, I inly added, *should de Montigny get wind of her here*, for he was ever a stalker of virgins, ripe for raping — 'to guard and shield,' I gabbled, parrot-wise, 'and faithfully watch over you — the right, I say, madame, to enrol myself your knight-at-arms if you will but give into my charge you and your — uh-uch!' This effusion was halted by an explosive belch that I managed to turn into a sob and which, to my discomfiture, was received with blushes and eye-blinking stammers while that rasping voice, not undeservedly likened by my mother to that of the ravens of Montfaucon, softened to a wheezing breath.

'Sir, indeed, sir, and truly, sir... I know not what to say or how to... Give me time, Messire François, to consider. I am greatly overcome...'

And so was I to perceive my manoeuvres on behalf of that brat, Marthe Rose, had been too eagerly misapprehended.

'Sir, I am beyond words gratified that the son — the foster-son — of my most Reverend Father Confessor should make me this offer. Yet reflect, messire, on the disparity of age between us. I am old enough to be your...' again that simpering blush, 'your elder sister. But sir, I understood you were destined for Holy Orders. Surely I am more than honoured that you should wish to renounce your chosen celibacy for ... dare I hope ... for me?'

Rising from her seat, she advanced, her hands outstretched to mine, and as I sprang from my stool to avoid a threatened embrace, I slithered sideways and knocked over my cup of wine. As I stooped to retrieve it the sleeve of my gown fell back to reveal a scarlet thread of blood from René's sword-thrust.

'Why, what have you?' Compassion most tender engulfed me. 'My poor, sweet boy... How did you come by this wound?'

'A mere nothing, madame,' I fabricated rapidly. 'A scratch from a rusty door nail.'

'So? Then let me bathe and bind it.'

She went to the dresser, pulled open a drawer and took from it a roll of linen. 'I keep this by me for emergencies. That child has yet to learn how to use a knife at table; she is always cutting herself instead of her meat.'

Pouring wine into a goblet, she dipped the strip of linen and washed the wound — with a damnable waste of good Barsac, thought I, nor did she offer to refill my emptied cup — and while she tended me, her fingers caressed my hairy arm, her eyes upgazing, moist with emotion, her heavy breasts rising and falling.

It was awful.

And what in the devil, I wondered, is the charm of my rat face and undersized body to whet the appetite of women, young and old?

'Come to me again, messire, come soon,' she croaked, 'and then … who knows?'

I fled from her, appalled.

That episode, unexpected as it was uninvited, caused me to avoid the house of Madame de Bruyères as if it were stricken by the plague. I had done what I could to warn her of possible danger to come, and if she went deprived of her marital joys, I was disinclined to recompense her.

Another week went by, during which time I applied myself to my studies with a fervour that earned me the approval of Dom Guillaume.

'How blessed am I,' he murmured, coming in upon me where I sat, deep in Aristotle, 'to find you turn from play to work and with such earnest will.'

Guiltily I watched a moisture slide from under his wrinkled eyelid, at sight of which a stone stuck in my throat as I replied, 'For your sake, Father, and in token of your bounty to one so worthless, I will do all in my power to satisfy you and my masters.'

'My boy!' That incipient tear — he was always one for tears — enlarged in volume, filling both eyes. Removing his spectacles he wiped them and laid a hand in blessing on my head. 'God has answered my prayers, praise be to the All Highest. Whatever your vocation, whether it were for Holy Orders, medicine or law, your choice must rest with you. Your tutors inform me you show an aptitude for metaphysics. So be it. Once you have taken your doctorate it will be for you to decide your future.'

I seized his hand and kissed it. 'I want only to please and repay you, Father, for all that you have given me in guidance and in love.'

'I am more than amply repaid,' was the gentle rejoinder, 'in so good and so grateful a son. And now, dear child, I must tell you — loath as I am to disturb you at your work — that Mademoiselle de Bruyères invites me to sup with her this evening, and graciously extends her invitation to you. Will you come?'

Anticipating some such summons I had prepared my answer to it. 'I would most gladly accompany you, Father, but for the next few months I dare not allow myself any relaxation from my studies. Pray, Sir, thank madame for me and beg her to excuse my absence.'

'A fair enough excuse, my son, which Mademoiselle de Bruyères will haply understand. God be with you.'

I watched him go off, well pleased with himself — and, I had not a doubt, with his hostess, whom I hoped he would serve with a more willing grace than I had served her.

I returned to Aristotle, and as ever when I gave myself to this greatest disciple of Plato, I was struck anew with the stark realism of his philosophy. Here is a man, the first of the Metaphysicians, who lived almost eighteen hundred years ago, yet sought to unravel the mystery of life and death as one continuous ascending scale from Matter. And what, I ask myself, *is* 'Matter'? Nothingness, a chimera, destitute of form. Yet, from this 'Matter', of which we know nothing, all Being may rise to pure Actuality, the Absolute, or 'Thought thinking Itself'. This, as I translate literally, Aristotle's meaning, is what he of an heathen age calls God; hence Theology given to the

First Philosophy: First, because it deals with the Ultima Thule of Being.

Exciting revelation! He, then, is my master, and on his rigid system of reason will I model myself, dispense with falsifying sentiment and seek truth where it is to be found, whether in bawdy-house or château, in the arms of Alma Mater, or the gargoyles of Notre Dame; for God, the Eternal Creator — this the Platonic ideology — could not make the world eternal as He Himself is eternal, since the world, the whole universe, is Matter and destructible; but He, the Indestructible, made the world, the Cosmos, in the moving image of eternity: Time. The soul of man, like the soul of the universe, is indeterminate between the corporeal and spiritual, ever rising from Matter to achieve the purest heights. Yes, I see how greatly influenced by, although converging from Plato is this great master… And so deeply engrossed was I with him that I did not hear the sound of a commotion out and beyond the cloisters beating like a muffled drum in my ears but unheard by my sense that could not differentiate between this peculiarly systematic distant throb and the usual buzz of the town before curfew.

Nor was I roused from my reverie, until — 'François!' — Madame Blanche, her face white as her coif, stood in the doorway. 'Thank God you are not embroiled in this latest devilment!'

'What devilment!' Impatient of interruption I swung round on her, glowering. 'Don't stand there gaping like a landed fish. Has the house been thieved?'

'Not this house, Lord forbid, but our scullion here whose mother serves in the kitchen of Mademoiselle de Bruyères has come back running as if the wolves were at his heels, and he says that they — the students — have robbed the lady of her stone.'

So they had done it, curse them! Working silently, as ants in the dusk, while Father Guillaume supped with madame and I was stuck here at my books.

I started up. 'I must go to him at once. The Father is her guest this evening.'

'No, you don't. There's hell's work out beyond.' Madame la Vache folded her arms and her lips, her portly back barring the door.

'If there's hell's work out beyond I'll be in it,' said I, 'to flay hell's demons. Let me pass!'

'Nay, now, François, keep yourself to yourself, and save your skin. You've been in mischief enough — stay quiet. The Father is safe in the house of my lady, and the stone is gone, so what can you do?'

'That remains to be seen. Let me pass.'

'Not if I know it. Go back to your books.'

'And you to your kitchen.' I pushed her aside; but she, who had spanked, scrubbed and nursed me since I was seven stood firm as a rock.

'I'll not budge. I see what you're after. Any mischief that's brewing is grist to your mill, my lad.'

At which, without further parley, I ducked under her arm that would have held me, and was off, clattering down the stone stairs and out at the door.

The curfew was ringing from Notre Dame when I reached the house in the Place de Grève. Lights twinkled in windows through the gathering dusk; the lamps of the city faded one by one, and from the Châtelet came the *sergents*, armed with staves and lanterns and followed by a squad of mounted Archers but — too late!

The students, led by René, had done their damnedest. A yawning chasm marked the site where the Pet-au-Diable had stood. None knew its origin or how it came to be there. Some said the Ancient Romans had set it up as a sacrificial altar to their gods; others said it marked the entry to the nether world where ruled the Prince of Darkness, hence its name. None the less the lady loved and cherished it as a monument of grandeur to her state.

How, I wondered, had they managed to uproot and lug it off unseen, unheard? They must have been well organised by René, timed to be done before curfew. The night was moonless, starless, and clouds low with a fog drifting up from the Seine to join the shadows and cover their tracks.

While I waited, undecided whether or not I should call at the house and report the theft of the stone to madame and my father, and so clear myself of any part in it, I heard from afar a triumphant uproarious shindy; a shouting and cheering and yelling and singing with a sound of pipes and tabor, located as coming from the direction of the Place Maubert in the heart of Sorbonne's territory.

I hesitated no longer.

Since the house in the Place de Grève, and madame, my father, and, not the least, Marthe Rose, had appeared to have suffered no harm, I would join in and partake of the sport, but not before I had lowered myself into the crater left by the uprooting of the stone.

Sufficient light from madame's windows and the candles at the foot of Our Lady's Shrine on the wall of the church, disclosed not a token of treasure overlooked, no coin fallen in the wrenching open of a casket. My scrabbling search on hands and knees gave me nothing but lumps of moist clay, oozing mud, and much evidence of deep and heavy spade-work. Whatever of gold had been found must have already been distributed among his confederates by René, who would certainly have kept the lion's share of it, blast him! I could have done with an *écu* or two myself. No such luck … So off I went across the bridge to the Place Maubert.

Past belief was the sight that met my eyes. A surging mob of *escholiers* run dancing mad around a bonfire in mock worship of the stone. They'd dug it in and set it up, propped with beams, at the foot of Mont St Hilaire, crowned it with rosemary and laurel, and were saying prayers to it!

I caught a glimpse of René in the fierce blaze of the fire on which he was piling wood and shavings, with a look of savage excitation on his wicked, handsome face as of some drunken young Dionysius. And there was Guy Tabarie, cursing and yelling himself hoarse. 'Not a sol, not half a one! We're duped.' And so, very thoroughly, they were, to dig up a spadeful of worms and no more.

Unnoticed I stood on the fringe of that crazed crowd who, incited by René, had no very clear notion what all this tumultuous frenzy was about, but given the flimsiest chance to run riot they would seize it, *diable à quatre*. First year scholars, Baccalauréates, graduates, clerks, incipient Doctors of Medicine, the Arts, Theology, were out and swarming round their captured prize like bees round their queen in her flight.

Wrapped in my cloak, hat well over my eyes, I watched their wild antics. I had no wish now to join them. What sense or reason in this foolery? Although Sorbonne was a city contained in itself and indulgently blind to the pranks of the students, I believed they would never get away with this. Besides, and even at the risk of madame's blandishments, I felt it to be imperative that I should keep an eye on Marthe Rose, since it was obvious that René, to say nothing of the others, was out to do his worst, gone berserk! And as if drawn by a magnet, back again I doubled to the Place de Grève to find the house shuttered and dark.

Long I stood gazing up at the lightless windows, waiting — for what? The trill of a song, a child's laughing whisper? Not a sound, which was as it should be. She was fast asleep and safe from molestation, or by now she may have been sent away to this — who was it — Madame de Vaucelles?

If so, you can wash your hands of her, I said to myself and dived into the darkness, a shadow among shadows, drifting home.

SIX

When the loss of her stone was discovered the next day, Mademoiselle de Bruyères, loud in lamentation, swept down on Civic Authority, demanding instant return of her Pet on pain of death to all concerned in this monstrous, outrageous, perfidious, malevolent, nefarious … and so *ad infinitum*. The string of adjectives was inexhaustible when, in duty bound, I betook myself to madame to offer my condolence and was treated to a similar tirade, with the peroration, 'And you, sir, I ask if, in view of your honourable intent on my behalf —' the lady induced a languishing look to turn my stomach — 'in view,' she purringly repeated, 'of your warm interest in me, which I dare not, for your youth's sake, encourage —' *Saint François,* thought I, *be thanked for that* — 'yet if you could give me but an inkling as to the leader of this dastardly crime, I'll have him roped and hanged on Montfaucon.'

'Alas, madame, I cannot name any one for such merited punishment, which indeed would be too merciful an end for him since name one, name all, except myself, your humble servant,' I bent my knee, 'who, you may remember, gracious lady, came to warn you of pending danger — a premonition of this evil that has befallen you.'

'Ah, how well do I remember! Would to God I had followed your advice, messire, and granted you the rightful protection of my house, my Pet, and … me.' Another of those looks, a tremble of her hand to mine that I, fingering my beads, eyes up, essayed unsuccessfully to parry.

'I can promise you, madame, that you will receive reparation for this most shocking…' My voice dwindled. Behind the lady's head the arras stirred and, watchfully alert, I saw the face of Marthe Rose peep out, withdraw, and peep again, to stay. Her comic little nose was puckered, her lips curving up in a faun-like smile that made her look half girl, half boy.

'But how — but when?' wailed madame. 'You speak of reparation and in truth I found the city sympathetic, but you know how it is. Authority has been ever indolent in asserting civic law against Sorbonne. Ah, if only my dear husband were alive! He, a notary of the very highest order, would not scruple to bring these malefactors — the whole university if needs be — to justice.'

I had but half an ear for this, since Marthe Rose, clad in her creamy woollen gown of nun-like chastity, had now revealed herself. Mind you, I hadn't seen her for a month or more, and seeing her again I perceived in her a subtle change, indefinable, elusive. It was as if a bud, tight-closed, yet full of the promise of flower, were unfolding, or about to unfold… Which poetic bathos, in this long retrospect, may be excused, for when I looked again there was nothing of flower in the bud unless it were of stinging nettle, where, soundless, she stood behind madame's chair to mime in dumb show every word, every gesture and trick of beard-plucking that I had all to do to hold my splutters and was brought to myself with an emphatic, more business-like end to madame's plaint…

'You, messire, will therefore understand that I demand and insist upon redress and full compensation for my loss.'

I rose; I bowed again. 'Rest assured, noble lady, you and yours will not go unprotected or unrecompensed.'

'Mine?' And now she was weeping. 'What is left to me of mine? Childless, widowed, bereft of my one and only treasure…'

My glance strayed to the oaken dresser adorned with those lavish carved vessels of gold, and to my inner man, *Your one and only treasure,* I submitted, *is something of an understatement.*

Marthe Rose, catching the return of my eyes to her, gave out a smothered giggle.

Madame's head jerked round as if pulled by a wire. 'What is it? Who is there?'

'''Tis myself, my lady.' Meekly Marthe Rose moved into madame's orbit.

'Oh, so! You. And what do you want?' her lady unamiably enquired.

'To tell you, mistress, that I have now my catechism word for word if you would care to hear it.'

'This is no time to come at me,' quacked madame. 'Do you not see I have a visitor? Pay your duty, girl, to Messire Villon. Where are your manners?'

'I trust,' said I sternly to the bob of Marthe Rose, whose lowering of an eyelid, well out of range of madame's vision, was saucily as near a wink as made no matter, 'that you have profited by the good office of your godsent benefactress.'

'Godsent my fiddler's bitch!' was the shocking reply from the corner of her mouth.

'And if,' I continued, uneasily aware of the tantalising uplift of that mouth as it widened to my words and aroused in me an urge to wring her neck or tumble her — or both — 'if Mademoiselle de Bruyères would permit I hear this child's catechism and report upon her progress?'

'Indeed, sir, yes. I am too distraught to catechise her, and if you will relieve me I would be much obliged. And you, too,

Marthe Rose, should be honoured that Messire Villon offers you his... Ah, ah, ah-ah!' A paroxysm of acutest pain appeared to overcome her. 'My head, my bursting head!' She raised her hands to it. 'I have had no rest, no peace of mind, no sleep since this calamity befell me... Rose, go with Messire Villon. Take her, sir, take her to the anteroom.' She pointed to a door in the arrased wall, at the same time calling, 'Marie, Marie!'

The maid came running.

'My phial, my physic, my drops... Fetch me my drops. I expire, I swoon...' And as Marie fled to her bidding, 'Messire François, your arm, if you please.' She leaned her head on my shoulder with murmurs of, 'Lend me your young strength. My heart ... it weakens. I die...' But she looked uncommonly robust for one *in extremis*. 'Recover me my stone, messire, and I will give you all, but all that you... desire.'

So what with the horrific implication conveyed in these fainting words, the uprolling of her eyes, her heaving bosom, and her hands that clutched at mine; and what with that brat behind her chair, pantomimically reflecting this performance, I came out in a muck sweat and was only saved unceremonious disentanglement from the lady's coiled weight by the entrance of her maid.

'Send for the doctor. Your mistress,' I said, 'is in need of medical attention.'

The maid, a rosy-cheeked pert little piece, received this with a knowing grin and the rejoinder, ''Tisn't medical attention, sir, my lady needs, no nor physic neither, unless it be physic of some other sort than Doctor gives her.'

'What?' Mademoiselle de Bruyères inclined her deaf ear. 'What do you say? Speak up.'

She spoke up. 'I was saying, madame, that your physic is turned stale being too long out of use. You'll be needing fresher, stronger drops than these to revive you.' And casting a meaningful saucy look at me, she tilted the phial to her lady's lips.

'Adieu, madame,' I made a hurried exit. 'May God send you speedy recovery. I will call again tomorrow to enquire how you do.'

Leaving Marie to her ministrations I grabbed Marthe Rose and hustled her away.

The ante-chamber adjoining the larger apartment of madame was, in contrast, of cell-like simplicity and size, unfurnished save for a chair and a round table. A window set high in the stone wall gave little light, but under it stood a shrine of the Holy Mother and Her Babe.

'I knew,' said Marthe Rose, 'that you would come today, because last night I burned three candles to Our Lady, and prayed Her you would come — and here you are. But why so long in coming?'

'I have more to do than wait on you,' I told her, brusquely. 'And now what of your catechism? Repeat it to me *verbatim*.'

'In a minute, but I've forgotten half of it already. My head is full of holes. You know, don't you, that I am soon to go away from here?'

'When? How soon?'

'Next week, she says, to the house of some old crab-fish who'll pickle me in brine if I —' she mimicked to the life, or as near to life as her young treble could make it, the raucous voice of madame — 'if I do not "mind my manners, conduct myself seemly, and cleanse my heart of evil."'

'Which,' said I, 'will need some cleansing, if I know you.'

'But you don't,' she nodded elfishly. 'You don't know me now — as I am. Can't you see how I am changed?'

She came close to me, so close that not a hand's breadth divided us. 'It happened on Friday the thirteenth of this month at full moon. They say Friday the thirteenth is an unlucky day, but it isn't unlucky for me. It's my birthday.' She put out a finger to touch my chin. 'You've a cleft in the middle — just here.'

I eased myself away from her, who, with the persistence of a virulent mosquito, pursued: 'And you've hairs growing out of your nostrils. Aren't you dark? Like a gipsy.'

I was tongue-tied; her nearness, the lure of her eyes so strangely coloured, green and gold, full of mischief incarnate or something more than mischief, was causing me acute discomfort. I heard my voice high up in my throat. 'You cannot evade your catechism by nonsense such as this. Come, child, recite me —'

Swiftly interrupting, sulky-mouthed, 'I'm not,' she said, 'a child any more. I thought you'd have seen by the look of me a … difference: "You are no longer a child, Marthe Rose".' Again that diabolic mimicry. '"Your womanhood has come upon you. May you find Grace in Our Blessed Lady's sight who conceived, at your same age, the Son of God.' And so I prayed that if I am a woman grown, Our Lady will find me a husband and that I shan't have to leave you. I could stay here in Paris and see you as often as I wish.'

Those eyes, golden-green, were fixed on mine, her upper lip shortened above her small white teeth. 'If the Blessed St Antoine — I prayed to him, too, because he always finds lost things for me, but I haven't lost a husband yet not having one to lose — and I did — I hope you won't mind, I know it's an impertinence and you a learned scholar — I *did* ask St Antoine to find for me — you!'

My heart gave an upward leap and sank with a queer dragging sensation as if my very life's blood had been drained from it. And there I stood, dissolved in drenching sweetness, when, with a swift confiding movement she put her arms around my neck and pressed her cheek to mine with the whisper, 'Don't you *want* to have me with you ... always?'

The man was made of steel who could resist her. I could not. I gave way then and took her. She let herself be taken, surrendering her mouth for my possession with a young impulsive innocence that smote me, pulled me up and gave me back my senses.

Out of breath and sullenly, 'I'm mad,' I said.

And she: 'I like you better mad. Won't you let me go with you ... away from here? I don't want to live with ugly old she-crabs who order me do this, do that, go there, stand up, sit down. Madame what's-her-name VauceUes — she came to look me over and I heard her tell my lady, for I had my ear to the door — that she would find work for me in the kitchen and out of it as I had been used to mind geese and she'd a plenty, and goose-girls were hard, she said, to come by. But I don't want,' tears welled and overflowed, 'to be minding geese no more. You wouldn't wish that for me, would you?'

And for my further torment she came close to me again her face upheld, eyes questioning, pleading. 'You took me from Fat Margot and gave me to my lady. Can't you take me away from her, too? Please, oh, do, messire, please...'

I was lost, submerged in the torrent of desire that overswept me. Desire? Was this fevered craving which, since first I saw her, had haunted me, had taunted me with longing unconfessed, desire only? A fleeting hunger to be fed and satisfied, forgotten? Or was it the deep ingrowing root of love ... and for a child of fourteen?

I clung to that reminder as a drowning man clings to a spar, and put her from me, harshly, while with inward mechanical insistence I repeated: *I am mad, I must be mad. Or drunk.*

Yes, drunk with her who, greedy for fruits unripened, infected by the storm of passion she had roused, eagerly returned her mouth to fuse with mine, while my fingers sought to probe beneath the woollen cuirass that enshrouded those twin buds, their tender stalks uprisen, firm and yielding to the sweet surprise of touch, until a small convulsion shook her and in my arms she slackened and lay limp.

I tore my lips from hers, gazing down at her closed eyelids. 'Unlock your eyes,' I whispered, 'look at me.'

Her lashes lifted; her eyes were wonder-charged. 'What,' her whisper answered mine in a shuddering long sigh, 'what happened? It was heaven.'

'I loved you,' I told her, and knew it for the truth, 'and I will love you while I live and … though I die.'

'Messire Villon! Rose! Marthe Rose!'

Recalled by the squawk of a raven from celestial heights to nethermost arid reality, we — at that moment both children, for I, too, was still in my teens — started guiltily, to stand apart abashed at the sight of the apparition at the door.

Alas for Marthe Rose. She, not I — no, I was not reviled. I, more sinned against than sinning, had fallen victim, as had the lady herself, to the treacherous tricks of a harlot.

'The scales,' madame uttered, awfully, 'are fallen from my sight, to see this serpent nourished in my bosom,' heavily her right hand thumped it, 'who, with her lies and masquerade of chastity deceived you, Messire Villon, to bring her here, into my house, that she be clothed and fed and taught the niceties of gentle life and go forth again, well schooled and tutored to demand a higher price for the sale of her tainted flesh that feeds the vile appetites of men. A trollop, a lying, foul and filthy, sluttish whore, a —'

'Madame!' I strode forward. ''Tis you who lie, defaming her. Take back your words! She is as innocent today as when I gave her to your mercy. I pray you to believe —'

'Believe?' The avalanche of madame's wrath descended now on me. 'Believe? You ask me not to believe the evidence of my own eyes? *You* to defend her, you —' she choked, clutching at the air — 'you, who are fallen prey to her lust. Did I not see you both entwined, embracing, clasped. And you would have me believe — oho, aha, ah — hah!' Hysterics were rapidly rising.

I glanced aside at Marthe Rose, who pale, scared, her underlip sucked in, her fingers crossed, was making tiptoe for the door.

'Stay!' The lady side-stepped with a hiss of silken petticoats as if she housed beneath them a colony of snakes. 'Stay where you are. I am not done with you yet. Sir,' to me again, 'you cannot right her who is sunk deep in sin. You, I'll grant, have, even as myself, been wrongfully misused, betrayed. But because of her youth I will not, have her thrown back to ply her filthy trade upon the streets. I will give her one last chance to save her soul. But not — *not* —' at each repetition of the word madame's voice rose to a shrieking crescendo — 'NOT in *my* house. She will go forthwith to Madame Vaucelles, who has a villa in the country outside Paris where this wanton brand, plucked from the burning, will serve the geese again and where, if she seeks the mortal sin of fornication, she can seek and find it — with the pigs!'

And that, when she paused to recover her breath, was the end, disastrously, of that.

But not for me the end of Marthe Rose, nor of the gnawing increasing anxiety when all my efforts to find her had failed. 'A villa in the country outside Paris' would, I thought, have offered little difficulty in my search for her. There were not so many houses of the upper bourgeoisie beyond the city's walls. I could not, for reasons apparent, approach Mademoiselle de Bruyères to enquire of her *protégée*, even though it would appear I had been vindicated as actively connected with her shame. I kept my distance from the lady and went on tenterhooks lest she should have spun my father the tale of that awkward contretemps in which I and Marthe Rose had been involved.

But when, after a week or two, no word nor sign from madame was forthcoming, I carefully pumped Father Guillaume. Did he know if Dom Pierre Vaucelles of St Benoît had any kin of his name who lived near Paris?

Surprise flickered mildly across that placid face. 'I know nothing of his kin, my son. Why do you ask?'

'Because I'd heard,' I had my answer pat, 'there may be no foundation for what is, likely, gossip of the students, that a kinsman of Dom Pierre, who lives somewhere beyond Paris, tutors scholars for their finals. And, as I am backward in Greek, I wondered if I might study under him for a few weeks? I greatly fear that without some guidance I may not pass with the honours you would wish for me — if I should pass at all.'

'You will, my son, you will. And it joys me to perceive in you such becoming modesty in respect of your work and your achievements. God has bestowed on you, François, an exceptional gift, the power to express yourself in verse. Yes,' a smile dawned, 'I have read your scribbled efforts left lying where they fell under the table in your room, and I think that your future lies, not in academics. Can a thrush be taught to sing by — academics?'

And as I stood there wordless, he answered my unspoken question: 'Yes, François, you see, I know — and know you better than you know yourself.'

'I shall never know myself,' I said, in whispers, and went from him, tear-blinded.

If only I were worthy of his all-seeing tolerance and all-loving comprehension. If only I could kill that lesser, baser half of me possessed by a hundred idiot voices all shouting 'This is I'. And what is 'I', the Ego, but an ephemera, the May-fly whose adult life exists only for one day? So snatch and taste whatever flux and flow of swift impressions the fleeting moment offers, for Life is short and Death is long, and in Death alone can consciousness be multiplied to find absolution, consolation, renaissance.

And still my search persisted. Dom Pierre Vaucelles, whom in desperation I determined to tap and extract from him some possible clue, had, I learned, left Paris for the Vatican and was not expected back until the spring. So, while I chafed and fretted and struggled with my work, faced by the nearing bogy of my finals, I abandoned my nightly haunt of taverns to steal out, like some starved hound in pursuit of its quarry, padding through dark open fields on the track of a glimmering light to find a lonely farmhouse, nothing of a villa, not a sign of one.

At last my questioning of farmers, for sometimes I would hunt by day, set me hot upon a scent... Vaucelles? Yes, Madame de Vaucelles and her husband, a notary, recently retired on account of his ill-health, lived at Bourg-la-Reine on the Orléans road.

It would seem that madame's indication of a villa 'in the country outside Paris' was little wide of the mark, and I walking round in circles to miss it! I must have passed it a dozen times in my perambulations, for, hidden deep in woods behind high walls, the house was not discernible from the road. But now so close upon the track, I determined to follow it up and would have done so had not a rising of the students flung the whole of Paris in a ferment to bar the city gates and put all of us who ventured near them out of bounds.

To appease the lady for the theft of her Pet-au-Diable, the city's Provost, Robert d'Estouteville, ordered Maître Jehan Bezon, his Lieutenant-Criminel of the Châtelet, to recapture and restore the stone to its rightful owner. Accordingly, Maître Bezon, attired in all the glory of his office and followed by his *sergents*, marched up the steep incline of the Rue St Hilaire, dug out madame's Pet, hoisted it on a cart and delivered it, not to her but to the King's Guards in the courtyard of the Palais Royal pending judicial inquiry.

You might have thought we would have been subdued by this warning. Not at all. Armed with sticks and hatchets or whatever weapons came to hand, the students stormed the Palais, bound and gagged the sentries, dug out the stone and dragged it back to Sorbonne.

This further desecration set madame on the warpath, declaring she would not wait for judgement to be passed upon the ruffians who had stolen her Pet. She was lost without her darling, so she put up another in its place.

No sooner did the students — and I was with them now having no more interest in madame, her belongings, or the inmates of her house — no sooner, then, did we sight this second awful thing than we tore it up and dragged it off to stand beside its twin on St Hilaire, crowned, not with rosemary and laurel but with one of our old hats!

Poor Mademoiselle de Bruyères looked to lose, as well as both her treasures, all her wits. Daily she bombarded Provost d'Estouteville with hysterical entreaty she be given reparation, that the villains who had worked this monstrous evil should be boiled, butchered, hanged, and her stones restored to her without delay, or she would herself take action to expose not only these illegal vile practices of the university but the disgraceful lack of principle and maladministration of the civic law, for which she held the Provost entirely responsible.

D'Estouteville, we take it, was in something of a fix. Since ever the College has been founded by Robert de Sorbon in 1256, receiving some twenty years later the sanction of Pope Clement IV, continuous strife had existed between the city and the State of university. The students, among whom had always been a smattering of riff-raff, felons, pilferers, and such, would stop at nothing short of murder. They knew they held the whip hand with the mark of the Church on their heads, for Provost, Parliament and the King himself were powerless to exercise their strength against the tonsure and the gown.

There could have been no man in Paris in more pitiable plight than Robert d'Estouteville. Torn between his duty to the city and obeisance to the Pope he was faced with a dilemma from which nothing but the sword could extricate him. Therefore, when not only madame but the town rose up in a body demanding these incessant brawls and riots of the students that disturbed their peace by day and sleep by night should be suppressed, he called his *sergents* and Archers — the mounted police — to arms.

It was a repetition, on a larger scale, of the earlier uprising in November when the long-suffering *sergents* had taken on themselves to beat us up. But this was not to end in any passing skirmish. The city was out for blood and meant to have it.

At the order of Lieutenant-Criminel Bezon to 'spare none, break all, take all, *kill* all who resist', the officers of the law charged down on us to make short shrift of the unwary. Some, and I among them, took refuge in l'Hôtel de St Etienne, the house of a priest, Père Andre Bresquiet who, luckily for him, was away saying Mass at St Julien le Paure.

I and René, Colin, Tabarie and others, whose names I have forgotten, forced our way in, terrorised the Father's servants and made a bee-line for the cellar where I, who had dined and wined once or twice with Père Andre, knew that he kept a goodly store, as also it seemed did the *sergents*.

Obeying their lieutenant's orders, 'Break all, take all,' they proceeded so to do. They hammered at the doors, broke through, and smashed the windows, ransacked the priest's cupboards, looted plate, books, bed-clothing, and finally trooped after us into the cellar.

We were no more than a dozen to about fifty of them, most of whom were already roaring drunk, having sampled the cellars in every house where suspected students might be hiding. With maniacal howls and at sword and dagger-thrust, they drove us up the stairs, arresting resisters right and left. I managed to escape by kicking my assailant in his — yes, my good old trick. But they got de Montigny and Tabarie — not Colin, for he, who had taught me that means of protection, used his knowledge to advantage. So we got away and hared for home.

I learned afterwards from René that the *sergents* bound them hand and foot, tossed them down like so many piles of faggots, sat on them and drained two casks of Father Andre's Beaune by turning the tap and lying under each in turn, until all were in a state of palsy which enabled their prisoners to loosen their bonds and get away quick. But the total haul of prisoners that night was near on forty.

I later heard from Tabarie that he had seen one of Bezon's men parading the streets in the gown of a scholar. His tale, borne out by others, rang true, or true enough to cap the injuries of Sorbonne with one last crowning insult.

For a while, however, nothing happened. Both gown and town preserved an inimical silence, while those thirty odd arrested students disconsolately kicked their heels in the Châtelet, and I sat, and stood, before Maître Conflans, to take, by the skin of my teeth and with no honours, my Master of Arts degree.

And in that same month of May, Sorbonne met in solemn council to consider the wrongs of her sons. It was finally decided that a deputation led by the Rector, Maître Jehan Hue and followed by eight hundred students, should cross the river and call upon the Provost at his house in the Rue de Jouy by the Church of the Celestines.

D'Estouteville received the Rector and his delegates with guarded cordiality, heard the address of Maître Hue, in which he demanded that all imprisoned scholars should be at once released, and brought before a tribunal for fair and proper trial, a request that was readily granted.

The deputation departed with seeming good will on both sides, and the whirlwind might well have blown over had not the procession, on its homeward way, fallen in with our natural enemies, the *sergents*, headed by Chief Constable Le Fèvre.

The Rue de Jouy was narrow and the deputation wide with its vast train of students marching eight abreast, and as neither we nor Le Fèvre would give right of way, there we were planted at deadlock.

While our Rector calmly stood awaiting a gesture from Le Fèvre to line up his men and let us pass, the chief constable, to whom the sight of a student was anathema, flew into a passion crying, 'Strike, in the name of the King!' Whereupon his minions, whipping out their swords and daggers, struck.

We, unarmed, as always, had the worst of it. A few of us, the cravens, fled. Not I, nor de Montigny, together with some of our toughest desperadoes who, never wanting in courage, formed a ring round our Rector to guard him from the brunt of the attack.

It was a confused, multitudinous frenzy of sight and sound, of brandished steel slicing the air, of mingled curses and triumphant yells from the *sergents*, cock-a-hoop to have us at their mercy to tease with dagger prick and, worse than that, a sword-thrust through the heart of young Raymond de Mauregart, a promising scholar who had taken his Master of Arts with me.

And still the Rector stood, his pale lips moving in prayer, his fingers on the Cross suspended from his rosary while we, having no weapon but our fists made of ourselves a human wall for his protection. He went unharmed, though Maître Pierre Quoque, one of his Canons, was trampled on and cut across the face. Other dignitaries of the Church and some of the students were found by Maître Pierre hiding in a corn-bin. Regardless of his gashed cheek, he rounded up the students, tended those less hurt than he, and only when he'd got them out did he drag himself away, half-fainting, to the nearest barber-surgeon to be treated. So was it given me by one of our fellows whom he rescued.

And now the fat was in the fire with a vengeance, to light a conflagration; for, not only did the university appeal to Parliament to right its wrongs, but banned all work and lectures for a year. This, the first strike in our history, was eventually ended by Parliament's complete capitulation with the payment of two thousand *écus* as damages to the parents of our slaughtered young de Mauregart — as if damages could compensate the loss of an only son. Another two thousand went to the Rector; and six thousand to the university.

Then came the turn of those officers who, proved guilty of murder and assault, were forced to do penance each with a halter round his neck, abased and grovelling together with Le Fèvre, crying, 'Mercy, and of the King, his pardon!' before the Châtelet and all Sorbonne, for our delight.

I have given full account of this, not for my negligible part in it, but that you may realise how unpredictable was the mind of my medieval Paris that boiled men alive for petty theft, tried animals and burned them for witchcraft — yes, they did, I've seen it done — and could fling itself into bloody insensate revolt at the cost to the city of ten thousand crowns for no more than a students' 'rag'.

SEVEN

My college days were over. The ban on lectures issued by the university did not affect me who had passed my finals, to find myself unemployed and unemployable. True, I was offered for my choice, the Church, the law, or Medicine. Had I chosen the first, my father's influence might have secured me a benefice; but the priesthood, I reasoned, was not my vocation.

My mother, who for so long had awaited my preferment, must have died a little death when I told her I had renounced the church and cloister as my calling. I remember how she took it to her heart, hands folded in her lap, her fingers feverishly twining until the swollen knuckles whitened as did her lips. She had lost most of her teeth, her face was lined as a skeleton leaf, she looked years older than her age that could not even then have been more than forty-five. In my day of child marriages, although these chiefly occurred in the higher strata of society and among those of Blood Royal, women were considered old at thirty. If unwed at twenty-one they were set aside as spinsters, unless they entered a convent to become the Brides of Christ.

And watching her, as she sat in a silence charged with her unfallen tears, 'Forgive me, *ma mère*,' I said, 'but I would be a traitor to Our Lord were I to give myself to Him unless with all my heart and soul.'

She moved her head a very little, spoke no word, until on a broken breath, 'Our Blessed Lady must know best. She has other ways for you, my dear.'

I put my arm about her narrow shoulders; her bones were small and frail as an elf's. 'Yes, my little, and I think I have been offered other ways. You remember, long ago, that you asked me to write you a prayer to the queen of heaven?' I dived into my pocket, produced a parchment and read what I had written. I think it gave her comfort.

As for Father Guillaume, he in his wisdom refrained from expressing opinion either for or against my renunciation of the priesthood, but he did, tentatively, suggest that I might find my metier in medicine. That, too, I refuted.

'Sir, the science of medicine has not progressed, it has regressed since the great Hippocrates gave his divine knowledge to the world. How could I follow a school of thought that prescribes as curative for various diseases the parts and excrements of living creatures? Take, for instance, this, as advised by your physician when I had a flux of the bowels last year. Before I gave it to the doctor's apothecary to distil I construed it from the Latin, no easy task for his writing is virtually illegible but I managed to decipher, among other savoury ingredients, that it included a bullock's spleen, the urine of a she-goat, the milk of a woman, the pizzle of a stag, and the liver of a hedgehog. All these to be dried, beaten to a powder and drunk in wine. Needless to say I drank the wine — without the powder, and my malaise ran its course to cure itself.'

I saw his mouth twitch sideways; his long, lean hand brushed away a smile. 'It is likely your Latin played you false.'

'Yes, but not so likely false as the doctor's physic would have played my bowels. No, Father, I could never take to medicine, any more than medicine would take to me.'

'So be it, my son,' he said; and that was all.

By tacit consent we avoided the law, which for me would have been easier to break than to make. None the less I suffered conscience qualms that I, a graduate, must still depend on my adoptive father's charity for my support. Even the tutorship of first-year students, by which I might have earned at least my board and keep, was denied me while the ban on lectures at the university remained in force. However, I did manage to scrape together an odd white here and there as scrivener to wealthy burgesses and tradesmen, many of whom were utterly illiterate.

I found it excessively boring.

No wonder, then, that I, at a loose end, gravitated toward those octopus tentacles of the Coquillards, a secret society that ringed, not only Paris, but the whole of France.

Its members, each of whom carried, concealed about his person, the badge of the Cockleshell, were drawn from all classes, the highest to the lowest; nobles, thieves, rake-hells, vagrants, counterfeit coiners, even clerks in Holy Orders who went befriended by their frocks. There were also a few among the students suspected of joining the Fraternity: René de Montigny for one, who in the summer of the university's great strike came to blows with a couple of *sergents* outside Fat Margot's brothel and in company with two others who may or may not have been of the Coquille. All three, by order of the Provost, were banished from Paris for six months.

In consequence of the secrecy maintained by the Coquillards, operating in gangs that numbered anything from five hundred to a thousand, the police were hard put to round them up. They were slippery as eels and, if not discovered red-handed in a crime such as the waylaying on the road of some rich merchant jogging homeward on his horse to be robbed of his mount, his money, his clothes, and left lying naked in a ditch, they, who knew all the tricks, invariably escaped the none-too-stern arm of the law. Moreover, there is little doubt that some of the *sergents* themselves turned a blind eye to these manoeuvres of the Coquillards for the consideration of their share in the spoils. But to give us our due we — yes, I can speak from experience, having later joined the Brotherhood — robbed only the rich, never the poor or any man, honest or dishonest, in distress.

There was a compatriot of yours, one Robin Hood, who lived a century before my time if he ever lived at all, and whose exploits have come to us by word of mouth in ballades sung by the *godons* during the occupation, to make of him a hero. It is possible the Coquille had him and his band of 'merry men' in mind when they organised a similar society in France. Not that there was anything merry nor heroic in the methods practised by our camaraderie; yet although defiant of the law, we adhered to a discipline almost hierarchical, serving an apprenticeship before we could be accepted an initiate. We had our own language, our *jargonne*, we had our 'lords' to whom we owed allegiance, and we also had our 'king'. Him we were sworn by the oath of blood to serve, honour and obey. None other than those of his chosen inner circle knew his identity. His name and person were as secret as the society over which he held dominion absolute.

While, then, I hovered on the fringe of the Coquillards, undecided if I wished to be received or not, I passed my time between two worlds. The underworld of Paris to which I had already been admitted was but a stepping-stone to lower depths wherein I was eventually doomed to sink, or swim.

Card-sharping, dicing, drinking, whoring, I tasted all in turn, and if the taste were bitter I spewed it out in verse, jotted down between drunken bouts in the most disreputable taverns of the town, to draw with vicious pen-strokes the life in which I wallowed — save my soul!

Not only was I Master of Arts but master in the art of dissimulation. Father Guillaume, God bless him, could not know nor recognise my dual personality. François Villon, MA, the embryonic poet for whom he augured a distinguished future, had naught to do with his sly-glancing, crapulous familiar, who boldly swaggered through the streets with a basket of fish under his arm, procured — shall we say — by sleight of hand? For if we would feast and had not the wherewithal to buy it we would steal it. Why not? The shopkeepers and haranguères, who could well afford the trifling loss of a haddock or two, grossly overcharged the students, particularly since our last rampageous orgy that the very sight of one of us caused the fish-wives to spit in our faces. We also had our ways of procuring a good supply of wine to lace the fish, flesh or fowl to which we, the sons of Sorbonne, felt we were entitled. For without the body's sustenance how could the brain survive? And these clods of butchers, poulterers and fish-fags, who had no learning and were ignorant as fleas, could well afford to give. If they wouldn't give, we took.

It was I who found the means of providing us with wine. It was quite simple; just a matter of two pitchers, one filled with water and one empty. This I would summon a drawer to fill with his best Baigneux. The drawer, who was rushed off his feet when the place was crowded — I would make sure of that beforehand — hastily did so, and went to attend the call of other customers who were impatiently banging on the trestles. Behind his back I adroitly changed over the two jugs, the one containing wine, the other water, and: 'Hola, fellow,' I shouted, 'here! You've given me the wrong wine. This isn't what I ordered.'

The drawer came hurrying. 'No, sir, pardon, Baigneux is what you —'

'Idiot! I asked for Beaune. Red wine, not white.'

'But no, sir, you —'

'Don't argue, sheepshead! I know what I want and what I ordered. Take this.' I handed him the jug of water. 'Empty it and fill it up with Beaune.'

While he with my pitcher, and too harassed by the clamour of unattended customers for any further argument with me, went to fetch the Beaune, I made off with the jug of Baigneux to join René and the others at the Mule.

And if, as was often the case, I reeled home at crack of dawn to clamber up the vine and sneak through the open window of my room and lie late a-bed of a morning, Father Guillaume contentedly accepted my excuse of having lost all count of time, writing through the hours of the night. 'But I've nothing to show for my pains,' I was careful to add. 'I sweat blood, Father —' that at least was true — 'striving for what? A glimpse, a shadow, a nebula that points to heights I can never attain. I sit struggling, I suffer — even you, *Mon Père*,' I was well away now — 'even you cannot possibly imagine the unutterable torture it is to sit hour after hour striving for a word that will satisfy my rhythmic sense to find only *non*-sense, jingle, balderdash, and then to throw away a dozen lines of verse to keep — one!'

'Which goes to prove,' soothed he, accustomed to these outbursts, 'that you are no mean poet. No great creative work can ever be produced without a struggle.' Meditatively regarding me he stroked his shaven chin. 'It is a pity that Paris has no Medici as patron of the arts. Were you born a

Florentine you would, without a doubt, have gained the patronage of Cosimo. Yet,' he mused, 'there is one here in France, at Blois, our Duc d'Orléans who, God be praised, is restored to us after his long imprisonment in England. He is himself a poet and encourages young aspirants of literary merit. If I could obtain for you an *entrée* to his court... Yes, I think it might be possible. We'll see, my son, we'll see.'

He didn't see, he couldn't see, fine scholar and visionary though he was, that the life of a court poet offered no appeal to me. I knew something of the chansonettes and rondels sung by troubadours and encouraged by that very minor dabbler in verse, Charles d'Orléans, but: 'I would be gratefully honoured, Father, if His Highness would consider my mean efforts worthy of his patronage.'

'He will.' Dom Guillaume refilled his cup and mine; we were at supper. 'Yes, he will. I'll write to my friend, his Abbé.'

He did not write, nor, having toyed with the idea, did he touch on it again. He had more to occupy his mind and his attention than me and my dubious future. The ban on teaching had affected the Canons of the Church no less than it affected the students. There were a number of priests, and few so well financially endowed as Father Guillaume, who must have suffered penury during the long strike. It was over now but had caused the university much hardship and disruption, for, not until the Court of Parliament, in 1454, ordered the Rector to resume his sermons once a week, was the ban on teaching lifted.

It was about this time, having settled the differences between the city and Sorbonne, that the Provost went out of his way to conciliate the higher dignitaries of the Church. D'Estouteville, always bon viveur, lavishly entertained all the *haut monde* with his charming wife, Ambroise de Lorède, daughter of Baron d'Ivry. She was the toast both of town and gown, or those of us privileged to be included in her circle.

The tale that d'Estouteville won his bride in a tourney at Anjou had been floated round the Faculty by one of my fellows who, when visiting an uncle in that part of the country, claimed to have witnessed the combat. His vivid account of it so captured my imagination at fifteen, that, although I knew nothing of a tourney or the tiltyard, I was moved to write a ballade grandiloquently dedicated to the (then to me unknown) *'Gentilhomme nouvellement marié pour l'envoyer à son Espouse par luy conquise à l'Espée.'*

The first two verses give in acrostic the name of Ambroise de Lorède. Poor stuff it is, too: the adolescent croak from a voice as yet untrained, flat and off the note, years later to be polished, licked into shape and presented with my humble duty to the Provost and his lady. It was the evening of their soirée, the highlight of the season, to which I and Father Guillaume, a personal friend of the Provost, were invited.

How could I know when I prinked myself in my brand new academic gown, a gift from the Father, that Satan, who was ever at my elbow, would set the seal upon my Destiny to release in me that fatal force, long dormant, from which there could be no retreat and no escape, with the crossing of my star by ... Marthe Rose.

BOOK TWO: LA DAMOYSELLE AU NEZ TORTU

(The girl with the twisted nose)

EIGHT

Let me take you with me to the house of the Provost in the Rue de Jouy on that August evening in 1454. An opulent mansion was this with terraced gardens sloping gently to the Seine and approached by a courtyard under an archway on which were emblazoned the arms of the d'Estoutevilles.

The Provost and his wife received me in a lofty apartment hung with tapestries, the patient handiwork of women long since dead. The wavering flare of torches lent a strange spasmodic movement to those figures of fair ladies, knights in armour magnificently horsed, of bowmen, huntsmen, and curious homed beasts pursued by leaping hounds. The centre of the floor had been cleared of rushes, and, against that dim but lively arras, the bewildering pageantry of jewelled gowns, gemmed hilt of sword and dagger, the bright harsh overtones of colour weaved a graceful everchanging pattern to the tune of lute and viol.

My father and I were late arrivals, after Vespers, and earlier guests were already disporting themselves in the dance, if dancing you can call such stately measure of formal bow and curtsy, point the toe, turn, chassé, touch fingertips; no more. Very different from my noisy jigs and romps with girls in taverns.

This was not the first time I had been entertained by the Provost and Ambroise, yet never on so lavish a scale as tonight. A cordial greeting awaited us. Then, on bended knee, I presented my ballade to our host who read it to his wife; both were pleased to praise it, insincerely.

'Exquisite, enchanting! Your son,' our hostess gushed, 'is greatly gifted, Father Villon.'

Madame d'Estouteville, a Junoesque brunette in a dazzle of azure brocade, her hair dark-winged beneath the steepled headdress from which floated a shimmer of gauze, allowed her eyes, for a second, to linger upon mine.

'You do not dance, messire?'

'Alas, madame,' a glance aside at the elevated eyebrows of my father who, to this invitation, offered me a warning hem behind his hand. 'I have never had the time nor opportunity,' I said, with sighs, 'to indulge in such pleasurable recreation.' Our eyes met again, and meeting, found it difficult to disengage. A dimple hovered at the corner of her mouth.

'That, sir, I can believe, to my loss.'

'Madame does me too much honour.' And be damned to my tonsure and Father Guillaume's hems, I would have led her out that instant but that more belated guests diverted her attention.

I edged away and found a vantage point half hidden by an elaborately carved column of stone supporting the vaulted roof. From there I could survey the decorous assemblage who, as the music ceased, dispersed, some to stand in groups, their trivial talk strung with rhyming rondels, for it was the mode of highest fashion to twist their phrases into verse. Others wandered out on to the wide flagged terrace where tables were set with finest silver and choice wines, viands, sweetmeats, and every sort of fruit in season.

The day had spread a bridge of dusk between evening and the night; faint stars glimmered in a sky of amethyst, outshone by the golden gleam of candles. I helped myself to wine agreeably conscious of the press of women's bodies close about me, each with a man in attendance offering this and that between sprightly jests and chatter, interspersed with ditties warbled to the music of lyre and lute.

Suddenly, above that gentle chorus, a solo voice rang sweet and clear, *'Ma doulce amour…'*

I stayed the refilled goblet at my lips, set it down with a jerk to spill its brimming contents, and wheeled round, eyes searching through that blur of faces that seemed to sway and dip before my sight, while all the blood in my veins throbbed to a maddened unbelievable expectancy of… what?

'Who…?' I turned to one beside me. 'Who is that singing?' But she was not singing now; other voices had chimed in and hers was lost; or had that memory, which never quite had vanished returned again to haunt me with chimerical delusion?

He whom I questioned, and gave no answer more than a negative shrug, was a callow youth with cheeks heavily rouged and white-leaded to hide pockmarks. Towering above my meagre height to survey the middle distance, his one supercilious over-glance asked as surely as the spoken word: *And who is this weasly-faced rat of a clerk that dares accost me?*

I drained my cup, and elbowing a path through the crowded company, regained the salon where the musicians were plucking at their instruments again.

'Messire Villon!' With a flutter of her hand Ambroise d'Estouteville called me to her side.

I bowed. 'At your command, madame.'

'Not mine, messire.' Her tinkling laugh, precisely tuned, was like a carillon of bells. 'It is I who am commanded by a lady desirous of making your acquaintance. Madame…'

The room spun and vision clouded. I saw and did not see or seeing disbelieved, while the past, the present and the future met and fused in that one second's pause of Time's recurrence.

'Messire François Villon … Katherine, permit me … Madame de Vaucelles.'

Our hostess left us, and in that moment brushed with magic — or did I dream the flight of years since I had lost her — reason clarified. I knew then that not one sordid brief encounter of a day, a night, an hour, nor all my reckless plunging into life's muddiest stream, had erased the hidden thought of her, close-folded.

The guests were at their dance again. I found her hand in mine, was led — no, dragged, for my feet were leaden weighted, out on to the terrace.

Night had dropped its curtain on the sky. The throng that flocked around the trestles, snatching eatables and tossing back the drink, had lessened. The trick-light of flambeaux, held by pages ranged along the parapet, gave an emerald metallic brilliance to the moon-dusted leaves of box and privet. Passing shapes of couples seeking amorous seclusion in the tree-girdled gardens rendered a vivacious impermanence to shadows flung across the lawns from plane and yew and cypress.

On a stone bench under a rose-embowered arch we sat in silence, broken by a sudden wonder of pure sound poured from some neighbouring bough: the nightingale's song that trembled through the fragrant air in consuming solitary passion to ravish and submerge the distant flow of voices. And as suddenly as it had come, it went.

She said, 'He's burst his little throat.'

I saw her face uplifted, her lips apart, and the gleam of her teeth between them. Her hair, as ever primrose pale, was star-silvered.

'Your name!' Frenetically I asked her, 'how come you by this name? *Is* it your name?'

Without moving her head from that rapt upgazing, she told me, 'Yes, my married name. D'you think he'll sing some more? I love his song. 'Tis cruel to prison them in cages. They were being sold at the fair last week in cages and I —'

'Married?' I crashed in hoarsely. 'You are married?' My hands clutched her shoulders swinging her round, forcing her eyes to meet mine. 'What foolery is this?'

'No foolery. It's truth. The old one died and he — her husband younger than she but old as sin himself,' a wrinkling of that comical uptilted nose, 'he took me to wife.'

A wife. And still a child, if not now in years but in her gamine immaturity, for all that my reckoning gave her seventeen, a marriageable age. Yet she had blossomed: the high small breasts defined by the close-fitting velvet gown, the slender waist, the fuller hips, betokened her unfolding…

'How? Who?' I croaked, 'where is he?'

She bubbled into laughter, pointing downwards. 'There, where he was spawned. The fever killed him in three days. I know we must be punished for our sins, and my marriage to him was a mortal sin, I'll say!' She clasped her knees, her jewelled hand were like white flowers, but I could remember them engrimed with dirt.

I made my voice firm to ask her, 'Did he rape you?'

She screwed a look at me from under her drooped lashes, and a lifting of them with a sidelong glint in eyes that shone greenly in the torch-light. 'Not to say rape. He hadn't the guts, though he tried.' The same tantalising impish grin. 'He caught me in the cow-shed and tumbled me down in the straw when I was milking. I was *fille à tout faire* in and out of the house, cowherd, swineherd, goose-girl — and were they mean with their money! And him so rich with the bleeding of the poor, but they fed me well and let me sit with them at table. 'My little foster daughter,' he'd tell his guests who came to sup, and then he took to pawing me with his hands up my legs whenever he could get the chance, which I was apt at dodging until he got me unawares, the dirty swine. No, swine are cleaner far than he. I'd have lief as lain with our boar. He was a good old boar and liked to have me tickle his snout. But him!' She made a feint of retching. 'Ooh-ah — ouch! And then his wife, poor soul, she had a seizure and was bed-ridden with her face all twisted so she couldn't speak — could only make noises. I had to wait on her — a sick nurse, and what with her and the pigs and the cows and the geese — and then she died and I confessed to Father Philippe of my mortal sin of fornication, though God knows I was unwilling and the old punk too far gone to make a stand, so you see I've been a wife and not a wife, but I did penance surely in being wed to him, for Father Philippe wouldn't have me live there in that house as his — he called it concubine — and the old man being scared of hell's burning took and married me in Holy Church.'

This monologue, glibly recited, and tinged with the country burr, came to a halt on a treble sigh. 'Ah, me!' Unclasping her hands she raised them in prayerful gesture, turning up her eyes to show the lower whites, 'I bore my cross with patience, humbly, and was all the better for it. Sorrows such as these are sent to try us.'

Said I, 'Your powers of invention are almost equal to my own, if less convincing. Every word of this is lies.'

Tu-dis, dis-tu?' Another of those looks that gave her back to me aged near about fourteen, with an exaggerated mimicry of the pointed accents of *l'haut monde*. And then she giggled. 'You were always needle-sharp, but not so sharp as might be. You have me wrong, messire. Marry him I did … when I knew him to be dying.'

I nodded approval. 'Not bad for a youngster of — how old at the time? Sixteen? So that as the widow of your patron you would come in for his money.'

'Why not?' She hunched a shoulder. 'I'd earned every sol of it.'

I stifled an urge to take her by the scruff and choke her, but it was I who choked on a burst of laughter with a shouting in my heart that cried to heaven. *She is mine! We belong each to each. She is of me and in me enshrined, for my life's torment...* That I knew as surely as I knew I loved her beyond desire, beyond hope, beyond regret. And cool as ice I asked, 'When did you come to Paris?'

'These six months since. The Father at Bourg-la-Reine found a house for me in the Rue St Martin. I live there in style.'

'With whom?'

Her eyes opened widely. 'With my servants — who else? I have no kith nor kin, and few friends save Father Philippe, who himself is a friend of Robert and Ambroise.'

'H'm! Christian names?'

'But certainly. I am a lady now and well received. I've learned to mind my speech and manners as la de Bruyères taught me. Ah, de Bruyères! You should have seen her face when I called on her dressed fine and attended by my maid. She didn't know that I'd been married. She didn't care what happened to me after she sent me there when you got me into trouble. A dirty trick that was. You were more to blame than I.'

'The woman tempted me,' I murmured.

'Yes. The same old Adam hiding under petticoats.'

'A fig-leaf, if I remember rightly.'

She didn't get that one. She was away again. 'You'd 'a laughed to hear the old girl saying I'd been saved by her prayers for my redemption and took five *écus* off me for the lost. My faith!' A hand clapped to her mouth. 'You never told her, did you, of Fat Margot?'

'Marthe Rose!' I seized that hand, crushing it against my knee.

'*Not* Marthe Rose,' she said, primly, 'I'm Katherine now. Here!' She freed her fingers from my fevered clutch. 'That hurts.'

Said I between my gritted teeth, 'So does it? And I'll hurt you till your soul yells out have mercy, for the hurt that you'll give me.'

'I?' Mock tenderness was in her voice. 'Would I hurt you, my dear, my very dear, you whom I love… What's that on your lip?'

I released a tooth that had bitten deep to leave an ooze of blood. 'Why,' I managed to articulate, 'did you change your name?'

'I didn't. It is my name, or one of them. I was baptised Marthe Rose and Katherine. Here!' She nudged an elbow in my ribs, 'not a word from you to Ambroise of where you found me, eh? Look, she comes. Be careful… Ah, madame,' she sprang to her feet. 'My good friend, Messire Villon, whom I've not seen since I was so small,' stooping to measure with her hand a midget's size, 'I thought I recognised him. My beloved husband who now is with the saints, he knew him and his mother very well. And how is your excellent mother, Messire Villon? Remember me to her most kindly. So charming a lady… *Dieu*! Is that the curfew?' Far distantly ringing from Notre Dame. 'How the evening has fled! Pardon, madame, I have outstayed my time and welcome.' Complimentary cries of contradiction from Ambroise and, 'No, no, madame, indeed I cannot stay, my man is waiting to conduct me home. Ambroise, my chère Ambroise!' That devilish high-toned mimicry again. She could have made a fortune as a mummer. 'I have been most sweetly entertained. A thousand thanks.' Curtsies, embraces, feline fond. I stood apart in wonder. Was there no end to the surprise of her who, it seemed, did not surprise Ambroise? Affectation, in which Marthe Rose, or Katherine, excelled, was *à la mode*.

'Messire,' she graciously offered me a hand.

'Madame,' bowing nose to knees I raised it to my lips, 'your servant.' *And, for my damnation,* I told her below breath, *your slave.*

Yes, her slave, her puppet, dancing on a string when she called the tune to make of me her fool, posturing before her in bedraggled motley. She had me utterly, yet I gave her not a sign of my subjection. Our relationship, thus far and no farther, was tacitly maintained: I, her 'friend', her 'only friend'. How she would harp on that: she, the forlorn waif rescued from 'worse than death' in her unsoiled 'innocence'… Innocence! What a game! And what a mummer I who should have worn the cap and bells as jester to the King, his court, not hers. Yes, I knew her if she did not know me for what I was, or for what she made me. She, whose devilish sweet spell drugged me with its poison, I but one of many. God! I knew that too, and was helpless as a moth drawn to the light of her damned sorcery.

I fought, I struggled, powerless, entangled in her coils and debased in my own sight. I cursed her in my heart; I cursed myself for my enthraldom, and played my part as she played hers, but I think I played mine better.

The months raced by. I visited her almost daily at her house, luxuriously furnished. She had money right enough, but how she came by it, or if the tale she had spun me held one grain of truth, or were she ever married still less widowed, I neither cared nor dared to question.

She received me with a charming naivety as likely feigned as not, and a horse-faced maid stuck behind her chair. We played at dice. I let her cheat, changing her aces to double threes, deaf to her prattle, conscious only of my unvoiced passion's hunger.

She had cultivated, with her gift for mimicry, the manner of *grande dame* in clothes to suit the role. I loved her best in a gown of green velvet and a close-fitted yellow jacket edged with miniver. Crocus-limbed was she in that green and yellow with her pale face, her pale hair, her mouth unpainted and so red you would have thought the slightest touch would cause the blood to burst from it.

Summer faded into autumn. Wild gales tore the brittle leaves from the wind-tossed branches in the gardens of St Benoît, and I was still her creature. What did I think to gain from here Her body, unpossessed by me save in my dreams as no sane man should dream and keep his reason? Mine was gone. My hate-tormented love for her, poured out in both my Testaments, is but a shadow of that fiercer flame, spun between ecstasy and craving, by which I was devoured.

Winter came with ice and snow and the starved howl of wolves across the frozen Seine. I had not been near her for a week. In my agony I vowed that this must end. I could not sit there in her salon like a dummy with her ogress of a maid behind her chair, watching us and listening to our chitter-chatter, for she couldn't talk my language, she could only talk her own, of empty gossip: of Ambroise d'Estouteville… 'What a cat she is! All milk and honey to your face to turn and stab you in the back. Yet men adore her, even you, François, with your rondeaux and ballades and what-not. She read me one you wrote to her and laughed to split her sides — "Such jingle-jangle. Why, my dwarf," she said, "could write a better." Thus on and on while she nibbled sweetmeats and I drank the wine she offered, which was all she offered me.

Then, at last, one day, her woman left us at the summons of a servant on some household matter, or maybe at her bidding, pre-arranged, for my excrucation. If so she had timed it well to have me on my knees.

'Marthe Rose!'

'*Tais-toi*. That name is forbidden.' She laid a finger to my mouth. I seized and bit it. '*Diable!* Are you a dog to bite? What have you?'

'Not what I have — but what I want. Why do you deny me?'

'Deny? When have I denied you? My house is open door for you to come and go. I love to have you with me, my friend, my only friend.' Always the same parrot-cry, the same wide-eyed child's look from under those negligible brows.

'Your friend?' My face upraised and mouthing with spittle on my lips, I gibbered witlessly, 'I am no friend of yours, you bitch. I have no words to tell, only my blood speaks for me in my veins! What have I to render you of this world's gifts who have so much that's worthless. I, beholden to my adoptive father for every morsel of food, every rag —' I tore my shabby gown asunder to expose my hairy chest. 'You see me? Hideous, unlovely, amn't I? You would prefer a shining fair young man, hairless as an egg, a fine broad-shouldered fellow stinking of amber, or some greasy burgess with coffers of gold to pour in your lap. But I can give you more than a dandiprat's jellified fumbling and more than all a merchant's money-bags can buy. I can give you my life's work that will live in my name — and yours when you and I are sizzling below in everlasting. You'll see –ß no, you cannot see, for your mind's eye is filled with sawdust.'

I buried my face in the velvet that sheathed her naked thighs. She wore no shift beneath her gown; her shoes were fastened with latchets of gilt cord over her bare insteps. I kissed each in turn, and my fingers sliding upwards, sought to find her greedy throbbing warm response to me. And knowing her for what she was I still could know, were I not rooted in her, I'd lack nourishment, turn rotten, lose myself... She, that tawdry little trollop who could take my very soul's strings and play on them as on a harp, a cracked false tune.

'If this sweet deflowered body were all I want of you,' I dragged my mouth's explorative delight of her to say, 'I'd take it as I've taken from a hundred other women but not, no, not as — wife.'

It was out, God help me!

And she, her blurred face flushed, lips parted, bruised and swollen from my frenzied taste of them, 'Your wife,' she breathed, in wonder, 'you and I to ... wed?'

I took her chin in my hands and whispered, 'If you will wed with me and breed with me ... I see our children in your eyes.' And, saying so, I loved her then with all my manhood's strength and might, beyond all doubt and fear. Words, broken, gushed from me to tell her, 'Love, my life is yours, my whole life's heart is yours if you will have me.'

'Have... *you?*' she echoed, soft as silk and stroked my cheek. 'This is more than I durst ever hope to have. Your ... wife. And you so fine a poet. Yes, you are, the Provost says so, no matter what Ambroise may think, and I...' she wrinkled her comical nose, 'I'm just a silly.'

I could have died for her there at her feet, while she, still stroking my cheek to add her subtle fuel to my fire, said in that small one-toned voice of hers with its soft country burr, for she gave me no airs and graces, 'Let me be sure. You know

I've always loved you from the first when you saved me from Fat Margot. It wasn't my fault I was there, you know that, too, but if you stay away from me awhile so … so I may be certain, not of myself. Of you.'

What new trickery was this? I was past guessing.

'Just to be sure,' her eyes glinted narrowly beneath their pale lashes, 'and if you stay away from me…'

'Away from you!' I broke in harshly. 'Listen!' I turned my ear to the window. Dusk had crept into the room. The charcoal brazier gave insufficient heat against the biting cold that shivered under doors and through the arras. From afar there rose upon the air a savage moaning howl. 'The wolves! You might as well bid them stay their ravening with only the wind for their food.'

'Just to make sure that *you* are sure,' she pleaded. 'I am unschooled — oh, yes, I am received by quite a few of the *haut monde* like the d'Estoutevilles, because I bear the name of him whom they respected as their notary, but how can I know that what you want of me and feel for me is … love?' And she put her lips to mine and murmured through them: 'Even now, and when you touch me,' a little frisson shook her, 'as no man has ever touched me, I am … gone.'

And what I would have said to that or what I would have done to her, sitting there in her green velvet gown, disordered from my love-play, as she weighed these pros and cons with a surprisingly practical insistence, heaven knows, had not the ogress returned to take her stance behind the chair and bring me in confusion to my feet.

'I let fall a bodkin.' The cool high voice that she affected excused my disarray while stealthily she put to rights her own; but I saw her woman, purse-lipped, throw a sniffing look that told me plain as speech she knew her lady's *passetemps*, not with me alone, with many others. 'Pray, messire, do not give yourself the pain of searching for so trivial a trinket. The men will find it when they lay fresh rushes. Jehanne, light Messire Villon to the door. It darkens.'

The woman lit a taper from the burning charcoal and stalked before me, curtsying me out. But although she spoke no word, I felt her secret knowledge of all that had just passed, and, in expectancy of tips, of more to come.

NINE

I kept away as bidden, seeking to satisfy my need of her in sordid little meals with those whose trade it was to comfort the uncomforted; and when at last I called on her I was refused admittance.

A manservant, not in livery, one whom I had never seen before, a thick-set, bull-necked fellow with a glossy, expressionless face, red and veinous from deep drinking, informed me at the door that madame was not at home.

Next day I called again. The same man appeared to my knock. Was he, or was he not a servant, whose glance, with veiled insolence raked me from top to toe?

'Mademoiselle de Vaucelles has left Paris.'

He stood above me, I on the step below, sucking at my tongue gone dry and tasting, suddenly, of lemons.

'When?'

'This morning.'

'Where?'

A shrug.

When would she be back?

He could not say.

'But look, I must —'

The door was slammed and bolted. I heard his steps retreating along the stone-flagged hall, and a sound of women's laughter with a mingling of voices indistinguishable, among them hers … or whose?

I stood there seething. Was this another of her tricks to rack me? And who could be this bodyguard, this animal, this beast to play the two-backed beast with her?

Snow began to fall and still I stood locked out and gnawing at my fingers, unconscious of the cold, while suspicion, like some dark uncoiled snake, wound its swift envenomed way into my heart...

This, then, was her answer, and I supplanted by her lackey, or her leman paid for service not in coin, but in that which she withheld from me.

And turning from that door I ran, choked with words of loathing for her and for myself and my enslavement. Yes, I loathed her and I loved her and I ran as one demented nor stopped till I was winded and fell sprawling, to struggle up and see, through the snow's sting in my eyes, a red light shining like a star in hell ... calling me to follow where it led.

So at the sign of La Grosse Margot, or in the roaring company of taverns I sought forgetfulness. I also made an effort to do some honest work by coaching students for their Baccalauréate who paid me not enough to souse myself in drink; and marking time between my bouts I turned again to versifying. Everything of life or death was seen by me in ballade. A church, a gallows, a brothel, or the joyous shrill clatter of women's tongues... *'Il n'est bon bec que de Paris'*, or a lash of my whip at the captains of the Watch who pull helmets over eyes to pass a felon, for a fee; at begging friars and mendicants exposing painted sores and stumps fastened to their hidden idle hands; or pert little trolls who promenade bare-bosomed to fleece some buckskin-booted dupe; at landlords, notably de Turgis of the Pomme de Pin, who water their wine to sell as double-price good vintage. All these came in for their share of my whip, but who was I to 'cry them mercy every one'? I was no better, if a trifle worse, than some who kicked the air at Montfaucon.

Yes, all of these, and all of this I jotted down and polished, to be crowned with laurels when five centuries had trodden me to dust.

You may believe my scribbled rhyming flowed painlessly. It didn't. I wrote and re-wrote every line a score of times and still was never satisfied. And of my ballades only two approached my self-set standard, or perhaps I aimed too high: one, the prayer I gave my mother for Our Lady, and the other my ballade '*Des Dames du Temps Jadis*'.

Dictes moy où, n'en quel pays,
Est Flora la Belle Rommaine…

…Berte au grant pié, Bietris, Alis,
Haremburgis qui tint le Maine,
Et Jehanne la bonne Lorraine
Qu'Englois brulèrent a Rouan;
Où sont-ilz, où, Vierge Souvraine?
Mais où sont les neiges d'antan?

If in versifying, tavern-crawling or teaching wooden-headed oafs to construe Aristotle I thought to find Nepenthe, I did not. I found instead Philippe de Sermoise whom I had known at Sorbonne, now ordained. He had a girl, on whose account, and according to him, he suffered even as did I. In our cups together we exchanged our maudlin confidences. Yes, a priest was he, but remember I am speaking of medieval France when Church discipline was, to say the least of it, elastic.

We who toured the taverns, were not unacquainted with a certain Abbess Huguette de Hamel whose reputation would scarcely bear strict scrutiny. Although the Convent of Port Royal, over which this redoubtable lady presided, was held in high regard by the Canons of the Church, the conduct of the Abbess beyond her cloistered walls was hardly in accord with her vocation. At masked balls, fetes, and in all the most famous, or infamous, houses in Paris, the presence of the worthy Dame was greatly in demand. Nor was she averse, so talk of her would give it, to the loan of her young novices to gentlemen who visited her convent. That is as may be; I can only vouch for what I saw, and often did I see the hearty Abbess masquerading as a man, jigging it and rigging it at the Popinjay, the Pomme de Pin, the Stag and, not ineptly, at the Nun-Shoeing-the-Goose. So you see Philippe de Sermoise, priest or nothing, was only following example of his elders to forswear his vows and take his fill of pleasure not entirely in prayer.

He brought with him one evening another priest, from Picardy, Dom Nicolas, whom Philippe had met on his travels while preaching in parish churches: so he said.

A brawny stout fellow was Dom Nicolas, full-bellied, bloated, and could he drink! I've seen him down a hogshead, nor turn a hair to have me under who could carry a good gallon, in good form. And spin a yarn, could he, to bring a blush even to the hardened cheek of the Mother Superior Huguette.

There also joined our circle at this time one Pernet de la Barre, dubbed by us 'The Bastard', for his much vaunted boast that noblesse obliged him to carry the arms, with the bar sinister boldly displayed, of his semi-royal father's house. A kindly foolish fellow was our Bastard, who attached himself to me with a limpet-like adherence that would not be shaken off.

Of all my former cronies only Tabarie stayed faithful. René, since his six months' banishment from Paris, had somewhat faded out, and Colin too, although both, from time to time, were back and forth in their old haunts with hints of a mysterious business on which they were engaged. It needed the least astute conjecture to believe that their activities were not unconnected with the Coquillards.

This company with whom I now consorted, as escape from Katherine *soi-disant* Marthe Rose, was, as you will gather, nothing of the choicest; yet it served its purpose to drag me from that dangerous quagmire where, like some love-sick mooncalf, I would stray to flounder on its brink, waiting, longing for a word, a token or a sign from her. None came. Her door was closed to me, her windows dark; no light nor sound within. The house appeared untenanted; no servant could be seen, nor any answer given to my knock. To all intent it would appear that she had vanished — but with whom? Not alone. Of that, for my discomfort, I was certain.

I might discreetly have enquired of Ambroise d'Estouteville as to her whereabouts, but I decided it were better not to ask. The fair Ambroise, with whom it was the fashion for the younger sparks of Paris to sing hosannas in praise of her beauty, and in lamentable verse, would brook no rival to usurp the interest of even such a scruffy out-at-elbows ballade-monger as myself, that is if I wished to retain the good grace of the Provost. His wife could pick and choose, discard, promote from her admirers, anyone — and why not I? — for some official clerkship in the Provost's Châtelet. His favour was too precious to be squandered at the caprice of this lady who had deigned to favour me.

I enjoyed my interludes with her, who, as others had before her and many others since, declared I pleasured her as no man ever could, or ever would, so I can well believe. For if I lacked looks, physique and riches, birth and breeding, I lacked nothing of a man that goes to make a lover. Yet despite the delights and demands of Ambroise which, in truth, I found to be a trifle *exigeant*, I still suffered from that ingrowing malaise which neither time, nor pastime, soothed. It festered till I became resigned to it as to an incurable canker.

Then, when lost to hope of my recovery, I determined to approach my father with the request, as he had once suggested, that he offer me with my credentials to Duc Charles at Blois. I even forced myself to contrive a pastiche of lays and rondels in the manner of the poet Prince, dashed off, tongue in cheek, to induce him to accept me as a possible court troubadour.

But when last year's snows had melted with a promise of spring in the air, and a breeze like a mischievous urchin played with the straw and refuse in the gutters; when bird-song and a burgeoning of blossom glorified the gardens of St Benoît; and when hope beyond all hope, for me, had died, she, with the swallows, returned.

It was the annual custom of the Provost and his wife to hold a civic soirée on May Day to which burgesses, merchants and wealthy tradesfolk were summoned to attend with a few personal friends of the d'Estoutevilles, among them my father and myself.

On nothing so lavish a scale was this city function as that of the preceding year to which only the élite were invited, and where Marthe Rose and I had met again.

The room was crowded to capacity. We, as usual, arrived late, and intended to leave early, which Dom Guillaume did, but I did not.

I sighted her among the dancers, partnered by a pretty youth, rouged, becurled, bedecked, whom I recognised as one of the de Montignys, a cousin of René, their black sheep.

From my post behind a pillar, with my heart like a drum at my ribs, I watched and marvelled at her poise, her graceful movements, learned never in a farmyard nor a bourgeoise villa.

Ambroise, busy with her guests, had not a glance for me, nor had Marthe Rose, although I could have sworn her eyes, quick darting, lighted upon mine and fled from them without one gleam of recognition. This did not disturb me; if evasion were deliberate it was with intent to pique. I knew my Marthe Rose.

The dance ended in a rowdy rigaudon. The townsfolk found it difficult to maintain the decorum required of *l'haut monde*. She joined in heartily, to the discomfiture, I noted, of her mincing cavalier. Then, in the general dispersion, I lost sight of her.

The company were flocking to the terrace, and I with them. There was a scramble for refreshment. I seized a flagon and filled a silver cup with wine, but as I lifted it to swill a draught I felt my elbow jogged to splash its contents on my gown. I wheeled round with an oath half-sprung that died in my throat, to find her there behind me.

'A thousand pardons, Messire Villon,' that lilting, high, affected voice trilling through the loud cacophony of laughter and rude speech was like a choir-boy's young alto. 'Someone jolted me. So many people here tonight. How do you do?'

That same gamine impudence — the same, yet not the same, as I, with every limb gone weak, recognised to see in her a new tormenting facet of enchantment. It was all about her; in her eyes, those strangely cat's green yellow eyes that still retained the half-awakened predatory look of *demi-vierge* belied by the seductive curve of her blunt-cornered mouth; the small rounded breasts, their nipples pointedly defined beneath the moulded satin of her flame-red gown; no crocus flower was she now, but a rose, rightly named, in its first blooming.

I drained my cup and set it down. 'Where,' I asked, 'have you been all this long while?'

'If long to you, much longer, then, to me.' Her white even teeth became visible. 'I have been in retreat to lose myself and find myself — in convent life.'

'A convent? Hah!' A hoarse crow escaped me. 'Which convent? Port Royal, well schooled by *l'Abbesse*?'

She fluttered her eyelids. 'How did you know?'

'There's nothing,' I said, 'that I don't know of you.'

'You may have known me as I was, but you cannot know me as I am.' Her hand slid down to mine. 'I told you wait and so you waited, but I … I can no longer wait.' I felt her fingers tighten.

My eyes were closing and I swayed, conscious of some indefinable sweet essence that came from her, suggestive, passionate. Imagination, machination, or anticipation?

'I am leaving now, and if you still may want me…'

'Want you?' All the ache and longing of these last empty months was in that breath torn from me on a shouted whisper between her words, cool, quiet.

'You will come to me tonight?' It was half question, half command. 'Stay here, and follow later. Take this.'

Something cold, hard, heavy was pressed into my hand. A door key! Then a darkness seized me, and to regain my senses I gripped the table's edge… What to make of her? Or what, dear God, what would she make of me?

I did not see her go.

TEN

Deux estions, et n'avions qu'ung coeur...

Yes, we were two, with one heart shared, as I, poor fool, poured out to her in a rhapsodic lay. This love of mine was no haphazard seasonal infection that comes and goes with youth's springtime like a crop of pimples on a beardless chin, but a fierce burning flame to leave a scar upon my soul, unhealed.

If I had been encoded in her web before our consummation, how much more now was I possessed. Did she say the sky were cheese, the clouds a calfskin, an abbot's paunch a fat sow's rump or God Himself the devil, I would tell her, 'Yes' and 'yes' again, so lost to Him was I in her.

We spoke no more of marriage: such union as ours asked no holy bond to tie us, as so she said, and I, 'Yes, yes', as always, and strove to strangle that secret serpent's head upreared to strike at me from its dark lair with subtle venomous reminder... The key. Are you the first to hold that key slid into your hand, or whatever other hand chance offered for her fancy?

I dared not probe too deep while she, divining my unease, would tell me, 'Dear, my very dear. I am so close to you even when most far from you. I knew you would be there that night at the d'Estoutevilles. I called you and you came...'

Like a breath on glass, as swiftly fading, was the memory of those long tortured months without her. Strange that one so frail fair, and colourless, as when she first revealed herself to me on her moonlighted couch as if her body were of carven pearl, not flesh, should be so urgently desirous, a tempest-torn implacable young Aphrodite. Yet my experience has proved it were fallacious to presume that your warm-tinted black-haired beauties are more hot-blooded than your blondes. In her exalted and complete abandon lay her power to make me hunger more where most she satisfied. And she, greedy for the passion-fruits of Tantalus with which I teased before I gave, was herself insatiable … We were well matched.

Then, from the reposeful void of our appeasement she would stir and, like a cream-fed kitten, stretch and yawn, and with inconsequential drowsy irrelevance would say: 'I bought a little monkey of a journeyman this morning. He's full of fleas.' And she would giggle and begin to scratch where the fair soft tendrils curled, 'I think I've caught one here. Shall I get him a mate and serve him to her just when you and I…? Monkeys are rare mimics. It would be droll to see them mimic us and learn them our love-games.'

If possible I loved her more for her childish inanities in these recuperative intervals than at the height of her transports.

All Paris in that sun-dazzled May time sang my joy of her. Never were the streets so filled with colour, movement, laughter. The poplars on the river-banks unfurled for me green banners; the Palais Royal gardens were a carnival of flowers, and even the beggars in their stinking rags, their scabrous sores stuck on with paste, grinned God-blessings at me who could ill afford the sols I flung at the feet of the blind and maimed — they who were neither blind nor maimed — to chase the rolling coins, and fight each other for first claim. The very house signs, newly painted, bright with varnish to greet the King's return to his palace for the summer, creaked breeze-swung songs at me as I passed under; and my old haunts, the Mule, the Pomme de Pin, where I'd not been seen for weeks, boisterously welcomed my return in early June.

A free drink of Barsac, corked, was offered from de Turgis, and a free meal from the too affectionately adhesive de la Barre. From Philippe de Sermoise the request to take me on at dice, or cards — 'the choice is yours'. He had brought with him, besides, the ubiquitous Dom Nicolas of Picardy, a fellow new to me, Master — *nota bene* Master, but of what Arts I never knew — Jehan le Mardi, a slouching shabby youth with a two days' growth of beard and watchful eyes set close together under black-shelved brows.

I chose the dice, played the three of them with mine, and won consistently to stand treat all round on my winnings. But when I challenged them to recoup their laggard luck, Nicolas, turned truculent, snatched my cubes and weighed them in his palm.

'Loaded?' queried Philippe, showing a mouthful of pointed teeth. Fox-haired was he, spare of build and tall; he carried his gown with a debonair grace as of one more accustomed to court than the Church.

'You said?' As suave as he was I to tell him, 'I am somewhat hard of hearing.'

His smile closed. 'Would you have me shout it in your ear?'

'To slice yours?' I was up and on my feet, a hand to my belt that hid a dagger in its sheath.

'Steady does it.' The Bastard de la Barre plucked my sleeve. 'He goes armed; you don't.'

'That,' said I, 'can easily be remedied. If the priesthood sets example, a layman may be advised to follow it.'

'Oh, *do,* my dear,' lisped de la Barre, 'be careful, He's so *shrewish* when he's roused.'

Shaking off my adhesion I bowed with mock humility to Philippe. 'I pray you, sir, repeat your accusation.'

'No accusation, my friend. A suggestion, merely, of small matter.'

'A suggestion I resent as of great matter to me and my honour. Dom Nicolas,' I rapped at him who, blear-eyed, peering at the brace of fives he held, let them fall bouncing on the table. 'Do you support this suggestion — merely?'

The fat priest reddened and, guarding a hiccup, replied in his mucus-thickened voice: 'Hum — a — ah — I find them somewhat heavier than those we use in Picardy.'

'If that be so,' I said, 'you know what you can do with them.' And in his wine-bloated face I flicked a cube. It hit him on his bulbous nose. Followed loud expostulation from the affronted Nicolas, in which de Sermoise joined, while, with the sleeve of my gown, I swept the scattered dice from the table to the floor. Then, stooping to grope in the rushes, I deftly substituted the cubes in question for a set I carried in case of such contingency as this.

'Bastard,' I turned to him whose vapid light blue eyes were almost starting from his head, 'and, de Turgis, you,' I beckoned, 'I request you both to weigh my dice and give these priestly gentlemen,' injured indignation blazed from me, 'your fair and just opinion. Should you decide my dice are loaded, then you, de Turgis, are within your rights as landlord to call the Watch for my arrest. I may be guilty of much, disapproved of civic law's sanctimony,' I proclaimed with unction, 'but never would I sink myself so low as to abuse my honour in a game of chance.'

By this time we had attracted some attention from those engaged in play at other tables, and to whom my words may have struck home. There were concerted cries of 'So say I!' 'And all of us!' and from Le Mardi who hitherto had taken no part in the dispute, 'Should any man suggest my dice are cogged or that these, my cards, are marked,' he produced a pack, shuffled them, dealt to each of us a dozen, 'then, by Our Lady, I'd demand my satisfaction.'

'*Qui s'excuse*,' murmured Philippe, 'but I accuse no man, least of all — a friend.' His glance skimmed mine to embrace those who gathered round us. 'Come, gentlemen, if any one of you has in your mind that these dice, as to *my* mind did weigh a thought too heavy, confess it so your hearts and spirits may be lightened.'

This pontifical address was delivered with a sidelong look at my balled fist, recalling memory, I have no doubt, of our College days when in frequent fight with me he had come off much the worse for it. 'I have often found that I, who am privileged by God Almighty's Grace to be ordained, can point the way of righteousness by parable, as did our Blessed Lord to those who sin. Thus these loaded dice do represent the weight of our wrong doing, for who among us here can declare 'I am no sinner?' But each of us —' He was talking now for talking's sake, well-oiled — 'may, if truly penitent, receive his absolution and depart in peace, to sin no more.'

'Come off your perch,' I growled, and shot a grin at Nicolas, whose beetroot face had turned a pale mauve at mention of the Watch; but the company, relieved by Father Philippe's sermonette, chose to take his hint and did depart in peace, if not to 'sin no more', to resume their play with caution. So that fracas being ended, we refilled our cups and I, rattling my substituted dice, called for another game, and lost every white I'd won.

The room, with the first bell of curfew, had become more than ever crowded. Street prowlers, dodging the Watch, slunk in, awaiting opportunity to slink out again and pilfer what they could from homeward bound unwary citizens. I, too, when my weekly dole from Father Guillaume was overdrawn did not scruple to help myself to a few whites plucked from the well-lined purse of some stout burgomaster. They, who amassed their wealth, not always fairly come by and increased by ruthless taxing of the poor, were hand-picked by the Coquillards. I, although not yet enrolled a full member of that august community, had learned to know by sight and name the 'haves' from the 'have-nots'.

It was easy work and without much risk to stand in the shadow of a doorway on a moonless night and trip up an unsuspecting burgess with out-thrust foot to send him sprawling in the mud. Then, from my hide-hole, I would rush forward to chase some imaginary urchin and return to the assistance of my recumbent gentleman… 'Good sir, allow me.' And as I heaved him up, I'd sneak his pouch, take half of its contents, and let it fall to pounce upon and hand it back to him with a — 'Yours, messire, I think,' receiving grateful thanks and liberal reward for service rendered.

I was about to quit the Pomme de Pin, for this night was moonless, too, and might again serve to reimburse me, with de Turgis sidling up to offer an account long overdue and all my winnings gone, when a name rang out, sharp spoken by de Sermoise above the racket of the inn. 'Katherine de Vaucelles? What! Do you know her?'

Le Mardi, complacently counting his pile of silver, looked up. 'Is there any man in Paris who does not?'

De Turgis was at my elbow. 'Sir, you owe me —'

'Get out! I'll pay you in my time, not yours. Who —' I feigned indifference, with my clenched fist at the ready to grind le Mardi's grin to pulp — 'who is this de Vaucelles whose name I hear on every lip of late?'

Le Mardi chuckled. 'Ask the Father here. He knows her, do you not, *Mon Père*?'

'Yes.' De Sermoise gave him a lipless smile. 'I know her.'

'Five whites, messire, for the wine you've had tonight.' De Turgis shoved at me a crumpled paper hieroglyphically scrawled 'And four plus six for two months still unpaid, which makes a total of —'

'Be damned to you! Take this.' I flung him my last coin. 'You can hold the balance over.' And as I watched de Sermoise preparing to leave, shadowed by the Picardy monk, it seemed as if a shutter had opened on some hidden corner of my mind.

'You, Philippe,' toying with my empty tankard, staring down at it I asked him idly, 'Were you not the parish priest at Bourg-la-Reine?'

'For a while, yes.'

I razed my chin between a thumb and finger. 'The name de Vaucelles is not uncommon hereabouts. My foster father was, I think, acquainted with a notary in Paris who retired to Bourg and who was, as far as I remember, a de Vaucelles.'

'Deceased,' said Philippe curtly.

I looked up from under my eyelids and saw his face inscrutable.

'Is that so? When did he die?'

'A year ago.' Philippe's lips unfolded to reveal his pointed teeth. 'I married him — and buried him within one week.'

Said le Mardi, 'A stroke of luck that, for his widow, young enough to be his grand-daughter, they say.'

'Who say?'

If ever I saw a lean fox stalk a moulting cockerel I saw him now in Philippe, on the tail of le Mardi whose shoulders went up, his chin down.

'The tongue of hearsay, shall we say?'

'You may say, but I say I know nothing of the Widow de Vaucelles since she left Bourg-la-Reine.'

'Did she sell the house, then, when she left it?' pursued le Mardi, undeterred.

De Sermoise, answering him, turned his eyes but not his head at me, who sucked a dryness from my tongue and, unclosing my fisted palm beneath the table, I saw four scarlet crescents where my nails had dug deep.

'I think not. She has her husband's bailiff there in charge. He manages the farm. But why this interest in the lady?'

And again Philippe's answer to le Mardi accompanied that slanting look at me.

'Messire,' de Turgis persistent at my elbow with his bill, 'I cannot allow you further credit. I insist —'

'Go to hell!' I got up. And pushing past him and the others, made for the door: and was followed.

'François, my dear! Let me go with you.' Pernet de la Barre, puffing and blowing, wriggled his hand under my arm. The swinging lantern above the tavern sign revealed his gentle moon-shaped face, pinkish, snoutish, sweating. 'Phew! It's hot in there, and such a stink of smelly feet. What a *beast* is that Dom Nicolas. I say,' he squeezed himself against me as we walked, 'de Sermoise *does* carry a knife. He uses it to carve his meat, or so he says — but I wouldn't trust him an inch. I am so *thankful,* my dear, you didn't stay. How wrongfully they used you. I could have killed them. As if you'd play with loaded dice — the swine — to turn on you simply because your luck was in. I don't know how I held myself from slashing them. I have a sword and so I may go armed, not being gowned. But who is this de Vaucelles?' He pushed his face so close to mine that his curled, tow-coloured hair brushed my cheek. He stank of scent. 'Do you know her? Does she keep open house to all of us — or all of you, for I've no use for her, being born, I thank my stars, under Virgo, the Virgin — he, he! — and not Venus. Women are so *drearily* insistent and so jealous. My dear, what do you think de Tabarie told me — *too* fabulous — that *la belle Ambroise*, just fancy! *She* is jealous, yes, positively — of our friendship, yours and mine. But you know what a liar Tabarie is. Just imagine! I've never stopped *screaming* — so ridiculous to think that you and I are — well, I mean Plato and all that, but still! Here we are at your red door. My dear, I'll have to fly or the Watch will have me. Such a fantastic hour to clear the streets at ten o'clock. It's scarcely dusk. Oh, my dear, I quite forgot. Tomorrow's Corpus Christi. Can we meet in the evening when it's over? I shall walk in the procession, I always do. I used to sing alto in the choir at Notre Dame. Goodnight.' He kissed me moistly on both cheeks, and holding me from him, said, 'Don't take this amiss, my dear, but if you're short of cash, having lost *all* to those abominations, the quarterly allowance from le Duc, my father, is due this week paid regularly by his agent. I never have to wait and I've settled all my bills outstanding. His Highness is very generous, so I owe nothing except to my tailor who always gives long credit knowing who I am, not that I've ever told him but one can't keep Blood Royal under the rose, it always *leaks* — so if a couple of *écus* would help?'

They would have helped exceedingly, but I couldn't bring myself to take from him, and told him so politely.

'Are you sure?' he urged. 'You're very welcome.'

Stifling a quite unwarrantable urge to kick his plump backside, I firmly disengaged and watched him go, weaving his careful way through the filth of the road to save his pretty buckskins, with hand-wavings and kissed fingertips over his shoulder to me. Poor Bastard! So fondly foolish, so foolishly fond, and the only true and honest friend I had.

Long I lay awake that night, picking over the scraps I'd gleaned concerning Marthe Rose. So, de Sermoise was her 'Father Philippe'; of that much I could be certain, nor had I reason now to doubt that she had been well and truly married to de Vaucelles. As to her life during those nine months after she left Paris, I would not wish, I told myself, to know where she had been. Better for my peace of mind not too closely to enquire… Yet I did, to fret me to a fever. 'In retreat', she'd said. At Bourg-la-Reine? With whom? Her husband's bailiff 'left in charge'. That surly individual who received me at the door to slam it in my face? I had never seen him since which rather pointed to the fact that he had not been given freedom of her house — and bed, as had I from curfew until dawn, in these six weeks of our reunion. Father Philippe, she told me, had found a house for her in Paris, and why not if she were friendless?

Philippe de Sermoise, as I knew him at Sorbonne, was a raffish young rip when at play, but when at work, which he took *au grand sérieux*, had been well-esteemed by his tutors. And then I needs must flay myself with the reminder that Philippe, when we met again, had confided in his cups that he too, had a girl, 'a feminine interest' he called it, which his vocation forbade him to follow. And what the hell, I asked me, has that got to do with you?

What 'that' had to do with me was the gnawing question: How close had been the interest of Marthe Rose in her Father Philippe, or Father Philippe's 'interest' in her?

And lying there with one star winking down at me through my dormer window, I chewed over to regurgitate each particle of jealousy's suspicion, creating vile fantasies to smear my love with poison until, worn out, I slept... And woke to the chime of church bells, and a chanting and a singing above the tramp of feet below, and White Coif at my bedside to jerk the pillow from under my head.

'Get up, or you'll be late for Mass.'

The Feast of Corpus Christi.

Lauda, Sion, Salvatorem
Lauda ducem et pastorem...
Bone Pastor panis vere
Jesu, nostri miserere
Tu nos pasce, nos tuere,
Tu nos bona fac videre
In terra viventium.

Every abbey, convent, church, throughout the city sang that glorious praise of the Host composed by St Thomas Aquinas; every shrine at every corner was decked with flowers, lighted candles; every window garlanded with evergreen and offerings from peasants of the fields. Flags were flying, banners waving, children running to strew rose petals in the path of the procession, preceded by servers bearing the tall gilded candles. Then, the long line of priests and monks and high dignitaries of the Church, crowned with lilies, laurel wreaths and roses. Silver swinging censers breathed their fragrance on the air; the sun enriched the gleaming jewelled vestments, and shone a golden blessing on the canopy shielding the Sacred Body of God in its monstrance, borne by the officiating priest... And all of us upon our knees before it, while above the murmurous hum of a multitude at prayer, above the chanting and the song, rose the epicene pure voices of young choirboys.

My mother knelt beside me. We were always together on this great day of days. I had fetched her from her home just in time for Mass in the Church of St Benoît. I heard her thin quavering voice join in the singing. I heard her tears and felt mine wet upon my cheeks, while my lips moved to words upsprung from a full heart.

...Je donne ma povre ame
À la benoiste Trinité
Et la commande a Nostre Dame
Chambre de la Divinité...

So in a blaze of glory passed the procession of the Precious Host. The organs thundered a last benediction, faded, sank; the day was dying. The candles on the shrines, the flowers at the feet of Our Sweet Lady holding her Babe, lay limp and withered in the airless warmth; and now it was sundown and all Paris in holiday humour, swarmed out to greet the evening.

I walked home with my mother through the joyous streets. She had prepared a meal of fish for me and begged me stay to eat it. 'Cooked fresh this morning early, baked in wine and spiced with herbs as tasty cold as hot, and see here —' she set before me a flagon of Barsac — 'our good Father Villon keeps me well provided but I drink little of it, saving it for you.'

I fell to with a will, having fasted all day; she, too, sat and nibbled, taking mouse-like bites, and loved me with her eyes and said, 'How thankful am I to God for His great bounty and the dear Father's grace. We talked of you after Mass — last Friday, was it? Yes, I'd been to market. Mademoiselle de Bruyères — she's grown so fat you'd think she had a dropsy — she asked after you. She was there, too, buying fish, a haddock at double the price I pay for if I know naught else I know how to strike a bargain. They can't palm off their white-gilled fish on me but she goes by size not quality and she said how you never call on her no more — "being so much engaged", I said, "with tutoring his pupils." Have you three pupils now, or is it four? The Father he spoke to me of your versifying, but I think it's a waste of your learning and time, unless you can earn money by it, which you can't. Now that prayer you wrote for me to Our Lady, I repeat it every day and that was God-inspired, and if you would write prayers in verse to be said in the churches then I'd believe you were favoured by Our Lord to use your gift, if gift you have, to some blessed purpose, but man must work to live and earn his keep unless he be a monk, which it has been my earnest wish as I was telling Dom Guillaume — don't eat so fast, you'll have the gripes.'

I passed my dish for more. 'You should be the King's cook, *ma mère*. This is a royal dish.'

She cut me another juicy portion and rattled on where she'd left off — 'as I was telling Dom Guillaume of my brother your uncle who is — or was — he may be dead by now, a priest at a Monastery in Angers. You've heard me tell you of my brother. I was born long after him on whom I've not set eyes since I was four. I wouldn't know him if he stood before me, but being of one blood with a holy man, I feel you ought to visit him in Angers, your only relative ,and maybe you'll find the priesthood through my brother. Father Guillaume says he'll write him a letter and tell him how I want you to visit him, but he don't hold out much hope that you'll turn monk. And Mademoiselle de Bruyères she said — now what was it she said? — Oh, yes, who are his pupils? Parish schoolboys? Looking down her nose at me as if I were a cod's head slung out to feed the cat. No, indeed, says I, he schools young gentlemen for their entrance to the university, which you did once, though you may not do so now, but I won't have her going round with her big mouth saying you are idle. There's a button off your gown. I'll sew it on.'

Then to her heart's content she fed and mended me, and had my hosen off to look for holes, found one in the toe and darned that, complaining: 'Madame Blanche don't keep you neat and tidy nor the Father neither who's so shiny at the seams it was on my tongue to ask him, let me have your gown to turn and press with a hot iron, I'd make it good as new, but I didn't like to be so bold —' And when she'd finished with me, reluctantly to let me go, I went.

It was nine o'clock and the day's heat cooling. The streets were busy with brawlers, drunks, and students out for a night's spree with the girls of the town. The hawkers in the Rue de la Juiverie had ceased to yell their wares; lights blinked in the lavender dusk on either side the river and in Father Guillaume's study window, but it still wanted an hour to curfew when I could steal out through the shrouded dark to Marthe Rose.

As I let myself in at the red door, White Coif announced that Messire de la Barre had called and would be back again before curfew to see if I'd returned.

'You can tell him I have not returned,' I said, and betook me to a stone bench under the belfry of St Benoît. From across the way at the Mule some little distance down along the Rue St Jacques, the sound of raucous song and voices fell harshly on the tranquil air, but few pedestrians were about in this quiet quarter of the town. The city's secret haunts of crime, debauchery and vice had not yet wakened to the night.

I stretched my legs, and watched the saffron-tinted sky deepen to a fiery glow, striking red sparks as from an anvil on the steeple of St Geneviève towering above me on the Sacred

Hill. All those angular grim spires of our great university, the soul and body of my Paris with her forty-two colleges clustered under her grey wings, looked to be bathed in liquid flame.

I sat there tranced; my head began to nod and I was half asleep, when suddenly a pair of soft palms were laid over my eyes, followed by a woman's shrill laughter and the words: 'I claim a forfeit, Villon!' shattering my peace.

I started up to find myself faced with the girl, Ysabeau — a girl no longer — whom in my first adolescence I had known too well; and with her one Gilles, a young priest new to Paris, just ordained, which is all I knew of him.

'Are you coming over to the Mule?' Ysabeau asked with a glance aside at the youthful black-frocked Father, who looked as if he wished himself a hundred miles hence.

'Not,' I told her, 'until I've paid my forfeit which is up and ready for your taking.' And I dragged her to my knees — she was something of an armful now — and kissed her full and plenty.

Young Gilles, mindful of his cloth, pulled a disapproving lip. It is likely that before this little by-play he had been innocently unaware of Ysabeau's profession, as I gathered from the wink she gave me and the whisper, 'I found him wandering about and asked if I could help him. He said he'd be obliged if I'd show him the way to St Benoît, so I brought him along. He's fresh as a daisy.' Which was evident enough in his haste to be off, having decided that neither she nor I were fit company for him.

'That's good riddance,' remarked Ysabeau watching his precipitate retreat. 'I'm no governess for half-baked boys, whether gowned or not.' Invitingly she pressed herself against me with her arms around my neck. The fading light was gentle to her once lovely face, her features blurred, her fair skin coarsened. And again, as often before, I was stabbed with the pitiful reminder of La Belle Heaulmière, the Fair Armouress, whose chink in her armour of beauty was the crushing of youth with age, to leave what? A husk, a shell... So that even while Ysabeau, perched on my knee, strove with her kisses to tempt, my mind wove a ballade for her and for all of her kind:

Filles, veuillez vous entremettre
D'escouter pourquoy pleure et crie...

'Girls, cast off grief with laughter,
Tears and sighs must follow after;
Time steals beauty's treasure
When life is lost of pleasure.'

Pah! Your English words are harsh to me who can only sing my own.

How long I sat there untouched by her enticements, waiting for the curfew to bring me to my love, I cannot say, but she, who found me unresponsive, redoubled her efforts until untimely interrupted by a shout of, 'Villon! I've found you now, caught in the act, by God!'

Philippe de Sermoise trailed by his shadow, le Mardi, bore down upon us. His hood had fallen back, his face was white, and whiter for the reddish tonsured hair streaked dark with sweat.

'What the devil!' I thrust Ysabeau aside and sprang to my feet. I saw Philippe's hand slide under his cloak, and caught the glint of steel.

Ysabeau tugged at my sleeve. 'For heaven's sake don't rile him.'

'Rile be damned. Go on, get away.' I gave her a push; whereupon she turned on me to spit abuse: 'You whoreson fornicating snite!' and sidled up to Philippe, with whimpers. 'See, Father, how a decent girl can't walk alone after Corpus Christi without she's followed and set upon by him who's known all over the town as one randy for a woman as a dog for a bitch in heat.'

This glib impromptu stoked Philippe's rising fury to a blaze. Striding up to me he shoved his face close to mine; he was wet about the forehead; his pointed teeth snapped together with a click, a tense muscle moved in his jaw. So we stood, taking each the other's measure with our eyes.

'Last night,' he bared his teeth to say, 'you threatened me that you would slice my ears. I am come now to slice yours!'

'No, no!' screamed Ysabeau. 'Let be! You can't have at him — you're gowned. You'll have the *sergents* on your heels.'

But he was stalking me like a fox that sights a coney, and paid no heed to her who gathered her petticoats and ran. Le Mardi, after a faint-hearted attempt to come between us, received a buffet from me that sent him flying after Ysabeau; and the next thing I knew was a blow from Philippe's fist to lay me flat.

I picked myself up, as rageful now as he, nor did I stay to question the reason for this onslaught, dropped like a bolt from the fragrant evening sky. I closed with him who had drawn a long dagger from beneath his gown. I ducked to save my vitals from his blade, but not in time to avoid a savage cut that slashed my upper lip in two. Then, with blood spouting in streams from my mouth, I felt for my trifling dagger to strike blindly and deep, and got him in the groin as I learned later. Howling with the pain of it, he came at me again and this time would have driven his weapon home into my heart had not le

Mardi, just at that moment, slunk back to tell de Sermoise, 'Put up your steel. Put up! Put up!' and wrenched my dagger from me with mutters of, 'You fool! Can't you see he's fighting mad? You can't fight a madman. He's out of his mind.'

I had no thought of his mind, only of my body deprived of its defence; and seeing Philippe mouthing and gibbering with foam on his lips, his eyes almost starting from their sockets, his steel flashing an inch from my nose — in very truth a madman — I heaved up a loose paving stone and hurled it at his head.

Down he went like a ninepin while le Mardi flopped on his knees beside him to glare at me across his shoulder, saying, 'You've done for him now.'

'He's done for me, more like,' I cupped my hands to my mouth and gurgled through the pouring blood. 'I'll call — gr-gr-I'll call you as witness that he —' I reeled and almost fell — 'attacked me first.'

Le Mardi cushioned the sagging head of de Sermoise on his arm and said, 'Best take yourself to a barber-surgeon.' And all this in a matter of minutes outside the peaceful cloister of St Benoît-le-Bientourné, where Father Guillaume's candle still shone in his window, and not a soul in sight to bear my word against le March's should I be called to answer for my part in this affair. Yet, as I staggered off almost senseless from loss of blood, my heart rejoiced. Whatever grievance Philippe nursed against me was not due to my relationship with Marthe Rose, but to a suspicion, in this case unfounded, concerning his 'interest' in the woman Ysabeau, which had nothing in the world to do with me.

The shop of Fouquet, the nearest barber-surgeon, was in an alley off the Rue St Jacques, not a furlong's distance from St Benoît. I waylaid him going out at I went in.

Fouquet, rodent-mouthed, sharp-eyed, and well accustomed to young gentlemen demanding his attention at all hours of the day and night for injuries received in a brawl, showed no surprise and little sympathy for my condition as I tottered in at the door. My gown was drenched with blood that dripped through my hands, still striving to staunch the flow. I must have fallen in a faint and recovered consciousness to find myself stretched on a settle. Placing a block of wood behind my head, Fouquet removed his moderately clean leather jerkin for one of rough wool, stained, greasy and splashed with the dried blood of ages. After a brief examination of my injury he pronounced briskly: 'This will scar you for life. How did you come by it?' Without waiting for an answer he took from a cupboard a flask, filled a phial and poured the contents of it down my throat. It had a bitter stinging taste that revived me sufficiently to tell him: 'I was attacked.'

'So were you?' Fouquet exhibited the coolest incredulity. 'We'll go into that later. Now let me have a look at you.'

He had his look with the aid of a probe that hurt like hell, and when he had washed the wound and swabbed the blood-flow with a handful of herbs he said, 'I'll have to stitch it.'

Then, when I was stitched and plastered, he removed the block from under my head and told me curtly, 'You can sit up now,' which I thankfully did and was ready to go, but he had not done with me yet.

It was the duty of a barber-surgeon to make a report to the police, not only of the condition of a patient who called on his services after a fight, but to extract all particulars as to the cause of it and to take the names of those involved. He demanded mine which I had sense enough left not to give, and invented the first that came to my mind — for my face must have looked like a decapitated sheep's — 'Michel Mouton.'

'And the name of the other party?'

'Philippe de Sermoise, a priest.'

'So you attacked a priest who goes unarmed?'

'He was not unarmed, and he, I tell you, attacked me. He carried a dagger or carving knife, though whatever it was it had a mighty long blade, and he came at me like one demented.' My mouth was throbbing, my speech slurred, for I was talking through my teeth with my lip curled back. 'I can't hope you'll believe me, but I've told you the plain truth. The fellow's a fanatic, crazy-mad. There was no reason why he should have come at me like a maniac. I was sitting there talking with a — with two others, one of them also a priest, whose name is Gilles and whom I met this evening for the first time. He is a stranger to the city. I exchanged no more than a few words with him of greeting before this lunatic came up and drew his knife shouting, "By God, I've got you!" and that's all I know. Can't you give me something to deaden this pain?

'There's worse pain in store for you, my lad,' was the discomfiting reply, 'should your statement prove false. And who was with you other than this Gilles, a priest?'

'A lady — a chance acquaintance.'

'Ho, a chance acquaintance. Of the streets?'

'Certainly not!' I denied loudly, to burst open a stitch. 'A highly respectable lady. She was accompanied by Father Gilles — here, I'm bleeding again.'

'And the name of this —' Fouquet's rodent mouth shaped itself to an inverted V, his nearest approach to a smile — 'this highly respectable lady?'

'I heard her addressed as Mademoiselle Ysabeau. Look here, I can't talk, it hurts.'

I have not reproduced the indistinct speech with which, deprived of labials, I jerked out my responses, and it is doubtful if Fouquet, laboriously writing, could transcribe the half of them correctly. I dreaded to think what hotch-potch would be rendered to the police.

'You *will* talk,' Fouquet said with ominous quiet, 'till I've done with you.' Licking his thumb he turned over a page of his tablets, re-dipped his quill in the ink-horn and continued: 'This other — Sermoise, is it? Was he accompanied?'

'Yes.'

'By whom?'

'Jehan le Mardi.'

'Ah. I know something of le Mardi. The *sergents* will take his statement. And now, Michel Mouton — do you spell it m-o-u-t-o-n?'

I nodded.

'Where do you live?'

I had that answer on my tongue. 'In Angers. I am only here today for Corpus Christi and leave Paris in the morning.'

I wondered if he'd swallow that. Apparently he did, for although St Benoît was nearby, I — cloaked and hooded and bleeding like a pig — must have been unrecognisable to one who could only have known me by sight. The barber who called regularly at the House of the Red Door to cut Father Guillaume's corns and trim his hair, attended also upon me; therefore I had never come to close quarters with Fouquet.

He held out his hand. 'Two whites, if you please.'

I made a feint of searching for my purse, to gasp, 'I've been robbed! Give me leave to pay you later — I'll return with the cash in half an hour.'

'Better make it an hour,' Fouquet said, 'for I shall not be here again till after curfew. I'm called to a case that may need amputation. If I am not here you can wait.'

I was surprised he let me go without payment. Mumbling my thanks I made off as fast as I could, being still shaky on my legs; and once clear of Fouquet and his questions I surveyed my situation. If Philippe had sustained a fatal injury I could see me charged with murder and its hideous penalty at Montfaucon; or even were it proved that I had killed in self-defence, the least I could hope for was a verdict of manslaughter and the penalty for that would be imprisonment, with the wheel, the rack, and all the horrors of the Châtelet administered, full measure.

It would be my accursed luck that I should find myself involved in a criminal offence of which I was morally guiltless, to be harried by Justice, unless I could evade it. Yes, if I would save my skin that was the only course to take. I must get away quick, nor wait to know whether Philippe were alive or dead. But first — to Marthe Rose.

Curfew had sounded; the streets were emptying and she, peeved at my late arrival, changed her tune to see me pale, my gown blood-stained, my lip in a plaster, one side of it drawn up; a sorry sight indeed to come a-courting.

I told her all, as well as I could with but half a lip to tell it, and finished by insisting she confess the truth. Was she or had she ever been the mistress of de Sermoise?

'I? By heaven's Grace I swear —'

'Don't swear,' I said, 'to swear your soul away. Has he had you?'

'He? A priest of God!' Her eyes rolled heavenward; she crossed her hands over her breasts. 'You defame his holiness and my honour by such evil thought.'

'*Your* honour!' I gave a hoot of laughter. 'Honour and you, my sweet one, walk at enmity with me.'

She wrinkled her funny little nose. 'You speak in riddles.'

'Wonder it is I speak at all with only half a mouth. So if Philippe is not your bed-mate he's your soul-mate, is that it?'

She nodded primly. 'Yes, that *is* it. He's my Father Confessor and cares for my soul.'

'And I care for your body. Come here.' I opened my arms; she ran into them, lifting her face to mine.

'I can't kiss,' I murmured, 'through a plaster.'

She put her lips to it, sought my tongue with hers, and drew away from me saying, 'We can love without kisses.'

She wore nothing but the sheerest shift of gossamer, and this I pulled off and carried her to our waiting couch.

Presently she stirred and raised herself on an elbow, stroking my damp hair from my temples. 'So hot with love you are,' she sighed, 'so splendid strong a lover... Our nights are all too short.'

'Yes, and this of all our nights — too short. I must leave you and Paris at once.'

'Paris! You'll leave Paris?' She leaned over me, her eyes fear-filled. 'Oh, no, you can't leave Paris and leave me!'

'I can, and must — or I'll be caught.' I got up and began hurriedly to dress.

She heaved her legs over the bed and sat there watching me, her arms dropped between her naked thighs, her hands loosely clasped. 'But where will you go?'

'Where my feet lead me.' I looked round for the wine she kept ready by the bedside and helped myself to a beaker-full.

'I'll tell you where you can go.' She slid from the couch to take wine in her turn. 'How thirsty loving makes one.'

'To thirst for more,' I said. 'Where can I go?'

'To my house at Bourg-la-Reine. You can bide there awhile. I've a man and his wife in charge, and my bailiff, Noë de Joliz, he is there too and will see to your comfort.'

I stayed the cup halfway to the unplastered corner of my mouth. 'Is he your bailiff, that Cerberus who drove me from your door when you were gone from Paris?'

'His name isn't Cerberus, it's Noë. I've just told you.'

'Oh, God! You're marvellous!' I stopped myself from the hurt of laughing, drank wine and said, 'What would I do at Bourg-la-Reine? It's uncomfortably near Paris.'

'You could hide in the attics until they're off your scent. Have you any money?'

'My purse is overflowing. I've had the devil's own luck with the dice this week, which is likely why he sent your Father Philippe to do his dirty work for him, regretful of his favour.' For I could not sink myself so low as to take from her.

She clung about my neck, sobbing that she couldn't — no, she couldn't let me go! How could she bear to be without me every night?

'You'll soon find consolation,' I told her airily; and seeing her lower lip bulge and her eyes suspiciously moist, I took comfort to believe her mine, as I so utterly was hers.

'What,' she whispered, 'if the Father dies?'

'Then,' said I, 'he dies.'

'And what of you?' breathlessly she asked, 'What — oh, what of you?'

'If the devil takes the hindmost he'll take me.' And I held her close and laid her down on our tumbled love-couch and kissed her with my broken mouth and left her. I think I never loved her more than at that moment when I looked back to see her lying there lily white and crumpled, and heard her voice, with tears in it, calling after me: 'I'll be behind you all along your way!'

It was just on midnight when I sneaked home, eyes and ears alert for stalking *sergents*, and my hand to my plastered mouth lest the Watch should already have taken Fouquet's statement with its damning particulars of me; but there was none about, not even a stray cat. All honest folk were abed. The night life of Paris in taverns and those hidden ways of stifled lusts was only just astir.

As I let myself in at the Red Door, a shadow emerged from the porch. I started back to see, in the dim hall light of guttering candles, the pop-eyed anxious face of Pernet de la Barre. Gripping my arm he dragged me in, closed the door silently, and hushed his voice to a hissing undertone. 'My dear! I've been waiting *hours*. You must get away, you're not safe. The Watch are on your track.'

'Yes, I know.' Disengaging, I told him, 'I must have a word with my father, then I'm off.'

'I'll go with you.'

'Don't be an ass! I can't let you in for this. What have you heard?'

'Oh, my dear! What *haven't* I heard?' Beads of sweat bedewed his forehead; the rose petal pink of his face was drained of colour, and his blond, carefully curled hair looked like a bird's nest.

'I must sit down...' He sank on to a stool. 'I've come over... When your old besom here said you had not returned at ten o'clock, I went to find you,' he gestured vaguely, 'and saw to my horror Philippe de Sermoise stretched for *dead* under the belfry with a dagger in his groin, and le Mardi kneeling by him—'

I took him up sharp. '*Was* he dead?'

'No, he breathed. I made sure of that — and le Mardi said — oh, my dear, it was *too* awful — how you'd attacked de Sermoise who drew his blade in self-defence and that he, le Mardi, had tried to disarm you but you were too quick for him and lunged at Philippe and that then you took a great flagstone and *hurled* it at his head after you'd spiked him.'

I drew a breath. 'So that's le Mardi's version, is it? Now I'll tell you mine which is almost the same — in reverse.' And I gave him the facts.

'Thank God!' The Bastard began to blub. 'I *knew* he was lying but I wanted to be sure because of last night. De Sermoise was so aggressive and peculiar — I wondered, and thought perhaps if you'd had a few drinks —'

'Well, I hadn't, and he hadn't as far as I could tell. Did you leave le Mardi there with Philippe?'

'No, I stayed till the *sergents* came.'

'Did le Mardi spin the same tale to them?'

'More or less.'

'Did he give my name?'

'Yes — the swine!'

'I gave a false one to Fouquet, the barber-surgeon, and that won't help me neither.'

The Bastard wrung his hands. 'Oh, why, *why* was I not with you when it happened? You've no witnesses. Le Mardi told them you were sitting on the bench there with a woman. They got her name from him — Ysabeau, a woman of the stews, he said, and that Philippe found you in the act of fornication.' He gazed at me miserably. 'Is that true?'

'She tried it on and was in a flaming fury when she found I wouldn't work. A fine witness she'll be. What did they do with Philippe?'

'They carried him to the Hôtel de Dieu, le Mardi with them blaspheming and cursing at you. Oh, François, what'll you do? Is there anything *I* can do to help? You've only to say and I'll do it.'

Striding up and down the hall, I halted and swung round to tell him, 'Yes, you can go to the hospital, enquire how he is and let me know.'

'But where will you be to let you know? You can't stay here. They'll be after you.'

I did some rapid thinking. 'Go to the moat outside the gates. On the hinder bank there's a scrub of thorn-bush. I'll tie a rag of sacking to it and if he's alive leave it there. If he's dead take it away, but you'll have to do it before sunrise for I can't hang about when the workers are in the fields. I'll have to remove this.' I touched the dressing on my lip. 'It marks me.'

'Oh dear, oh dear!' The Bastard moved his head from side to side and burbled, 'Suppose he dies *after* you've gone? How can I let you know then?'

'I'll know soon enough,' I said darkly.

'I can't *bear* it!' blubbed the Bastard. 'It's too awful! To think of you wandering about with those hounds on your heels. What if they catch you?'

'That will be too awful,' said I in his bleating falsetto; and seeing his spherical blue eyes dribbling tears, I patted his shoulder as one would pat a dog. 'Don't fret yourself, my pretty. You do what you're told and St Christopher, God bless him, will be beside me on the road. I've nothing on my conscience — here, wait a minute.'

I heard the door of Father Guillaume's study open, and dashed up the stairs to meet him coming out of his room. 'Father, a word with you.'

The light of his taper fell full on my face; his jaw dropped as his startled gaze travelled from my plastered mouth to my bloodstained gown.

'François! What is this I see? You're injured.'

Hurriedly I gave him the bare facts. 'Father, you believe me? You must believe I was not the aggressor. What I did was done in self-defence.'

'You say he is a priest and went armed?'

'Yes, many of them do. They carry knives to cut their meat, but if so his was the fiercest carving knife I ever saw. A sword, no less.'

'And you, François, you too, carried a knife?'

'Yes, Sir. I had a dagger in my belt. It is not unlawful, surely, that I who am not in Holy Orders should carry a weapon as protection from attack?'

He thumbed his chin. 'I have no forensic authority to say yea or nay to that, but in the eyes of the Church even a layman should not take up arms against his neighbour whom Our Lord bade to love as himself and to forgive his enemies.'

'But Father, would you have had me offer my other cheek — or t'other side of my mouth to be sliced?' And while he pondered on this I followed it up with, 'After a century of war should we forgive our enemies, the English?'

'God works in His own mysterious ways, my son, beyond our comprehension; yet after a hundred years of tribulation and disaster France emerges, saved.'

Such talk as this could bring us nowhere.

'Sir,' I danced impatience, 'I am come for your advice how best to save myself. I am innocent, but if this man dies I shall be guilty of murder.'

'No, no.' He drew me with him into his study, lit the candles on his desk and scrutinised me closely. My heart was wrenched to see his poor old eyes, pink-rimmed behind those spectacles, his face grown haggard, drawn and worn in these last few minutes, 'If what you tell me is the truth, and I do not doubt it, you will be fairly judged. And for this present, and your safety's sake, I advise you to leave Paris. Go to Angers where your uncle, a holy man, will give you sanctuary. I have written to him at your mother's wish, and yet I fear he may be dead. If so, the Abbot will protect you. Should this priest die, then you must come forward and protest your innocence, and plead —' his voice faltered — 'manslaughter.'

'The penalty for that,' said I, 'is worse than hanging.'

'God forbid.' His pale tongue came out to wet his lips. The ready tears welled and flowed down his furrowed cheek.

'Father!' I knelt to kiss his hand. 'I am unworthy of your love and care. I bring you only sorrow who should have brought you only joy. I am guilty of much that is sinful but I swear to you before Almighty God that what I have told you of my part in this is the truth, and if I am to be judged, pray Our Lord that I may receive justice.'

'You will, my son, you will.' He raised me up and blessed me. Then going to a coffer ranged against the wall he took from it a purse containing five pieces of gold.

'This will help you on your way. Go to Angers, and my prayers go with you. I will set in motion all means in my power to clear your name.'

'Father,' I too was now in tears, 'I gave a false name to Fouquet, the barber-surgeon who dressed my wound.'

'That was wrong. The truth is always right.'

'Yes, but I was almost unconscious at the time, and didn't know what I was saying, and, Father — I told him I'd been robbed of my purse and that was also a lie. I hadn't, but I knew I must leave Paris at once, and needed the two whites which was all I possessed. I said I would return and pay him within the hour. Will you, Father, pay him for me?'

He nodded; he could not, just then, speak; but he made the sign of the Cross on my bowed head, and I left him on his knees before the ivory crucifix of the tortured Christ on the wall above his desk.

I groped my way down the stairs to the hall where the Bastard waited.

'My dear!' He thrust three *écus* into my hand. 'Take these. I insist.'

'My father,' I said weakly, 'has provided me with —'

'Please, I'd feel happier.' He closed my fingers on the coins. 'You must have money, and the more you have the better that you may be well lodged and fed. Oh, if I could only go with you!'

'You can serve me best by staying here and keep your ears wide for news.'

'You may be sure of that.' He tiptoed to the door, opened it, peered out. 'All's quiet. Now you can go, and God be with you. I'll burn a hundred candles to St Christopher and I'll not forget the rag. Watch for it, and do, *do* take that dreadful plaster off your mouth. You're so right. It *will* identify you.' Somewhere in the distance a cock crowed. 'Oh, do, my dear, do go!'

He fairly pushed me out.

ELEVEN

For four days and nights I lay in hiding beyond the city's walls. I bought a knapsack from a pedlar, and into this I stuffed my academic gown; and because I chose to sleep in a ditch or under a haystack rather than a bed in a farmhouse or an inn lest I be traced, my shirt and breeks were soon earth-soiled that I looked like any tramp. I ripped the plaster from my mouth to cause a gush of blood again, but I staunched the flow with grass and let the sun dry and heal it. I fed myself on eggs thieved from hen-roosts with an occasional meal at a farm, and gave out I was bound for Orléans. When asked by a farmer's wife how I had come by so ugly a wound I explained I had fallen and cut it on a jagged stone, to receive from her a soothing balm of hog's grease.

The weather favoured me. The haymakers, busy in the fields, were glad of my help, sharing with me their dinner of bread and goat's cheese. None questioned me, yet for safety's sake I assumed their country accent since my Sorbonnical French fadged ill with my tale of seeking work in Orléans as a locksmith. Each night under cover of the dark I would return to the thorn-bush, crawling on my belly as I neared the moat, for the moon was at the full and I dared not risk the light of a *sergent*'s lanthorn. The rag of sacking was still there; but in the dawn of the fifth day it was gone: the faithful Bastard's message to me that Philippe de Sermoise was dead.

Then I took to the road, stopping at wayside inns to drink and eat, and on again, fearful of every stranger that I passed; skulking behind trees when a party of horsemen galloped by.

Once I was almost caught by a couple of mounted Archers who sighting me pulled up and called, 'Hey, you! Come here.'

I shook my head, conveying by signs that I was a deaf-mute. At which one of them got off his horse and came to grab me by the shoulder. I had sense enough, on seeing them, to chuck my knapsack in the ditch and my money with it. Then he went over my pockets, shoving his hand inside my shirt while I stood there making animal sounds, my mouth open and pointing to it foolishly.

Finding me witless, speechless and with nothing on my person to identify me, he took me by the scruff, whirled me round, kicked me in the buttocks and left me sprawling in the grass where I gave a fair imitation of an epileptic. His fellow, disfavourably watching this performance, yelled out an order: 'Let be! Why waste your time with the village idiot?'

That was a near shave.

I lay quaking where they left me till they were out of eye and earshot before I dared retrieve my money; it took an hour to find, and then I made off across country skirting Bourg-la-Reine. I decided it were better I avoid the house of 'Katherine de Vaucelles', for I had no wish to meet her bailiff, Noë de Joliz, who would as likely give house room to me as to a rattlesnake.

I must have covered two hundred leagues, back and forth in the ensuing months, halting at village inns, footsore, weary, sleeping under hedges, never in a bed, for my money was soon spent on food and drink. My broken shoes were worn to their uppers, and my toes sticking through, for even had I enough cash left to buy myself a decent outfit I deemed it wiser to go in rags.

Then one evening, I arrived at a tavern a few kilometres from Tours to see, seated at a trestle, René de Montigny and Colin de Cayeux.

'Well met! This is my lucky day!' I cried, holding out a hand to each, and got from both a cool stare of suspicion. Not surprising that neither recognised their one-time boon companion, the tavern-poet, Villon, in this weather-stained vagrant whose scarred lip was drawn back in a permanent sneer.

However I soon revealed myself by spouting a verse or two of a ballade I had scribbled down and read to them during one of our orgies at the Pomme de Pin: *'A Ceux de Mauvaise Vie'.*

Traistres, pervers, de foy vuydez
Soyes larron, ravis ou pilles:
Où en va l'acquest que cuydez?
Tout aux tavernes et aux filles.

Which, as near as I can give it in your English is to say,

'Traitors, perverts, no repeal
For you who cheat and ravish, steal
Where go your pickings of a purse?
On taverns, girls, or something worse.'

We split a bottle on the strength of it and my escape. It was indeed my lucky day since both René and Colin were now full members of the Coquillards. It was a point of honour among the Brotherhood — for I can tell you there is honour among thieves, and maybe more than you will find among your honest folk — that the Coquille, whose eyes and ears were everywhere in that vast web which cast its mesh across the length and breadth of France, were well aware of my danger.

As I was high on the list of novitiates to be enrolled an associate companion of the Coquille, I was entitled to their protection. René and Colin had heard from headquarters of *'l'affaire Villon'*, and had received instructions, passed from mouth to mouth, that should they or any members of the Company meet with me upon my way they must aid and abet me by all means in their power or their province.

'You can set your mind at rest,' René flashed me his engaging smile. 'You are no murderer. De Sermoise confessed, at his last gasp, that you drew against him in self-defence. He admitted that he was the aggressor and told those who were standing at his bedside in the Hôtel de Dieu to take his statement, that he was entirely at fault.'

Philippe seemed to have come out of this sorry business better than I who had fled from justice, leaving him to clear me on his deathbed.

'So all I have to fear is a verdict of manslaughter?'

'I doubt it. Bide your time and it will blow over. Father Villon is pulling every string he holds to obtain a royal pardon, and you have the Provost and his wife on your side. The fair Ambroise has her uses both in the alcove and out of it. Yes?'

His amber-coloured eyes were full of mischief. He smoothed back a lock of hair fallen over his temple: as handsome a devil as ever I saw. I'd have given my poet's soul in exchange for his charm. And as if he read my thought he said, 'You, François, with your wizened weasel-face, your narrow chest and spindle legs, can, if you will, have all Paris, women *and* men, at your feet; you, whose salt wit and spiced tongue weave banal words into glorious verse, while I —' he paused and drank, and wiped his lips — 'I can weave nothing but a hempen rope to hang me. Drawer! Another flagon of the same.'

Colin, well in wine, slanted me a cock-eyed look.

'Our Villon knows where — hic — to sow his oats. Your pretty filly, Madame Provost, eats out of your hand. She'll not see you stre-stretched to spin on any wheel but hers.'

'Do you lie here tonight,' I asked René, 'or are you on the move again?'

'We've been on the move this last month or more, but — yes, we are here for the night. There's a mort of trouble brewing for the Brotherhood, to which yours is no more than a pimple on a pumpkin.' He glanced around, eyes narrowed. There were a few tables occupied, and those by farmers or yokels stolidly drinking, with occasional gaping looks in our direction. René, point device in mulberry cloth, gold-trimmed, long scarlet hose and fawn buckskin boots, Colin in his disguise of a servant, and myself in tattered shirt and ragged breeks, must have seemed an incongruous trio. 'Walls,' muttered René, 'have ears. Hey, you!' He yanked up Colin, whose head had dropped on his arms across the table; and to me, for the benefit of the company at large, 'Come, give a hand to this oaf. Lug him to bed.'

Taking my cue from him I touched my forelock, with a 'Yes, my lord,' dragged Colin from his stool and up the stairs, followed by René.

'In here,' he opened a door into a room containing two truckle beds.

The landlord came puffing after us. 'Is all to your liking, my lord?'

'My fellow,' René said disgustedly, 'can't stomach your filthy wine. This clod here, my baggage man,' he waved a hand at me, 'will see to my needs.'

'Will your lordship have me bed him in the stable?' asked the landlord, doubtfully eyeing me.

'No, he can lie here in the straw.'

And as the landlord stumped away, 'The eccentricities of the noblesse,' I murmured, 'are manifold and manifest, but I'm damned if I'll lie in the straw when I've the chance of a bed.'

And having lowered the comatose Colin to the floor where he lay contentedly snoring, I flung myself down on one of the truckles and was slipping off into oblivion when René called to me: 'S'tt!' and got up to light a candle. 'I can't shout this for mine host to hear.' And seating himself on the edge of my bed, he said, low-voiced: 'I'm to warn you that Colin and I are for the Pot, and you with us if we're nabbed. We're on the run from Dijon where they've rounded up our leaders.'

And he told me a harrowing tale of how their Commander-in-Chief at the Dijon headquarters — a brothel kept by one Jacquot de la Mer — had been raided and their Commander, Regnault Daubourg, who served as a wagoner to the Duke of Burgundy, was seized with two of his lieutenants; one, a fellow known as Sunday the Wolf — 'not your Wolf, the duck thief,' grinned René, 'another, turned traitor along with le Fournier, a barber. All three fell foul of the public prosecutor, Jehan Rabustel, who got wind of our organisation and sent a body of *sergents* twenty strong, armed to the teeth. They battered down the door of de la Mer's bawdy-house where our Commander was holding a meeting, and took the lot.'

'Phew!' I whistled. 'How many?'

'Two dozen or more. You wouldn't know who, but some were our staunchest supporters, including a Scotsman, Jehan d'Escosse, a fine upstanding fellow with a crop of wild red hair, and brave as a lion. He's banished, but they seized

Daubourg, Sunday the Wolf, and le Fournier for — manipulation.'

It needed nothing of my imagination to supply the cause of the momentary spasm that contorted René's face. Behind my eyes I saw the torture chamber, heard the creak of chains and pulleys and the agonised shrieks of the racked.

'Yes,' René nodded. 'It was a triumph for Master Rabustel, but he got not a squeak from Daubourg, to whom he gave the whole bag of tricks, including the Water Cure.'

I gritted my teeth. I'd heard tell of that most favoured and most fearful method of extraction.

'Yet Daubourg, God rest him,' René, for an instant, closed his eyes, 'that stoutest of all stout campaigners, never made so much as a moan nor uttered so much as a word. The other two, after the first turn of the screw, squealed and gave in and gave up, with a list of near on eighty names. By Holy Cross!' He clenched a fist. 'If I could meet with those two I'd —'

'What,' I interrupted, 'did Rabustel do to Daubourg in the end?'

'Boiled him,' said René briefly.

I saw that too. The smoking cauldron of oil, the fettered victim carried on a hurdle, the excited crowds of watchers, the stretched and naked body hoisted up the wooden steps and flung... I felt my face stiffen and whiten, and watching me, René said, 'Those of us who stood by to see the last of him — even then, he made no sound nor gave no sign.'

'And you,' I steadied my voice to ask him, 'did those two yelping jackals list you, also?'

'Oh, yes, I was well up among the damned, but not Colin although he was there and I wasn't when they raided the house. He belongs to another company, l'Isle de France, so they hadn't got his number. I was in Dijon at the time of the raid, visiting my uncle, le Vicomte de Montigny, and they've got me on their list, thanks to those squealers. Lord!' He flung back his head with a burst of laughter, 'Such a to-do as never was at the Château when the news of it leaked out — hithering and dithering and gabbling and babbling and myself in the midst of it, loudest of any. My uncle had to hold me down for I was up and ready to join in the hunt for these scurvy knaves, these double-dyed villainous what-d'ye-call-ems — Coquillards? I stayed there well covered by the bosom of my family until the hue and cry died down, and then left with my uncle's blessing, and,' he added with a grin, 'a pouch of gold. I sent word — we have our ways of communication which you'll learn in our king's good time — for one to meet me outside the prison in the Rue des Singes where the jailbirds were taken to be plucked. I hoped to have had a last word with Daubourg as they dragged him out, for I went disguised, but I couldn't get a glimpse of him. They didn't keep him long in the condemned cell. Then I got my orders from headquarters to take the road as a gentleman of leisure with Colin for my lackey. So here we are, and here I am — heigh-oh-ah —' He yawned widely, got up, and unfastening his tunic, laid it on a stool. 'If you care to risk keeping company with me, and this,' toeing the huddled heap in the straw that was Colin, 'I've a spare suit. It will fit you well enough. You can't go about in that revolting guise. You must be verminous.'

'I am.' I began to scratch at the reminder of an itch between my legs. 'And I'll borrow your razor. I've two months' beard on my chin.'

'Grow all the hair on your face that you can,' advised René, 'it will hide your sliced lip. They'll be looking for it, and when you're dressed fine you can pass for a Spaniard, Don Francesco Desperado. How's that? But I warn you —' he stripped off his scarlet hose and examined each carefully — 'Here's a hole. I'll get Colin to mend it. He's as nimble with a needle and thread as with a picklock — but I warn you, if you throw in your lot with us you may run your neck in a noose.'

'It's a risk we all run,' I said, half asleep, 'so we might as well run it together.'

We left the inn at Tours next morning. The suit supplied to me by René, consisting of a tunic of forest green embossed with silver, long hose and the fashionable fawn leather boots, was a welcome change from my vagabond's rags which I would have thrown over a hedge but that René advised me to keep them and rid myself of my academic gown, still carried in my knapsack. 'For that,' he said, 'would give you away to any who rifled your bag. Best burn it.' We burnt it with the aid of his tinder-box, having first smeared it with the remains in the jar of hog's grease given to me by the farmer's wife. It made a good bonfire, and Colin, who had got us a plump cockerel — we didn't ask him how — heaped faggots on the flames and we feasted well at dead of night, squatting on our haunches in a field.

Then, off again, René and I travelling as *seigneurs*, I as a Spaniard with my beard and dark growth of moustachios hiding my lip. I assumed a broken French accent, René acting as interpreter for his friend, Don Francesco Desperado, Duc de Castille, to impress the innkeepers who, never having seen the like of us before, offered the best accommodation their houses could afford. René had also managed to procure himself a horse, borrowed from his uncle's stable.

We took turn and turn about in the saddle, leaving Colin as our lackey to follow on the pack-mule provided by the Coquillards, an arrangement that joyed him not at all.

I passed a pleasant week with them, playing dice at taverns with likely customers. You may be sure René had about him a set of cubes that would give him a profitable game to share with us his winnings. There were girls in plenty to be picked up along the way, but none to my taste. Those wide-hipped heavy-hoofed peasants with breasts like cows' udders and arms red as hams, had no appeal for me. Colin and René were nothing so particular, and when they quizzed me for my continence I told them hard drinking had rendered me inactive; and to lull the ache and longing for the primrose loveliness of her who haunted my empty nights, I soaked myself in wine to seek oblivion and left those two at their wenching.

We were some dozen leagues from Angers when René told me we must cut adrift. News had come to him that the description of a trio, to the very clothes we wore, had been circulated from the Procurateur at Dijon. We were suspect, and the Archers would lose no time in searching.

'How,' I asked, 'did you obtain this news?'

He gave me a shrug and a grin. 'From the barks of trees, the droppings of a leaf, the song of a bird — or,' he added slyly, 'a rag of sacking tied to a thorn-bush, Michel Mouton.'

Was there anything the Coquille didn't know?

'If the police have us marked by our dress,' said I, 'I'll take to my rags again. But what of you and Colin?'

To that he made no answer more than, 'The devil looks after his own. As for you and your finery —' he tore a button off his tunic; beneath it was hidden the badge of the Cockleshell which he unpinned and handed to me — 'if you follow that track,' he pointed to a path across a field, 'it will bring you to a poplar where you'll find a jack-pudding of a fellow waiting for you. Show him your badge, give him the password, and he'll give you another change of clothes. You'd better get out of these.'

I effected the change without more ado, regretfully gave up my forest green tunic and fawn leather boots, and put on my broken shoes, while Colin, on the pack-mule, kept a look out. Not a soul passed us, we had chosen an unfrequented by-lane far from the highway.

'Here,' René drew a dagger from his belt, 'you can have this. You may need it.'

'What of you? I can't take yours.'

His face closed like a trap. 'You can take an order, and,' he held out his hand engulfing mine; his gay smile returned, 'you can go.'

So we parted in that barren field with the evening sun behind us, his horse cropping the grass, man and beast outlined against the reddening sky. I looked back across my shoulder; he was still there, his hand raised in a gesture that seemed to linger...

Dusk was falling with a dampness in the air, for it was now four months since I had left Paris on that fifth night of June. The land here in the level-lying valley of the Loire sloped gently upwards, breaking into black-browed pasture where sheep, grazing in that dim half-light, looked like crawling maggots.

I had walked half a league or so, eyes straining for the poplar, not easy to find in the gathering mist. The path here had narrowed and was water-logged with the overflow of a trickling stream swollen by recent rain. My feet squelched in mud and I lost a shoe, no loss to me who walked on the bare soles of my feet, the leathers having long been worn away. Presently I discerned a tall tree standing isolated from the sparse ranks of poplars that lined the rough-hewn track, and hurrying my steps, having cast off my remaining shoe, I saw the shape of a man seated with his back against the tree-trunk.

I came up to him, gave him the password in the jargon of the Coquille and showed him my badge. He produced his from under his hat. He was uncouth, untidy, unkempt and ferret-faced, in a stained leather jerkin, patched hose so faded and filthy that their original colour, which might have been yellow, could only be guessed; but the few words he spoke, after that first greeting, were in purest French. He said, 'You are not *au courant* with our jargon, I take it,' with a penetrating stare from under hooded eyes that seemed to strip me to my skin; and stooping to his pack he took from it the brown frock of a Francescan friar, a pair of sandals and a rosary. 'This,' he told me curtly, 'you can wear over your shirt and breeks. The nights are turning cold and you can do with some warmth.'

'And where do we make for now?' I asked when I had covered my rags.

'You make for Paris.'

'In this guise?'

'Why not?' Shouldering his pack he pointed westward. 'This is my road. You go north. Have you money?'

'A few whites.'

'A holy friar,' those hooded eyes twinkled, 'can always be fed and housed. But for this night's rest, over the hill here,' again he pointed, 'you will find a shepherd's hut, a flagon of wine and food. From there you will receive further orders.'

Then, without another word or backward look he strode away. I watched his receding form vanish into the ghost-like vapour that crept up with the rising moon, hiding in a grey mantle of mist the silver waters of the Loire, winding like a translucent snake through the wooded valley.

I was to learn more of the methods of the Coquillards before my journey's end; yet I must surely have been favoured by those in high command, for I found myself mysteriously guided on my journey back to Paris. Directions as to the route I was to take were left for me in Latin at the shepherd's hut where I feasted on a cold roast duckling, a fine cool Barsac, a loaf of white bread and Brie. I slept on a pallet of straw, rose at the crack of dawn and resumed my way. Following the itinerary discovered on a folded paper wedged in the crust of the loaf, I made tracks across country, bearing northwards. The same message gave me a list of signs by which I would know what inns and villages must be avoided, so carefully organised was my every move. I might have wished less supervision to allow of more adventure which my friar's frock debarred. Cards, dicing, wenching, even had I hankered for a woman, were forbidden. I must play the part allotted me however much it irked, and I played it well enough to gull the *sergents*, who were combing the countryside to seize me. Although I had been absolved from a verdict of murder by Philippe's deathbed confession, I still stood to be indicted for manslaughter. Moreover, the recent rounding up of the Coquillards at Dijon, and my friendship with de Montigny and Colin des Cayeux, both known to be members of 'this dangerous society of felons, bandits, vagrants, marauders, card-sharpers and counterfeit coiners' — there was no end to the litany of our documented crimes — had got me well marked and charged with manslaughter or any other proven criminal offence, to be punished as prescribed by the law and the King, his pleasure.

Winter was ending when I received instructions to present myself at the shop of a barber, one Perrot Girart, in Bourg-la-

Reine. Genial, pot-bellied, and much respected in the town, he was a trusted fence of the Coquille, a receiver of their stolen goods. This I learned later; all I knew at the time was that he would give me bed, board and safe conduct to the gates of Paris.

Cheerful news was this; and a cheerful host to welcome me with exchange of the badge, the password, and a rigmarole in the jargon, which I had not yet mastered but understood enough of it to the effect that: 'Your priestish rig has done its turn to slip the cops and now you're out to knap a yack or smash a rag or rattle tats or strip a dame and blow the swag and booze the lot!' He roared with laughter, slapped his thigh, and fetched another bottle from his cellar, of which I took every advantage. There appeared to be no woman, wife nor maid about the place, which was spotlessly clean as himself. We supped in his bed-chamber for my safer hiding, and when we had eaten our fill of the fat capon fresh killed in my honour, he, picking his teeth with the wishbone, said, 'Villon, you may wonder why you've been led by the hand as you were the son of our Khan —' their jargon name for King — 'and given a free pass all along your way, nor will you be charged a sol for this spread or any bite nor sup you swallow. Them's my orders. Well, what of it? Shall I tell you for why?' With his forefinger he tapped his red nose, so like a chunk of raw beef, his little eyes almost disappearing in the rolls of his fleshy cheeks; and he told, in the jargon of which I was hard put to interpret more than the gist of it, that: 'You, Villon, being a poet and a man of parts as marked by our Khan, for while we have among us nobles, wise men, rich men, pawky men, jailbirds, cut-throats, thieves, and learned doctors of your Sorbonne, we have nary such a one as you. There be troubadours and mumpers, tumblers, barbers,' he chuckled fruitily, 'and I could name you more than a sergent or two o' the Watch. Oha, yes! And they be the first to claim their share o' the pool. For this I'll tell you, brother, we none of us takes but what's fairly divided and much of it goes to the needy.'

Refilling my cup I asked with a grin, 'Would I be considered the needy?'

He shot me a sharp look, with an answering grin that revealed his broken teeth. 'The Khan,' he said, 'helps those who help themselves.' And he helped himself to another cup of wine.

From under my eyelids I saw him take stock of me where I sat, warmed and replete, my head against the chair back, my thumbs in my girdle.

'You have been given,' said he, 'full protection.'

'And who more deserving, by your account, as honoured by the Khan?'

Reflectively he sipped; his eyes, like boiled gooseberries, never left my face. At length he vouchsafed, 'Orders have come from the top down each step of the ladder, passed from the lords of our High Court to the least of us, that François Villon, Montcorbier, des Loges, alias Michel Mouton, shall be watched and guarded and whosoever lets him slip into the noose will pay the penalty — Wait! What's that?' He cast a furtive glance around him, got up, went to the door, opened it, peered out, returned. 'My shop is closed for custom after curfew. I thought I heard a step below. Did you?'

'I heard nothing but the creak of your sign in the wind. You are over-cautious, brother.'

'One cannot be over-cautious. The wind carries voices, and mistakes have been known to occur even from the topmost.'

I stretched my legs, twiddling my bare toes in the thick-soled sandals that had served my journey well. 'Do you think I'm a mistake?'

He licked his lips, liking not, as I could see, my lopsided smile. 'If so, your blood be on our heads. Not a man of us who is not pledged to follow to the letter, for his life's sake, the command of the All Highest.'

'So! The Lord God has a competitor.'

Girart chortled and served his teeth again with the wishbone, brought forth what he found sticking to its fork, and popped it in his mouth. It struck me that he did not altogether relish this charge of the All Highest, but since I had been planted on him he must fulfil his obligations or take the consequence. It would seem the Coquillards were nothing if not thorough.

Having emptied between us two flagons of wine and picked bare the capon to its bones, Girart pointed to a truckle bed in the corner of the room, bidding me curtly, 'Lie you there.' Then, divesting himself of his jerkin he laid himself on the floor in a heaped bundle of rushes. I fancy he slept as little as did I, for guessing him wary of me and my credentials, the badge of the Coquille and the password which might have been falsely obtained, I thought best to be on the alert. I had seen him slide the knife with which he carved the fowl into his belt before he bedded down, and I felt for the dagger I carried under my friar's frock, given me by René when I parted from him some five moons ago. 'You may need it,' he had said. It looked as if I might.

The arrest of the leaders of the Coquillards at Dijon had resulted in an elaborate system of espionage, organised by Rabustel, in which certain of his officers were detailed to mingle with the Brotherhood and secure further evidence concerning the activities of the Burgundian Coquille. I had learned of this on my travels, for we, too, had our spies, and Girart would certainly have been warned of Rabustel's secret service.

However, the night brought nothing more eventful than the dawn when, weary of watching the dark, I fell fast asleep and was roused by Girart dragging me up from my rude couch. 'Come on. I must rid you of your beard,' now a sturdy growth that took all his time to shave. Regarding me critically when I was shorn, he remarked, 'This won't do. You're piebald.' Having no mirror, for only the most wealthy could afford a looking-glass and these were imported from Venice, I had to take his word for it that my chin and cheeks, deprived of hair, were, in contrast to the rest of my weatherbeaten face, pale as a bone.

'I'll have to stain you,' Girart said, eyeing me mistrustfully and, still on his guard, not yet convinced that I was whom I claimed to be; but he did what he had to do with the aid of a phial of walnut juice. Then he brought from a chest a graduate's gown and a pair of new shoes. 'You can throw off your friar's habit,' said he, 'and be yourself again, Maistre Villon.'

'Does that mean...' The joyous shock of all that it might mean arrested further question, which I gathered Girart was not disposed to answer, more than the spread of his palms in a negative gesture.

'You will bide here with me until further orders. I have customers awaiting me below. You too can wait — to have your hair trimmed. There's another way into my shop,' he indicated a door at the top of the stairs. 'This will take you to the yard and so to the front entrance.'

The 'yard', as he called it, was a wide grass-grown plot where hens picked and scrabbled along with half a dozen pigs. A fat sow lay on her side, suckling her newly farrowed young. From the yard a gate led to a field where several more pigs, their heads in troughs, were guzzling. Girart, it seemed, combined his barber's trade with more profitable business, as so I soon discovered; for, during my visit he, having perforce accepted me as a ward of the Coquillards, fed me on fat pork at almost every meal.

Picking my way in the mud with a care for my shoes, I found a cobbled way round to the front of the house and walked in at the door of the shop where Girart was shaving one of his two clients. The other was in the hands of his apprentice.

Bidding me a polite good-day, he offered me a stool. I sat, and with a heart-leap of surprise saw that the second of his customers, attended by his underling, was none other than Colin des Cayeux. Well-groomed and spruce, he could have passed for a prosperous tradesman. He gave no sign of recognition, and I, taking my cue from him, sat aloof, feigning impatience, tapping my toe, while I awaited my turn.

Having finished with his gentleman whom I took to be a burgess, and who was ushered out by Girart with bows and hand-washings, he offered the vacated stool to me. 'Your hair, messire, is sadly in disorder. Will you have a full cut or a trim?'

'A full cut,' and I added below breath, 'See that you cleanse me of nits. I'm full of 'em.'

I was seated next to Colin, who gave me a wink but no word; and when washed with some concoction that stank most evilly, Girart vigorously dried and cropped me, cut a square fringe across my forehead, and rhapsodically pronounced, 'I have seldom seen so fine a head of hair as yours, messire. Two whites, if you please.'

'Be damned,' I muttered from the corner of my mouth, 'you know I haven't a sol.'

But at a warning look from him I made a great to-do of searching for my pouch to find some silver slipped there by Girart, as I guessed. I tendered him a couple of whites, with loud complaint of surcharge, demanding that he spray my hair with amber. 'For God knows what dog's turd stench you've put on me.'

'Messire,' more hand-washings, 'I have treated your hair with a tincture of camomile, bay-leaf and juniper, as prescribed by the King's physician to preserve the scalp from dandruff. And my charge of two whites, messire, I do assure you, is a reduction of my usual fee in consideration, maistre, of your gown. I make always special terms for a Master of Arts. Good-day, messire, I thank you.'

I did not look at Colin, towelled and lathered there beside me, but as I rose from my stool, Girart, waddling to the door to bow me out, whispered, 'Go to the church and wait.' And for his underling's ear: '*Bonjour*, maistre. Your servant, sir. You were asking could I lodge you here. Willingly, messire, at your convenience, there being no hostelry that I can recommend as worthy of your honour.'

Greatly mystified by this I made my way to the church. In the pocket of the gown with which I had been provided, I found besides the purse containing money enough for board and lodging, a set of tablets; and to allay suspicion of the sacristan who might well have been an agent of Rabustel, I made feint, as of interest to a Master of Arts, to examine the beautiful porch of the church, a very fine example of the transitional Gothic, while I jotted down notes on my tablets.

I had not been there long before I heard myself hailed: 'François, what happy chance brings you here?' Colin, his face full of smiles, seized my hand and wrung it, for the benefit of the sacristan, still watchfully hanging about, and who at this seeming accidental meeting between friends, backed into the church.

'What news?' I asked, 'and why all this mystery? That fellow Girart — is he to be trusted?'

'He's safe enough, he's one of us but —' he glanced furtively around — 'Rabustel is on my track. I had orders to meet you at Girart's shop — I'm on my way to Paris, and although I was not listed in the round-up at Dijon, they are after me, having wind of my whereabouts from l'Isle-de-France.'

'What happened to René?' I asked.

'God knows. He's done a bunk — probably visiting his noble relatives at Chartres, where I last had news of him. Come away. We can't talk here.'

Leaving the church we came out into the village street. It was still early morning with a bite in the air, for March had come in boisterously with frosty nights and snow, but the first breath of spring was sweet above the stench of an open sewer. We turned into a lane hedged with blackthorn, its starry frail blossom just unfolding; and so through a turnstile into a meadow where pied cows grazed. Colin spread his cloak for us to sit for the grass was wet; and there he told how he had heard from headquarters to pass on to me, that thanks to the efforts of Father Guillaume and Provost d'Estouteville, I had been granted royal pardon.

'The Watch can't nab you now and they've nothing on me, neither, more than that I am, or was, connected with the Coquillards, but that's enough for them.' Colin plucked a sprig of sorrel and nibbled it between his teeth. Still freckled, sandy-haired, snub-nosed, he looked the merest boy, yet older by a year than I. 'I'm on my way to Paris, but was told to halt at Girart's and give you this latest news.' He spat out the sorrel stalk and slapped me on the shoulder, his face a-grin. 'You're free!'

Free! The quiet green of the meadow, the slow-moving, munching cattle were dissolved in a blinding upsurge of relief that was almost a physical pain. After nine months of exile, never knowing when I would be seized, shackled, flung into a cell, I could not yet believe myself saved.

Too joyfully dazed to ask Colin how he had come by this news, yet knowing something of the inner workings of the Coquillards, I guessed they had been as active in obtaining my release as Father Guillaume and the Provost.

From Colin I learned also that Letters of Remission had been issued absolving me of the accusation of manslaughter on the statement of Philippe de Sermoise. My foster father, not knowing my whereabouts, could not communicate with me, nor I, for safety's sake, with him. 'And now,' Colin said, 'you can. Write him a letter. I'll take it.'

But the formalities were not even yet complete, since every statement made by me, the accused, and written down by Fouquet *verbatim,* had to be verified, and if any flaw were discovered I would be further detained. 'Which being so,' Colin told me, 'and in order to satisfy Authority that the documents, every one of which is curry-combed, are proven, all Letters of Remission must be confirmed by the Court of Inquiry.'

'How long — O God, how long,' I cried, 'have I to wait?'

'A week at most, as Girart's lodger. He'll feed you well, and l'Abbesse Huguette at Port Royal will provide you entertainment.' Colin gave me a meaningful leer and got up, pulling his cloak from under me. 'Damnation! It's soaking wet. Write your letter to Father Villon and I'll deliver it — be quick, for I must be on my way.'

I scribbled a hurried note to my father, expressing my grief for all the anxiety I had caused him and my mother, and gave it to Colin with injunctions to hand it to Dom Guillaume in person.

I made the most of that week at Bourg-la-Reine and the hospitality offered me by l'Abbesse Huguette at Port Royal in the Chevreuse Valley near Paris. If Girart knew of my nightly sorties to a certain tavern in the village frequented by the blades of the younger squirearchy, and a favourite venue of l'Abbesse — masked and cloaked — he made no question of my comings and my goings.

How this extraordinary woman, the Mother Superior of Port Royal — or Pourras, as locally known — had retained the high opinion of ecclesiastical authority for fifteen years before action was taken against her, is inexplicable; but I can vouch for it that during my visit to Bourg-la-Reine she, who was cutting her capers before I was cutting my teeth, had the *entrée* to every house of repute, or ill repute, in the vicinity. I did, on one occasion, make a survey of the villa of 'Madame de Vaucelles', to find it shuttered, closed. I received no answer to my knock, and enquiry of a farmer's lad working in an adjoining turnip field elicited the information that the bailiff had gone to Paris.

'And the lady of the house?'

'There be no lady here,' he said, and said no more.

I passed an hilarious week in the company of the rollicking Reverend Mother, who urged me stay longer but I would not be persuaded. Girart, too, who still not certain whether or no he harboured a murderer and stood to be arrested as an accessory after the fact, seemed anxious to be rid of me. To be hanged for no fault of his own and despite the vigilance of the Coquillards must have caused him some disquiet. I am positive that he lost weight during the week I boarded with him; his rosy-gilled face had turned a mottled mauve, and his pendulous belly was as the shrunken bladder of a sheep. But as Colin had advised, he certainly did feed me well on a surfeit of pig.

On the morning of the seventh day of my sojourn at Bourg-la-Reine, I received an answer to my letter from Father Guillaume.

All was well, God be praised. I could return to Paris unmolested. I was pardoned. He begged me not to delay a moment but to come to him at once. My mother and he were counting the hours... The dear kind anxious soul, and my poor little mother; I could picture her at prayer before the altar of Our Lady in the Church of the Celestines...

And so, hot-foot, I sped for home again, and Paris.

TWELVE

It was late afternoon when I passed through the gates of the city and plunged into the welter of her streets. All the way along, my head in the air, my feet winged, my heart had trumpeted its gladness of this moment when I would come, a free man, into my own; for Paris was my own, the very heart of me.

Above Montmartre a broad ribbon of gold was banked with storm clouds shaped like dark somnolent dragons, but the last of that clear cold day etched every roof and spire in strong relief against the fading sky as if a master's hand had limned it.

My steps led where they willed, seeking to refresh me with every dear familiar sight and sound of the city, lovelier for me than all the wooded valleys of the Loire, or the wide plains and vineyards and pastures where I had wandered during these long weary months of exile.

On the Petit-Pont I stayed awhile, leaning my arms on the parapet, a shelf inlet between the clutter of gabled houses, clinging close together each to each, their walls greened with the mists of the river rushing fiercely under the five bridges, and steel-grey now beneath the deadened sky. And there, in this same place, where la Belle Heaulmière had found me, a ragged urchin, all those years ago, I sniffed again the savour of the fish-market, intermingled with the reedy stench uprisen from the flotsam of the Seine. The haranguères were packing their day's unsold surplus into baskets for the morrow, to be bought, unfresh, at bargain price. The one with the wart on her nose, who had used to give me flyblown guts to take home to my mother, was still there, thinner, greyer, more than ever warty. On I strolled, mingling with the crowd under the painted signs; the same hurry and flurry back and forth of men-at-arms, short-gowned students casting respectful eyes at me, a graduate; and here at the end of the bridge was the Shrine of Our Lady with the lamp glowing at Her feet among a handful of wild flowers, such as I used to pick for Her from the fields beyond the city walls and offer them up with my Hail Marys ... And there goes a Dominican priest in his black-and-white habit; and here, arms linked, Marion l'Ydolle and Bertha Broadfoot, those two who always hunt in pairs, more blousy and broader in the beam than when I had known them; and now a troupe of mumpers, and a showman prodding with a cruel iron-pronged stick his pitiful starved bear to make him dance at the end of a chain. And what, St François, do you have to say to that?

And here one of the fairest sights to see crossing the bridge; a bridal procession, she in her high steepled headdress and silver-white gown, with two silver-clad pages behind her, and her groom in his red velvet tunic preceded by boys in scarlet and yellow, their pipes and tabors giving out shrill slender music; and relatives and guests following in the gaudy colours of their festive dress to see the newlyweds upon their way. And I felt a great throb and a sinking somewhere in my middle, for I too might have had a wedding such as this if she and I... Then I scoffed at cloying sentiment and said to myself, *What you have of her is more than that simpering groom can ever have or know of his young virgin bride this marriage night or any other night, for marriage stales love-joys.* Yet marry I would, and will, I vowed, if she will have me. Maybe now that I'd come back to her we could talk of it again, for I thought of her as a wife to me in all but holy giving. I had known no woman since she and I were one, and that's God's truth, but … would she believe me to whom all women once had been fair game?

And with that thought of her I was seized with such an ache for her that I reeled and almost fell, and cursed me for a fool to love — for love's undoing.

The day was almost done; soon the Angelus would ring its evensong from every sweet-voiced bell of every church, and I must to my mother and give her first joyful surprise before I went to my father who would now be preparing for Vespers. But when I came to the house where she lodged, by grace and favour of Dom Guillaume who charged her no rent, I was told she had gone to the church: and there I found her.

She knelt, a little bent bowed figure at the feet of Our Lady. Light from the stained window barred her shabby veiled black with a glory of crimson, purple, turquoise, gold. None but ourselves was in the church, her Church of the Celestines. Silent as a cat I trod the aisle, seeing through a mist that curtained my full sight of her with small mouse hands uplifted, and veined like withered leaves. Her lips moved, wordlessly voicing the prayer I had given her, the prayer that was hers alone.

I slid on my knees beside her. She looked up startled, turned her head and saw me. I heard her quick intake of breath; her eyes were round with terror as a hare's that sees a fox. I think she took me for a ghost until I spoke and put my arm round her shoulders, so thin they were, and told her: 'Mother, my mother, it is I, your François. I've come home.'

O, that reunion at the altar of the Mother of us all, whose tender compassionate face looked down to bless our meeting. And how my little mother sobbed her thanks to the queen of heaven — 'You who have guided and saved him for me. I knew it! I knew you'd be saved for you did no wrong to save yourself from murder. God has forgiven His priest who confessed to his sin, absolving you... O, most loving Virgin,' up went her praying hands again, 'it is a thing unheard of that anyone — even so humble a creature as myself, ever implored your help and went forsaken. There is no single prayer, so you have promised us, that goes unanswered if it be your Son's good will in His good time. O, dear Lord God, this joyful day! O, my François, whom I, forgive the doubt most precious Lady, sometimes have thought I might never see again on earth. I rode the night mare in my sleep when the devil thrust his evil imps between me and my guardian angel and saw you mauled by wolves or set upon by robbers or catched by the *sergents* who were after you...'

And all this going on in the church, myself gulping down stones in my throat and buying candles from what was left of the money given me by Girart and which I hoped had been honestly come by, but if not it was used to blessed purpose in such a blaze of candles as to run out of stock, so I must seek the sacristan and give him the three whites left over to buy more; and then my mother too must empty her purse of the few sols it contained to burn candles to St Antoine. 'For he has found you for me at Our Lady's bidding.' Then home I went with her to the House of the Red Door.

Here another joyous welcome from the Father, who sat us at his table to such a feast as I think must have been prepared, in anticipation of my coming, for a week. A larded fowl and flawns, and mackerel sauced with Barsac, a fine fat goose, frumenty, my favourite dish, and cheese tarts, all washed down with Hippocras laced with cinnamon and ginger, and three flagons of Beaune.

My mother, after one cup of Hippocras and two of the Father's good wine, was in that state when laughter comes more readily than words; and Madame Blanche, grown stouter in my absence, who by the gleaming look of her had taken her full share of celebration in serving us, heaped my platter with every conceivable mixture of dishes, and every now and then darting back to fetch more and pile me with cream and rice — 'to fatten you who are nothing but a bag o' bones,' and, 'Did I not tell you, Father, that he'd come this very day? O, blessed day that brings him back, for I'd a pricking in my thumbs and saw two magpies perched there on the sycamore outside my window — one for sorrow two for joy — Lord! Aren't you brown. And your lip! What have you done to your lip?'

Then my mother who, in the excitement of our meeting at the church and from unaccustomed wine, had not noticed my scar being so taken up with me, looked and saw, and wailed, saying, 'God forgive me if I speak ill of the dead who confessed to save you — let me see, then, child — Holy Grace! your mouth is cut in half and there's marks of stitches here and very poor sewing it is I stitched my cere-cloths better and him a barber-surgeon to sew you up as if you were a sack!' And the good Father Guillaume, blowing his nose, full of tears and chuckles, and pouring more wine into our cups and telling my mother: 'Dear soul, be thankful that he has a mouth to speak with after so savage an attack. All is well, and you stay here the night for there's a gale blowing and it rains. You must not walk through this foul weather to be drenched.' It was evident to him that my mother could have been in no fit state to walk through any weather, foul or fair. 'Blanche will make ready a bed for you, my daughter. I insist.'

So, garrulous with thanks, she curtsied herself, a trifle unsteadily, out of the room; and supported by White Coif, in scarcely better case, they took themselves to Madame Blanche's quarters, to talk of me all night I had no doubt.

Alone with my father I gave him a fairly accurate account of my exile, reserving only my contacts with the Coquille. 'I dared not write to you,' I said, 'for I was watched every step of the way.'

'I guessed as much.' He shook his head. 'I have been most exercised to know how you managed to live all these months on the little money I could give you when we parted.'

'I lived sparingly, sir,' I avoided his eyes, 'and worked when work I could find, in the fields.' That at least was true. 'And for the rest — I managed somehow.' I knelt to kiss his hand and left him standing at the foot of the stairs, his lighted taper softening the lines of grief and anxiety my worthless cause had carved there; and I swore within myself that I would never give him reason to suffer so again, and fell asleep with that promise in my heart...

Mais, que veux-tu?

Car jeunesse et adolescence...
Ne sont qu'abus et ignorance.

A poor defence of what I was instead of what I might have been had I not dipped my wings in mud, that though I struggled like some storm-swept gull to flounder in Seine's garbage, I could not free myself to soar above the filth that wound and bound me.

Yet so filled was I with good intent and pious resolution that the next morning saw me in the confessional pouring out my sins, making much of my illicit love and my association with dishonourable companions, as so I named the Coquillards, and, with vows to sin no more, I was absolved.

Then, eased of conscience-nagging I took me straight to Marthe Rose, in full determination to present myself as suitor for her hand in marriage. All should be as circumspect as any bourgeois burgess would have wished it for his daughter, or any prince for his.

The door was opened to me by her bailiff fellow, Joliz, for I called there in broad daylight. I was done with pass keys, stolen meetings, the hushed ascent up the unlighted stairway to her chamber. I had nothing now to hide. I, François Villon, Master of Arts, acquitted by the King his royal pardon, of a wrongful charge, had come to claim and announce her my betrothed before the world.

'Madame de Vaucelles is within?'

Joliz, Noë, Noël, or whatever his hell-blighted name might be, directed me a lethal look, standing square and bull-chested in the doorway. 'Madame is not at home.'

'When is she expected to return?'

'I cannot say.'

'I will wait.'

He made attempt to close the door but I, foreseeing this, had shoved my foot in it. Short of a tussle on the doorstep indicated by my upraised fisted hand, which I guessed him loath to encounter, there was left him no alternative but to let me in.

'I'll wait here for madame,' I said, and seated myself on a stone settle in the vaulted entrance. Cold as charity it was, or cold as the shoulder he turned on me with another stabbing look that I threw back at him with multiple aversion. I watched him mount the stairs, glaring down to see if I were glaring up at him, to find me engaged in contemplation of my navel.

I must have waited with increasing impatience for near on half an hour before I heard the peal of a bell answered by the horse-faced maid who threw me a look, inconceivably malign, and tossing her head like an ill-tempered mare, opened the door to her lady. It was evident she had been to market, for besides numerous packages borne by the diminutive page at her heels, he carried a brace of duck slung across his shoulders.

She, giving orders in an undertone to her woman, did not see me seated there in the dimly shadowed hall until the boy let fall on the stone flags one of the packages with a sound of splintered glass, to call forth from her a volley of abuse concerning his mother and his misbegotten birth, that he deserved to be disparaged of his parts and himself strung up on Montfaucon — 'It is my fine Venetian goblet you've broken, you lousy *(adjectival)* bastard! I'll hide the skin off you for this!' And seizing him by the ear she whirled him round, beating her fist into his face with such violence that blood spurted from his nose, when I thought fit to interfere.

Starting up from my seat I dashed forward, seized the bawling infant by the arm and put myself between him and his rageful mistress.

'You!' She drew back a step, and, composing her face which a few seconds before had been unrecognizably distorted to render it the mask of an avenging Fury, she exclaimed with every semblance of delight: 'Messire Villon! After all this while! What a gladsome surprise. You, Pierre,' to the blubbering child, who had slunk close to me for protection, 'you're a bad boy and deserved a whipping for your clumsiness. But here's something for your comfort.' She stooped to the packages scattered on the floor to find a piece of marchpane and popped it in his mouth that showed a gap where one of his milk teeth, dislodged by her blows, dangled over his bruised lip on a thread.

I relieved him of his tooth by a gentle pull and, lifting his chin, examined his battered button of a nose.

'There, there,' I soothed the whimpering brat, whose years at the most could have been no more than seven. 'Madame has grievous cause to beat you, but no harm's done.' Doubtfully I felt the bridgeless tissue to find — as long ago my father had found after one of my scrimmages with Colin — a fracture of the tender unformed bone. 'Whatever hurt you have will soon be healed. I advise that it be bathed in a concoction of witch-hazel if there is any in the house, if not send to the apothecary hard by here.'

Although this was addressed to Marthe Rose I did not look at her, but handing the child over to her woman, 'See to it,' I said, 'he be well tended.'

'Go, Hortense, and tend him as you are bidden.' She gave the order coolly, yet a thievish glance from me discovered her bulging underlip above the tremble of her chin, that I was hard put not to shake and take her there and then.

'Madame.' Profusely I bowed, watching the retreating back of Horse-face and her bellowing charge, who, having found so ready a champion in me, redoubled his howls to receive a silencing cuff from his wardress.

'Sir,' Marthe Rose, very much the *grande dame*, with one eye on the staircase where in a shaft of meagre sunlight I discerned, or thought I did, the burly shadow of de Joliz, 'I much regret you should have witnessed this unfortunate domestic scene, but if you could only know what I suffer in the training of that poor little orphan whom I found lost and straying on the Petit-Pont, and brought him here to save him from starvation and the dangers of the streets —'

'*Tu quoque?*' reminiscently I murmured.

She pinkened, darting me a narrowed look. 'You said?'

'That your sorely tried indulgence does you credit.' Again with exaggerated courtesy I bowed. 'I must apologise for my intrusion but am only just returned to Paris and hastened to pay you my respects ... Madame, allow me.'

She had dropped to her knees on the flagstones to recover a fragment of ruby glass. Regarding it ruefully:

'That,' she said, 'cost me an *écu*. Put yourself in my place! Would you not have been enraged?'

Whatever doubt I might have had of her for her uncontrolled attack upon so young a child, melted before the tantalising uplift of her blunt-cornered mouth.

'Marthe Rose!' In that stifled cry wrenched from me was all my unslaked hunger for her soon to be appeased.

'Sh!' She hushed me with a finger to her lip, and rising, whispered, 'Come into the solar.'

I followed her to a room seldom used except in winter. Closing the door she stood facing me, defiant. 'You had no right to interfere with the beating of the boy before my woman and Noë — my bailiff — on the stairway listening, all ears.'

'Aha!' I felt my jaw stiffen. 'Your Cerberus. He guards you well.'

'I pay him well. He attends to my affairs at the farm and keeps account of wages and such. I have no head for figures. I can't add two together.'

'Couple two together,' I said, 'and you have one. Come here.' I held out my arms to her but she evaded me and sat herself, lips primly pursed, in a high-backed chair. And: 'Is there no end,' I marvelled, 'to your delicious inconsistencies? I know you to be possessed of all allurements synonymous with woman, even to those of the wild-cat as your remarkable performance in the hall did so admirably render, but I have yet—'

She sat sulky-mouthed, picking at her thumbnail. 'Such a fuss to make because I beat him. Haven't you been beaten when you was a boy?'

' — have yet,' I went on softly, 'to see you close-lipped as an oyster or — my maiden aunt.'

Her eyes opened widely. 'I didn't know you had a maiden aunt.'

'Sancta Marie! The joy of you!' With a burst of laughter I flung myself at her. 'The artifice of dalliance is not for us, my love, my only love.' I knelt and took her hands, turning them palm upwards each to kiss. 'I'm here. I'm yours to do with as you will.'

She dragged her hands from my fevered clutch and said, 'Your mouth, your poor, poor mouth.'

I fastened it on hers; and at the eager tremble of her body, 'My little nymph,' I taunted her with slow adventurous caresses, 'are you still so greedy?'

'Yes.' Her hurried breath was on my lips, 'Yes … yes. Tonight. I can't wait. I've wanted you, I've longed for you … and … You have the key?'

Between the hot rain of my kisses, reeling sense was clarified to ask, 'That man, your bailiff. Will he be here?'

'Only for today. He goes to Bourg-la-Reine this evening. He had business to discuss with me.'

I drew away from her, searching her flushed face. 'I have come from Bourg. Your house was uninhabited. I prowled about — saw no one.'

A little crease appeared between her faintly surprised eyebrows, slanting up and outward like the wings of a bird in flight.

'He comes and goes. He may have been to market to buy livestock for the farm. My dear, my very dear,' she stroked my cheek, 'I've missed you every hour of these long lonely nights.'

'Not again. Never again. We'll be together always now. I want you, not as mistress but —' my arms tightened round her — 'as my wife.'

A truant look dawned in her eyes.

'No!' A shiver seized me. 'I'll take no denial.' I heard my voice shake to its pleading. 'If it is love with you as so enduringly it is with me, then we must be bound in God to sanctify this loveliness, that from a seedling growth has flowered in our…'

I stopped myself and added, mutely questioning: *Our hearts, or only mine?* And as if in answer to that doubt of her, unspoken, she said, withdrawn from me and downcast, 'I am afeared of marriage. It kills love.'

Still kneeling there before her: 'Not such love,' I told her fiercely, 'as we have found.'

'I wonder.' Her face shadowed.

I got to my feet. 'So may you wonder, for love *is* a wonder, God-given.'

She looked down at her hands. 'If we were to marry, all I have,' she half whispered, 'would be yours.'

'All you have is mine already.' Then I caught her meaning and a coldness came upon me. 'You fear not the loss of love in marriage but the loss of your worldly goods, your house, the wealth of your coffers. You are no better than a whore who sells herself for money as you sold yourself to him on the edge of his grave that you might be his widow.'

She sprang up in blazing protest. 'Cruel! You wrong me! It is that I — I love too much. I have seen how marriage cools a man who takes to wife his mistress.'

'What man?' I stormed at her. 'What do *you* know of men who never knew your husband in his dotage as you have known me in the heat of my youth.'

She drooped her head, and like a lightning flash her moment's passion passed.

'I have been your harlot,' her words were a woman's but her voice was a child's. 'How can I be your wife?' and she fell to quiet crying.

I took her back into my arms. She hid her face to hide it against my heart. 'Love, my love,' she whispered, 'how fast it beats. Is this hurry all for me?'

'For you. Always and only for you.'

'So you may think, but afterwards,' her slender body strained to mine, 'I've seen it so often that husbands who were well content in their first year of marriage sicken of the wife bound to them by the nuptial Mass, and seek to satisfy themselves with other women. This I know, and fear to lose your heart.' And where she thought to feel the beat of it beneath my gown she kissed and said, 'If this is all and only mine, then let me keep it. I would not lose it to another. You must want me always as you want me now.'

'Until,' I bent over her, 'such time as I'm your husband, and then ... I'll want you more.'

THIRTEEN

That night, O God, that night when we two were one again in the perfect unity which only comes, so I believed and trusted, with the yielding of desire to the soul's expansion. Yes, so immersed was I in her that I could only sing of souls, and much she understood of it lying there in a moonbeam, her head pillowed on my arm, her flower-like body tranced and scarcely breathing.

'Such a pretty piece of poetry,' she yawned a very little. 'Did you make it just for me?'

'Just for you. All that burns and beats within me, my heart's blood and my heart's song, all I am and ever will be, here and hereafter is yours.'

I saw the gleam of her teeth in the moonlight.

'How clever you are but ... am I the only one for whom you say these pretty words? Do you write and learn them first, or make them up as you go along?'

'Yes, *ma damoyselle au nez tortu*,' I pinched her nose, 'I make them up as I go along.'

She moved her head in momentary petulance. 'Why do you call me that? My nose isn't twisted.'

'Yes, it is. The loveliest twist of a nose in Christendom. It points to heaven.'

She gave a gratified giggle. 'Say me some more.'

I said her some more.

Le souvenir de vous me tue
Mon seul bien, quand je vous voy,

Car je vous jure sur ma foy
Que ma joye sans vue et mue.

'That's a pretty piece, too. But if you truly mean that you would die with nothing but the thought of me and without the sight of me, you should have been dead these nine months past.'

'Part of me *was* dead, lost of you and all of this,' I kissed again where I had loved, 'and this.'

'Ah!' She shuddered sweetly. 'Yes, I too. I can't think how I've lived without you, so wonderful a lover as you are. We have never been so close together as tonight, but look there,' she pointed to the first grey finger-thrust of dawn piercing the curtained dark. 'You must go. The servants will soon be about. They mustn't see you.'

'Tonight?' I leaned over her when I was dressed. 'I'll come to you tonight.'

'No,' after a second's pause, 'not tonight. I have guests for supper.'

'And I am not invited?'

'How could I invite you? I didn't know you were in Paris.'

'Who,' I demanded, 'are your guests?'

Another pause; in the hastening light I saw her brow puckered.

'None of interest to you. Some old people, friends of him — my husband — a lawyer and his wife. They're from Bourg-la-Reine and will be here a night or two. So, dear love, you mustn't come until you hear from me.'

'How soon — how soon,' I was pleading with her like an adolescent cub, 'can I proclaim you mine before the world?'

'Not too soon, sometime, only... Wait a little longer so I may be sure, not of you but of myself.'

I took her by the shoulders. 'I think you never will be sure unless I make you sure, to take — or break me!'

And with that I left her.

The evening saw me at the Pomme de Pin where I received a boisterous welcome from my fellow taverners. Tabarie was there, full of drink and talkative as ever, Nicolas, the Picardy monk, and Colin, just arrived in Paris and at no small risk, so under cover of Tabarie's babble he told me. 'But better I am come and boldly, undisguised, for they have nothing on me yet beyond suspicion.'

'How,' I asked, 'have you accounted to your father for your absence?'

He laughed shortly, and lifting his horn cup drank full of it before he answered: 'My father has a workshop at Bourg la-Reine. He sent me there with two apprentices to learn them their trade.'

'Of lock-picking?' I slipped in, drily.

Disregarding that superfluous remark, 'My father,' he said, tilting his cup to take the dregs of it, 'cannot spare me from his business here in Paris. He is getting old, and hopes soon to retire. Drawer, another flagon.'

Since it was clear I would get no more from him than what he chose to give I refrained from further question.

We were a company of five seated there at table, Nicolas, Tabarie, Colin, myself and another, a stranger to me but not to Colin and the rest of them. He went by the name of Petit-Jehan, was himself a locksmith, and 'A master of his art,' so Colin presented him to me, 'who has forgotten more of his trade than I could ever learn.'

A dwarfish stumpy individual was this Petit-Jehan, with a short black beard and eyes set close together under heavy jutting brows. I noticed, in particular, his hands, sensitive, long-fingered, and ever on the move. He had little to say, yet his eyes, those crafty darting eyes, were everywhere.

Colin called for dice. 'You, François, have you brought yours?' I had not.

'Which,' said Nicolas, his voice rumbling up from his distended paunch, 'is to our — and my — advantage when I recall the last time I had the honour,' his thick lips were drawn back in a snigger, 'of playing with you.' In the flickering light of candles his gross dew-lapped face had the appearance of a dark distorted moon.

'Well, who has the cubes?' I cried, with a glance around the table.

Tabarie produced a set, grabbed by the Picardy monk, peering to weigh and examine them closely.

Tabarie gave a hog-like grunt. 'They're not loaded,' and began to hold forth on the intricacies of cogging and how the bone must be drilled and the lead inserted — 'a careful tricky business and not worth the pains since any but a dolt-head can tell the false from —'

'Here, come on!' Colin rattled the dice, threw them down, and the play began.

It was nearing curfew hour and, like rats driven into their holes, men with their women picked from the streets came crowding in to pass the night in gaming, drinking, whoring, for de Turgis could supply a *cabinet privé* for those who were willing to pay.

Luck was with me. I won consistently in the first three throws, dispensing my gains in four flagons of wine to celebrate my safe return.

Tabarie was full of it: how it had been bruited all over the town that Father Villon and his friend, the Provost, had got me my freedom. 'Which only goes to show how unjust is justice when favour of the Church is brought to bear upon the law, not,' babbled Tabarie, 'that you yet may go untrailed. The Watch'll have you marked, so guard your step.'

'And you your tongue that runs too free so you may lose it!'

Then, as I gathered up the dice, Pernet de la Barre arrived, breathless with haste, and, holding his side, announced, 'I've *such* a stitch with my hurry to beat the curfew.' He flopped down on a vacant stool beside me. 'My *dear!* how wonderful to have you back again! I went first to the Mule and not finding you there I guessed you'd be here. My dear, your lip!' He gazed at me with intolerable adoration. 'What a pitiable scar.'

The others, exchanging amused glances fell silent, all but Tabarie, well in his cups, who gave an hiccupping imitation of the Bastard's falsetto. 'Yes, my dear! Your barber-surgeon could surely — yip — have made a better pre-hic-servation of your beauty. Who'll play me now? Bastard, my *dear!* You've money to lose. Will you take me on?'

'Well, I don't know.' His plump pink face, so like an amiable pig's, shone with sweat. He took a silken scented handkerchief from his sleeve and mopped it. 'How hot it is in this inferno. Are you staying, François?'

'No.' I got up. I'd had enough of those four; enough, too, of drink. The close atmosphere of the low-ceiled room, its rafters blackened with brazier smoke, was stifling. 'I'm going home.'

The Bastard buoyantly sprang to his feet. 'I'll go with you. We've just time before curfew.'

Clinging to my arm he walked with me through the emptying streets, but before we reached the cloisters of St Benoît, the city's curfew rang its warning note.

'My dear! We must be quick. Oh, when I think of the last time I saw you — shall I ever forget it? You can't *believe* how I suffered not knowing if you were dead or alive, but Father Villon was an angel to me. What a *saintly* man. I used to visit him and talk of you for hours. I told him all about the rag you had tied to the thorn-bush and I would hang about there *freezing* in the cold, hoping to see you but I never did. You were elusive as a sprite. *Do* tell me, have you written any more poems? The Father spoke of your writing. He said he is always finding pages torn from your tablets lying on the floor of your room, and he takes and treasures them. He considers you a poet of "the greatest stature" — those were his words — but that you lack concentration. He says you are unaware of your own strength as a master of expression, but he only voices what I've always known. If you would —' He stopped abruptly. His hand tightened on my arm. 'Jesu! The Watch, and I've no pass. Have you? No? Oh, Lord! Get under this porch. Quick.'

A steady tramp of feet, preceded by the light of lanterns, proclaimed the advance of the patrol. The Bastard dragged me into cover and stood, breathing heavily, beside me. The night was clear with a full moon, the sky a starlit canopy.

A couple of *sergents* passed us by with measured tread, their lanterns sweeping a path of light before them.

'Let's wait,' the Bastard panted, 'until they're round the corner. Such a waste of the city's money is this night prowling of the Watch. Set a thief to catch a thief — I'm told that one in every three would rob us first before they run us in. Oh, my dear, I quite forgot to tell you. I've taken lodgings in the Rue de Grève, near by the house of Mademoiselle de Bruyères. Do you know her?'

Did I not?

'She,' he tittered, 'has a penchant for me and, my dear, it was too *awful*! She invited me to visit her and I found her there alone. My dear! I was terrified. I'll never go again unless I'm chaperoned. And what a beard! A positive *broom* growing out of her chin. And what do you think? She tried to *kiss* me! I simply staggered away and fell flat on my — but really, those old widow-women, they're not safe. Talk about ravening wolves!'

By this time we had arrived at St Benoît. He followed me into the cloister, and while I fumbled with my key to find the lock of the red door, he said, 'You must take supper with me in my rooms. I have an admirable servant, he cooks *à merveille*. Can you come tomorrow?'

The door swung open. 'Not tomorrow. Some other time — perhaps. And you'd best get to your lodgings before the Watch come round again, if you haven't a pass.'

He was edging in beside me.

'Go along, my little cabbage.' I patted his cheek. 'It would be too awful to have you collared by the Watch.' I fairly pushed him out.

The house was silent save for the steady muffled rhythm of Father Guillaume's snores when I took myself to bed but not to sleep. Moon-dazzled, restless, I lay turning over in my mind her evasive half-consent — or no consent? — to be my wife. And if she were, would my love for her be strengthened by the closer bond of marriage? Yes! Love's passion fruit is sweet but God's acceptance of it sweeter. Yet, was not woman man's perdition as in the beginning from his fall? Or, had I taken Holy Orders, would I then have been immune from this same betrayal? No. A thousand times, no! I would have sinned against the Church to take her, for my soul's destruction. That much I had been spared, and if now my sin were love unsanctified I must and would make reparation.

Je meurs en aymant pas amours
Languir me fault en griefs douleurs

Sprung from my inner voice those words whispered to me and I groaned aloud. *Be done with falsifying sentiment to cloy you. Your want of her is avarice; the guarding of a treasure that must be yours alone, unshared as a miser guards his gold!* And then that thought, like smoke, wind-driven to obscure the creature I had made in my own image and not God's, was cleared to see her as she was, more worldly-wise than I. And why, cold reason argued, should she sacrifice her freedom, so well-endowed, for me, a vagabond at large with nothing to offer in return for her wealth more than a smattering of scholarship and a few indifferent ballades tossed off in taverns. 'A poet of high stature,' as that good patron saint of mine who loved his wastrel son so blindly, did deceive himself as I deceived myself, in her.

Ah, if only she were still that forlorn waif as when I found her, would I then have taken her in marriage as I would take her now? And unable to endure this fevered wakefulness I threw off the coverlid and going to the window opened it for air. Although the night was chill in its last hour, I burned and was hot, shivered and was cold as with an ague, while a deep-sunk urgency possessed me to be done with indecision. I would go to her now and stake my all upon her answer. But … she had told me not to come to her tonight, and why? What should I care for her guests? Let them know. Let the whole world know her mine.

Stars were fading, dawn was nearing, the Watch ending, the moon high-riding, and somewhere in the distance a cock crowed. I dressed quickly. My fingers shook as I fastened my gown and tied its rope girdle.

By the window I stood listening. All was quiet, but the city soon would be astir. With my shoes in my hand I crept down the stairs, one eye on the door of Madame Blanche's room. She wakened early... No sound yet in the house; even Father Guillaume's snores had ceased.

I let myself out and, speeding through the shadows of the cloister, made a circuit along narrow hidden byways that would bring me to her house in the Rue St Martin. The bells of Notre Dame heralded the day's approach and the end of the Watch.

I was safe.

I stood below her window, gazing up. All was in darkness, but every minute the sky lightened. I had held in my keeping the key to her door, hidden on my person whatever my disguise since I fled from Paris on the night of Corpus Christi.

I needed no candle to guide me to her chamber; the weakened moon gave light enough. Her bed faced the window, its curtain half drawn to reveal not one couched there, but two, close bound, their bodies blanched in the lifting light.

A spark of red flashed behind my eyes to blind me before reverberation came with a strangled cry as of some wretched animal, trapped.

They stirred, those two, and he, bronze naked, head reared like a snake's about to strike, sprang from her arms to me where, dry-tongued, my scarred lip stretched in the grin of a skull, I stood.

I heard her scream, and then my ears were plugged with the shock of impact that felled me to the ground. A second only, and I was up and battering with all my strength against that of the bull-chested beast.

'Noël!' A whimpering bleat broke through our struggling silence. 'For God's sake, hold! You'll kill him — he's no match for you.'

He had stripped me of my gown and shirt and had me under him, his great thighs straddling my buttocks, to thrash me with my girdle's rope as the washerwomen thrash their linen in the Seine. Powerless as a gnat in a hurricane under the storm of his blows, I felt myself lifted, locked in a hideous embrace, and flung like a sack with a dead dog in it, rolling over and over and down, into unfathomable dark.

BOOK THREE: ROGUE ERRANT

FOURTEEN

Christmas Eve, 1456, and a night of bitter cold. I am writing in my little room at Father Guillaume's house. The Angelus is ringing from the steeple of Sorbonne. My lips move to the Salutation: *'Ave Maria, gratia plena...'*

Blowing on my fingers I dip my pen again. The ink is freezing in its horn. I scrape away the film of ice that has formed on its surface and continue to write. I am at work on my Petit Testament, written in verse, as was the fashion of my day among dilettantes who could neither read nor write, could only spout to scriveners and earn me a white or two by taking to dictation their jingling bequests enlivened by additions of my own.

I intended to leave Paris in the morning, had bidden farewell to my mother, received Father Guillaume's blessing with a letter of introduction to the Abbot of Angers, and one, of more value, to Son Altesse, le Duc d'Orléans. So, on this Eve of Christendom and my departure and in view of a journey to be undertaken, not without hazard in winter along almost impassable roads, and provided with such means as my father could spare, I thought to make my will. And here I am, filling sheets of parchment with my scribble, my fingers so cold-stiffened they can scarcely hold the pen.

L'an quatre cens cinquante six
Je, Francoys Villon, escollier...
En ce temps que j'ay dit devant
Sur le Noel, morte saison,

Yes, I can hear the wolves, driven from the woods of Montmartre howling at the very gates of Paris in search of food, having nothing for their hunger but the wind that whistles down the chimney of my closet with a flurry of snowflakes falling on the hearth logs to hiss among the last glow of the ashes. I hug myself in my gown against the icy breath that sneaks through every crevice to mantle Paris in a shroud of white.

I had in mind to bequeath my worldly goods — God save the mark! — to my associates, and some who were not, to slash them with my bitter mockery. I doubted they'd see the joke.

To Jehan Le Loup and Casin Cholet — you remember those two with whom, as gosses, we poached farmers' geese and ducks from the moats beyond the city's walls? To them I leave a stolen duck and a friar's frock as once did serve me well to dodge the law, and would serve them equally as well, I hoped.

To René de Montigny I leave three hounds, insignia of his noble rank, that he may hunt the wild pig; he, poor devil, ripe for hanging who will hunt no more. The Pig hunts him.

To Pernet, the Bastard de la Barre, I leave three trusses of straw that he may have a bed to lie on for his comfort — with a girl. For which he will not thank me.

To three poor little orphans, Colin Laurens, Jehan Marceau and Giraud Gossyn whom I have befriended with my scanty means, I leave my wealth — so much it is! — that they be clothed and fed through the long winter. Ah, François of the tender heart, may you be pardoned for your sins in this good act of charity that offers up your all to those unfortunates. Suffer little children... Yes, indeed I have, and suffered for and through them, blast their eyes! Who were they? I'll tell you. Three grabbing money-lenders whose shady dealings had ruined half our gilded youth and any gull whom they could lure into their net. I was one of them when, after a run of ill-luck with the dice, uncogged for my conscience, I found myself neck deep in debt to de Turgis who was dunning me that I must needs go cap in hand to borrow off a pair of them — at accumulative interest. The third, Giraud Gossyn, a speculator in salt, lent me the wherewithal to make a deal with him and win a fortune, so let him burn! And now the three are on my heels with threats to take their due from Father Villon, or screwed from me upon the thumb-rack in the Châtelet. And that's one reason why I must leave Paris. The other…

My pen slackened. I sanded the ink and swept aside the parchment. The cream of my jest was turned sour. Supporting my chin on my hand I allowed lacerated memory to limp across the screen I'd raised against it.

Several months had crawled by since that fatal dawn when I had found myself *cocu et battu*: cuckolded.

Like some unshelled crustacean I shrank beneath the merciless recurrent stab of my excruciation… How long I lay there in a huddled heap at the foot of her stairs before consciousness returned I cannot tell; but this I know, when sense and feeling were restored it was day and I out in the street, stumbling to fall and puke in the gutter.

If passers-by observed my plight it occasioned less pity than laughter. Townsfolk were accustomed to young gentlemen reeling home in early morning; nor was it unusual to see them sore and bloody from a thrashing, were their amours in a brothel or a lady's chamber interrupted by a rival or a husband.

It was unfortunate, however, that I should meet with Tabarie before I reached the shelter of St Benoît. He, too, had made a heavy night of it on his winnings at La Grosse Margot, after I had left the Pomme de Pin, and was in highest fettle. The halting explanation I offered for my gownless state, the bleeding weals on my back, and my general disorder as result of being set upon and robbed by thieves on my homeward way, sufficed to satisfy him — for the moment, as it satisfied my father to whom I gave a similar account.

'But what use could be your gown to them?' the good man in horror-stricken sympathy enquired. 'These miscreants were not students, surely?'

'No, sir.' I could confidently deny that. 'Nor can I give you any adequate description by which they may be identified before I was knocked senseless.'

'My poor, poor boy! This,' cried my father, 'is an outrage. The Provost must be informed and the Watch doubled. I have always maintained that Sorbonne and its environs are not sufficiently guarded. Get you to your bed, my son. Your back is beaten raw.' He adjusted his spectacles the closer to examine it. 'I will apply a soothing balm to this. Your flesh, thank God, is healthy and these are but surface wounds. They will soon heal.'

They did, after a week or so, during which time I slept face downwards, for even Madame Blanche's finest linen caused an agonising friction. Yet, although the outward and visible signs of my humiliation faded, the inner, deeper wound of it stayed with me to fester. Moreover, Tabarie, his nose ever scenting a scandal, had run it to earth having tracked the trail to its source: de Joliz.

It went the round of all the taverns and the stews, embellished by Tabarie to make me the hero of a ballade in which I figured as a mutilated comical grotesque, who entreats the gods to crown his head with horns that he may prove himself, if now deprived of action, as one whose codpiece had been lost in goodly cause. Nor did her name escape the filth they flung at mine. The mud of it stuck, to couple us in fleering badinage and twist a knife in my hidden wound, while I, with chuckles, improved upon their doggerel.

But their puerile jibes and baiting were nothing to the anguish I endured in the knowledge of my self-deception: not hers. I alone — may I be cursed for it, and am — was to blame for my wilful blindness. Yet, for all the abuse of her that I poured out in lays and ballades, chucked aside, discarded, though some of them were saved by those who seized on any scrap of jottings ascribed to the dead Villon, the shade of her persisted in the guise of Marthe Rose, or of her double, the exquisite *hetaera*, Katherine de Vaucelles, courtesan par excellence, whose spontaneous response to love, or what to her did pass for love, was in itself a poem, unparalleled. She haunted me till shape and sense were rent apart. I loathed her, I despised her, I wanted her, I loved her. Yes, God help me, and I love her still. There is no forgetting.

I sought refuge in my misery with Margot to find a bitter savage joy in my debasement… *Bad rat, bad cat.* How choose between the two of us? I, her pimp, paid for what I gave in return for what she earned, snatched in our drunken orgies to flagellate myself with disgust of the thing I had become. I could sink no lower.

And here another reason why I must leave Paris, that by all severance from my degradation I might start life afresh, purged of its poison. Yet no sooner had that thought flashed a spark of hope into my darkness than I scarified it with a jeer at mawkish humbug. You are as you are, as black is from white, but… what am I? Shall I ever know who knows all, except myself?

And taking up my pen again I dashed off the 'Ballade de Villon à s'Amye,' with her name in acrostic with mine.

Faulse beaulté, qui tant me couste chier
Rude en effect, yporite doulceur
Amour dure plus que fer a maschier...

So to its whining end; and then I wrote a preface:

C'este ballade luy envoye
Qui se termine tout par R...

or for your reading:

This ballade I now send to her,
Each line of it ending in R.
Who shall deliver it? Ah,
I'll call on Pernet de la Barre
And if he should meet as he goes
My girl with the twisted nose
He will say 'you dirty whore
With whom have you been before?'

Having got that off my chest I let it bide. I did not give it to the Bastard to deliver, and so may have deprived him of an errand he would, I think, have gladly undertaken. I placed it in a casket along with the 'Ballade to my Love and my Little Testament', discovered, seared and yellowed after fifty years, to be seized upon and published in the infancy of print.

The night was still young enough for me to slip over to the Mule, drink a cup with Colin, and glean from him some means of communication with the Coquille should I fall into trouble on my journey. He had invited me to sup with him, but I, deep in my writing, had lost count of time. I found the tavern full of Christmas cheer, and Colin at table with Tabarie, Dom Nicolas and Petit-Jehan, their heads together in close talk that ceased on my arrival.

'Why so late?' Colin dragged forward a stool for me to sit, and with a sweep of his arm indicated the remnants of a feast: the carcass of a capon, scraps of roast pork congealed in fat, and a dish of nuts and raisins. Pouring me a tankard of Morillon, a dark heavy wine of Bourgoyne, he refilled his own, and cried a toast to: 'One last fling before you leave us. Are you game?'

'That,' I answered cautiously, 'depends.'

'Much depends,' he said, 'on your discretion.' He screwed a glance at Petit-Jehan who returned him a quick nod, and, thus encouraged, Colin proceeded in the Jargon: 'Will you pitch a snide with us to make a crack?'

'And leave my hair and hide behind?' I shook my head. 'My skin so far is whole. I've no wish to lose it.'

'Come on! If nix we find then nix you'll have, but the fruit is ripe for plucking, and you,' he regarded me steadily, 'can lead us to the tree.'

'I fancy not your metaphor,' I told him, cool. 'The only tree I know, and have so far avoided, grows on Montfaucon. Am I your ape to hang there from its branches?'

He emptied his tankard, refilled it again, passed the flagon to me and licked a dribble of wine from his lip with a grin. 'An ape hangs from a tree by its hand.'

'And you,' I flashed, 'are handy. I am not.'

'But you have knowledge at your fingertips.'

Petit-Jehan beside me spoke. Not unlike an ape himself was he, with his melancholy eyes, long arms and stunted body. And watching the restless movement of his fingers delicately touching the wooden surface of the table as if they played upon some instrument unseen: 'Such knowledge,' I retorted, 'lies more in your province than mine.'

'Not so,' he murmured, gently. 'There is no knowledge more enviable than that of the scholar, which, messire, in your case flows from the mind spiritual to the hand that drives the pen; the finance in control of your Muse.'

I regarded him attentively. He was not young; his dark hair receded from a low wide forehead that gave height to a brow uncreased and mild.

'You, too, I think, have scholarship?' I put it to him as a statement rather than a query.

He stroked his pointed grizzled beard. 'In my youth,' a reminiscent smile came upon his lips, but his eyes were infinitely sad, 'I suckled at the breast of Alma Mater, yet any scholarship I drew from her is lost.'

'*Deliramenta doctrinae,*' quoth the monk from Picardy. 'The mad delusion of learning, hah? or conversely, *haud aequum facit qui quod; dedicit, id dediscit.* He is wrong to unlearn what he has learned. Is there any more in the bottle?'

He tilted it to find it dead. I called for another flagon.

'Which being so,' Petit-Jehan referred himself to the blear-eyed monk, 'Maistre Villon, if it please him, can impart to us his knowledge since *Sapienta qua sola libertus est.* Wisdom is the only way to liberty, *via*, shall we say —' he spread his hands, palm outwards — 'a game of skill?'

'Here, what's all this?' Tabarie, roused from semi-coma raised his lolling head, his wide foolish mouth a-grin.

'We were discussing,' replied the bland Petit-Jehan, 'a game that requires not only knowledge but skill.'

'If there's a game afoot, I'll foot it with you.'

Tabarie, taking a walnut to crack between his teeth, flicked a morsel of shell into the mottled dew-lapped face of Nicolas, and giggled delightedly at the monk's glare of detestation. By this time we were all well steeped in wine, with exception of Petit-Jehan, a careful drinker. Yet I can swear that I knew no more than Tabarie of the master-stroke those other three between them had devised. But, as always when wine worked in me whose stomach was stronger than my head, I would give rein to honour, duty, reason and ride headlong into any mad adventure.

Much that followed is amorphous.

I remember how Nicolas drew the babbling Tabarie aside in solemn conjuration to take his oath on pain of murder, that he would not divulge to any living soul whatever he would see or hear this night. I remember how Colin questioned me about a certain house adjoining the College of Navarre. 'You know the house. It belongs to Robert Saint-Simon but he doesn't occupy it now. Your Father Villon is acquainted with Saint-Simon, and you too have visited him there.'

I had; nor did it strike me as singular that Colin should have obtained this information, since he of the Coquillards would have eyes and ears in every house in Paris. Moreover, he drove home to me that I, if not yet admitted to the Inner Circle, was bound to them in loyalty and gratitude for their care and guidance during my exile and their efforts to secure the Letters of Remission on behalf of my release, which I doubted, unless they had their spies in the centre of Authority.

'And in return,' proceeded Colin, 'you are called upon to aid the Brotherhood by all means in your power should we demand your service, as now we do. So now you know — and here we are.'

Which left me little more the wiser as to where we were indeed.

One conclusion, however, despite my whirling head, I had drawn from this ambiguous cabal: that both Petit-Jehan and Nicolas, the latter, who it seemed, had wondrously escaped unfrocking, were likewise of the ubiquitous Coquillards. If I needed confirmation it was offered by Petit-Jehan who showed me the Cockleshell badge pinned inside the lining of his cap.

The streets were deserted when we five left the Mole. Snow had fallen, leaving tracks for the Watch to follow if they could, but they couldn't. The venture had been nicely timed. Soon the bells would ring for Midnight Mass with people flocking to the churches, their footsteps crossing ours in the trampled slush, for a rapid thaw had set in and the nipping wind had softened from the west. A moon in its half quarter and a starry-blossomed sky gave light enough to see our way along. Nicolas with Tabarie walked before, I and Petit-Jehan behind. Tabarie, ahead of us, was burbling to a monosyllabic Dom Nicolas. I was uneasily silent. Braced by the sharp fresh air I asked myself to what foolhardy enterprise I was now committed; and as if in answer to that thought Petit-Jehan beside me said, 'The first of the Ten Commandments of our Order, as you, a novice have already learned, is, "Thou Shalt Obey".'

This was something new; but I let it pass. 'You have been honoured with a trust,' continued Petit-Jehan, 'and if you fail it—'

His pause was eloquent. Colin supplied the deficiency by stopping to confront me with a dragging of his finger across his throat, a hideous uprolling of his eyes, and a significant protrusion of his tongue; which disagreeable mummery, if designed to threaten, fell short of its intent. I gave a whooping laugh, fetched him a flip on his nose and told him, 'You'd do well to play your part on the St Denis road, and to a better audience than I.'

Which grisly allusion to the Montfaucon gibbet was, though neither of us guessed it, in the nature of a prophecy.

The College of Navarre was no more than ten minutes' walk from the Mule. The courtyard of the house, once occupied by Saint-Simon, abutted on the College. That much our three ringleaders knew. What they had yet to know, and looked to me to tell them, was of an entrance to the Chapel of the College through Saint-Simon's house. 'For many houses,' Colin said, 'that stand beside a College have a door into the Chapel.'

I could tell him of none in the house of Saint-Simon.

'But you must at least know this,' he persisted, and proceeded to interrogate me as to where a certain coffer in the College Chapel could be found.

I now realised why I had been drawn into their plot. I, who in my student days had attended lectures in the Great Hall of the College and service in its Chapel, could guide them to the coffer for what purpose I was yet to learn.

'Yes,' I admitted, 'there used to be a coffer in the sacristy. But why —'

'The College and the Chapel,' Colin curtly quenched that question, 'should be as familiar to you as the palm of your hand. So come on!'

There was access to the garden of the house from a side alley by means of a low wall. Over this we climbed, Tabarie hysterically giggling and nudging Colin's ribs to ask, 'Hey! What's to do? Does the College run a brothel? If so, it's the only one in Paris that I've missed.'

Colin rounded on him, hissing: 'Get this in your thick head. *You've* naught to do but shut your trap and stay on guard and if

221

you hear so much as the squeak of a mouse give an owl's hoot for warning.'

Tabarie shivered. 'I don't much relish staying here alone. The wolves are rabid at the gates. Suppose they should come hunting and find me?'

'You'd make a juicy meal for them. Here, take this.' He handed him his cloak, and rapped an order. 'You others, give him yours. They'll only hamper us.'

The garden of the house and the courtyard of the College were divided by a wall some ten feet high. A ladder stood against it, easy to climb once we were rid of our outer garments. By the dim light of a shaded lantern, held by Petit-Jehan, I saw, when Nicolas of Picardy threw off his monk's habit, that he wore under it the jerkin of a forester complete with hunting knife and horn.

I was reminded of the legendary Robin Hood and his Friar Tuck, bawled in ballades by the *godons* and handed down to us.

'Keep your eye on our cloaks till we come back,' Colin bade the goggling Tabarie, 'and hold the ladder steady. Up now — and over! Villon leads the way.'

How often have I relived that night, possessed again by a reckless fierce excitement to exterminate discretion. I see myself swarming cat-like up the ladder, poised for a second on the top of the wall to take the jump and land on my toes. Petit-Jehan, no less agile than I, followed me, then Colin. I see Nicolas puffing and blowing as he labours up and plumps himself astride the wall while Colin hoarsely urges him, 'Come down, you greasy bladder of lard! We can't stay here all night...' I see the grim grey-faced old College, its great height lost in abysmal dark. I hear Nicolas, muttering curses unclerical, hanging on by his hands to the top of the wall, his sandaled feet wildly kicking; and Colin on edge with impatience, leaping up to grab him by his legs and pull him down to send him sprawling on the flagstones with groans and moans that he has broke his ankle.

'Wish it was your neck,' growls Colin. 'Lie you there, then, and stay out of it.' And lapsing into the Jargon, 'We three'll blow the dibs and melt the swag.' Which brings Nicolas in haste to scramble up and hobble after us, remarkably recovered.

'Is the College door the only entrance to the Chapel?' Colin asked me.

I told him, 'There's a window here. It could be forced.'

Petit-Jehan said, 'No. We'll try the door.' For locks were more in his line. The heavy oak yawned wide to his swift manipulation. We three slipped through, ghost silent, followed by the quasi-monk.

The Great Hall was a black chasm, its penumbral shadows lit by the faint gleam of Petit-Jehan's lantern. Again Colin questioned me. 'The sacristy, where is it? Can't see an inch ahead in this hellish dark.'

I felt my way along the wall under the tall windows, guided by the pale glimmer of a star.

The coffer, a large chest, studded and bound with iron, stood just inside the sacristy. A second door gave entrance to the Chapel. I heard Colin's whisper, 'This is our work, not yours. You and Nicolas stand by to give the alarm if need be. We can't rely on our jackass Tabarie.' He lifted the latch of the Chapel door. The altar lamp gave out a thread of light.

In awed wonder I watched that master craftsman, Petit-Jehan, kneel before the coffer as before a shrine. I saw his supple fingers caress the four great locks, feeling each with the sensitive touch of a surgeon. He, too, had his instruments, but his scalpel was a crotchet, a frail wisp of a skeleton key. Colin held the shaded lantern while he picked and probed with no sound, until the great lid creaked as it lifted slowly ... slowly, and a grating breath from Colin: '*Diable!* Another!'

Yes, the first contained an inner casket of walnut wood, treble locked and iron-bound.

With imperturbable precision and infinite care, Petit-Jehan sorted his instruments from a leather case strapped to his belt.

A leaden hour passed. Nicolas had flopped on to one of the stone benches in the College Hall and was snoring. I went to him and shook him roughly. 'Wake, you fool! You're supposed to be on guard.'

Time crawled, and still those crotchets picked and probed with little elfin scratches, and then a smothered croak from Colin across the muffled dark: 'Heave — heave up!'

The locks had yielded.

Something between a sob and a sigh shook the meagre frame of Petit-Jehan as the lid of the enclosed treasure-chest was wrenched open. Those two plunged their hands inside dragging out the heavy money-bags. Then, with the same masterly skill that he had lent to their breaking, Petit-Jehan repaired the damaged locks, left all in order and got up, bending his knees to ease their stiffness. In that ribbon of light from the altar lamp his face had a look of exultation.

The account of that night's robbing of the College of Navarre has been carefully documented and presented in its original Latin; but not for two months later was the burglary discovered, so excellently did our Petit-Jehan conceal his handiwork. And had it not been for that gawping windbag, Tabarie, nothing of my part in it would ever have been known. For, emboldened by success, those other three raided the house of a worthy Friar, Guillaume Coiffier, stole a quantity of silver plate and five hundred crowns in cash, to set the hounds of Law upon their heels. Luckily for me I was far from Paris then.

The beetle-headed Tabarie must needs go blabbing of this latest exploit in a tavern to an elderly amiable party, a total stranger to himself but not to the Friar who had been robbed of his plate and his money.

Tabarie, hauled before the Provost, was dragged off to the Châtelet to have his evidence extracted under pressure. This I later learned at Bourg-la-Reine from my friend the barber Girart, who had it, word of mouth, from one or two of the Fraternity.

Much of that screwed out of Tabarie in the torture chamber was invention to save himself a still more drastic treatment. This, known as the Question by Water, was a last resort much favoured by Inquisitors and often with desirable result. I can speak from experience. I've had it.

The victim is bound to a board while one interrogator holds his nose and another pours water down his throat through a funnel to swell his bowels and stomach to bursting point. Two pipkins, each containing a litre, sufficed for Tabarie, who even under pleasanter conditions could never hold his drink. Squirming and squalling under renewed administration Tabarie, between his yells, spilled all he knew and a deal he didn't know, to confess himself a minor accessory after the fact, his part in it having been confined to guarding our cloaks and steadying the ladder for us to climb back.

After more internal irrigation he admitted he had received ten crowns for his pains. The rest of it, he said, had been equally divided between the four perpetrators of the crime. They got our names from him. Mine topped the list. I can see Tabarie, mewing and spewing it out along with those litres of water… Equally divided? Yes, so it would appear to Tabarie who stood by in the shadow of the wall while Petit-Jehan counted the cash, handing him his ten crowns and bidding him be off. He went, not without some heated argument that he'd been rooked of his rightful share, but he pocketed the money and that is all he knew and saw of that night's work.

Yet, while we four were allowed ten per cent each of the proceeds as reward for our successful coup, the remainder, in the region of three hundred crowns, must, as I understood from Petit-Jehan, be retained by him and rendered to the treasurer of the Coquille.

'You will appreciate,' he said, 'that our Brotherhood relies on the activities of its members to finance us.'

I might have reminded him that I was not yet a member of the Brotherhood, and had been drawn into this particular activity with no previous cognizance of it, and upon compulsion. However those fifty crowns clinking in my pouch overcame my scruples to content me.

We parted; the others with their money-bags, and I home to fetch my knapsack. I had already bidden farewell to Father Guillaume, for I intended to leave Paris at daybreak; but with my pocket full of stolen cash I thought it best to get away at once.

The House of the Red Door was sound asleep when I crept up the stairs, took my bag and a stout staff, and was out again within five minutes. The streets were silent, the curfew bells had long ceased ringing. I hurried along, following my footsteps where they led. And where did they lead? Not to the city gates, but to a house in the Rue St Martin.

Her window showed a streak of light through its drawn curtain. I stood, as so often I had stood before, gazing up. My hand slid beneath my gown where, on its slender chain, I still held the key. Should I go in for one last glimpse of her? To find her with him and be flung out or stabbed to death?… Then, while I hesitated, I heard a sound of voices loud in song, a clapping of hands, and, above the last fading note of a lute, a girl's voice, high and sweet, *'Ma doulce amour'*.

I turned and, stumbling like a blind man, began to run. I ran till my breath gave out and I found myself propped weak-kneed, against a wall, my body bathed in a cold sickly sweat. Where was I? My straining eyes pierced the dark to find that I had come to the Church of the Celestines.

I went in and knelt before the altar where candles shone like golden lilies. Head bowed on my hands I tried to pray, but no words came. Footsteps shuffled down the aisle and halted. I looked up. An old, old priest was there beside me, his wrinkled, parchment-coloured face shadowed by his cowl, was calm and gentle. I struggled to my feet.

'Father…'

'Yes, my son? Ah!' A look of recognition dawned. 'You, François.'

He remembered me from long ago when I had used to come to that church with my mother to lisp my sins to him, my Confessor. I had often seen him since, at Father Guillaume's house. My hand sought the pouch attached to the belt of my tunic under my gown. The stolen money seemed to burn through into my flesh.

'Father, I … I would wish,' I stammered, 'to give a donation to … to the Church.'

Then reason cautioned me: *Don't be over-generous.* The old man was certain to tell Father Guillaume who would question how I came by it, he having given me barely enough to sustain me on my journey to Angers.

I handed him two crowns and said, 'I wish, *Mon Père*, that it were more.'

He took it, quavered a blessing, and shuffled off again to drop it in the offertory box. I was in half a mind to ask him to confess me, but fearful of the complications that would ensue with the return of my share in the theft from the College, I left the Church, unconfessed and unabsolved: a thief.

Yet there was still something I could do by way of penance. Making my way through the dark silent streets I came to the meat market by the Grand Châtelet. Under the butchers' stalls lay huddled heaps of human refuse: beggars, maimed, blind, starving; children, too. I caught one by the leg, his bones were like a bird's. Gently I lifted him. He moaned in his sleep, but did not wake. Into his small cold fist I slipped an *écu*, and laid him down; his eyes opened and he smiled; then his lids sank and he slept again.

I crawled about on all fours, to let fall coin after coin among those fleshless mounds of rag and skin and bone whose only surcease from their life's misery was sleep, or death... Did they dream lying there, twitching, scratching, snoring? Did they see me, or if seeing, did they think me but another dream, of an ugly black-winged carrion with the face of a man, or a devil, hovering to swoop, its scarred lip drawn back in a snarling grin as its foul droppings clinked on them in their fall?

One, a noseless hag, mowed at me, gibbering, mumbling: 'The angel, Gabriel, his blessed self.' And clutching at the air, she dropped her head on her shrunken breast. Her mouth sagged. Her eyes were open, sightless, dying...

I scattered what was left of the money I had stolen; and as I slunk away I heard their waking mutters, saw those scarecrow shapes heave up, the stronger of them grabbing at the coins with blows and curses and a scrambling to seize and take, and in the taking, kill.

My pouch was empty now of all but the five *écus* my father had given me in parting, and with my knapsack slung across my shoulder and lighter now in pocket than in heart, I took up my staff and walked through the gates of the city out to the open road.

FIFTEEN

When in the soggy dawn of that Christmas Day I sneaked through the gates of Paris, I had every intention of visiting the barber Girart at Bourg-la-Reine. With him I would stay before undertaking the journey to Angers; but in the mist of the morning, as I neared the outskirts of the village, I was met by a shepherd driving his flock. To my word of greeting he replied with the sign of the Coquille and a warning, in the Jargon, *'ne soiez plus sur les joncs'* — 'See you watch out for the cops.' I further understood that he had instructions from headquarters to tell me not to linger here in Bourg, but to make at once for Angers, thus to keep a safer distance between myself and the city police before the burglary at the College were discovered.

I went on my way marvelling at the co-operative system of this intensive secret service; a system whose disciplinary allegiance and control was far more effectively conducted than that of those who sat in judgement on them.

I still had the money given me on parting from Father Guillaume, and this I managed to increase at roadside inns by playing my personal dice to procure me food, drink, and a bed for the night with easy company thrown in.

Once well away from the danger of pursuit, which lessened with each kilometre I covered, I took my leisurely time, guided by signs carved on barks of trees intelligible only to the Brotherhood, or a muttered word in a tavern from some well-to-do farmer obviously much respected in the neighbourhood; or some loitering fellow at a cross-road. Any of these would advise me at which inn or in what village I could, with safety, stay. On one occasion, when having bought a meat pie at a cook-shop, its counter open to the village street, the owner called me back as I turned to go, insisting I'd paid him in false coin, which admittedly I had, having collected a few here and there from my friends of the road.

A heated argument ensued with exchange of invective on both sides, capped by my injunction that he, a mangy gobbet of dung, should shove his stinking pie a-crawl with maggots where it could be put to better use, much to the delight of passing villagers. At which the pie-man, clambering over the counter with threats to call the *sergents*, one of whom I saw approaching to investigate the row, I thought it healthier to pay him his due, and found my counterfeit coins returned with a note slipped into my hand bearing the roughly drawn sign of the Cockleshell. I hurried off quick, leaving the cook to deal with the sergent.

Once out of the village I sat under a hedge to decipher the message. Partly written in the Jargon, it contained the news that the robbery at the College of Navarre had been discovered; that an inquiry was to be held within the next few days and that those three, Colin, Petit-Jehan, Nicolas, and another, Thibault, a name unknown to me, acting under orders, had burgled the house of a priest, and fled from Paris; Colin to Normandy, Petit-Jehan to Le Mans. Nicolas and Thibault were still at large, their whereabouts not yet traced by the Coquille. I was also forbidden to play with loaded dice in taverns as my continuous run of good luck had aroused suspicion. This was something of a blow for my purse had run dry and I looked to my gaming for livelihood. However, I got over the difficulty of procuring food and drink by methods that had served me in the past. I can well believe that taverners and housewives may have much regretted their hospitality to the shabby young Master of Arts who, despite his threadbare gown and ugly face, had a pretty wit to entertain them with impromptu verse and risqué jokes, and was evidently a man not only of parts but of means, demanding the best room, ordering lavish meals and wine, regardless of the cost; and who slipped away leaving his bill unpaid. This by the simple expedient of getting out of the window before the household was astir.

The high road from Paris to Angers ran through two towns only, Chartres and Le Mans, but, in view of what I'd learned from my friend of the cook-shop, I deemed it wiser to avoid any hostelry or village where my methods of obtaining bed and board had become a trifle too familiar.

It was a safer, if a harder way along unbeaten tracks, wading ankle deep in mud, but my wits and the mild weather favoured me, and when it rained the woods afforded shelter failing that of better sort. Hen-roosts from outlying farmhouses also served me handily, and a tinker of the Brotherhood gave me a cooking-pan. With that and faggots lighted by my tinder-box I feasted well on eggs and chicken, fried.

The winter was passing, chased by the winds of March, yet, while I much preferred the city's voice to that of rural song, my eye was pleasured by the tender green of field and pasture, the delicate tracery of trees against the sky-line, beaded with buds like the nipples of young virgins. Primroses, violets and little white anemones — those 'lilies of the field' — patterned the joyous grass of meadowland. Every hedge was starred with the frail blackthorn blossom falling in silver showers at each careless breath of Spring.

And so to Chartres.

I arrived at daybreak, fagged and footsore, having walked half the night with barely two hours' sleep in a deserted shepherd's hut; and when I passed into the town I saw, towering in all her gracious height, lit by the first rose-torch of morning, the glory of France carved in stone.

The air was clean and clear, and as I climbed the hilly steep that drew me in awed wonder to those portals, others walked behind, beside, or rode before me; they of the Faithful come to see and homage the Tunic of the Virgin.

There were knights in armour, their saddle-cloths magnificently broidered, followed by their squires no less grand than they. There were mounted nobles and their dames on palfreys merged together in brightly coloured raiment like figures in a tapestry, immensely rich I will say. There were youths and maidens, lovingly entwined; and beggars in their rags, and lepers with clack-dishes striking a harsh and dismal note above the happy jingle of horse-bells and the song of minstrels plucking at their lutes. There were burgomasters, housewives, vagabonds and peasants, and one scurvy down-at-heel and out-at-elbows object clothed in a mud-bespattered threadbare gown that may once have been a scholar's, joining in the singing with a voice about as tuneful as a corncrake's. He, too, went with them into the House of God, lining up to kneel before the altar and burn a candle to our Blessed Lady, and tell his beads and say a prayer, and slink out, tail down.

I did not stay in Chartres; I took the road again, and was within some seven leagues of Angers when I met with an opulent stout burgess in a scarlet fur-trimmed surtout, riding a tall grey horse. In him and in this guise, I did not recognise my barber friend of Bourg-la-Reine until he leaned from the saddle to give me the sign.

He dismounted, turned into a side track and, leading his horse, beckoned me to follow. Screened from observation by the hedgerow he flopped down on the grass, mopping his sweaty face, for the day was warm and he unused to exercise, as evident from the rolls of fat around his middle. He told me he was come from Angers where he had been called to a 'conference' — the nature of which I could guess — and was now returning to Bourg-la-Reine. Also, that having been informed of my destination, he had orders to keep a sharp look-out for me with instructions that at all cost must I avoid Angers.

It was then I heard how Tabarie, that imperishable babbler, had loosed his tongue in a tavern to an affable old gentleman, none other than the Prior of Paray who had come to Paris the night before on business. Exactly what 'business' engaged this venerable priest in the Trois Chanderliers — not the most reputable tavern to have chosen — was of no concern to Tabarie.

From Girart's account of it I can reconstruct the scene enacted when this ill-assorted couple met at breakfast, later to be confirmed by the Prior who proved himself an admirable witness at the trial.

Tabarie, delighted to find one so ready, not only to listen but encourage him to talk, he talked. The inn parlour at that hour of the morning would have been fairly free of custom. One can picture those two seated at the trestle with a goodly spread before them: the Prior, for all his years a hearty trencherman, ordering a breakfast and abundant wine for both at his expense, warming the heart of Tabarie to tell of a mysterious 'adventure', in which he and others — but no names mentioned be it understood — had, in the dead of night entered a certain College — no, indeed, he must not say which College and with no intent, upon his word, to rob — great heaven, no! Neither Tabarie nor any friend of his would stoop to felony. All was done in purest jest, being Christmas Eve and

His Reverence would understand that on such a festive occasion young gentlemen were hot for amusement and innocent fun.

His Reverence understood that very well. He, too, had been hot for his innocent fun, in all likelihood the night before and in that very inn.

What Tabarie meant to say was, 'I thank you, Reverend Father, yes, I will take another cup, an excellent good Barsac, Sir.' Now, what was it Tabarie had meant to say?

'To do with an adventure,' prompts the beaming Prior.

'Ah, yes, now my mother,' babbles Tabarie with startling inconsequence, 'is well to do, but I am not. She keeps me cruel and meanly.'

'Dear, dear,' tuts his sympathetic Reverence, 'how very distressing — for you.'

'It is, when one wants to stand treat to one's friends and finds oneself short of the wherewithal. But,' kindled by that excellent good Barsac, Tabarie expands, 'I have learned a craft by which an honest — a — ah — useful living can be made.'

'And what is this craft, my son?' coaxes the wily Prior. 'Come, let's hear it. Fill your cup. You were saying —?'

The cups are filled; and if Tabarie had left unsaid anything further to say, the persuasive Prior pumped it out of him, full measure. For this delightful old gentleman had already heard from his brother churchman, the unfortunate Friar, how he had been robbed of his silver plate and almost all his money.

'To tell you the truth, *Mon Père*,' says Tabarie, his idiot's face rosy with wine and importance, 'for one must always tell the truth to a holy man…'

'Yes, yes,' agrees the Prior, eyes upturned. 'Truth is wisdom, godliness, and the key to heaven.'

'Aha!' giggles Tabarie. 'And I can tell the truth to do with keys. I have — or I did have — a set of keys, till I threw them in the Seine.'

'The Seine!' the bewildered Prior echoes. 'Why throw them in the Seine?'

'Because the Seine,' Tabarie solemnly winks, 'can't throw them back at you. They're sunk. Y'see?'

The Prior, we take it, did begin to see. 'And what — h'm — do you call these keys you so rashly threw into the river?'

'We call them crotchets and they can open anything — but anything!' Tabarie licks his chops. 'Coffers, caskets, church doors, Anything. I've done it myself or as near as damn — pardon me, *Mon Père* — as near as, well's near enough.'

'Now this,' cries the Prior, sniffing a rat and more than ever charmful, 'is of singular interest to me. I know something of these — um — crotchets, but have never seen one.'

'Ah,' brays our imbecile, by this time fully soaked, 'I have. An I can show you one or two or several or's many's you like. An if you're ripe f'raventure — he, he! — hic — Paris offers all sor'ss to all kinds s'even to the godly, being — yip — but 'uman. An ess-ss'lent good wine, yr Rev'rence.'

'Help yourself, my son. Now what of these crotchets? Go on.'

And Tabarie, gurgling with Barsac and pleasure, goes on. 'You sh'should've been with us at the College of Navarre —' How the worthy Prior's ears must have pricked at that! — 'Now there's a fellow if you like! Not a *crocheteur* in Paris to hold a can'le to him. Yes, there is one, but muss'n tell you's name.'

'Why not?' The Prior exhibits toothless gums in his most winning smile. 'As between friends? And don't forget that what you reveal to a priest is in strictest confidence...'

And in strictest confidence Tabarie reveals all of our night's doings at the College; how he had believed Petit-Jehan — every one of our names hopped out of him now — to be the finest pick-lock in Paris until he saw another at his work.

'And who,' wheedles the Prior, 'is the other?'

Thibault was the other. 'But,' hee-haws our jackass, 'if I tell you there's not a casket, not a coffer, not a —'

'Yes,' the Prior interposes hastily, 'so I understand.'

'Not a prison door,' Tabarie determinedly continues, 'that he couldn't open with his crotchets. Why, not all Villon's learning — *he* was in with us the night we robbed the College —'

'Ah!' The Prior blinks. 'So you *did* rob the College!' The gums are seen again, and to their fullest with the shock of this, swiftly changed to admiration: 'That was very daring and courageous.'

'Yes.' Tabarie preens himself. 'But the most cor-c'rageous — me. I had to stay behind and be eaten by wolves while they went in. A dirty trick, was'n' it, Reveren' Father, to make me stay behind and then all I got was ten *écus*, an' Villon an' the others took the lot an' Villon went off nex' day. You know Villon? He wri'ss poetry. He said he was going to Angers to visit the Abbot.'

'So!' nods the old Prior, with more blinks. 'My good old friend the Abbot of Angers will make Master Villon very welcome, I've no doubt.'

'Yes. Thass' where he's gone, but the others are still here in Paris. Would yr' Rev'rence like to meet them?'

Decidedly would His Reverence like to meet them.

'And believe it or believe it not,' exploded Girart in conclusion, 'that animal, that ape, that bumble-headed jobbernowl meets the Prior by arrangement — by arrangement, I ask you! — the next morning and walks him off to Notre Dame where Colin, Petit-Jehan and the other two had taken sanctuary. The police are after them for that little affair to do with the Friar. He, we understand, has coffers full of money and can well afford to lose a small proportion of it to give —' Girart showed his yellowed fangs in a leer aside at me — 'to give to charity.'

'And the Prior — did he meet those four at Notre Dame?'

'Yes,' Girart said with bursting emphasis, 'he did! And could not have been more civil, but they were spry enough to guess that his interest in pick-locks and the use of crotchets was not confined to idle curiosity.' From his vast scarlet-velveted abdomen came a series of internal squeaks and rumbles. Ruefully patting himself he remarked, 'I ate of stewed oysters last night. I take not kindly to shellfish. It leaves me sickish.'

'With exception,' I suggested, 'of the Cockleshell?'

'Hah!' snorted Girart. 'And that will leave *you* sickish if you don't keep away from Angers.'

'So it seems,' said I, close-lipped. 'By St Denis! If I could lay my hands on Tabarie I'd wring his neck!'

'The Châtelet,' said Girart grimly, 'will do it better for you.' He got up to mount his horse, quietly grazing the tussocky grass; and, as he heaved himself into his saddle, 'You made the mistake of your lives to bring with you that blockhead.'

'A mistake,' said I, 'which is likely to cost us our lives — may he rot!'

'You'd best be rid of your gown,' advised Girart. 'Get yourself a pedlar's pack and grow hair to cover that scar. You're marked by it. And now, thanks to Tabarie, they're after you too. Have you any cash?'

'About three whites.'

'That won't last you long.' He took a handful of coins from his pouch. 'This will buy you enough cheap-jack stuff to start you off. No, you don't have to thank me. It's from the Pool. Where were you bound for after Angers?'

I told him I had intended to make for Blois with a letter from Father Villon to the Duc d'Orléans. Girart was suitably impressed. 'Still, you've got to get there. Keep your gown but don't wear it till you come to Blois. Take your time and a roundabout route. You'll be advised along your way.'

Then as he turned his horse's head, I caught at the bridle. 'My father will expect to hear from me at Angers. He is a friend of the Abbot who would certainly write to him of my arrival, so what if I don't present myself?'

'Have you your writing tablets with you?'

I had.

'Very well, write to Father Villon. I'll see that he receives it.'

I wrote a few words saying I had called on the Abbot of Angers but was told he had left on a mission to Chartres and would not be back for some weeks. I would write again in due course when I had further news. I sent him my dutiful respects, with all my love and gratitude, and was as ever his devoted son.

I folded the letter and gave it to Girart, who read it before he put it away.

'That should satisfy Dom Guillaume. Goodbye. Good luck. Bon voyage.'

I watched him ride off, bumping in the saddle, a mountain of a man. Then I took up my staff and keeping clear of the road to Angers, made my way across country to Poitou.

239

SIXTEEN

It was full May time as I trudged along the valley of the Loire where meadows, cornfields, vineyards lay bewitched by the sun-dazzled sky to a ripening green. The weather held. The good earth was my bed, my roof the interlacing boughs of forest trees; my company, the birds and wild creatures of the woods, for I still kept well away from humankind save at dusk, when I would halt at some sleepy village to buy bread, cheese, wine, and so to pass the night beside a forest stream, and tickle trout at wake of dawn and fry them for my breakfast.

I discarded my gown and allowed the hair on my upper lip to sprout and hide my scar. My shirt was in tatters, my breeches soil-stained when I took to the high road again for Parthenay. There I furnished myself with a pedlar's pack and stuffed it full of gewgaws. At a mercer's I bought a pair of parti-coloured hosen, a new shirt, and a cap with a jaunty pheasant's feather: this outfit, procured by exchange of false coins, for I had now run short of the money given me by Girart. And I walked out of the town as bold as you please, leaving the mercer lamenting his loss, never to be traced to me.

Keeping south of the Loire I followed the high road to the village of St Generoux. It was midday when I arrived and found a likely spot to tout my wares upon the green, where women with their buckets came to draw water from the well. Soon they were joined by others; girls and farmers' lads, yokels, and children trooping out of cottages to cluster round me where I stood with my tray to offer irresistible enticements in glib vernacular:

'*Voilà, mesdames,* come take your choice. I have here buckles, bodkins, laces, gloves, ribbands, beads, a rosary? A chalice? What am I bid for this chalice? Two sols? Ah, no, *ma damoyselle!* I am philanthropist, truly, but man cannot live by bread alone. Two sols! It cost me ten — if I tell you, *ten écus.* 'Tis solid gold, this chalice, yet you are young and lovely, yes, you are, and will be more lovely than Proserpine if you buy this chalice for it possesses a magical quality... What? Proserpine, who is she? Why, she used to live here, a bit before your time, a daughter of the gods was she and beautiful beyond compare to ravish Pluto, son of Saturn, as am I who inherited part of my father's land many leagues under the earth and if you as did Proserpine would ravish every man whether he be saint or sinner, god or mortal, then you'll find this chalice that I give to you for six sols, only *six* — just fancy! — and worth a fortune too, so sweetly carved and chased with nymphs and satyrs — if, as I say, you fill it with this potion brewed by me from the flower o' the broom and clover buds and bats' eyes and tongues of butterflies...Yes, my pretty, certainly butterflies have tongues. D'ye see that couple now — white as last year's snows? Look up above your head. D'ye see them kissing in mid-air? How could they kiss together with no tongues to tell of love? Invisible and silent their tongues are, truly which is more than yours or his will be when you drink of this potion to bring a laggard lover to his knees — and a powerful potion it is, never known to fail. But I must warn you, the potion will not act unless that it be shared sip by sip with him when the moon is in her quarter as she will be tonight, and if the draught should fail I give you my solemn word to return your money, so whoever buys this chalice buys the potion with it... Going for three whites, going, going, one, two... three! Ah, to you, Proserpine, with the vixen-red hair and a face as freckled as a cowslip. Three whites. I thank you, *chérie*, he'll be in luck to have you to his bed and *Deo volente* I'll dance at your wedding.

Now who'll buy my balm? I have here a powerful balm. One rub of this — yes, madame, you, so sadly pock-marked — one rub of it only and see your skin clear as a marguerite daisy of pimples and boils and blemishes, warts and moustachios. What am I bid for a pot of my balm mixed with holy water and blessed by the priest, a cure guaranteed after one application... What I say, madame, is true for I'm an honest man by nature not by chance. You doubt me? Do my ears mistake? Never in my life has my word been doubted... You ask how can I swear to the good of my balm? Madame, I swear by the gods — if I tell you Son Altesse, King Charles, will bear token to dub me knight of his Court for did I not cure la Duchesse de l'Abracadabra one of his loveliest ladies of a carbuncle the size of an egg on her — well, never mind, but so unsightly and painful where the King's Highness would wish she were least to be rendered inactive. Nor could all of the Court physicians called in to consult on the lady's discomfort, ease her one whit of her misery nor the King his impatience until having heard of my wonderful balm he sent for me and — *hola!* Hey presto! One fingertip rub of the unguent and... Yes, but I was blindfold, madame, and la Duchesse de l'Abracadabra embraced me with tears and thanksgiving and she to the King and their pleasure again. So mesdames, take heed, what I sell to you now I sell to kings and commoners alike with equal benefit for I am very knowledgeable, yes I am. I know more than'll sit on a codpiece, ha, ha! And here is a ballade to prove it:

I know horse from mule
And wise man from a fool,
I know fair from foul

And a monk from his cowl
I know jargon's patter
And much that's no matter.
I know every trick of the game
Je congnois tout fors que moymême.

I did a roaring trade that day to find my store of gimcracks more than half depleted when the bells of the church on the green called villagers to Evening Mass. Having stowed away the remainder of my wares I went over to the sign of the Striped Ass for my supper of pigs' trotters, flawns, and goat's cheese washed down with a flask of the native red wine. I had just finished eating and ordered another two flagons, standing drinks to the pippin-cheeked landlord and his regulars, mostly farmers and the few tradesmen of the village, when three itinerant minstrels came in and seated themselves at my table. The rest of the company were grouped on stools around the empty hearth.

While the newcomers ate I took stock of them. Two were exactly dressed alike in full-sleeved tunics of some coarse brown stuff and the tall narrow-brimmed hats of the troubadour; but the third, whom I took to be their leader, wore a tabard embroidered with a device in tarnished gold and silver thread of viols, lutes and pipes and harps. A lean tow-haired fellow was he, whose ferret-face seemed vaguely familiar. I caught his eye, a sharp hooded eye, and in a flash I knew him for my guide of the poplar who, during my first escape from Paris some eighteen months ago, had set me on my way to Bourg-la-Reine.

I gave him the sign; he returned it as did those other two. Whereupon I called for more drinks and a song from the three, who obliged with one of our popular sickly prosodical ballades to do with lasses and lads and kisses and blisses and dew drops a-sparkle on leaves, and swallows that nest in the eaves, and sweethearts and love-darts and so on... Which went very well with the company, who made them repeat it *ad nauseam* until the landlord intimated it was time to close his house for they kept early hours in those parts.

Then, when all had dispersed and we four remained, he enquired would we wish to stay the night. The minstrels, conferring, decided they would stay the night and demanded a bedroom for three. I rose to go, when, at a meaningful glance from Ferret-face, I also asked for a room. Since, however, our host could provide only two beds, he suggested we should all turn in together.

The room to which we were conducted though moderately clean, was low-ceiled and stuffy, the floor strewn with stale rushes which, by the stench of them, could not have been renewed for years. For my part I would as soon have slept in open air.

The landlord then lit a rush-candle and bade us goodnight.

The two companions of Ferret-face, whom they addressed as 'Capitaine', shared one of the truckle beds. They were a young and sturdy pair of almost identical twins aged about eighteen and recently 'initiated', so Ferret-face informed me. It seemed our meeting here had not been accidental, my way closely followed by the Coquille under command of Ferret-face, or to give him his name and title, Seigneur Enguerran de Grigny. He, I gathered, was chief of the company operating between Poitou and Touraine. While the other two slept, de Grigny said although not obligatory that I should be enrolled a full member of the Coquillards, it would be to my advantage as a fugitive from justice — 'Such,' he smiled wryly, 'as justice is — that you take the Oath of Allegiance and Brother in Blood. This can be effected by me and my lieutenants here as witnesses before we part tomorrow, or today, for it is now past midnight.'

He then outlined the tenets of that ideological system born from insecurity and unrest of a nation disorganised by a century of war. 'You will appreciate,' he said, his thin hands clasping his knobby knees encased in purple hose, 'that a communal democratic movement such as this, for which we strive, can be subject to grave abuse both of internal discipline and external misjudgement. We live today in a world of transition; a chimerical world of cause and effect. We, of the Brotherhood, are motivated by a universal mission. Seigneurial tyranny is tottering, to fall. No nation can survive on oligarchical didactics. Feudalism must bend and ultimately break before the new social order that is dawning on our bleak horizon. There is no shame in servitude if those who serve are paid their due for service; but the odious exactions imposed on the persecuted brothers of submerged humanity is a blemish on the face of France which must and *will* be eradicated.'

In the feeble flame of the rush-light I saw his eyes, fanatical under their hooded lids, gaze past me with a burning challenge in their depths, as if his spirit were at grips with some mighty unseen force.

'And do you believe,' I asked, 'that by brigandage and unlawful seizure you will achieve a paradisiacal community wherein all men are equal?'

He moved his eyes to mine. 'I believe,' he said slowly, 'that those who live on the blood and sweat of the overtaxed labouring poor are homicides, and that the seizure of mortmain is sacrilege. Such as they desecrate the souls of the dead. What answer do they give us when we attack them for taking some wretched peasant's cow? 'Why should he complain? I've left him his calf and spared his life.' Everywhere one sees the strong oppress the weak, the great devour the small. I, born of the *Seigneurie*, am a traitor to my kind. The only son of my father, I renounced my lands, my heritage, my wealth, when I and others of as high a rank,' again that bitter smile hovered, 'if man's quality be judged by his rank, did give ourselves to this, our Cause.' He flexed his thin fingers, staring down at them. 'Yes, and I inherited more than my feudal rights. My ancestor on the distaff side, Enguerron de Courcy, in the year twelve hundred and four, received en masse the emigres of seventeen villages, the persecuted serfs of the Bishopric of Laon. He harboured them, fed them, and housed them to incur the wrath of his peers and the rebuke of Holy Church. But the seeds of Brotherhood were sown and the harvest will, in God's good time, be reaped.'

'By bloodshed, pillage, insurrection?'

'By enlightenment, my friend, when we render to Caesar the things that are Caesar's.'

'Meaning *your* Caesar, a rapacious hydra-headed Caesar, yes?

And what then is left to be rendered to God?'

'Man's soul — to be judged,' said de Grigny. He got off the stool, and unlaced his tabard. 'The birds are waking now, and I must sleep.'

We both slept; he on the bed, I in the rushes, dog-tired; and was roused by de Grigny shaking me and saying, 'Time to be up and about. There's more for you to do and more for me to tell.'

What to do was quickly done; the pricking of my wrist at de Grigny's dagger-point to draw blood, and with it trace on my forehead the sign of the Cockleshell. Then the swearing of the oath of allegiance to our Khan, 'Who demands that my life be dedicated to the service of the destitute: to annihilate iniquitous exactions from those who have not eyes to see nor voice to speak. To nourish and sustain by all means in my power the suffering and beggarly, and, if needs must, to take the bread from the mouths of the rich to feed the poor.'

I went through this performance in all due solemnity, and signed the document that gave the oath in writing, witnessed by him who was now my captain, and his two lieutenants; after which we breakfasted, paid the landlord in good coin, and left. The twin troubadours went on ahead, de Grigny and I followed after, for I had still to hear what he had to tell; and I heard it as we walked along the road to Parthenay.

His news was of René, who, arrested in Paris for stealing a valuable chalice from the Church of St Jean-en-Grève, had been thrown into the Châtelet charged with theft; not the first of a formidable list of his misdeeds that, since last we met, had landed him in prison, successively at Rouen, Tours and Bordeaux.

'But,' said de Grigny, 'he has the devil's own luck. Each time he has been released by Letters of Remission and payment of heavy fines by the de Montignys backed by the Bishop of Paris who maintains that as René has received minor orders he comes within his diocesan jurisdiction. The usual tussle between canonical and civil law.'

'I find it difficult,' I said, 'to reconcile the robbing of a church with your — with our,' I hastily corrected, 'ideological doctrine of equality for expansion of the soul of man.'

'The Church,' was the inimical reply, 'feeds the soul of man and starves his body.'

'Yet was it not St François of Assisi, the apostle of poverty and renunciation, who sought to resuscitate the Church as founded on love and charity, Our Lord's gift to us by His Word?'

'Yes, and if the Church had followed the true Christian communal spirit of love for his neighbour, feudalism would have been a thing unknown, unborn, a paradox. But the serfs of the Church are no better off than the serfs of the nobles. There are some of our highest clergy who uphold serfdom as a legitimate necessity and a divine institution.'

I chewed this over before I put to him: 'I take it, then, that René robs the Church and I my Alma Mater from entirely disinterested motives — to nourish those who starve in poverty unthinkable, as I, when a child was reared in it, suckled from it; but of such, thank God, there are fewer today. Serfdom is dying. Men are no longer the slaves of their masters. The old seigneurial rights will soon be obsolete.'

'Never!' De Grigny stayed his steps; his eyes, with that same burning light in them, gazed along the straight white dusty road where his underlings had halted, looking back. He waved them on. 'Tyranny under our present conditions can never be obsolete. Its roots are dug deep in the heart and entrails of France. Cut down the tree and its branches will sprout. Its roots, spread underground, will spring up to pollute and destroy the whole social fabric unless, or until —' he clenched a fist — 'we, of the Brotherhood rise as one man and wipe it out of existence. That is our aim and our Ultima Thule.'

I refrained from enquiring if the encouragement and condonation of larceny, felony, theft, and other unlawful occasions approved by the Brotherhood, would achieve them their Ultima Thule. Instead I submitted: 'It charms me to know I may steal, conscience clear for the good of our Cause, though I swing for it.' And I stooped to my shoe that had picked up a stone, and I gave him a grin and I said, 'Here's where I fall by the wayside. I've tramped my feet sore in these last weeks. I may see you later in Parthenay.'

I squatted on the grass verge while he rejoined his fellows and watched them out of sight. Then I shouldered my pack; but I did not go to Parthenay, for I'd had a bellyful of Brotherhood by this time. I bought all the stuff I needed for my peddling in the very first village I came to and was back in St Generoux by sundown.

SEVENTEEN

All through that golden summer I travelled back and forth along the byways of Poitou, peddling my trayful of trumpery in scattered villages between La Vendée border and the Marches of Bretagne. Round-eyed children excitedly would watch for the coming of the Va-nu-Pieds with his toys and his trinkets, his wisecracks, his quips, his needle-sharp wit and his ballades, croaked in their patois picked up as I went. At times, if I'd had a good day, I would sleep at an inn but more to my liking in a dry ditch or a field. And in those sun-warmed evenings I would lie on my back watching the scorched sky fade from flame to rose, from rose to lavender, and a sickle moon swing up among a powdering of stars, till night overlaid the dusk in a silent dream-tranquillity... And then my waking to the early sound of bird and beast and toiling men, and the distant laughter of a girl, to bring with it the throbbing ache of memory.

I was at St Generoux again by harvest time, working in the cornfields, loading wagons, raking in the gleanings, binding up the stooks; and there in the stubble I met not one but two Proser-pines. She, the red-haired nymph of my magic potion, came at me sour as curds with a grievance.

'What! You say it didn't work? Impossible! Unless... Aha! I see. The draught was not for him but for another, and he'll not lag behind in coming forward. Look for him at your door tonight when the moon rides high above the steeple of the church.' And look for him she did, with good result.

She had a sister, a nut-brown maid whose eyes were like dark pansies. Their ages joined were less than thirty-five. And how we romped among the corn, that pretty pair and I, in play as innocent on their part, as strange to say, on mine. True, Proserpine, the elder, turned seventeen that month, admitted that my potion did work wonders when she drank it sip by sip with me beneath the moon... No, I cannot tell you more than that, but you can take it as you'll find it in verse ninety-four of my Great Testament, that these two delicious creatures were indeed:

> ... *Tres belles et gentes*
> *Demourans a Saint-Generou*
> *Près Saint-Julien de Voventes*
> *Marche de Bretaigne en Poitou*

And they taught me to speak *'ung peu poictevin'* in their lovely rich dialect.

I loitered in the meadows of Poitou until September, when with tears and sighs and kisses from the girls, and promises from me of my return, I took to the road again. At Châtellerault I fell in with a troupe of strolling players, feather-brained, light-fingered vagabonds who roamed the countryside juggling, peddling, pilfering, miming, exploiting their flea-bitten apes and tumbling dwarfs, scattered by the mounted guard of some noble returning to his château on the Loire.

My dexterity with dice and ballades were a welcome asset to this imbroglio, until I discovered they were bound for Anjou to pass the winter in or near about Angers; and so we parted company, not without regret on either side.

The days were shortening. Fierce gales tore the yellowed leaves from the clustered fruit in the vineyards of Touraine, where men and women trod the bursting grape, their bare feet purple stained. Still keeping south of the Loire, I followed a winding track through copse and wood and vale, till I came upon a signpost pointing to Chinon. In the falling dusk the little grey town, overshadowed by its sturdy castle, was already half asleep, but light shone in the windows of a tavern. Here I stopped to buy a flask of Beaune and a hunk of bread and cheese; and sighting a garden at the rear of the house I took my food and drink outside, for the day had been sultry and the inn smelt rank to me after months of God's fresh air.

On a bench under a vine-trellised arbour I sat, and listened to the rattle of dice from within; the clink of coins, the hoarse wrangle of men's voices and a woman shrilling a ruttish song to wake the drowsy birds with faint sweet chirp; then silence, broken by the savage cry of some swift-winged killer, and the shriek of its captured prey; sound symbols of nature, carnal and ruthless here in this twilit solitude as in any teeming city. A fugitive bat, blindly darting, swooped over my head and away. I drained the bottle, felt for my cubes, and decided to play for a bed.

As I rose from the bench a figure, cloaked and hooded, came out of the shadows and stood in my path. My hand sprang to my hidden dagger, but before I could draw it I heard the muttered password of the Coquillards, and throwing back his hood he revealed me the face of de Grigny.

He had been told from those I had met on my journey that I would likely come through Chinon on my way to Tours, and had taken a chance to find me here. Bound for Poictiers he had engaged a room for the night which he insisted I should share.

On his advice I covered my dusty hawker's rags with my scholar's gown lest our host should be chary of housing a tramp. De Grigny, who had exchanged his minstrel's guise for that of a well-to-do merchant, now wore a doublet of fine murrey cloth, leather leggings, and over these his riding boots. I asked news of de Montigny and got it — to lose me a night's sleep.

Despite the combined efforts of his family and the Bishop of Paris on René's behalf, he had been condemned to death. As a last desperate resource his sister, young Jehanne, of whom he had often spoken but I had never seen, pleaded his cause with the King. A few months married and expecting her first child, she knelt at the feet of Charles beseeching him to spare her brother's life and save her own, for his death by hanging would, she swore, kill both her and her unborn babe.

Moved by this appeal, the more touching for Jehanne's beauty, the King commuted the death penalty to one year's imprisonment only, and a pilgrimage to the Shrine of St Jacques de Compostelle.

'As you know,' de Grigny said, 'Charles never can resist a woman be she fair and under sixty, and Jehanne is an uncommon pretty girl and just sixteen.'

I breathed thankfulness. 'René, then, is pardoned?'

'By the King, not by those who dragged him from his dungeon — sit down!' For I had started up with a question unuttered, its answer forestalled. 'Not so. The death sentence had been passed before the Royal Letters of Remission with all the final formalities were issued, and thus the King's word is worth less than a scrap of torn parchment.'

'And René, did they — what of —?'

My throat closed.

'No more,' said de Grigny, 'of René, than his name inscribed, as a gesture of grace to the Montignys, on the gibbet where he hangs at Montfaucon.'

Frères humains qui après nous vivez,
N'ayez les cuers contre nous endurcis…
De nostre mal personne ne s'en rie,
Mais priez Dieu que tous nous vueille absouldre!

'Brothers, men, who after us will live, harden not your hearts against us nor mock our misery, but pray God he will forgive…'

Those words, as yet unwritten and unsung, drummed in my ears a formless dirge while I ploughed through the valley of the Loire. That René, my boyhood's friend, had fought his last fight with fate and lost was a bitter shock to me, even though I knew that anyone of us who ran before the hounds of justice ran to outrace death. Nor could I dispossess myself of a gaunt spectre that, day by day and night by night, swung from a creaking rope. Storm gales snatched the rags from its rattling bones as it tossed its legs in the air to the dance and the yell of the winds, its eyes a feast for carrion, its once gay laughing face a blackened bone; he, who for his reckless courage, his audacity, his charm, I had loved, as I think, in his fashion, he loved me.

Sickened of tramping and trickery, reduced to begging or stealing for food, I trudged beside the Loire, where, mirrored in its silver depths, the gracious spires and castellated turrets of châteauland lay drowned. Tattered, penniless, burnt by summer suns, drenched with autumn rains, and more than once the loser in a brawl, on and on I went, crouching in a ditch to dodge the mounted Archers after me for theft. Yes, I'd picked the pocket of a fellow I met in a tavern at Tours. He was bragging of his money and the shady deal he'd done to get it, so could well afford to lose more than I had ever earned, or thieved. But before I could slip him he had caught me, and it was touch and go which one of us would come off best. I did, with a buffet on his jaw to lay him flat... Then on again, dogged every step of the way, fearful of each squad of horsemen pounding by, dashing under cover, running for my life, hiding in a brothel with some dirty drunken wench, loathing her, myself, and all the world. And so, empty of purse and of belly, I came to the Castle of Blois.

Rain had been heavy in the night but my dice had bought me shelter in a swineherd's hut. Caring less for his verminous company than that of his pigs I left him at cockcrow, snoring in the heap of straw that served us both for bed.

Drearily footing it in that sodden dawn, squelching through mud and rotting leaves, I followed the road to the crest of Bon Bec, and from the hill-top looked down upon Touraine.

A giant's coverlid of faded green and gold and autumn bronze threaded by the serpentine translucent Loire, lay below me. I saw Orléans, a mirage in the distance, and nearer, wrapped in the haze of morning mist, an ivory fortress, its towers lit by the first sun-gleam from a sky crystal clear, the Castle of Duc Charles; a glorious sight but not for one whose heart and soul and lovesickness was Paris.

On a moss-grown rock, elbows on knees, chin in my hands I sat, and gloomily considered my next move. How could I in my soiled shabby gown — I had discarded my pedlar's rig — present myself to this prince of ballade-land? What sort of reception, I jeered, will you get from the seneschals, who'd as lief offer the devil himself to His Highness as a draggle-tailed vagrant wanted by the police? The introductory letter from my father could serve me nothing now, reduced to pulp, its ink illegible.

I took it from my rain-soaked pouch and laid it on the rock hoping for the feeble sun to dry it. I could, of course, have chanced my luck, or my fingers, to get me a fresh sheet of parchment, pen and ink, write a facsimile and forge the Father's signature, but I still could do better than that…

Figure to yourself the effect on the flunkeys, at the royal portals, of a blackguardly tramp claiming privilege of audience with His Highness to offer his credentials on the strength of clerkly honours.

Was he hurled by his scruff into a dungeon to be brought before the Procurateur for trial? Which would undoubtedly have been his lot but that his luck, or Saturn, for once did play him fair.

Certainly the seneschal, whom this rascally impostor demanded should be called to hear his case, ordered he be taken into custody while awaiting judgement of the Prince, when, at that specific moment, His Highness returned with his entourage from hawking.

See now the brilliant pageantry of colour, the gaily caparisoned horses, the hooded falcons perched on jewelled gauntlets, the gauzy veils floating from women's steepled headgear; the gold and green and scarlet splendour of men's liveries embroidered with the ducal badge of broom and peacocks' feathers; the running foot-pages, all spindle legs and pourlaines — those long pointed shoes stiffened with buckskin — leading the panting dogs on golden chains; and the gentle , grey-bearded, gouty, slightly deaf, heading the cavalcade in a violet tabard, sable-furred and sewn with pearls and silver pomegranates, asking in his careful, hesitating voice as he halts and is dismounted: 'Who is … this?'

And 'this', with unexampled impudence born of desperation, inspiration, what you will, prostrates himself in homage to kiss the royal hand and to declare:

'My clement Prince, I beg you of your grace
To learn that I know much but have lost face.
What do I ask? The right of common law,
A living wage that I may rise, not fall;
Though well received I am rebuffed by all.'

'Well received?' A moot point that, if derisive squeals of laughter from the ladies, grunts of disapproval from the gentlemen, and an ear inclining from His Highness with the command to: 'Repeat … a little louder,' could lay the odds in favour of reception.

I repeat, much louder, with additional embellishment to the duke's delight and my amaze.

'Pardie! A poet of quality. Your gown proclaims you academic. From where?… Ah, so! Sorbonne. But this is excellent. We are always joyed to meet a fellow bard. Your rhythm, sir, enchants us. Gentlemen,' he addresses his squires who look anything but enchanted, 'you have here a competitor. We will set a first line to your impromptu, sir, and you, my lords and ladies, and messire — eh — ah — what name did you say?… And Messire Villon will enter with you in … a poetic tourney, shall we call it?'

Or a fairy-tale as the whole performance and mise en scène did seem to me. Ridiculous, apocryphal, incredible: but true.

EIGHTEEN

Great as would appear the incongruity of an intimate association between a royal duke and a down-and-out adventurer, the Prince and I shared this much in common. We both had suffered life's humiliations. Certainly Charles, grandson, uncle and father of Kings, had tasted his bitter dish in an enemy's castle while my scavengered grubbings were wolfed in a den of thieves. Nevertheless, the duke, himself a ballade-maker of graceful and not indifferent parts, was naively gratified to claim a similar devotion to the Muse of song as those who sang it. Others before me had found in this amiable, if not highly intelligent prince, a sympathetic patron. But, when summoned to his presence, he, in confidential session, would inform me: 'None, my dear Villon, has ever so moved us with the vital certainty of absolute creative force in its supreme essence as do you.'

Flattered by laudatory unguent I chose to believe him sincere, for I think were he cast in a different mould, had he been born as was I of humanity's dregs and not of Blood Royal, bred passionless, thin, his poems would have lived as more than lilting ditties, light as summer cloud yet fraught with pathos in a music of their own.

When I came to him he was in his middle sixties, of which twenty-five years had been passed in captivity. Taken prisoner at Agincourt by your Henry V, he was brought to England and held there throughout his youth and middle-age. I remember him telling me with his abstract wavering smile in which a hint of humour lurked: 'Of all my miseries the crossing of that trough of water which divides Calais from those white staring cliffs, was the worst. I would gladly give to England dominion of the seas.'

He was well treated in the Tower and at Windsor where he had his own suite. 'But guarded, my friend, always guarded.' He spoke with a gentle precision as if his thin spinsterish lips caressed each word. His personality was as elusive as his poems, which he would read to me in that same gentle monotone. I found it hard to see him in the forefront of the battle that lost him his freedom. He told me of the joyous jubilation of the English, the shouts, the singing, the clangour of bells that followed your prize captive to his prison, and still rang an echo in his heart. Yet he bore no malice against England nor her monarch. He would speak often of his boyhood and his father, Louis de Valois, Duc d'Orléans, brother of a mad King and patron of the arts. He would dwell on the beauties of his father's châteaux and the decor of the rooms designed by him, which he had reproduced, wherever possible, at Blois. 'This apartment, for instance, is almost a facsimile of my mother's salon.' A green room with a ceiling full of angels, flying birds and cherubs; and a tapestry where a knight and his lady, ensconced in a pavilion, played interminable chess; a carpet of cherry trees and children plucking fruit, and much of shepherdesses in a garden wrought with rose and gold.

At fifteen he was married to his seventeen-year-old cousin Ysabeau, virgin-widow of England's Richard II. 'A desirable match financially,' he said, his light-coloured eyes, that seemed never quite to hold his sight in focus, gazing past me, 'but we both could have wished I were older than she, who thought mine a contemptible age. Also, I think she felt deeply the renunciation of her title as Queen to that of duchess. She died three years later in childbirth, for I was not too young to beget me a son, or, at least,' again that faintly ironical humorous smile, 'to accept him as mine. I wept copiously at her death but did not greatly grieve.'

It is doubtful if his second marriage at fifty was any more felicitous than his first. Yet, although the amours of his youthful duchess were the scandal of the Court, her grandfatherly husband turned, *faute de mieux*, a deaf ear to them. But despite her girlish peccadilloes, the duchess fulfilled her obligations as a wife by presenting the duke with a daughter while I was attached to the court.

A far cry from pot-houses, brothels, and my chosen company of mountebanks, gallows'-birds, prostitutes, thieves, was this royal household to which, with my chameleon adaptability, I soon became accustomed. Nor did the entire reorientation of life, as I had dangerously lived it, discolour or detract from the exaggerated overtones of this new environment. In the course of my chequered career, association with the d'Estoutevilles and others of the Parisian elect, had, in part, prepared me for the artificialities of a more spacious, higher sphere.

I now went clothed as befitting my state as Court poet; not, to be sure, the only one so honoured, since Charles, that gentle visionary, would turn from his gates none of small or mediocre accomplishment who could string a rhyme to pique his fancy; or it might be a troubadour, a jester in his motley to sing him a rondeau spiced with innuendo; or those three English minstrels who claimed descent from Blondel, lute-player of your Richard *Coeur de Lion* and who, I've always understood, could speak no word of English more than could his English King. All of those would be welcomed and sent away with liberal gratuity; yet I was commanded to stay and endowed with high office. This the result of the duke's 'poetic tourney'. All his household from his herald to his smallest page — for he, an advocate of child education, did himself instruct a special class of little boys in Greek — were invited to enter the lists, since every one of his attendants, lords and ladies, seneschals, butler, stewards, chefs, and even the lackeys were encouraged to speak in the ballade-tongue, with embarrassing effect.

For his competition His Highness set the first line:

Je meurs de soif auprès de la Fontaine

I, who often had thirsted, but not beside a fountain, won an easy first with a lamentable effort of despairing self-pity and sentiment to declare me 'naked as a worm, my laughter diluted with tears,' that brought tears from the ladies and a handsome stipend from the duke.

The novelty of a royal court, its puerilities, its indolence, and the feasting, dancing, flirting, playing at tennis or chess, strolling on terraced lawns where peacocks bowed and strutted in unconscious mimicry of the bowing, strutting nobles was to me, a mere spectator, an amusing pantomime. But a few months of this incessant masquerade that bore about as much relation to life as the woven figures in the arras on the walls: those polite purgatorial banquets where, every fibre on edge I sat, supplementing bathetic banalities to the flowery rhyming of finical lords; the constant strain of conforming to ceremonious ritual — one dared not even get decently drunk — reduced me to an almost suicidal desperation.

I saw no beauty in the women who were either too fat or too thin, with not a word of wit to share between them while they giggled and cast suggestive eyes at me, who could not have obliged if my stipend were doubled. Their idiotic simperings, elaborate gowns, the hair on their foreheads hideously shaved, according to fashion's demand that their brows were bare as billiard balls, seen through a film of jewel-banded gauze, gave me no desire to see more of any one of them.

While in lower regions I found diversion from surfeit of a finer grain in coarse-bodied ribald kitchen-maids, whom I rough-and-tumbled to their content and mine, none of this could lessen boredom. I felt to be mentally palsied. My creative sense demanded an emotional concussion as stimulus to vigorous activity; and from a source as sudden as it was unforeseen, it came.

I had suffered royal bondage for near upon a year when Jehan Le Nègre of Lombardy, champion chess-player, arrived at Blois with a retinue of servants and a nationwide repute. Lithe as a greyhound, coffee-coloured, woolly-haired and of evident Moorish extraction, he was a frequent guest of the duke who took great delight in the game. I, having learned the rudiments of chess from Father Guillaume had, while at Blois and under the guidance of my patron, improved my play sufficiently to challenge any practised hand and to beat the duke upon occasion.

Le Nègre, summoned to the castle, was commanded to organise a tourney in which all interested players were invited to take part. He had been two weeks at Blois when the duke desired me to play against the champion.

I had hoped to get out of this for although I had not spoken with the fellow, I had taken an instant dislike to him. He was oily, exuding a perpetual shine. His hair, charcoal black, shone with bears' grease. His nose, a proboscis with wide curving nostrils: that shone. And his teeth glistened white between his dark lips in a shining, self-satisfied smile. I had noticed, too, that he seemed to be inordinately interested in the remarks of Maistre Caillaux, the duke's physician, when at breakfast one morning on the terrace, concerning my gashed lip.

A bright-eyed sparrow of a man was Maistre Caillaux, with too little to do and too much to say, and an unfortunate habit of picking at any stray bit of information to feed the yawning mouth of gossip as a bird will pick up grubs to feed its young. How, the little doctor wished to know, had I come by my disfigurement that, in his opinion, had been very clumsily treated. What type of surgeon was he to brand me with so deep a scar? To which all eyes at once were drawn; not many to be sure, for the duke, the duchess and their personal attendants breakfasted in their private apartments.

I peeled a pear before I answered sighingly: 'Hélas, Maistre Caillaux, I was born with this mark, a species of hare-lip, I am told.'

'Parbleu! Who tells you that? What you have is no hare-lip nor birth-mark, or if so it is the first of its kind I have seen, and an abortive phenomenon.'

'Could it have been caused in a duel?' spoke Le Nègre, his smile split to show every one of his teeth.

The doctor pounced. 'Hah, yes! I think so. Very likely. Our friend has been engaged in an affair of the heart that involves a lady. Am I right, Maistre Villon?'

'Villon?' Le Nègre took him up sharply. 'Did you say — Villon?'

'Assuredly! Do you not know Maistre Villon, our court poet?'

If he had not known me before he knew me then, with a close look from black syrupy eyes and a smile stretched to say, 'Who indeed does not know the name of Villon, nor —' a pause — 'of de Montigny. So sad an end. Your *bel ami*, I think, messire?'

My hands were clenched to keep them from his throat.

'De Montigny?' twittered the doctor. 'Let me see now — yes, a noted criminal but of high nobility. He was hanged in Paris, was he not — a year or two ago? Time flies.'

I swallowed my wine, set down my cup, rose from the table and strolled over to a sundial pedestaled upon the terrace. 'Time flies indeed. It is past ten hours, and I must to my work.'

'Your work?' The jetty eyebrows of Le Nègre were arched to the fringe of his shining hair. 'On what new work or *magnum opus* are you engaged, messire? Or is it secret as are all the workings of a master's mind?'

'Secret, as you say.' I flicked him back his look, turned my heel and then my head to see him lean his toward the doctor, while the other three of the household who had taken no interest in this talk being eagerly engrossed in their own, to do with the latest fashion of tunics, now craned necks to listen and stare after me... So what the devil comes of this, I wondered?

Nothing came of that; and if Le Nègre knew or guessed enough to damn me with the duke he surely would be disinclined to endanger his professional position or lose his ample fee by bringing a charge against one who stood high in His Highness's favour, unless he could produce sufficient evidence to support his allegations. Still, I thought it best to keep my distance from Le Nègre and did, until forced to meet him at chess.

As I took my seat at the chequerboard, his teeth glittering between his brownish lips, he said, coolly, 'I play you without my queen.'

A hush emanated from the courtiers grouped around us. I heard the duke mildly expostulate: 'I think you discredit Messire Villon's capability. You are matched against not only the greatest poet of the day, but a player whom I judge to be a combatant well worthy of your skill.'

Le Nègre was on his feet, low-bowing to that courtly figure in its long black velvet gown and jewelled cap, who stood fingering his beard, a puzzled pucker lodged between his brows. 'Your Highness honours me,' and down he sat again, but not to play.

I said, 'Replace your queen or I give you the game.'

And, his thick lips scarcely moving, he returned an answer for my ear alone: 'Poet you may be and of His Highness favoured, but I only play with gentlemen. I do not play with rogues.'

And then — it all happened in a moment.

I sprang up to overturn the table and sweep the chessmen from the board. My fist shot out and caught him full and square on his thick nose. I saw the dark blood trickle, saw him reel, heard the screams of women, and, above the tumult of men's voices, the duke's ringing clear, peremptory: 'Remove him!'

Halberdiers rushed forward. I was seized, dragged, unresisting, to the door and out into the courtyard. There, uncertain what to do with me, one of them went back to ask. He returned, followed by a pair of lackeys and a seneschal who ordered: 'Have packed and bring to him Messire Villon's baggage. Sir, His Highness, in consideration of your office, does not wish that you be taken into custody for your disgraceful misbehaviour in His Grace's presence, but desires me to say — you are dismissed.'

NINETEEN

Once more my own master to go my own way, foot-slogging it along the river-valley, with the earth for my bed and the sky for my roof and a song in my heart for my freedom. Better far be a prince among beggars than a beggar among princes, a jay rigged out as peacock squawking nonsense rhymes of nightingales, hawthorn buds, butterflies and posies to mimsy rodomantadors in literary gardens.

It was sundown and high summer when I turned my back on the castle following the Loire that would lead by easy stages to Orléans; but although I passed through isolated villages where I could have found a lodging for the night, I preferred to sleep under the stars.

I had come to Blois a penniless tramp, lean as a hungry cat. I came to Orléans well-fed and well-clad with money burning in my pocket: not for long. After one riotous week of drinking, dicing and wenching, I found myself the biter bit. I had picked up a girl of the town known as Macée, with a look in her eyes and her blunt-cornered grin to bring me nostalgic reminder. Judging my state by the fine clothes I wore and my liberal purse, she stole it from me while I slept, and woke — to find her gone, the bitch, and all my money with her.

I could have raised a hue and cry to have her rounded up and charged, but not caring to draw attention of the Watch to me, and since I had suffered no worse at her hands than others had suffered at mine, I let her go.

Having nothing now with which to pay the landlord of the inn who had obliged us with a room, I told him I would stay

266

another night, waited till his house was closed for custom, and took myself, presumably, to bed. Then, when all were sleeping, I resorted, as on previous occasions, to the window for my exit and was away before he could have missed me.

Sancerre, Bourges, St Amand, Moulins … A long, sore-footed weary road was mine, zig-zagging across country, guided by the secret symbols of the Coquillards on walls of stone and barks of trees, joining with them in a hold-up of some rich lord or merchant, to seize and bind his servants while we robbed him of his horse, his pack-mules, his gold and his garments to leave him trussed with nothing on him but his shirt, until he and his lackeys should be rescued and we would be far from pursuit.

In most of these raids we were acting under orders of the captain in command of the Orléannois-Bourbonnais regions; not de Grigny, whose province was chiefly Angers and Poitou. Our commandant was a Spaniard, son of that Villandrando who had fought with us against the English, and, in the last years of the war, had organised a band of marauders attached to the Armagnacs in their feuds with the Burgundians. I knew Villandrando by name and repute, but I soon discovered that the Bourbonnais Coquille did not conform so readily to discipline as did those who worked under de Grigny. Although we were forbidden to seize from our victims more than three fourths of their merchandise or chattels, there were some who would risk the penalty of insubordination by prigging the lot, and rendering false statements to our commandant with regard to the quantity and value of our plunder.

While I hold no brief for my part in any of these cool-blooded forays I soon sickened of hunting in packs, and the spring of the year 1460 found me a lone wolf again.

It was now four years since I had sneaked out of Paris a thief in the night. I had lived in a castle, the protégé of royalty: I had limped into villages begging for a crust at cottage doors to be sent packing, more often than not, with a flea in my ear. I had starved and fought and brawled and thieved in pot-houses and brothels, scrounging for a livelihood by fair means or foul, tramping up and down the countryside peddling my wares, stolen when I had no cash to buy them, and always hunted by the police. But I was not yet to be caught, and when at length I faced the gibbet, I stood charged with the one crime of which I was not guilty. An ironical twist of Saturn's humour, that!

After six months of this hand-to-mouth existence, down to my last farthing and racked by a rheumy cough due to exposure in all weathers, I turned back, like some stray cur, toward Blois to try my luck with the duke again, and cadge, if not a lodging for the winter, at least enough in pocket to keep me clothed and fed. At Bourges, on that long weary way, I fell in with a gang of the Coquille operating in the district under direction of — Colin des Cayeux! An agreeable surprise.

One of his fellows brought me to him at the house of a goldsmith in the town: an undersized scrag of a man who had lost his wife, his children and almost all his custom in a recent epidemic of the plague. This I learned from Colin when I had eaten my fill of the first round meal I'd had for weeks. Then, drawing our stools to the hearth, where a cheerful log fire burned, and, with a bottle between us, Colin gave me account of himself since we parted after robbing the College of Navarre.

He too, had been a fugitive hunted through Dijon as far as Britanny, where he lay in hiding till they gave up the chase. He was now in charge of a section with temporary headquarters here at Bourges. He told me how Tabarie had got off lightly, having squealed on us under the 'Water Cure', as I had heard from Girart. 'Yes,' blazed Colin, 'damn his soul to hell, and his mother paid up fifty *écus* in gold to get him out — with a free pardon. He takes good care to keep away from us, the swine, but we'll have him in the end though we swing for it ourselves!'

He spoke of René, 'who died as he had lived, cocking a snook at death,' and of Petit-Jehan and Nicolas, 'vanished none knows where.' And lifting his tankard he called a toast, remembered from the time when the *godons* used to bawl it about the streets of Paris. We put it into French but they gave it us in English:

'Here's to them wherever they be
And here's to me as bad as I am
But as good as they are and as bad as I am
I'm as good as they are as bad as I am!'

Colin was little changed since I had seen him last; carrot-haired and shifty-eyed as ever. He told me that he and others of his company had been employed in the profitable practice of thieving gold and silver chalices and candlesticks from churches. They had come to Bourges to plant their booty on this wretched little goldsmith, inveigled at a tempting price to melt it down. 'And then,' Colin said with chuckles, 'we hand it over to our Mint for coinage. We've done well here. The Cathedral is rich in chalices. They've already had two stolen. I reported to the Watch that I'd seen an ugly type hanging round the altar when I stayed for confession one evening after Mass.' He gulped a swig from his tankard and grinned at me above it. 'They took a full description from me and were profusely grateful, and they'll be more grateful still before we've done! If

you like to come with us and take your share of the proceeds
—'

'And,' I filled in his pause, 'of the risk?'

'Which we all run.'

'A tempting proposition,' said I, 'but not if I hope for further bounty from the duke. I'm too near his domain to chance falling foul of the Watch.'

'Yes,' Colin seized on this, 'you can serve us better at Blois if you stand well with d'Orléans. My faith, what a coup!' His eyes kindled. 'Good Lord alive, man, you were there — how long? A year with all those jewels and gold, and pouches bulging, and not a pin's head to show for it! Get back there quick and do your damnedest, and you can leave the rest of it to us.'

Warming to the prospect he proceeded to enlarge. He would appoint a man to meet me at or near the castle gates. 'I'll get a message through to you somehow. It will be tricky with those sentinels posted there, yet if you're of the household you can come and go as you please. Small stuff can be carried on your person, but if it should be heavy — say a dish or cup of gold — you can tell him where you've cached it. He may have to scale the walls by night. I'll have to think this out,' muttered Colin, chewing his thumbnail as he always did in school when confronted with a problem that required concentration. 'Yes … and I'd best send half a dozen, well armed against attack. If you are there for the winter you should bring us in a haul.'

He watched me with eyes narrowed as if to probe my silence, not knowing what to make of it; and, relinquishing his thumb, thrust forward his face. 'You, as one of us now, must follow our creed, that France and all she holds is as much the right of every man born and bred from her soil, as of the King and the lords of the land — a lot o' ghouls who pick the flesh off the bones of the poor to fill their coffers and none but us of the

Brotherhood to speak them fair, and right the wrongs of those who can't speak for themselves.'

I felt my lips quirk, detecting in this tirade an echo of de Grigny.

'And do you think a chalice cribbed from a church or the gold from a prince's table will right the wrongs of those who have been always with us since the fall of man? I applaud,' I said drily, 'your altruistic motives, but for my part I profess to no such scruples. I steal for the good of myself and none other —' I slid him a grin — 'as do you, and so it will be until the State is the thing of the people. Not in our time nor in any time while the Word of God, in Whose sight all are equal, is defied.' I gathered up my pack and stood, and said, 'I must be off and on my way before nightfall. I've many leagues to cover yet. You'll hear account of me from those I meet — maybe.'

And out I went.

I passed the little weasly goldsmith crouched on the stairs, all ears. His eyes were big as an owl's and he was shivering.

'I'd have had naught to do with it,' he whined, 'had I known the gold they brought for me to melt was of the Church. I've lost all — my wife, my children, my livelihood, and now I've lost my honour I have nothing more to lose.'

He bowed his head on his hands. Through his thinning hair his scalp showed bleached as a bone. I patted it.

'But more to find. There's a vein for the silver, and a place for the gold As for the earth, out of it cometh bread, and the stones of it are sapphires ... ask Job.'

He stared after me in wonder.

TWENTY

I was on my last legs when I came to the hamlet of Baccon on the outskirts of Meung-sur-Loire in Orléans. Luck had been churlish all the way along. I had slunk into taverns bawling a ballade to pick up a copper here and there, always hunted, always flying from the Archers who had me marked for a score of petty thefts: the stealing of a purse, the robbing of a hen from a roost to wring its neck and pluck its feathers, squatting in a ditch to tear it limb from limb and wolf it raw. I had grubbed pigs' swill when nothing better offered. I had blasphemed, fighting drunk in village inns, my head in a whirl with a ballade calling down curses on all who denied and betrayed me. I can tell you of one: François Perdrier, a fellow I had schooled with at the Faculty. He was a scribbler of a sort; had tried his hand at versifying when we were *gosses* together. I ran into him after parting from Colin at Bourges, and over a bottle in a tavern we talked of old times. He, too, so he told me, had presented himself and his drivel to d'Orléans at Blois and been refused an *entrée* to the Court. He got his own back on me who may have bragged of my conquest with the duke to rub him sore. I didn't let him know I'd been kicked out.

I played him for my supper, then he caught on to my dice, accused and denounced me, started a row, and sent for the Watch. They came charging into the tavern with the landlord on his knees praying them not to defame his house. Never would he harbour or encourage false gamesters, and so on ... I thought I was done for that time, but wriggled out of it by swearing the dice were not mine. I had been what you would call 'framed', and produced my fair set, turning out my pockets to show them empty. I gave my name as Montcorbier, a name to conjure with in the neighbouring Bourbonnais district; and for want of evidence they let me off, but not without a warning that my next offence, proven, would be the end of me.

I hurried out of Bourges spitting venom at the viper Perdrier in my ballade entitled 'To Envious Tongues' in which I fry them and all others who snarl at me their spite, in red arsenic, sulphur, saltpetre, quick lime. In reeking pig's dung and pitch. In serpents' blood and the brains of a toothless old black cat. In cauldrons filled with suppurating sores. And in the froth of dogs run mad. In the filth of soiled breeks, and a dozen more delectable concoctions… I was still mumbling it in a delirium of hate, fevered, sick and aching, when, in the evening dusk, I crawled into the church at Baccon and before the altar knelt and tried to pray, but no words came.

How long I stayed there in the empty church I cannot say, but as I staggered to my feet I heard a stealthy step behind me and saw a muffled figure stealing out. I saw too, that the votive lamp on the altar was gone. I could have sworn it had been there when I went in; or maybe not. I was in no state to know, to hear, or see. My head was in a buzz; yet now I had no hunger, only a raging thirst. At the door I paused to dip my fingers in the holy water, crossed myself and dipped again, carrying the drops to my dry tongue; then I bent my head and lapped, tottered out into the porch and sank.

For a moment I must have lost consciousness, and was roused from a dizzy void by a sudden metallic clattering sound. I looked up to see a shadow creep and vanish in the shadows of a yew, and on the stone bench beside me I saw a glinting object: gold.

I took it up: a votive lamp, its wick guttered and still smoking. I heard the tramp of feet. A lanthorn flashed a light at me and on the thing I held, while a voice bayed: 'Seize him!'

I let fall the lamp. Hands snatched it, grabbed and bound my arms; my wrists were fettered, and the breath of the beast was on my face.

'We've got you now, caught in the act, you skunk!'

No act of mine, nor could I have denied it, for I had not strength enough, dazed as I was, to speak; but as they dragged me off, laughter shrill and cracked broke from me with the words:

'Run to earth!'

Words prophetic as they proved to be when I found myself lowered in a basket down, deep down, to the bowels of the earth; a pit in the Tour de Manasses, the prison of Meung-sur-Loire.

In that foetid dungeon, its walls that oozed a greenish slime sucked by the waters of the moat, I, with none but crawling toads and rats for company, could laugh again to flout at Fate that had the laugh of me.

I had ample time to chew the cud of meditation as supplementary diet to my daily bread, a mildewed crust flung by my gaolers, while I damned to hell *le traistre chien* — the treacherous dog who had sent me there: Monseigneur Thibault d'Aussigny, Bishop d'Orléans — behold him!

A right proper man was he, a man of sternest will, of quality and justice; a dispassionate, cool-headed disciplinarian, undiluted by indulgence. No quarter could be asked of him before whom I was brought to be questioned after twenty-four hours in a cell, where I languished in a fever and no fit state to undergo examination. The Bishop, in duty to his calling and his

God, decreed that I be tended and sufficiently restored to offer a defence in the hearing of my case. Yes, he was just, but what a hope! With the evidence against me, black as this hole in the ground, where, chained to a staple I re-live that scene in the court chamber.

Nothing of the clerk, as he claims to be, is discernible in this human scarecrow who, despite its rags, its shaggy unkempt hair and its gashed lip accentuated by a defiantly sardonic grin, stands, head up, between his gaolers rapping out repetitive denial to the charge of sacrilege.

What a contrast is here presented between accused and his accuser; my Lord Bishop, portly, impressive in purple. His smooth-shaven face is cold and motionless as stone, while the charge against François Villon, Master of Arts, is read by the Clerk of the Court.

From those granite lips comes the question: 'Do you deny the charge?'

'I do, my lord, deny it. I am innocent of sacrilege. I did not steal the votive lamp from the church of Baccon-sur-Loire.'

'The lamp was found on your person.'

'With every respect, my lord, I repeat, I did not steal the lamp. It was placed on a bench beside me by a thief, unknown, a moment before I was arrested.'

Not the flicker of an eyelid marred that mitred immobility. 'I cannot accept any such implausible denial.' The episcopal finger with its amethyst ring is poised above a sheaf of documents upon the table before which he sits enthroned. 'I have here a list of certain other misdemeanours of which you are accused.' Then, gazing not at me, nor at his velvet-capped and robed officials but at some inner focal point, he pronounces judgement.

'I sentence you to prison pending further inquiry…'

Prison, mark you! A dungeon, at its worst, as I thought it would be, not this lightless pit that bandages my eyes with walls, where there is neither day nor night, nor sound more than the scuffle of toads, the patter and squeal of rats, or the clink of keys when my gaolers slide the grating high above my head to drop me a crust or let down the pannikin of water by which I am kept alive. For the wages of sin are death, but not by starvation. My Lord Bishop, judicial servant of God, has ordained I can escape the final penalty if I make full confession of my guilt.

The methods by which the Most Reverend Monseigneur Thibault d'Aussigny hopes to obtain it, are, though persuasive, not entirely successful.

After some weeks or months — I have lost count of time — the door of my tomb is unlocked by those in charge of me. They do not descend to my depths by the steep winding stairs to deliver my food; one broke his neck falling down those slippery steps, since when they have been avoided. Moreover, human contact, even with my goalers, is denied me; but now the door is opened by my two ruffianly keepers. They unfasten my shackles; they haul me out and up the spiral. Is this the end of me? If so I welcome it. Nothing, not hell itself, could be worse than the noisome dark of this inferno that feeds my soul with hate for him who has cast me here.

Half-blinded by the unaccustomed glare of day, stumbling with weakness, I am untenderly guided to the Chamber of Examination — or Extermination, as to many it has proved to be — where the Bishop, my hospitable host, invites me to the treatment of the rack. I am stretched, pinioned, screwed, but they cannot wrench from me admission to a charge of which, between my groans, I gasp, 'I am not guilty.'

I am unbound, unscrewed, and lugged into the Chamber of the Question Ordinary, a procedure which in most cases, as in that of Tabarie, is an infallible means to confession from the obdurate. And now, having been given a taste of it, I can understand why Tabarie succumbed, as I too might have done, if all they asked of me had been admission of the charge against myself; but they wanted more than that. They demanded the whereabouts of one Colin des Cayeux, an associate of mine, known to be the instigator of a series of thefts concerned with the stealing of church chalices; and of one Seigneur de Grigny, a dangerous rebel, and any others of that infamous band of criminals, the Coquillards, with whom they had reason to believe I was connected. A free pardon to be granted me if I will supply the required information.

I will not. I know nothing of de Grigny nor his name; nor had I seen or heard of Colin des Cayeux since my student days in Paris.

Very well, then. They must wrest from me the truth under further pressure.

I am stretched again and gagged, my nose held, my mouth forced open to receive the horn funnel through which the water is poured down my throat to flood and burst my bowels, to distend my body in choking, drowning torment... A brief interval for question, and, when writhing there I still refuse to answer, it begins again, till at last, unable to endure the agony of that hellish torrent, I give in and gurgle: 'Yes ... yes ... I did steal the lamp ... I admit my guilt but know nothing ... nothing ... of those ... others...'

It was enough. They had got my confession and could hang me for that alone, unless...

I am unscrewed, ungagged, unbound. They turn me over, head downwards, to pour out of me what they'd poured in, and were now disposed to pleasantry. 'Another little treatment and you'll spill all you know for a pardon, hey? Come on, you hank o' gallows' meat!'

I am packed in a basket and lowered to my lair; and sit, trussed in my shackles, until they come to chain me to the wall.

In all fairness to those in charge of me I am bound to admit that visitors to my dark underworld were not prohibited. Madame la Baronne Bufa, a buxom matron, was one of those well-meaning ladies who, from the best possible motives, endeavour to cheer the solitude of prisoners.

In personality and general demeanour she bore an elusive resemblance to Mademoiselle de Bruyères. Her bright beady eyes would regard me with the same overpowering approval, from which I gathered she desired entertainment more than my fettered state and frugal fare could give. She had a dun-coloured belly, a green speckled back, a broad intelligent brow, and ineffable dignity. She would climb on to my foot and squat there in aloof expectancy of crumbs.

She had a numerous progeny whose soporific attention I much preferred to that of the Rodentia, an ill-mannered noisy crew who disturbed my fitful sleep with explorative invasion of my person, that was even less agreeable than the ravages of lice.

While diversions such as these enlivened my gloom I knew nothing of time, since day and night were one. Rain dripped through the grating of my circular roof; I could hear the howl of the wind but could not see the sky, nor sun, nor moon. I believed my existence was forgotten, or that Monseigneur Thibault had condemned me to lifelong entombment rather than curtail my end on the swift and more merciful gibbet; an end that could not be far off in this walled grave that squeezed the breath out of my lungs, coughed up in blood-stained gobs. Hah, good! I would soon be gone, to disappoint the worms who would find no better food than skin on my fleshless bones.

Had I my tablets I would write an elegy to this double-damned bishop who blesses his flock as he passes in state through the streets, deaf to mercy; righteous, just, God's servant.

> *Dieu mercy et Jacques Thibault*
> *Qui tant d'eau froide m'a faict boire…*
> *Manger d'angoisse mainte poire,*
> *Enferré… Quand j'en ay memoire*
> *Je pry pour luy,* et reliqua…
> *Ce que je pense* … et cetera

Yes, I'll pray that nothing worse can come to him than this he offers me: these stygian waters to drown him, and *la poire d'angoisse* — the pear of anguish — to eat, that his teeth like the teeth of a rake be broken on the iron gag as are mine … If I could get a message to Father Guillaume I might yet be saved. But how? For even though I had the cash to bribe my gaolers, I am not permitted contact with them other than the hollow echo of their voices from above, warning me of my approaching basket lowered to rest on the stone floor of my pit near enough for me to snatch and gnaw its contents, my daily crust, and take to drink the pipkin full of stagnant water… No, not that, I've had water enough for a lifetime!

Once I quavered up to them, 'For God's sake, parchment, ink, a pen!' To be answered by Homeric laughter and the gleeful information: 'If you want a change o' diet you'll find the rope more tasty than pen and ink and parchment. You've not long to wait before you join your *confrère*, Cayeux, who frolics in the air at Montpipeau!'

Colin! So they'd got him. How? And when? No matter, I had played him fair, and now it was my turn. But I'd like to know the sneaking hound who, with the Archers after him, framed me. Not any of the Coquillards, of that I can be certain. We have our code of honour, among thieves. 'Not long to wait…' If only I could send a letter to my father with full confession of past sins, and of my guiltless end; and a message to my mother of my undying love… And to her on whose sugared lies and loveliness I'll never feed, to starve again. She for whom I'd suffered torture more agonising than the screw, more shameful to my pride, more destructive to my parched soul than all those gallons of water pumped into me. Yes! I will write her epitaph. I think of her as dead, for dead to me she is. No, not an epitaph, a rondeau to her passing.

Death, I deplore your harsh decree
That has seized on my lady to slake
Your discontent, turned now to take
All that is left of my vigour and me,
My strength and my life to slay
But what harm has she done to you, will you say,
Death?

It was in these haggard hours that I conceived a metaphysical debate between my heart and body, groping to find a reason for Fate's diabolic persecution that entombs me in this sarcophagus. Yes, Fate or Saturn, who packs my baggage full of spite, has done this thing to me.

Pourquoy est-ce? — Pour ta folle plaisance — Que t'en chant-il? —
J'en ay la desplaisance? Pourquoy? — For my pleasure's cost? To

hell with that! What do you think you are? A puling infant? You, in your thirtieth year. Yes, I'll soon be thirty, a mule's age, with as much sense. Death will bring me peace. You think? God, what a hope! Why blame the Fates or your dark planet, Saturn? Remember Solomon who said, 'Wise men can sway the stars'… But you — you whining cur — have only yourself to blame. As that I am, so will I remain. *Veux-tu vivre?* You do? You don't. What's life? A load of misery. What's faith? The weakling's anchor. Turn penitent and pray. God help me that I may… If I come out of this I'll cast off folly and the piddling lusts of fools that skim life's surface. I'll dive deep and salvage words of wisdom, to find what? *Plus ne t'en dy et je m'en passeray.* Who cares? Who! Madame la Baronne, do you care? Yes, you, too, seek a change of diet in these mouldy crumbs, more appetising than a fly. Phaugh! How you stink. Your tongue darts poison… Give me your hand. You're cold, but you're God's creature, too. He, who, without beginning or an end, has made this world and countless other worlds of which we can know nothing: He who made Himself a man and died for us, He stoops and has made… you! But why has He made me? I can't answer that one yet. Soon will.

And sooner than I had hoped, with a clinking of keys at the door, opened only when they came to fetch and take me — where? To the Horror Chamber of the Question Ordinary for another Water Cure? Or to the hangman, Petit Robert, Monseigneur the Bishop's aide-de-camp? We'll see.

They burst in on me, a pair of them, blue-chinned, swart and brawny. A lantern's ray pierces my darkness. 'Now you're for it. Out you come!'

I am unshackled, dragged to my feet, and, wrists still fettered, am lugged up the spiral stairs. My cramped limbs are unwilling but my spirits soar as step by feeble step I go, prodded by one behind, pulled by one before who turns to cuff me when I stumble… Up and up, a slimy Jacob's ladder that will lead me to my heaven. Death. Extinction.

I find voice to croak: 'A priest…'

'You'll have your priest. He waits for you.' Loud cackles indicate a winsome jest.

We have come into the light of day, still walled, but open windows show the sky and give me sound of cheering, loud.

I cannot see but may believe they cheer a gloating welcome to speed me on my way. For them a hanging is a raree-show, and I, chief actor in it, bow my grateful thanks for their amiable applause, and receive another cuff to burn my ear.

'Stop that! This is no time for foolery!' They turn me right about along a stone-flagged passage terminating in a door that gives on to the courtyard with its entrance gates flung wide and guarded by sentries. And now I see a huddled group of jailbirds, shackled as am I in charge of keepers… Another burst of cheering and the tramp of marching feet, the vanguard of a procession: bowmen, Archers, banners waving, children strewing flowers in the path of knights-in-armour, townsfolk flocking — a hell of a send-off is this. I'll not die in obscurity! They're out to do me proud… And here are men-at-arms and burgesses in scarlet, nobles robed in cloth of gold. The velvet trappings of their chargers edged in ermine, sewn with gilded bells, jingle to the chimes of ringing steeples that vibrate in the sunlit air to multitudinous shouts of: *Le Roy! Le Roy est mort, vive le Roy!*

My shrinking eyes, seared by the strong light of day, glimpse a hunched figure in purple on a tall white horse. His lizard face is shaded by a shabby old black hat, its brim hung with leaden medallions. Glancing neither right nor left, staring straight before him, he acknowledges the greetings of his people with marionette jerks of his head… The King? What King is this? And why am I and those others unearthed from our graves to watch his entry into Meung? A royal concession? Is this all, and am I to be buried and dug up again?… I lift my fettered wrists to jog the arm of him who holds me by a chain as a showman holds his dancing bear.

'The King,' I quack from a dry throat, 'is the King dead?' My question goes unheeded. They are shouting with the rest… I had not known nor heard of the King's death, but how could I, enclosed in my stone coffin down below, know or hear of happenings above? This, then, must be the Dauphin, son of Charles Sept, now Louis Onze, our King. One knew something of him, and nothing to his good: a crafty schemer who murderously coveted his father's throne. Much cause have his subjects, yelling loyal homage, to rejoice! This blood-sucking spider, whose web is France, will sit in wait to seize and devour these unwary helpless flies whom he will tax beyond all harsher means than ever have gone before. Yet it is to this repulsive abnormality, whose unscrupulous intelligence made of him a great and a powerful King, he, who believed that every man had his price and who paid that price where he could strike a bargain even to the length of his own life, handing his physician ten thousand *écus* a month to keep him alive: to this would-be parricide, feared by his people, detested by his nobles: to him, this eleventh Louis, King of France, I, at my eleventh hour, owed my life — by the breadth of a hair.

It is over, the clatter, the marching, the cheering, the excited surge of the welcoming crowd — poor devils, little do they know what is coming to them with the coming of him. Nothing is left of that triumphal entry into Meung on his journey to Bordeaux from his crowning in Paris: only its tail of gossiping wives, of children gathering the faded flowers that lie heaped in the dust; and straggling loafers, beggars, and us, still herded by the gates like so much cattle, awaiting the drive to the slaughter-house… No… No! Good God! What nightmare fantasy is this? I am unchained, my wrists unfettered by these two swarthy fellows sharing one broad grin.

'Satan, or Louis, takes care of his own. Go on, be off. Get out!'

Hustled to the gates I am speeded by a parting kick into life again. My resurrection.

TWENTY-ONE

'Yes, my dear, you *must* drink this bouillon. It will strengthen you… that horrid cough. I *insist* you see a doctor… No, don't talk. Drink it up, and *don't* leave this little piece of chicken liver… That's the way.'

The Bastard, more than ever stout and porcine pink, stood over me, cosily beaming. 'I'll leave you now to sleep while I do my shopping.' At the door he turned to ask, 'Could you fancy oysters for your supper? So nourishing. I'll be back in half an hour.' He breezed happily away.

Propped by pillows I lay on his bed, his own that he had given up to me — when? Was it only three nights since that I'd limped through the gates of Paris not daring to show my face by day for I was still in hiding, a criminal at large, my respite an indefinite reprieve. Not by the will of Monseigneur the Bishop but by the law of the land that rendered to a newly crowned King on his first triumphal entry to a city or a town, the royal prerogative of commanding a general gaol release of all prisoners.

I can well imagine with what reluctance my Reverend Father in God, whose Christian duty it was to exact from me the ultimate penalty incurred by my confession to the mortal sin of sacrilege, did relinquish his prey to the mercy of the King. Not for one moment did I flatter my ego that Louis had singled me for his especial favour, although, as I later learned, when informed of my impending doom, he had said that: 'While France can afford to lose a hundred thousand less deserving of death on the gallows than Villon, he could not afford to lose his greatest poet.'

It is likely that his uncle and my patron, Charles d'Orléans, had a hand in this, for it must have come to the knowledge of the duke, if not from the Bishop from some other source, that I, a captive in the prison of Manasse within his province, had been sentenced to hang. Yet Louis, that extraordinary being, half-genius, half-madman, wholly ruthless tyrant though he was, had more respect for men of letters than for men of rank. He enjoyed, he would say, to gather fruit grown in his orchards. I, then, was one of his fruits to be plucked, stored and served at his table for dessert, in his good time.

But it mattered not to me how or why my freedom had been granted. My life was mine again to make the best or worst of it.

I had been helped along my way to Paris by the Coquille who were hunting the country between Orléans and Bourbon for the traitor who had planted on me the votive lamp, thieved from the church at Baccon. They were hot on the scent for a kill, but since I could give neither adequate description nor a clue to his identity, they were unlikely to draw covert.

Those long months of frozen despair and desolation, that had shrunk the flesh from my bones and broken my body, could not destroy the vital spark within myself: it kindled, burned, and leapt to flame, snatching at vision dizzily revealed in a flash of ecstasy transcending mortal consciousness. In such moments, when waves of words in music struggled for expression, I suffered torture worse than any yet endured or yet to come. More than my craving for Paris, and for her who had crippled but not killed my love, did my soul's essence, that for so long had shared imprisonment with me, seek its fulfilment. All that weary homeward way, my famished spirit — or 'muse' as Duke Charles would call it — fed on soundless song woven from my inner world of thought and feeling where every drift of sight or action is retained in its own image.

The Coquille, acting under orders from headquarters, had supplied me with a change of clothes and money enough for bed and board along the road. It was slow going in my weakened state with the muscles of my legs turned to jelly after three months' disuse, that I could not cover more than six leagues in one day.

At Bourg-la-Reine, my last halt before Paris, I stayed the night with my barber friend Girart. He was shocked to find how I had changed — 'A living skeleton. I wonder you survived.'

'Perhaps I haven't. Death has his claws in me, if not to choke out my life on the gallows, then —' I was seized with a fit of coughing, tapped my chest and spluttered — 'here. He sits in wait.'

'Bah!' ejaculated Girart, his gooseberry eyes uneasily darting away from my grin. 'You must have the constitution of an ox to have come through what they did to you with no worse than a cough, which good food will soon cure — at your age.'

'My age. Yes. When I left home my age was five-and-twenty. In these three months I've lived my three score years and ten.'

'I only wish I had as many years ahead of me as he ahead of you.' His juicy voice held in it an unconvincing geniality, and reaching for the bottle he refilled my cup, cut another slice of his prime pork, placed it on my dish and said, 'This will fatten you.'

His table lacked nothing of bounty; and while he trotted to and from his back room and his shop, shaving and bleeding his clients and drawing their teeth, he told of Colin's capture, caught red-handed by the Watch in the house of the goldsmith at Bourges — 'with four chalices he'd lifted ready for the melting pot.' Girart allowed a thoughtful look to creep over his fat face. 'Too cock-sure, y'see. You get careless, you young 'uns, when you've had a run o' luck. They took the goldsmith too, as accessory after the fact, but on his plea of poverty and with no previous charge against him, he got off with a month's imprisonment and a strong recommendation to mercy. I must go and see what my leeches are doing with the Mayor. He has the dropsy.'

I finished the wine and sat sombrely brooding. First René, now Colin. Who next?... I passed my tongue across my lips.

'Yes, and it was *your* luck,' continued Girart, coming in from the shop with a basin full of swollen black things, 'that brought Louis into Meung that day, but don't you go thinking you'll get off so easy. They're out for blood.' With a somewhat too apposite attention he gazed upon the glutted occupants of his pewter bowl. 'There'll be a rounding up of all suspect of association with the Cockleshell. I must put these away.' After depositing his surgical assistants in a cupboard he took from it another bottle, uncorked it with care and replenished our cups. Seating himself he drank heartily, and leant forward to say, 'Here's a word of advice. Don't go to your home. That's the most likely place they'll look to find you. Lie low for a while. Is there anyone in Paris you can trust?'

Yes, one, if he were still there.

I left for Paris the next day, arriving at the gates an hour before curfew, but I did not go directly to the house of de la Barre. Ignoring Girart's advice I let myself be drawn, as if by invisible hands, into the heart of the city. Although October that saw the King's entry into Meung had passed, the evening still held a gentle warmth as if late autumn clung to summer in a sky tint had been blue all day, darkening now to a sapphire clearness. On either side the river, lights, like a necklace of jewels on dark velvet, were brighter than the early stars. Paris… My first and my last love, more fervent than the love of woman, claimed me for her own again. Nothing was changed; the same motley crowd surging through the narrow streets to take their fill of all she had to give; taverns loud with song and laughter, whining beggars, priests, and *filles de joie* shadowing cloaked gallants; the mournful mew of seagulls mingling with the clack and chatter of haranguères on the Petit-Pont; the same familiar smell of fish and garlic, offal, open drains, dead cats and rotting refuse: the same ribbed mud of the river at low tide, the same thronged bridge. Over it I went, past the Faculty of Arts, into the Rue de Fouarre, so named for the straw that gave to schoolboys' frozen feet numbed comfort in the winter. And here the Mother of all Universities, grave and grim, disgorging her troops of students, some with lexicons hugged to their breasts stopping to browse at open bookstalls; some spectacled and earnest, all tonsured, gowned; these at a glance, for the priesthood; others whooping, shouting, heading for the Pomme de Pin. And there go the Archers, mounted *sergents* of the Châtelet spurring a lane through loiterers. Must hide my face, but they're not after me… They always ride out at Vesper time to keep a watchful eye on citizens and mendicants, and most of all those devils' kin, the students. But who is this, or am I hallucinated? No, it can't be… yes, it is! The Bastard de la Barre, rubicund, rotund, cherubically snoutish, and oozing self-importance, wearing the red, white and green of King Louis.

Well, here's a coil. What's to do? How, if Pernet represents the law, can I lie low with him as advised by Girart? Just my luck.

Then, while I turned from those twelve clattering by, their horses' hooves kicking up clouds of dust, reason jogged my elbow. Luck indeed, and in my favour since I held a royal pardon and nothing proved against me more than my admission, under torture, to an uncommitted crime. By which token, if the Bastard's apocryphal bar sinister had got him appointed to the Châtelet, I would have a friend at court ... Ah, but now another problem. Would he be lodged at the Châtelet, or where? I knew that certain of the *sergents*, in particular the Archers, were permitted to retain their private quarters. I would have to take a chance.

I did.

And that is how I came to be lying on his bed, when, after prowling the streets on the night of my return, I waited at his door, hidden in the sheltering dusk of the porch. If he failed to come I would have to seek a lodging somewhere, for apart from the risk of being tracked to my father's house, I would not have him see me a starven scrag of skin and bone, lost of half my hair, balding, haggard, aged. Nor did I know if the Letters of Remission, granting my release, had been confirmed. If not, or if too long delayed, they could seize and take me as they had taken René... No, God, not yet. Not until that which I must do is done. I saw now why I had suffered, sinned and died, to live again, with the stir and heartbeat of conception striking, from long muted soul-strings, the fanfare of my life's passion and life's work.

I was in a sweating fever from the woollen shift and blankets heaped on me by the Bastard. I had asked him to bring a set of tablets. Had he done so? My head was a spinning-wheel, the room a ship at sea, rocking like a drunkard ... but I must write ... must write.

I got out of bed, stripped off my shift — it was sopping wet — and went to the window. Opening the casement I let the crisp air cool my fretted body, hawked up a lump of gob that had been sitting on my chest, and felt the better for it. My eyes travelled to the table set with parchment, ink and tablets. Good Bastard! He must have brought them while I dozed.

Stark naked I sat and wrote: first a letter to Father Villon to tell him of my return, and briefly of my imprisonment, on a false accusation, at Meung. I made the least of those agonised three months, and the most of the King's pardon. Pernet would take it, and the Father would come to me here if I could not go to him. Then, this sanded and sealed, I penned the first lines of:

LE GRAND TESTAMENT
DE
MAISTRE FRANÇOIS VILLON

It begins, as those who have read it will know, with a hymn of hate to Thibault d'Aussigny, my gentle Bishop… No Bishop of mine, may God have mercy on him who had no mercy, in his holiness, on me. I had already sketched the first four stanzas, to my dissatisfaction, a hell of a lot of revision needed here, when the Bastard came bubbling in with the superfluous query: 'My dear! Are you sitting there with nothing on? Go back to bed at once. Oh! and the window is open. Who opened it?'

'*The Bishop, whose harsh hand* … shall I read you what I've written?'

'No. Let me cover you.' He seized a blanket and flung it round my shoulders. 'Now *do* go back to bed.'

I remained static, reciting: '*In this, the thirtieth year of my age, I who have drained grief's bitter cup, not wholly fool am I, nor sage…* What rhymes with *cup*?'

'Up?' brightly suggested the Bastard. 'Please — *bed*.'

'*Sup*. No, I can't have *cup*. *Brew* … *true*… Damn, damn and damn! I'm no rhymster. Bastard, I envy you and turnips who are not born with hell's striving for … what? Why should I struggle to dig from my innermost depths every nuance of feeling and thought to transmute it into the Absolute without losing the balance between concept and spirit. Why? Why? Will you take this letter to Father Villon?'

'Presently. I'm not on duty tonight. My man is opening a dozen oysters for your supper. They are very good and fresh.' He bustled about, ordering the bed and urging me into it. 'Here are the oysters.' He took the dish from his servant and sat by me while I ate.

I had given him an equally brief account of myself as that I had given my father, dwelling at large on my visit to Blois, and watched his eyes grow spherical in the reflected light of my glory.

'But it's *monstrous* that you, the Poet Royal, should have been detained by those *canaille*! We must get the Letters of Remission through at once! D'Estouteville, unfortunately, has retired. We have a new man now, Seigneur Jacques Villiers de l'Isle-Adam. So many innovations since the death of my beloved Uncle Charles.'

D'Estouteville retired! That was no good news to me.

'How,' I asked, 'did you come to join the Archers?'

'Well, my dear, between ourselves in *strictest* confidence, Louis is so unpopular that the city feared there would be riots at the coronation and asked for volunteers to increase the Guard. And being of the Blood in direct line of succession, more or *less,* I thought it my duty to offer myself and my service to the Crown, even though I'm paid the barest *pittance.* Did you notice our new uniforms? Aren't they hideous? Green and red are colours I abhor. But I felt I *must* oblige my Cousin Louis because — now this is *lèse-majesté* so don't listen to me — he has *no* discrimination whatsoever. He loads his court with bourgeois who can't even speak the King's French and has thrown out *all* the advisers of my good Cousin Charles. As for the Châtelet — they will take anyone now. We have a fellow there called Cholet, my dear, a *wine-cooper's* son — a rude coarse type who has the impudence to claim you as an old friend of his, and he said how you used to go duck-stealing in the moats when you were boys. My dear! Wasn't it *dreadful* about René? I can't bear to *think* of it, and after he had the King's pardon, too. Oh, and did you know that Colin —?'

'Yes,' I broke in hastily, 'and I all but followed him to Montpipeau.'

'Montpipeau!' A horrified gurgling sound issued from his parted lips. 'Not really?'

'Really.'

'But what had you *done*?'

'Nothing.'

'Nothing?'

'I perceive,' said I, 'a singular dearth of originality in this duologue.'

'But,' the Bastard adhesively persisted, 'you must have done something.'

'A case of mistaken identity. These are excellent oysters.'

'The Law,' said the Bastard profoundly, 'and in particular the Watch, are quite, *quite* mad. Only last week a case of larceny was committed to the Pot, and after they had boiled him they discovered he was not their man. Both had lost a finger but the man they should have taken had lost an ear as well. They had an idee fixe upon the missing finger — so inefficient.' He eyed the empty shells on my platter. 'Have you finished?'

'Quite, *quite* finished.'

'You look tired.' He removed the dish. 'Try and have another little sleep while I run round to Father Villon with your letter. He *will* be pleased to know you're safe with me. He must be *longing* to have you home again, and don't you dare to let me find you out of bed when I come back.' Tenderly stroking the hair from my forehead he said, 'This sadly needs a trim.' And, as if on eggs, he tiptoed from the room.

Returned from harsh captivity
Where life was almost lost to me
If harried still by Fate I be
She may have reason in her sight
To judge if she has done me right
On my return

…And when my soul is fled from pain
God give me life with Him again
On my return

Home at last, re-united with my father in the House of the Red Door. What need to tell of his thanksgiving, he whose prayers had followed me through all this dreary time? As for my mother… Will I ever forget that day when I found her in her room kneeling before the Image of Our Lady, bought with the first money I had earned as scribe, so long ago?

At the door I waited, saw her rise from her knees and turn to me, her face transfigured, but her hair was snow white. The rosary dropped from her outstretched hands.

'Is this a vision? O, blessed Virgin, is it he… François? Not dead?'

She swayed. I caught her and held her. 'Yes, Mother. I am here, never to leave you now.'

The sorrowed years slipped from her in the glory of her joy, unmarred by me who gave her nothing of these past tortured months, making much of my travels and my visit to the duke at Blois, of which she had already heard from Father Villon… 'So proud was I even when all Paris spoke of you as lost to us my Faith remained unshaken although 'tis said no man is prophet in his own country — which led me to fear that with such honour gathered to your name you were dead and writing poetry up in heaven and Father Villon has collected all your scribbled verses compiled in one volume to be given to the world… Oh, my love, my son, my heart, how am I blessed! I, an ignorant poor creature who cannot write nor read have borne a poet of whom all learned men — the Provost too — he's no more in office we have another now — they don't think so high of him, speak of you with reverence, they do, they do!… And Mademoiselle de Bruyères, she asks after you and deigns to invite me to her house but I don't want her patronage. I told her flat, I thank you, Mademoiselle, when I was scrubbing steps to earn a sol or two you had so much use for me as I for a mule's piss — Yes, I spoke her plain when we met as always in the market. I was buying mutton — I can afford meat now and then thanks to that angel man our Father Villon who insists I take from him two *écus* a month besides my board and lodging free since he says that in your absence he saves your keep but I put it by for you and sometimes buy a joint of mutton — not for myself I mislike meat but for those who hunger as once I did. How great is God! You're thin.' She put me from her, gazing up with tear-wet eyes. 'You shouldn't be so thin living on the land's fat in the castle of a prince —

and Father says he also is a poet, not such a one as mine, but well enough. I knew you was destined for grandeur…'

I let her talk and stayed with her till evening to hurry home under cover of the dark, for although the Letters of Remission had been received and passed I was still wanted by the police, thanks to Tabarie, for my part in the burglary at the College of Navarre.

I had confessed all to Father Villon, who readily chose to believe me innocent of premeditated theft, and having assured himself that his scapegrace son was a truly reformed character, 'renounced and withdrawn', as he joyfully noted, 'from your former low debauched associates who, but for God's Grace, would have led you to the Pit,' was prepared to defend and uphold me against importunate enquiry.

His cronies of the cloister, in particular Maistre Laurent Poutrel — mark well the name — a Canon of St Benoît-le-Bientourné, a Grand Beadle of the Faculty, held me in lowest opinion viewing this fatuous forbearance toward a hardened criminal as a sign of an old man's senility. However, he allowed him his illusions and me a frigid welcome, expressed by Maistre Poutrel in 'the Hope,' with an emphasis on capitals, 'that I would profit by Experience and so Repay my Reverend Father for the Enduring Anxiety I had caused him in the Past by Stern Resistance of Temptation in the Future, and turn from the Lure of the Flesh to cultivate the Gift bestowed on me by God that it be not scattered to the Winds.'

'Have no fear,' was my father's staunch assurance, 'François is working day and night at what I think will prove to be his masterpiece.'

'Let us pray it may be so,' which Maistre Poutrel's tone implied would be unlikely.

Yes, day and night I worked, for I knew my time was short, writing as one possessed through those sharp winter months of 1462. Much that I wrote had been conceived while I lay chained to a prison wall... A song saga of my life. Seldom was I seen in the night haunts of Paris. The friends of my youth were no more. Two had met their end on the gallows, and the rest gone. Where? None knew.

Harboured in the cloisters of St Benoît I lived a full year in Paris undetected, but still shadowed by the Watch in wait to seize me on the evidence of Tabarie as an accomplice in the unforgotten College of Navarre affair. But as time went on I took heart to believe that the Châtelet, under new administration, had more to do than nose around for Villon, reformed and pardoned, with the Letters of Remission confirmed, leading an exemplary existence under the protection of my much revered adoptive father. But, as warned by Girart, I was too cocksure. Saturn had yet to have the laugh of me.

It was on an evening in November, a year after my return, when with my last work nearing its completion, and while I rearranged the earlier Ballades in the order as I wished them to appear in the Great Testament, that I came upon her name of bitter memory.

Qui me feist maschier ces groselles,
Fors Katherine de Vausselles?

Yes, she who made me chew the cud of shame. Be done with love.

Je renye amours et despite
Et deffie à feu et à sang

I renounce, I curse, I defy them all, all loves with my blood and fire ... But even while I cursed her in my heart, the old wound throbbed and ached for just one sight and touch of her. The cold had crept into my bones and I sweated in a fever, as always at nightfall, but I took no count of that. The air would cool me.

Wrapped in my cloak I stole down the stairs and out at the red door. The city roared its evensong in the flurry and hurry of the lampless streets under the heavy-eaved houses. A blanket of fog rose from the river to shroud me. It wanted an hour yet to curfew, but the gathering dark had crowded the taverns bringing shadow shapes of women to hang around the doors. One, old and dreadful in her paint, came at me with whispers, pointing her tongue at me.

I shook her off and hastened on along the Rue St Martin to that house at the upper end of it. I no longer held the key to the door. It was lost with all else of me.

A light shone in her window; a figure moved across it. My heart jumped. No, not she ... her Gorgon, recognised in one fleeting glimpse when she turned to draw the curtain, shutting out the night.

I pulled the bell, heard its clangour and running footsteps on the stone flagged hall. Whose? Not hers.

The door was opened by a liveried page staring up big-eyed under the square-cut fringe of hair.

'Madame de Vaucelles is within?'

'Yes, messire.'

'Tell ... no, take me to her.'

'The name, messire?'

'No name. I will announce myself.'

I slipped past him. He closed the door and pattered after me as I made to mount the stairs.

'My lady is here, sir, in the solar.'

I followed him to a room to the left of the hall, but as he lifted the latch I thrust him aside and went in.

She was seated on a settle by the open hearth where logs blazed and tall candles on the chimney piece, rayed down upon her hair, lighted it to ashen gold. She turned her head and, seeing me framed in the doorway, her face sagged, was drained of colour, her lips wordlessly moving, and one hand out-held, not in greeting but in fear, to guard her eyes.

'Yes,' I made my voice sepulchral. 'I am risen from the dead.'

She gave a little shriek and started up, backing in terror. The heel of her shoe caught the edge of the stone hearth. She toppled forward and into my arms.

'Take care lest you fall in the fire,' I said, 'and burn before your time to trick the devil of his due.'

'Oh! Oha! No … yes!' Between laughing and crying she laid a finger to my scarred lip. 'This … is it … are you…?'

'I am.' Flaming at her touch I put her from me, and said in the words but not the tone of a lover, 'As for all time, beyond forgetting, you are and ever will be my perpetual enchantment and … my whore.'

She was fiercely white. 'Now I know you are no ghost. Only you would dare so to insult me.'

'You are well schooled,' I grinned, 'in high dramatics, and well formed, too. A little stouter, richly gowned, and … let me think now, yes, you're twenty —'

'— two,' she prompted sulky-mouthed. 'A hag.'

'Not yet.' My glance voyaged round the room extravagantly furnished and returned to the sparkling jewels on her neck. 'The wages of sin,' I murmured, 'spell death to youth.'

The petulant bulge of her lip, the same mutinous shake of her shoulders almost shattered my defence of critical detachment. Her pallor, her gem-encircled throat, brushed by the firelight, held the luminous quality of tinted glass.

She looked at me aslant. 'Why are you come?'

I crossed to a table set with wine and heavy silver cups. I lifted one to examine the ornate carving embossed with a crest. 'This is worth more than a night with you. How many nights do you give for one of these?' I filled two goblets, passed one to her. She snatched it from my hand, put her lips to it, but did not drink.

'I ask again. Why are you come?'

'To discuss a slight emotional conflict with myself and … myself.'

I drained the cup. She put hers down untasted.

'You talk in riddles. I thought I had done with you when I heard you were hanged.'

'Don't be too sure,' I told her airily. 'I'm a cat o' nine lives.' I took her discarded cup from the chimney piece. 'If you won't drink this, I will. You keep a good cellar, Madame la Veuve de Vaucelles. I presume you are still a widow?' I stared down at the wine in the silver cup, filled to its brim and glowing red. 'A ruby,' I murmured, 'imprisoned.' I drank, and smiling, asked, 'What have you done with your Minotaur? Have you cast him off that he may grow a second pair of horns? Mine have rotted, fallen to decay. You see?' I slapped my forehead. 'Gone — for good.'

Her face, so pale, crimsoned. 'If I tell you that he — that I am not what you think. He was my servant. I dismissed him. He took me and — and raped me. He did! That time you came upon us was the first and only — and against my will. Never before or since. I swear — you *must* believe —'

'Believe?' My voice dropped cool as rain to drown her flash of heat. '*Faulse beaulté qui tant me couste chier, rude en effect, ypocrite doulceur* … I have put you in a ballade that you may live when this, and this,' I touched her crudely, 'so sweet and precious, flower-fair, turns foul and stinking in death's embrace with me — we two together. Always.'

A tremor shook her body and, as if released by that involuntary movement, the scent of her flesh, a mingling of honey and apples entirely her own, overswept me. I took and held her, felt her quicken in my arms. There was something pagan in the strained pressure of her flanks to mine, in the sting of her questing mouth, her broken words.

'No man… none but a god could give me this. Love, my love, how I have longed for you. Never, never will you leave me … promise … promise.' Stealthily her fingers unfastened the laces of her corsage to slide it from her shoulders. 'Take me,' she whispered. 'Take what is and ever has been yours.'

I had her now to know her weakness and my strength; and my resistance, schooled in torment to deny and flagellate myself.

'Would I promise not to drink when I thirst, or to feed when my blood cries out in hunger for the fruits you offer to my … emptiness?' Leashing the surge of desire that consumed me, I drew away from her. 'My life has nothing left to give *ma damoyselle au nez tortu*. Pardon, madame, you are disarranged.'

I ordered, carefully, her gown and was treated to a volley of gutter filth accompanied by a battering of fists against my chest.

'Beast! Beast! A lousy impotent ******! What else do you lack besides horns, you —'

I caught her hands that climbed to claw my face. 'You've reaped a choice variety of seeds sown from where? Fat Margot's garden?'

'Pig's offal! Pimp!' Sucking her cheeks she spat in my eye.

'Well aimed, madame, this will spare me a tear.' I bowed, I turned; but as I reached the door one came in, apish, old, prinked in youthful fashion of short tunic and long hose. His spindle legs were knobble-kneed and bent, his lips stretched wide to show a mouthful of juvenile teeth drawn by an expert barber-surgeon from some child's skull in the Cemetery of Innocents, an expensive process much favoured by those who could afford it.

'*Seigneur!*' Her voice, high-pitched, shrilled at him. 'What a delightful surprise. Allow me to present Maistre François Villon.' She came close, loudly to repeat in his inclining ear: 'Villon. François Villon. He's a poet … POET.'

'Ah, so?' A clawlike hand was shakily extended. I bowed over it.

'*Enchanté, Seigneur…*' The name had escaped me, but not the drop from shrivelled gums of those childish white teeth, hastily replaced with a click; nor the bleared dart of a suspicious eye from under wrinkled lids at her, low-curtsied to his entrance.

I closed the door on them, and stood listening to a mumbled wheeze of, 'What is he to you or you to him, this … who? A poet? Villon… Don't know him.'

And she, cooingly, 'Why should you? He is of no account. A mendicant. He came to beg. I met him long ago at the d'Estoutevilles who thought well of his ballades, but he has never written anything as yet and never will.'

'Did you give him money? Don't you go giving my money to vagabond students.'

'He's not a student now … I said he's not a *student* now.'

'He wears the gown.'

'They all do. Will my lord take wine?'

'I have bought you a set of gold cups, and this.'

'How my lord is gracious… Oh, a necklet of pearls…'

'In token of my gratitude. Give me a kiss.'

'More, *much* more than a kiss…'

I retched.

'Messire!' Her page was beside me, not the child I remembered; another, spruce, well trained, an embryonic major-domo, his tunic embroidered with a coat of arms, his pursed lips holding back a grin. 'Messire is sick?'

'Unto death.' Sliding a coin in his hand, 'Is Papa,' I jerked my head, 'a frequent visitor?'

'Yes, messire.' His chubby face was supernaturally solemn.

'What's his name?'

'Sire Denys Hesselin, messire.'

'And these,' I touched the device on his tunic, 'are his arms?'

'Yes, messire.'

'Goodnight.'

'Goodnight, messire.'

Hesselin. I knew the name: a municipal overlord, retired from office, a flaneur in his dotage, often seen at the Pomme, paralytic, lugged home by his lackey.

It was long past curfew when I left the house, strolling through the empty streets. Forgetful of the Watch, or deliberately careless of danger, I turned to tread the mill of my thoughts… *Thrice besotted ass, did you not ask for it? You knew her for what she was and is, and ever will be until, like La Belle Heaulmière, she ends in a ditch or on a dung-heap, a bag of bones. But don't we all? What's love? You're happier without it, safer too, safe as a witch astride a broomstick. She's got a head on her shoulders, yes! She'll get her price while she lasts, before she's poxed… Those furnishings, her jewels. Wish I'd had the sense to pinch one while she panted in my arms for what she'll never have again from me… A poor revenge to spite myself, filling an open wound with salt. Pleasure is bred from pain as hate from love and death from life… I'll remember her in my last Will and Testament. Item.*

M'amour, ma chère Rose, ne luy laisse ne cueur ne joye, elle aymeroit mieulx autre chose... *I'll leave her neither my heart nor my liver, she wants something more solid than that.* Une grant bourse de soye, *a great silk purse stuffed with gold, which is all the stuffing she'll get from her old leman.*

I burst into a laugh to catch my throat in a paroxysmal cough, and didn't hear the Watch till they were on me, their lanthorns flashed in my face to bring a shout of recognition.

'Villon! There's no two men in Paris with that sliced lip. We've got you now. Come on!'

TWENTY-TWO

Yes, these bloodhounds who so patiently had waited, licking their chops for a kill, had got me again, hand-fasted, a prisoner, hauled to the Châtelet charged with a six-year-old crime.

What use to plead as defence to the raid on the College of Navarre that I, an innocent accessory after the fact, had been tricked into it unwillingly, when that yelping skunk Tabarie had sworn to have seen me take my full share of the loot? Just my cursed luck that d'Estouteville was not now in office. This new man would be a harder nut to crack. Nor could I hope for help from the Bastard who had nothing to do with the administration of the Châtelet. The work of the Archers was to arrest, not to judge. Moreover, the recently appointed Lieutenant-Criminel, Pierre de la Dehors, ex-master of la Grande Boucherie, aptly named 'the Butcher', exercised his power *sans merci* and with particular attention to the clerks of Sorbonne. As one of the city's high officials he did not readily forget the riots, no student 'rags' to him, caused by the theft of the Pet-au-Diable in open defiance of civic authority.

Nevertheless, my incarceration in a cell, not a dungeon, and comparatively clean, was a very different proposition from my entombment in the Tower of Manasse.

For thirty-six hours of devilish suspense was I detained, fearing the worst, for I couldn't believe that having caught me I would be let off with less than my life.

However, I bribed my warder to obtain me pen, ink and parchment, and take a letter to Father Guillaume telling him of this latest unwarranted charge, and received a note from him imploring me to make full confession of my part in the Navarre robbery, with the hope-giving avowal that he would stand surety for me, whatever the cost.

No! I couldn't let him do it. Where would he find the money? I wrote a second letter saying that if money must be raised for my release he must sell all my collected poems for what they were worth. But who would print them, and if printed who would buy? Nothing I had written would appeal to the *vox populi* except a few indifferent ballades.

On the third day of my imprisonment I was brought before the court for examination. It was brief. My judges, Maistre Jehan Collet, Procurateur of the Faculty, and Maistre Laurent Poutrel, the Grand Beadle, questioned me in turn, reading out the damning evidence of Tabarie who had named me and those three others as guilty of a raid on the College of Navarre between ten o'clock and midnight on the Eve of Christmas, 1456. A coffer containing five hundred gold crowns had been forced open and the money stolen. One of my confederates, Colin des Cayeux, had paid his well-deserved penalty of death. Two others involved — Nicolas of Picardy, a defrocked monk, and one known as Petit-Jehan, an expert pick-lock — were still at large. My sentence would be lightened if I could inform them where these two were to be found.

I could not.

'Do you confess to this charge of robbery of which you stand accused?' was the question yapped at me by Maistre Collet, angular, dog-faced, his sharp nose pointed, not at the prisoner but at the vaulted roof of the stone-walled chamber.

'I do.'

A gratified buzz from the Clerks of the Court. What now? The sentence?

A crackling of parchment, spectacles poised, a murmured consultation with Maistre Collet's learned friend, the Beadle, enthroned on the dais beside him: a thumb is wetted to turn the documented sheets; more crackling, and the scratch of quills as the scribes, at the table below the dais, write their reports for the registers of the Criminal Court of the Theological Faculty.

My knees shake. How much longer must I stand between these two effigies, my gaolers, waiting … waiting? *For God's sake spit it out!*

'Are you prepared —' more rustling of parchment passed to Maistre Poutrel for confirmation. The scribes, expectantly, are staring up, quills at the ready.

Dog-face clears his throat. 'Are you, François Montcorbier *dit* Villon, prepared to refund the sum of one hundred and twenty gold crowns in yearly instalments of forty *écus* for a period of three years?'

The ponderous words drop like stones in a pool, spreading wide uncomprehended ripples.

From some dizzy vacuum I hear those words repeated, and my parched answer: 'No. I cannot … have not … that amount of… No.'

'You are aware of the penalty if you refuse repayment?'

This from the Beadle, Maistre Poutrel whose gimlet eyes bore holes in my head.

I nod it, choking back a whoop of laughter at the thought that if I go on nodding long enough it will fall off. *And what'll you do then, you old chuff-cat, with nothing but my carcass left to hang?*

'Take him away.'

Back to my cell, locked in with a warning from my gaoler. 'You'd best raise the cash or else,' a ghoulish chuckle, '*you'll* be raised — to feed Madame la Montfaucon. She has a healthy appetite, and nothing much from this month's haul to fill her maw. Our governor prefers the Pot. 'Tis more hurtsome and takes longer.'

It was darkening when the door of my cell creaked open to admit the Beadle, Maistre Laurent Poutrel. His hand held a scroll, his face a look of greedy satisfaction that struggled with suitable gloom. Drawing his fingers through his grizzled beard as if to measure the weight of his words, he pronounced, 'I am come from the House of Father Villon who —'

'My father!' I broke in. 'Is he — does he —?'

A podgy hand was raised. Please. No interruption. My good friend, Dom Guillaume, with whom I have conferred on your dastardly behalf, is agreed to stand surety upon this undertaking as follows … Hahum.' Unfurling the scroll with a flourish he read: *'Pro littera condempnacionis passate per dictum Villon de somma sexvigniti scutorum auri quam promisit solvere Facultati et execucione defuncti…'*

He plodded on while I stood in a blinding rush of light, as did Paul on the road to Damascus, to receive my redemption… Yes, my father had bound himself in my name to repay to the Faculty the prodigious sum of a hundred and twenty gold crowns as from the time of my immediate release.

'You will affix your signature hereto.'

I signed the bond.

'Father, my father! Why do you impoverish yourself for me? I am unworthy of such sacrifice. I've sinned and was prepared to pay the penalty even with my life.'

I knelt at his feet, that great old man of God, on whose face the lines of suffering and anxiety engraved there in my cause were less deep now and lightened as the blurred imprint on some ancient coin. Nothing of reproach was in those dimmed eyes, nor in the tremble of his voice made firm to say:

'We, who tread the downward path of time, re-live our youth in the young. Is it not a bitter thing to see the flower of April fruit frost-blighted? How much more bitter, then, for a father…' The brave voice broke. 'O, Absalom, my son, my son, would God that I had died for thee, as would I not for you?'

I bent my head to his knees, so thin beneath the habit of his order. Shuddering with held-in sobs my fingers sought his girdled rosary and raised to my lips the Cross. 'May Christ our Lord and Master make me worthy of your love and His.'

'He will, my son, He will, if you give of yourself that which is good to edify those who have the wisdom to read what you have yet to write.' A smile like a momentary rainbow gleamed through his clouded eyes. 'When the Beadle came puffing up my staircase and, less to spare me pain than to reimburse his pocket, did offer me your freedom, could I refuse repayment to receive what is mine? God sent you to me for His purpose that I might nurture the great gift He has bestowed on you, so to raise a pillar on which future generations will read and honour your name.'

'*Your* name, Father, and I will honour it, so help me God.'

And in so far as lay within my power I did keep my word to him and to my God. I did… But I had reckoned without my demoniac inexhaustible pursuer who had me marked from birth. I had slipped him twice too often. He was not one to take defeat, give up the chase and leave me to fulfil my destiny in my own way, not his.

Let us see how he played one last Saturnine trick with *his* cogged dice — to win.

TWENTY-THREE

It was during that month of November when, after signing the bond on my father's surety, for my release, I set myself to work at fever pitch on the revision of my Testaments. I seldom left the House of the Red Door save to attend Mass and to visit my mother. I saw no friends, for I had none now, other than the Bastard who, when off duty, would come to my room with offers of assistance in the re-arranging of my manuscripts. I must have a second copy of my poems for fear the first were lost or thieved. Since, therefore, it was necessary for me to have a scribe, as the Bastard's script, for all his good intent, was quite illegible, I engaged the service of one Fremlin, a pimply youth with a formidable stammer and poetic aspirations, whom, before I left Paris, I had coached for his entrance to Sorbonne. It was some three weeks after my release from the Châtelet that the Bastard called to see me, big with news.

'My dear! Who do you think I saw last night when I was on foot patrol with two of the Watch? Tabarie! He simply *shot* away as soon as he saw us but I don't think he recognised me. We tracked him to the house of Robin Dogis at the sign of the Chariot. You remember Dogis? He used often to come to the Mule. I wonder Tabarie dare show himself in Paris after implicating you in that unfortunate affair. We couldn't arrest him as his mother paid up, but we have had orders to watch him. My dear, if *only* I'd been with you at the Pomme that *aw*ful night, I would never have let you get mixed up with that villainous canaille. Yes, and *please* believe — I've told you this so often but I *do* want you to know — that not until you left the Châtelet did I *dream* you were there! I could have come to see you and bring you things to eat. And now I must tell you something else. When I heard what an *enor*mous sum they'd screwed out of Father Villon for your pardon I implored him to let me go halves, but he wouldn't. He said he'd sold his vineyard in — now where was it? Oh, yes, at Vaugirard. Now don't look like that! I'm sure he did it willingly, as so would I, if I had a vineyard. My father has dozens in the Bordeaux country. And my dear, Dom Guillaume paid me *such* a compliment. I blushed all over. He said I am the only friend you have of whom he has ever approved. *Isn't* that nice?'

'*Isn't* it! What did you do about Tabarie?'

'My dear, what *could* I do except to report that I'd seen him? His mother paid the fine so he goes free.'

'You say you saw him with Dogis?'

'No, I saw him go into the house where Dogis lives, but others live there too, so he may not have been visiting him.'

'We'll soon see about that.' I got up to take my cloak from a peg on the door.

The Bastard eyed me apprehensively. 'Where are you going?'

'To find Tabarie.'

I did not find Tabarie, but I found Robin Dogis at supper with Fremlin, who lodged at his house, and two others unknown to me: Hutin de Moustier, a Châtelet *sergent*, off duty, and Roger Pichart, a young 'blood' of Sorbonne.

One glance sufficed to tell me that wherever Tabarie might be it was not here, and I gave as excuse for my intrusion that I had come to ask if Fremlin were free to work with me the next day. Having secured his promise to appear at 'nine o'clock in the m-m-morning', I was about to depart when Dogis invited me to stay.

'There's not much left to eat, though we have drink enough.' And more than the three of them could carry, but as I had missed my midday meal I made do with the carcass of a goose.

Dogis, when I knew him at Sorbonne, had been studying Law and just managed to scrape through his finals when the death of his father, a wealthy advocate, made him independent. He was never more to me than a casual acquaintance, although I'd tapped him once or twice at the Mule for my supper and a bottle or two. He was free with his cash when he had it, but most of it went in wenching and drinking. I had rarely seen him after midnight anything but soaked.

It was Pichart, the youngest of the trio, who suggested we should go on to the Mule. Fremlin, at a warning glance from me, refused. 'I m-must k-k-keep my h-h-head c-clear for my w-w-work with m-m-m-maistre —'

'Yes,' I said, 'and see you do, and so must I.'

'Well, why not le'ss go to your house fir'ss?' floundered Pichart, well in his cups. 'An' then you can read's some of your late'ss work.'

To that request I did not commit myself, for while my father in the past had long-sufferingly endured the sound, if not the sight, of my choice companions smuggled to my room, wakening the house with ribald song and drunken laughter, I, now reformed and repentant, held fast to my resolution never more to stray from the path of righteousness... I wonder for how long I would have kept to that?

On this occasion, however, my halo firmly adjusted, I left the house at the sign of the Chariot, cold sober, as those three most certainly were not. Down the Rue des Parcheminiers and into the Rue St Jacques we went. The bibulous off-duty *sergent*

Moustier, having rid himself of superfluous drink in the gutter, was in better case than Pichart and Dogis who had gone on ahead supporting each other and making the devil of a row with catcalls and screechings and a lively chant to do with the gibbet of Montfaucon *'où estoit toute assemblée, avec chascun une fille … À mort! À mort!'* Lunging, daggers drawn, right and left, at imaginary foes.

'This,' said Moustier, 'is where we leave them to it. That young Pichard is red-hot for a fight — Here! what the hell!'

The street was dark, the moon cloud-hidden, but a shaft of light poured through the window in the house of Maistre Ferrebourg. No, you have not met him, yet, and nor had I. Until that doomed night of nights he was no more than a name to me, a much respected lawyer who employed some half-dozen clerks. From the opposite side of the road I could see them through the unshuttered window, busily copying legal documents; and there Pichart, hanging on to Dogis, halted to let off a lusty torrent of abuse to the effect — in modified English: 'A pox to you, you coin-griping niggish deformed sots who serve your writs with codpieces of the law. Goats'-noses! Pelf-lickers! May Pluto disparage your parts!' And a good deal more, unprintable.

At first the clerks, loftily ignoring this amiable address, continued to write, but when Pichart scooped a handful of horse dung from the cobbles to hurl at them through the open window, they sprang up from their desks, dashed out into the street and began to pummel the intruders with their fists. I, within a stone's throw of my home, kept my distance, yet near enough to see — before I deemed it wiser to be off — Moustier, tardily reminded of his duty, bearing down upon the combatants in attempt to enforce order, only to find himself dragged into the house by a couple of infuriated clerks. His yells of, 'Let be! Let be! I'm a Sergent of the Châtelet. I'll arrest you for assault!' brought Maistre Ferrebourg hurrying from his private sanctum to find two of his clerks belabouring Moustier in the front room, and the remainder of his staff actively engaged in dealing with Dogis outside.

Meanwhile, Pichart, first cause of the disturbance, had made off top-speed for the safety of St Benoît, where I, although a mere spectator judged it expedient to follow him. I was just about to go, when Ferrebourg, shouting, 'The Watch! Call the Watch!' seized hold of Dogis, who having struggled free of his assailants, was shoved aside by the highly indignant lawyer and with such violence that he fell asprawl. He was up again in a trice, and drink-inflamed, drew his dagger to thrust at Ferrebourg. I heard a yelp of pain, saw Dogis take to his heels, and stayed to see no more.

But Ferrebourg had seen me, the only one of the four endowed with a criminal record. Yes, he knew all there was to know of Villon. Was there a notary in Paris who did not?

I went to bed. I had no premonition, no pricking of my thumbs to warn me of disaster. Conscience clear, I slept… And was awakened by the too familiar dreaded tramp of feet in the cloisters of St Benoît-le-Bientourné. I heard the mutter of their voices and their halt below my window. I got up and looked out. Four of them: the Archers.

Their steel breastplates caught their lanthorns' light flashed in my face with a shout of recognition. 'Here, you, Villon! Come down. You're wanted, charged with assault!'

My one thought was for my father. He must not hear them. He need know nothing of this. Ferrebourg having seen me must have given them my name, not necessarily as one of those two drunks who had reviled his clerks and attacked himself unless… my heart narrowed, unless having spotted me he had come to the most obvious conclusion that I, Villon, ex-jailbird who so often had escaped the grip of justice, was their man, chief instigator of this night's latest devilment… Let them take me then. Twice had I been given to the power of the dog, and twice escaped his savagery. This time I would beat and bring the cur to heel. What charge had he, who held between his jaws the whip of justice, against me and my foolproof defence? On that I would stand.

I went down to his men of the kennel.

Ah, yes, and if my good friend, d'Estouteville had been still in office I would have been detained no longer than it took to tell of my negligible part as eye-witness of the brawl. But d'Estouteville's successor, Villiers de l'Isle-Adam, was a man of iron whose god, the law, would be untempered by reason or mercy. De la Dehors, his Lieutenant-Criminel, 'the Butcher', but lately bereft of his prize by my father's reimbursement of my share in the spoils from the coffers of the College of Navarre, was one after the Provost's own heart. Should the 'Butcher' find a single flaw in my defence, he would condemn me out of hand. I could see him indefatigably studying my dossier, a rich harvest there for him to reap.

Item: the assassination of one Philippe Sermoise, a priest, whose deathbed confession had vindicated this incorrigible reprobate, which none the less had blackened his record. Item: a common thief, a burglar who had broken into one of the Colleges that nurtured him. Execrable! And worst of all he was a flagrant robber of the Church, committed for sacrilege, saved from the gallows by the death of a king. No king was dead now for a newly crowned sovereign to exercise his royal right on his accession. No matter that this charge against a thoroughly bad character was unproven. Whether guilty or not of stabbing

Maistre Ferrebourg, he had committed crimes enough to hang him. So dangerous a criminal, known to be associated with the infamous Coquillards, was not fit to live.

'Bring him out!'

They brought me from my cell in the Châtelet to the torture chamber, again to undergo the agonising Question by Water. God, O God, why do this to me? Have I not suffered enough? Between my shrieks of torment I was racked with more than the relentless torrents that gurgled through the funnel to my bursting bowels, while at intervals they removed the gag that I, at my last gasp, should be enabled to confess. Yet they could not drag confession from me, who, with what breath was left in my lungs, gasped out: 'Kill ... if you must. I die ... innocent.'

He was there, the 'Butcher', his face a mask, inscrutable; but even as he gestured his servers to suspend their infernal rites, since only on the altar of his holy gibbet must he offer up his sacrifice, I discerned in his eyes the burning light of the fanatic. Exquisite satisfaction did he derive from this adherence to his faith in the execution of his duty. I am positive that he, with all who administered the law, taking to themselves the advocacy of the one Supreme Judge, believed he did obey His Word made Flesh.

Of all contradictory insensate peoples were these whom I give you out of my mouth as I knew and lived with them. What a world was mine, and what a world is yours, of shiftless unrealities: you, who preach of God and in one breath do murder Him. Yet this much have I learned: that the boundless mystery of the Infinite, to which the secret things belong, contains within itself worlds incalculable, among which yours is but an embryo, blind and seeking.

They unfastened the ropes that bound me to the leathern mattress. I was led to my cell and there I sank … to die? No. Such peaceful passing out was not for me.

When I came to myself a sense of raging resentment convulsed me to the exclusion of my body's pain. Why was I here? I had done nothing, nothing to deserve this monstrous misdirection of their justice'. Why, why did I go after Tabarie that night? They could never have had me on so paltry a charge … or could they?

For three days I was held in gnawing suspense before they came to take me… where? Again to flood my belly with their hellish waterfall? No, not this time. They would have me up for question in that same court where, only one month before, I had undergone examination; but now Provost Villiers de l'Isle-Adam, scarlet-robed almighty judge, sat on the dais, supported by his Lieutenant-Criminel.

I stand between two Archers while the clerk of the court reads, at interminable length, my indictment, of which only the last words convey to my dazed sense their awful meaning.

Pendu… 'hanged'. *Étranglé.*

No, no! You can't do this to me! I try to speak but have no voice. *You can't…*

They can.

Two Archers, like heraldic symbols supporting, take me, not ungently, by my flaccid arms. Head up — never let it be seen that I cringe — I walk with them back to my cell. And now that I know the worst, I can face death with hope renewed … of life.

My gaoler brought my evening meal, no dry crust for us, the highly favoured who tread the road to Montfaucon. They can afford to feed us at the King's expense for our last day on earth.

A dish of goat's flesh and a flask of wine is set beside me on the straw where I sit to ease the riven muscles of my back against the wall.

'What's this? His Honour, the Provost, is a liberal host!'

'Not he.' With a stealthy glance at the door he leaned over me, exuding an effluvium of garlic. 'You'd have had bread and water as will be till the end, but that Marchant de la Barre of the patrol sends you this and bids me say he's going to see your father.'

I stared at him, a florid fellow with a broken nose and a cast in his eye, that fixed itself not on me but on the narrow barred window while his other eye explored my feet.

'Will I be allowed to see my father? He's a priest.'

'A priest, eh?' He sniggered, 'Your father outside o' the Church?'

'I'm his son by adoption. And remove that grin from your face or I'll remove it for you.' Tilting the flask of Bordeaux I drank, paused in my draught and passed the half-emptied bottle to him. 'Take a swig?'

He shook his head.

'Go on, it's a rare vintage.'

His squint eye hovered to light on the middle distance. 'It's not regular to drink with prisoners.'

'I won't be a prisoner for long. You can give me a toast to speed me on my way, or — no, I'll drink to myself. Hand it over.' I took the bottle from him before he drained the lot, sucked down what was left and gave him an impromptu: 'How's this? *I am François, fortune's toy* … No, that won't do … Wait, I've got it.'

'Fortune's fool am I, François
Born in Paris near Ponthois

When from the six foot rope I sway
You'll know how much my buttocks weigh.'

'I'll write that down and leave it to you in my Testament that you may tell them how I hid a chuckle in my shroud. Lord, man, don't look so glum. *Je ris en pleurs…*'

I could see he thought me a cool customer; and, strangely cool I was, unafraid, fearful only of delay. But as the solitary hours passed, this uncertain waiting for the end keyed me to a pitch of passionate impatience to burst forth in an epitaph, much of which I had already written, now to be completed. All night I paced my cell in a fever of creative urge. My one regret at leaving life was that I must leave my work unfinished.

Morning came. I had not slept, revising that last of my Ballades written on my one remaining scrap of parchment and long ago conceived when I learned of René's fate.

With the first grey finger of dawn I knelt and offered up my heart and soul to Him who died that I may live … hereafter.

Through my barred window high up in the wall I watched the waking day spread its light across the sky. Footsteps resounded in the stone passage. Had they come to fetch me? Bolts were drawn. The door creaked open on its rusty hinges, and, pushing past my gaoler, in walked the Bastard. He wore his Archer's livery and a well-assumed air of authority.

'The Provost has granted you permission to send a message by me to your relatives.' And to my gaoler, 'Wait outside. I'll deal with the prisoner. Go.'

He backed, and, as he went, his roving eye lowered its lid at a rafter in the roof.

'My dear! Father Villon — you had my message that I'd seen him? — he has appealed to Parliament. They are considering your case. There's every hope of a reprieve, but you will have to make a statement. Write it now. I've brought pen, ink, and this.' From the pocket of his tunic the Bastard produced a sheet of parchment. 'I've stopped that fellow's mouth, always open for a bribe. Now write! You are entitled to appeal against injustice. Father Villon says you have a *prima facie* case. He has questioned Ferrebourg who admits that you didn't attack him although you were one of the four who insulted his clerks.'

'It's a lie!'

'Then *write* it. They've had Moustier in the Châtelet but they let him go. They believed his word because he's a *sergent*, and they will and *must* believe yours... Oh, do be quick. They mustn't know I'm here or they'll have me for connivance.'

I was writing while he talked in gusty whispers, not hearing half he said.

'Have you finished? Let me see.' He took the parchment from me. 'How *beautifully* you word it! They *can't* refuse you this appeal ... Oh, my *dear,* how I've prayed! I *know* all will be well.'

'Have you any more of that parchment?'

'No. Why?'

'I have something that must be written. Tell that fellow there to bring me a set of tablets. You can say I wish to make my will.'

'Oh, my dear, don't *frighten* me!' He raised his voice. 'I'll see that your message is delivered.' He went to the door calling: 'Warder! Bring the prisoner a set of tablets. I will pay you for them. Here —' the chink of coins, a rattling of keys, one backward look at me and he was gone.

Did I believe my appeal would have effect? I did not; nor, in this last hour, did I greatly care.

The warder brought no tablets but a grubby strip of parchment and stood over me while I wrote the Envoie to my Ballade of the Hanged:

Prince Jesus, Lord and Master, heed
This prayer born of our bitter need
Preserve us from Hell's fiery pall;
Men, judge us not by your harsh creed,
But pray God He will forgive us all.

In the sundown of evening the road lay like a cloth of gold spread between the level pasture-lands of Poitou.

I had wandered far in these six months since Parliament commuted the death sentence to ten years' banishment, with, one dared to hope, a guarded reprimand to Provost Villiers de l'Isle-Adam for blatant miscarriage of justice.

To the outburst of gratitude and thanksgiving in the form of a ballade which followed my plea for mercy, I added a postscript imploring the Great Court, good Mother and Sister of Angels, to give me three days' grace that I might take my leave of those two most dear to me, my mother and Dom Guillaume, my Father in God.

I would have given much to have seen the faces of that august body of parliamentarians when they succumbed to this hysterical farrago, but it secured its desired effect. Even such as they were not proof against flattery heaped on them in honeyed verse from one, who, if still a criminal unhung, was recognised, too late, as a poet of promise. Banish him for ten years that he be given his chance to prove his worth, with the implacable proviso that should he reappear within certain bounds of the city, he would be put to instantaneous death, not on the gallows but by the sword.

Thus was my three days' grace granted before the gates of Paris closed on me for ever.

My road ran down to a valley where the river flowed clear and strong. I had walked through the night untired and now was glad to rest. Bells were chiming matins from some distant church unseen, and the sun rose high in heaven to flood the world with light.

Where the meadow edged the water, with the blue above, the green below, I saw a reaper at his work, and as he scythed he sang. His song came to me borne on the wings of the echoing past into a timeless day.

And when my soul is fled from pain
God give me life with Him again
on my return.

ENVOIE

None knows what became of him when he left Paris on that bitter January morning in 1463. It is likely he lived no more than ten months of his ten years' banishment, for, although he may not have been aware of it, the symptoms he so graphically describes in his Great Testament are indicative of advanced phthisis, doubtless the result on so frail a constitution of the starvation and tortures he endured in that awful dungeon at Meung.

It is possible he wandered back to Poitou, as suggested by Rabelais who, unborn in Villon's time, recreates him as Panurge. And I like to think that perhaps he did again meet, in the meadows of St Generoux, those two country girls '*très belles et gentes*', on whose laughing faces he lifts the curtain for one delightful moment during his first long exile.

But if we know nothing of how or where he died, whether in a drunken brawl at some wayside tavern, or in a brothel or a doss-house or a ditch to be buried in a nameless grave, we do know how he lived.

I have chosen to present his story in the first person for that is how he gives himself to us in his word pictures of that turbulent teeming medieval Paris which is his whole life's song.

Those I group around him and many more besides whom he meets in the taverns, on the road, or with the Coquillards, whose '*Jargonne*', in which he has written some of his most roystering ballades, rendered into crook English by Henley, all are there in his Testaments. They call to us across the ages in the voice of this greatest of ballade-singers, as vital and alive after five centuries as if he sang of them today.

There is, however, one voice clearer than any whose song remains a mystery: that of Katherine de Vaucelles, or Marthe Rose, his heart's obsession.

Who was she, and who this Rose, or Marthe? I have joined their names together, for to me they are inseparable as they appear in acrostic with his name in the *Ballade de Villon à s'Amye'* and in the same breath in which he reviles his 'False Beauty', Katherine.

Did he ever send that scathing letter by the hand of the Bastard de la Barre, with each line of it ending in R — for Rose? Were Katherine, Marthe and Rose one in three, his love's trinity and torment? I believe they must have been, for none in that long procession of *filles de joie* who flit through his verse and vanish as they pass, have left the faintest bruise upon his memory. Only the name of Katherine or Marthe Rose recur, an unhealed wound in all his songs of her, and, since this is a novel based on his life, I first introduce her as a child; she who tricked, deceived, bewitched, humiliated him and finally had him kicked out of her house by his rival Noë, or Noël, de Joliz, 'thrashed', so he tells us, 'as the washerwomen beat their linen in the Seine'.

Many are the attempts to translate into English the incomparable verse of this supreme poet, but while Rossetti's somewhat laboured rendering of the most exquisite of his Ballades, *'Des Dames du Temps Jadis'*, is the best known, I can recall none other than Swinburne who comes anywhere near the interpretation of Villon in that tremendous soul-cry, 'The Ballade of the Hanged'.

In these few excerpts I have translated into our language that does not remotely lend itself to his, I make no attempt more than briefly to use them as illustrative of the context in the telling of his story.

Yet despite his reckless defiance of law and order, judged by such standards as men held law and order in his day, cursed, as he gloomily believed, by Saturnine malevolence, there runs like a silver thread through the storm-tossed fabric of his life, a strong spiritual faith, exemplified in that loveliest of prayers to Our Lady, written at the request of his mother; his deep devotion to her and to that good old priest, his foster father, who gave his name and his works to the world.

A NOTE TO THE READER

If you have enjoyed this novel enough to leave a review on **Amazon** and **Goodreads**, then we would be truly grateful.

Sapere Books

Sapere Books is an exciting new publisher of brilliant fiction and popular history.

To find out more about our latest releases and our monthly bargain books visit our website:
saperebooks.com